MAGPIE'S FLIGHT

Allison Pang

IRONHEART CHRONICLES III - MAGPIE'S FLIGHT

Published by Outland Entertainment LLC
3119 Gillham Road
Kansas City, MO 64109

Founder/Creative Director: Jeremy D. Mohler
Editor-in-Chief: Alana Joli Abbott

Paperback ISBN: 978-1-954255-45-6
Ebook ISBN: 978-1-954255-46-3
Worldwide Rights
Created in the United States of America

Editor: Danielle Poiesz and Double Vision Editorial
Cover Illustration: germancreative
Cover Design: germancreative
Interior Layout: Mikael Brodu

Printed and bound in the United States of America.

Visit **outlandentertainment.com** to see more, or follow us on our Facebook Page **facebook.com/outlandentertainment/**

— A WORD FROM THE CRITICS —

"Pang delivers a fascinating storyline, strong character development, and plenty of plot twists which will draw readers into the first book of the IronHeart Chronicles and leave them eagerly anticipating the next tale in the series. Maggy is a plucky and loyal character that will fascinate readers but what makes this novel so enthralling is the relatable and carefully drawn characters coupled with vivid imagery throughout every scene."

–4 Stars – *RT Book Reviews*

"Allison Pang's *Magpie's Song* is exactly the sort of thing I love to read most. Beautiful prose, interesting characters that I want to know better, a carefully crafted world of that is both mysterious and almost inevitable. It's rare that a book surprises me on so many levels. Powerful stuff with enough surprises to make me smile and enough twists to keep me on my toes. I can't recommend it enough!"

–James A. Moore,
author of the *Seven Forges* series and the *Tides of War* trilogy

"Vivid, thrilling, clever, and imaginative, *Magpie's Song* is a genre-bending gem built around a kickass heroine and a compelling, beautifully-wrought SF/fantasy world you'll want to explore further. Allison Pang's talent is on every page. Fans of Pierce Brown and Wesley Chu will love *Magpie's Song*."

—Christopher Golden,
New York Times bestselling author of *Ararat*

"Pang has crafted a beautiful world with a ticking mechanical heart and a story that flies with fast-paced action. Utterly enchanting!"

—Laura Bickle, critically acclaimed author of *Nine of Stars*

"Maggy is an unlikely heroine, but Pang makes it easy to root for the foulmouthed scavenger.... [U]nique worldbuilding and impressive character work.... Readers will be eager to know what comes next."

—*Publishers Weekly*

"The world-building is a true delight, having a feel of Sanderson's old *Mistborn*, a touch of hardcore steampunk, but most of all: pure and distilled fantasy dystopia."

—Bradley, *Goodreads*

"Finally, a book that has left me speechless."

—Melissa Souza, *Goodreads*

"From the very first pages I fell in love with this story."

—A Book Shrew, *Goodreads*

"Every once in a great while I come across a story that knocks my socks off. This is one of them... This world that Allison has created is stunning. The characters are people that I want to know and go "rooftop dancing" with. Clockwork hearts, a mechanical Dragon that can sit on my shoulder, and eat pieces of coal? Yes, please. The entropic city below, and the floating, shiny city above? Yes, yes, yes. Even this plague? Again, yes! I can't wait to visit this world again. Highly recommended!"

—LIsa Noell, *Goodreads*

"Love, love, loved this book. Can't wait to get my hands on book 2."

—Seleste deLaney, *Amazon review*

— ALSO BY ALLISON PANG —

Graphic Novels

Fox & Willow: Came a Harper
Fox & Willow: To the Sea

The Abby Sinclair Series

A Brush of Darkness (Book One)
A Sliver of Shadow (Book Two)
A Trace of Moonlight (Book Three)
A Symphony of Starlight (Book Four)
A Duet with Darkness (a prequel short story in the *Carniepunk* anthology)

The IronHeart Chronicles

Magpie's Song (Book One)
Magpie's Fall (Book Two)

Standalones

"Respawn, Reboot" (a short story in the *Out of Tune, Book 2* anthology)
"The Wind in Her Hair" (a comic in the *Womanthology: Space* anthology)
"A Dream Most Ancient and Alone" (a short story in the *Tales From The Lake Vol 5: The Horror Anthology*)
"A Certain TeaHouse" (a comic in the *Gothic Tales of Haunted Futures* anthology)

To Magpie, Ghost, and Sparrow.
You know who you are.

A ragged singing is my cry
Broken wings on which to fly…

A roving gambler is my trade.
Winning wagers, bets are made.
With Death, the biggest cheat is fated,
Alas to find His dice were weighted.

— CHAPTER ONE —

Mags, Mags, dressed in rags..."

The voice is eerie and familiar, but I can't tell who it is. It's like a whispering shadow of everyone I've known or lost in the tunnels of the Pits. Penny. Conal. Anna. Georges. Even Buceph, his wheedling sinister cadence tumbling through my mind. I dodge through the caves, my feet scraping over rock, ignoring the cuts and bruises.

The sound grows louder, becoming less like words and more like heavy, sad moans. I am nothing but air moving through the lungs of the earth, dark and damp and without meaning. My hand slides over a wall, sticky.

On instinct, I pull it away and wipe it on my shirt. The smell hits me then, the sickly-sweet scent of blood. Rotter blood, decaying and stagnant. I turn away, not wanting to go forward, but the walls shake, rocks crumbling as the ceiling begins to collapse. I writhe, the air growing hot and thick and hard to breathe, the tunnels filling with blood and filth.

Penny's head goes rolling by, her broken teeth bared in the rictus of a grin. "Don't be a suck-tit, Maggy." She laughs cheerfully. "Give us a kiss, aye?"

I jerk awake, trembling in a pool of sweat, my hands scrabbling in the bedsheets as though I might somehow bury myself in the mattress. But my stomach spasms, and I roll from the bed into the private bathroom to vomit noisily into the toilet.

"Are you all right, Mags?" Ghost murmurs the question from the threshold but doesn't come in.

"I will be." I wash the sour bile from my mouth in the sink. I'm sucking in great gulps of air, my lungs burning. The bathroom is Meridian-made, of course, but I've paid scant attention to the details. I suppose the suite itself is simple enough by Meridian standards, but marble sinks and stone tiles are a luxury I've never had.

I haven't bothered to turn on the light, but then, light isn't exactly necessary for me. I catch a glimpse of myself in the mirror, my hair and eyes glowing with a soft luminance in the dark, a play of shadows scattering over my face as I move. I don't linger. My face is too gaunt, my cheekbones stark, my collarbone jutting from beneath my shirt. All evidence of lack of food, lack of light, lack of air.

Lack of humanity.

Penny's chuckle echoes in my ears, and I push it away, swallowing down another queasy shudder. Shivering, I emerge from the bathroom, pausing to wave off Ghost's questioning look. He hands me a glass of water, and I sip it gratefully.

"I had a nightmare," I say, not fighting it when he drapes a blanket around my shoulders.

He nods in understanding. After all, we both spent time belowground in the Pits beneath BrightStone—me as a victim of the Tithe and him in a haphazard attempt to rescue me. But now we are here on Meridion, whisked away to a hotel inside one of the silver towers that dotted the landscape the moment the airship docked. I've been here for nearly a day, ensconced within our room while my skin itches with the need to finally see the city I've given up so much for.

In hindsight, the delay gave us a chance to bathe, eat, and rest a moment before making our next move, whatever that is, though I'm not sure if I am completely ready for such a thing. The day before was a blur, running through the streets of BrightStone, avoiding Rotters, trying to save Lucian from being hanged on the gallows by the Inquestors…

My bones weigh heavy with exhaustion, but that doesn't quite quell the vibration of excitement that rattles down my spine. I glance toward the window with its heavily drawn blinds. Not even the barest crack of light emerges through the thick cloth. "What time is it?"

"Almost dawn. We'll be meeting Lady Fionula for breakfast in a few hours so there's still time to rest." He sits on the bed opposite mine, his own face bleary with weariness, but his smile is kind when he looks at me, his lips curling gently.

We'd shared the room, of course. His brother, Lucian, is in the suite next door, but I'm glad enough for Ghost's company. Nightmares are hard enough when you're sleeping alone, and they certainly don't seem as though they'll be stopping any time soon. That we hadn't shared the bed was more a circumstance of being exhausted and tumbling onto the nearest mattress as opposed to any issue against the matter.

I pick up the glasses with the dark lenses I need to wear to face the day, a souvenir of my time belowground, and slide them onto my face before carefully peering around the curtains. The sun hasn't risen quite yet so the glare isn't terrible, though the lights of Meridion glitter all about us like strands of falling stars.

It was overwhelming the night before, and it's just as bad today, but I ignore the sharpness of it to stare down at the city. My clockwork heart quivers in anticipation, whirring in response to my reaction.

"It's beautiful," I mumble, trying to take it all in. The great glass buildings, the flashing lights, clusters of airships and wind balloons streaming past us in some metaphysical dance that I don't understand. From up here in the tower, I feel like a bird nesting in a great tree. But it's new and different, and despite all my longing to be in this place, unease trots over me, leaving tingling footsteps upon my skin.

Ghost makes a soft sound of agreement behind me, and I turn. He's facing away from me, stretching his arms as he puts on a shirt. "You'll get used to it. It's going to take Lucian and me some time, as well. After all, we haven't been back here in, what? Fifteen? Sixteen years?"

"You seem so calm about it," I point out.

He lets out a low chuckle, capturing my hand and pressing it to his chest. "I'm not, as you can tell. I'm just better at hiding it."

And indeed, his heart is galloping beneath my palm. Still, barely an ounce of emotion is reflected upon his face, that stoic expression barely changing. His high cheekbones are sharp, the dark eyes soulful and serious while he watches me.

While he had always been long limbed and wiry, the time underground didn't do him any favors, either. His expression is far less hollow than mine, though his hair is just as white. Moon Child hair, the telltale sign of mixed blood and limited social status.

A knock on the door interrupts anything I was going to say, and Lucian pokes his head into our shared suite. "Ah, you're awake. Good."

Brothers or not, his skin is far lighter than Ghost's, with a hint of red in his shoulder-length golden hair. He eyes me critically when he crosses the threshold, his doctor's gaze measuring me as it always does. He says nothing, but I already know he disapproves of my emaciated figure. But then, I'm not exactly thrilled with it either, though I'm grateful he's too polite to mention it right now.

"Why are you here?" Ghost yawns at him, flopping down on the bed. "It's not time for breakfast yet, is it?"

"No, but I thought a little privacy in which to discuss some things might be prudent." He tosses Ghost a small cosmetics tube. "Here. Go dye your hair."

Ghost rolls the tube between his fingers, glancing at me. "Are you sure?"

"Only you, yes. There are too many uncertainties right now. Until we know what we're working with, I think disguising your Moon Child status is for the best."

"I hardly think anyone will be paying attention to me," Ghost grumbles, heading into the bathroom with a grimace.

"We don't know that. If Lady Fionula manages to snag us an audience with the Civil Court this morning, we don't want to be making excuses for your appearance." Lucian scratches his chin. "Not that we all couldn't use some new clothes and a visit to the barber beforehand." He gives me a weary smile. "Well, we'll see to all that after breakfast. There's quite a lot to do, but nearly all of it takes money. Our mother had many holdings and accounts, of course, but all of them were frozen when Ghost and I were forced into exile."

"I suppose that's the practical thing to do when your mother is considered a criminal," I say archly.

He flushes. "A bit of an understatement there, but I see your point."

"Should we get our mother's estate restored to us, money won't be an issue. It's certainly the easiest route to take—and the most obvious one." Ghost leans his partially darkened head around the corner. "People here are very silly, Mags. Appearances mean everything."

"Indeed." Lucian gestures at him. "You're dripping all over the floor. Hurry up and finish."

Ghost rolls his eyes and disappears again. I straighten my loose-fitting shirt. It's a bit ragged, but at least it's relatively clean considering I slept in it. "I don't suppose there will be some money in the budget for me?"

Lucian smiles tightly. "But of course. You won't need to worry about that. We'll even give you your own line of credit. You'll be able to buy whatever you want, whenever you want it."

It's a heady thought. I've always been poor. The idea that I might simply waltz into a clothing shop or a candy store on a whim seems ludicrous. I don't want to get too excited about it, though. So many things have been pulled out from under me, too often. But I allow myself to hope at least a little.

Lucian retreats into his room, leaving me to sprawl out on the bed to wait for Ghost to finish. I whistle aimlessly at my clockwork dragon, which has taken refuge on the decorative mantle, its tail twitching like a cat's as it peers at me peevishly. For a mechanical device it has a remarkably intelligent way about it. I haven't managed to figure out its secrets yet, other than the fact that it was most likely created by Madeline d'Arc, Ghost and Lucian's mother. Not only was she the brilliant architect and inventor who created many of the functionalities that allowed Meridion to fly, but she stole the mechanism and fled the city, leaving chaos in her wake.

That she placed said mechanism into my own chest, where it allowed my clockwork heart to function, was another matter entirely. But here, upon Meridion, anything was possible, wasn't it?

Somewhere along the way I doze off, only to be awakened later by Ghost, his hair now a light chestnut. "We're off to breakfast, Mags."

I stretch and gather myself to my feet. The dragon gives me a sour look when I gesture at it, and it alights on its usual perch upon my shoulder. Ghost waits until I'm done lacing my boots, though I can't help but tug on his newly darkened locks when I finish, a bit of the ink staining my fingers. "Shame you have to do this."

Lucian made Ghost dye his hair during his younger years in BrightStone as well, partially as a disguise and partially to keep up the illusion that he was still a Meridian. Which technically he is. Although not an actual half-breed like me, he has the appearance of a Moon Child, given to him after his mother injected him with a serum, something none of us knew the reasoning behind. Her notes mention it in passing, but with details no more definitive than her needing a Meridian test subject.

Ghost had not been keen on the concept when he found out, and I couldn't blame him. Family was supposed to protect you, not experiment on you. His face falls a little at my words, but he shakes it off. "It's just for now. Hair doesn't make the man, right?"

"Fair enough." My fingers linger on the curve of his jaw, and I'm sad at the idea. As though the Ghost I know will somehow disappear, lost in the potential of Meridian privilege to which he'd been born. "But don't let Lucian pull you into machinations simply for the sake of appearances. Survival is one thing, but you are who you are. And that's enough for me."

Something unreadable flickers behind the darkness of his eyes, but he merely smiles. "I'll remember that," he says, studying my face. "Are you sure you feel well enough to eat?"

I tuck my ever-present hammer into my belt, its weight a comfort. "Do I ever refuse food? Lead the way, aye?"

He laughs then, his teeth flashing as he opens the door and ushers me out.

"Have you thought about what I said?" Lady Fionula asks pensively. She's sitting across the table from Lucian, using her spoon to stab her grapefruit with deadly accuracy. I try to do the same to mine, though it takes most of my patience not to simply bury my face in it, the citrus scent driving me mad with longing.

I force myself to take small bites, ignoring the way the spoon wants to slip from my grasp, the juice electrifyingly tart upon my tongue. Ghost is across from me, and he hides a smile, ignoring the way I kick him under the table.

The four of us are seated in the small hotel restaurant. It's empty except for us. Lucian was good enough to choose the table farthest from the great glass windows on the far side of the room. Not that I wouldn't love to take in the scenery, but the glare is already causing my head to ache, even with the welcome darkness of my spectacles.

"What is there to think about? Nothing's changed since last night." Lucian generously slathers a piece of toast with a creamy slab of butter. "Our mother's estate is to be restored to us, of course. And then once we're reestablished among the Meridian Houses, we can focus on Moon Child reparations." He inclines his head in my direction.

Lady Fionula's attention flicks between us briefly, her eyes lingering on the dragon perched quietly on my shoulder, before she returns to her breakfast. She's gorgeous, with a royal bearing that looks as though she is very used to having her words heeded. Even this early in the morning, her dark hair is done up in extravagant fashion, curls rolling down her shoulders and back, nestled against the emerald-green of a gown that glistens like the scales of an exotic fish. I can only imagine what sort of duties she actually has as the liaison between Meridion and BrightStone, but I'd only met her the day before and I have no idea what the protocol is for interacting with her.

Her face is emotionless, but tiny streaks of lightning flash over her ebony skin. It's fascinating to watch, though I try to keep my curiosity hidden. The skin illumination is an odd phenomenon I've only seen a few times. Once in BrightStone, when I found the body of a Meridian after it apparently had been pushed from the floating city, and once in the Pits, where the Meridian scientist Buceph had corrupted the effect by using mushrooms that glowed in the dark. Mushrooms that contributed to my own luminescence, in fact, though we still aren't sure how it worked.

But despite being Meridians, neither Ghost nor Lucian have lightning skin. Something about living in the city itself is the trigger. They and the Meridian Inquestors, who had been exiled to BrightStone, both lost the ability somehow. Would they get it back? Would I, as a half-blooded Meridian react the same way? And if the lightning reacts to a Meridian's emotions, would I be able to utilize that to my advantage? An unkind thought, perhaps, but I've been used my whole life by Meridians and those in power. What harm would it be to use it against them now?

"Reparations, is it?" Lady Fionula's plump mouth purses in pretty amusement, and I savagely bite down on my grapefruit to keep from barking something rude at her.

"It would not be so odd a thing to pursue," Lucian retorts mildly. "While I understand you have been removed from current events in BrightStone as of late, do not assume that Meridion bears no responsibility. We owe these children more than you can possibly understand."

"They bear all of it," I snap finally, unable to contain myself. "Or nearly so." I thrust my spoon in Lady Fionula's direction. "I didn't ask to be born, and I surely didn't ask to be used and forgotten—same for the others in my clan. You Tithed us, made us lead a parade of the dying underground in some ridiculous ritual meant to both appease the ignorant masses and hide the research *your* people were conducting. Our immunity to the Rot made us test subjects in an experiment so vile as to be incomprehensible. So yes, reparations would be the least of what you owe us, aye?"

"Mags." Ghost lays his hand on my leg under the table. *I am here...* He gives it a gentle squeeze, and I relax beneath the heat of his palm.

"No one is forgetting you," Lucian says, one brow cocked at Lady Fionula. "Are they?"

"Indeed," she says a moment later. The lightning beats unhappily at the base of her throat. "It was not my intention to offend, but things are different now than they were years ago. There were always rumors, but no one wanted to believe them. To think that Meridians were breeding with the citizens of BrightStone in some...contrived plot to search for an immortality serum... Well, it seems like a tall tale."

She raises her hand before Lucian can protest. "I have read the recent reports, and obviously, with the plague—the Rot, as you call it—clearly things are far out of hand. I will do my best to investigate the issue and work with BrightStone to try to remedy the matter. But understand, for Meridion, the Moon Children are less...a curiosity and more of a quaint concept most people would prefer to ignore." Her look grows more pointed. "I have heard Moon Children essentially run wild in the streets. Even if I wanted to come up with some sort of assimilation plan for them, however would it be managed?"

"We're not rats living in a sewer," I grind out. "We live in clans, yes. Before the Pits collapsed, we were split into several groups spread out across BrightStone. But now...now we're mostly under one clan with a couple of leaders. Josephine, who runs her operation from the ruins of the Brass Button Theatre, is one of them." I pause, uncertain of how much detail to give her. "And Bran is the other. He was in the Pits with me, though I'm not entirely sure where he'll be now."

"If you need to get a message to one of them, contact the Chancellor of BrightStone," Lucian interrupts before Lady Fionula can respond to me. "In fact, you should be exchanging information with her already. Chancellor Davis has a unique grasp of the pulse in BrightStone and the people living there—including Moon Children."

"My thanks for explaining to me how to do my job." Lady Fionula gives him a withering stare, her skin lighting up briefly before she schools her expression into something more professional. "Ahem. My understanding is that Moon Children are unable to reproduce, correct? There will be many here who will assume the reparation issue will die out as soon as no more of you are born."

"Well, as long as I know where I stand. The honesty is refreshing." I finish the grapefruit and set down my fork, the fruit sticking in my throat like poison.

"It isn't you—not directly. It's what the Moon Children represent. Meridians always like to think we are above such pettiness. Moon Children make it abundantly clear that we are not." Her mouth curves into a self-deprecating smile. "Forgive me."

I shrug at her as Lucian inclines his head, as if unsure of how to respond. "Forgiven," he murmurs. "What is the timeline, then? How soon can you get us an audience?"

Her face smooths in an instant, the lightning becoming quiet. "I have already sent out missives. They'll be expecting my report on what happened in BrightStone yesterday, of course. I will endeavor to be as clear about the situation as I can be. As far as your house goes..."

"There's nothing to say," Lucian insists, pouring himself a fresh cup of tea. "It belongs to us, and we *will* be moving in."

"The city took it as an asset once you were exiled. Nothing was done with it as far as I know, but I'm fairly certain they've got it locked up. I doubt you'll be able to enter without a writ from the city declaring the ownership transferred back to you." She pauses carefully. "Jeremiah could help you with that, if you want me to ask him."

Lucian's smile turns bittersweet. "I see."

Ghost squeezes my leg in warning. Jeremiah had been Lucian's lover before he and Ghost were forced to flee Meridion. Lucian doesn't talk about the other man much, but even I can see how desperately he's trying to hide his emotions. I can only imagine how Lucian has held himself together this long, instead of rushing off to find his lost love.

But then, Lucian always put his brother's safety above everything else, even his own happiness. I suspect that won't stop now simply because we're on Meridion.

"He spent quite a bit of time at university after you left. He's a barrister now. You know how he is: once he sets his sights on something, he rarely turns away from it. Much like you, I suppose." Her expression grows gentle. "He has never stopped searching for a way to undo your exile. Believe it or not, he's been in front of the Council several times to plead your case."

Lucian stills. "I thought he might have moved on by now."

She scoffs ruefully. "Please. I'm sure he hasn't become a monk, by any means, but there's a part of him that's just as trapped as you are. I could tell him you're here. As your fiancée, it would be the… compassionate thing to do."

My head whips toward Lucian, but I'm nearly biting through my tongue as it is.

"That would be kind of you, yes." There's a shiver in his voice, as though the very words are breaking inside him.

Blotting at her mouth with a napkin, Lady Fionula stands up. "I think we've discussed things enough for now. I have another meeting shortly. I'll let you know what the Council says when I can. Where will you be staying?"

Lucian blinks. "Our house. Like I said."

She frowns. "But the locks…"

Ghost side-eyes me. "Somehow I don't think that will matter much."

Lucian snorts, the three of us exchange a quick look that speaks volumes. In whatever odd bit of fate twisted our lives together, Madeline d'Arc's inventive clockwork heart not only keeps my blood pumping but contains a key of sorts that can open every Meridian lock ever made. Or so our current working theory goes. Thus far, I managed to open several unlockable doors over the last several weeks, but there is no sense in showing our hand this early in the game.

When none of us volunteer any more information, Lady Fionula sets down her napkin. "Well, then I leave you all with a bit of advice. The Council abhors paupers. You'll do better if you look more respectable." She points at Lucian's face. "You've got the appearance of someone who just left a bar brawl."

Her comment rings true enough. A set of purple bruises blossoms over his jaw and right cheekbone, one eye sporting a swollen lid, courtesy of the Meridian Inquestors who took him captive and sentenced him to death.

"Next time I'll make sure to preserve my dashing good looks as I'm being dragged to the gallows," Lucian retorts. "That way the Council can pull their respective beards at the handsomeness of my corpse as they deny me my rights yet again."

"Point taken." She inclines her head toward me, and I bristle. "This one, in particular. Moon Child or not, the least you could do is make her seem civilized."

My eyes narrow, whatever charitable thoughts I might have had about her flying right out the window. "Less like a Moon Child, you mean?"

Lucian pinches the bridge of his nose. "That's enough, 'Nula. Don't take my sins out on them." She blinks at his casual tone. "Lady Fionula, then. Or would 'Your Eminence' be preferable?"

"We may have been children together," she says. "But you must try to keep things as formal as possible if you want the Council to take you seriously. Even if you think they're not watching." Her mouth presses regretfully. "I'm sorry. I really am." Glancing at the serving boy, she waves him over. "Charge their meal to my account. I'll send my factor to make amends this afternoon."

And with that, she glides out of the restaurant, her hips swaying gracefully.

Ghost slugs the rest of his juice in a quick swallow. "Well, that was fun, wasn't it?"

"You have an odd definition of fun, aye?" I snag another biscuit and pocket it for later. "Now what?"

"Weren't you listening?" Lucian stares at the space Lady Fionula left behind at the table. "Now we go home."

Millet seed and silken threads,
My bed is made of these.
Silver stars in the night sky spread
Upon a dress of woven weeds.

— CHAPTER TWO —

The world tilts through the window of the airship, making my stomach ripple with a queasy excitement. Below us, the city of Meridion sprawls out like a chessboard, tall buildings scattered about like pawns made of glass and steel, silver and green and shining like the sea. But none of this is a game that I can truly play—at least not with the rules I've been given.

The airship we're in is smaller than the one that brought us up from BrightStone. A taxi, I suppose, meant for short trips with only a few people. It certainly seems more convenient than one of those larger ones, though the inside spares no expense, and it's easily as luxurious as everything else in Meridion. Even the seats are plush and thick, made for comfort and a quiet ride.

"What do you think?" Ghosts nudges me to drag me from my momentary stupor.

My eyes tear up despite my glasses, the glare forcing me to blink. "It's bigger than I thought. The maps in the BrightStone Museum really never did it justice," I say, trying to match what I know with what's unfolding below us. "How will we ever dance on the rooftops? I'll be lost in an instant."

In BrightStone, travel by rooftops is the main way Moon Children get around. It isn't always a choice. Most of us don't have enough money to hire a cab, let alone be welcome to do so. But here, the buildings are so tall…

Lucian clicks his tongue sharply. "There will be no rooftop dancing. At least not that I'll be aware of," he mutters a moment later. "I mean it. Not until we get a few things straightened out with the Council."

I stick my tongue out at him. "So what am I even looking at?" I wave imperiously at the window.

Ghost's mouth purses, and I flush at his obvious amusement. "The maps you saw in the museum were probably a bit outdated And they weren't really maps of Meridion, so much as maps drawn by Inquestor memory, I suspect. The thing to remember is that the city is set up like a spiral, but there's an Outer Spiral, where we're headed, and an Inner Spiral. Our hotel was on the edge of the Inner Spiral. The closer you get to the center, the more expensive things become."

"What's that?" I point at what appears to be a shining stream snaking its way below us.

"Ah, that is the Oubliette River. It runs around the city between the two Spirals, but there are any number of bridges that can be used to cross it by foot." He eyes it fondly. "I seem to remember searching for frogs in it when I was younger, but I don't believe I ever found a single one."

Lucian grunts. "It was never intended to support wildlife. It's used more as a way to produce energy via a series of waterways and tunnels that run beneath the city. It's really a rather complex system when you get right down to it."

"And your mother's house is on the Outer Spiral?" I frown. "Seems a bit shabby for the woman who actually built the place, aye?"

"One of her houses," Lucian admits. "She had a lab and an estate in the Inner Spiral—in one of the Five Towers, of course. But when it came to her children, she preferred to raise us in a more rustic environment. I'm sure there was a method to her madness, but I never got around to asking her the reason."

"What are the Five Towers?" I crane my head to see if I can get a better look.

"They're on the far side of the Inner Spiral, but they're a little hard to see from where we are just now," Ghost says. "The elite Meridian Houses and families have estates there. It's considered a privilege. Space is at a premium here, if you haven't guessed, and the higher up you literally are, the higher status your family name."

"Makes things easier when I have to know who to bow to," I murmur.

Lucian wrinkles his nose. "No one's doing any bowing. It's simply enough to be polite and keep a civil tongue. The results come slower than we might like, but we do try to avoid direct confrontation here as much as we can."

A bitter laugh escapes me. "The Inquestors certainly have no issue with direct confrontation, aye?" The Inquestors are nothing more than Meridian bullies, keeping BrightStone citizens in check through fear and an authoritarian rule. The gods know I had enough run-ins with them—and suffered the loss of more than one friend at their hands. The death of my dearest clanmate, Sparrow, had been the worst loss of all.

Lucian nods. "And now you know why they were sent down to BrightStone in the first place. We couldn't control them up here."

"Meridion has always thrown its garbage upon BrightStone. Why stop with mere objects?" The words slip out before I can stop them, though I know it's not fair of me to say. He and Ghost certainly had nothing to do with Meridion's laws. The two of them had been living in squalor in BrightStone for many years and had taken me in without a second thought, even if their initial hope was to enlist me to their cause.

"Fair." Lucian smiles tightly, and I realize I've hurt him. "Well, let's see if we can change that, shall we? If nothing else, with the arrest of the High Inquestor, their place in BrightStone is likely to be diminished, if they are not outright disbanded."

"I'm sorry," I say, flushing. "I didn't mean it like that."

"I know. But you're entitled to your thoughts. And you certainly have cause. I simply ask that you give us a chance to try to make it up to you before you judge everything about Meridion under the same harsh light." Lucian reaches out to hold my hand for a moment. "Things here are going to be very different, Mags. You've never been anywhere like this. Meridion has its own way of doing things, much as Moon Children do."

I nod, trying to swallow my anxiety. Here, with the exception of these two men, I am utterly alone and without resources. I've tightroped my way from one scrape to another nearly my entire life, but there's always been a Moon Child clan at my back, even in the darkness of the Pits.

Not knowing what to expect or how to move about this city makes me far more nervous than I want to admit. My fingers twitch, itching for a cigarillo, but I simply return Lucian's squeeze before retreating to look outside the window again. I get lost in a hazy swirl of kinetic movement and a dizzying array of lights.

Before long, we're sinking slowly toward the ground, and I realize we're docking at a small airship kiosk. It's got a shaded overhang and dark blue bench. We step off the platform, taking the steps to the main thoroughfare. Lucian lags behind, handing something to the driver of the airship.

Ghost thrusts his head toward the kiosk. "You can grab an airship from pretty much anywhere in the city at one of these. Most people don't carry a lot of those Meridian chits on them like we saw in BrightStone, but each family has a crest stamp that can be used to pay for things on short notice."

"I still have some chits—that should do for a few necessities," Lucian says with a hint of relief. "It's not much, but with any luck, the Council will grant us access to our mother's accounts. I'm fairly certain she had a rather large sum hidden away somewhere, though without her personal crest stamp it might be a while before we can retrieve it."

"Ah, I see," I say smartly. I've never had more money than I could carry in my pocket. Keeping anything of any real value on you in BrightStone is simply an invitation to have it stolen. Jingle comes and goes within moments, no matter how it's earned. Having another mechanism to pay seems wise. "What happens if someone steals it, aye?"

Lucian and Ghost exchange a quick look. "Well, technically, the stamps are keyed in via a code." Lucian's mouth purses wryly.

"So you're saying I can potentially unlock the code of someone's stamp with my heart? That...opens a rather large world of possibilities, don't you think?" I wink at Ghost, and he shakes his head.

"Don't do it at all," Lucian warns me. "If you're looking to make a good impression for Moon Children up here, I highly recommend *not* stealing."

"I'm sure I wouldn't know anything about it," I say, studying the sky.

He rolls his eyes, and I let him take the lead. Ghost casually snags my hand. Bemused, I stare at him but don't try to pull away. It's not about showing weakness at this point anyway. This is his world, not mine. Or at least it was. Seems only fair he show it to me.

The road here is flanked with trees and flowering bushes, delicate fountains and exquisite sculptures of great beings with wings, odd creatures, and men and women of such beauty that it nearly hurts to look at them.

Ghost told me about them once, long ago, when I admired the statues outside the now destroyed Brass Button Theatre. I thought he was bragging, making me feel stupid for enjoying such things.

But now I see what he meant, and I can only sigh inwardly for being so naive.

Ghost squeezes my hand, though I don't know if he understands the source of my melancholy. His own face is drawn to the buildings about us with a fierce longing, a clear excitement to finally be among his own people once more.

We're attracting a fair number of stares, all the same, and I draw my hood over my head to hide both my pale hair and the dragon on my shoulder. I'm not quite ready to be gawked at.

As though reading my thoughts, Lucian leads us away from the bustle of the main thoroughfare and down a series of narrow streets and back alleys. Such places in BrightStone would be filled with gutter trash and the stink of dead fish, but even the shadows in Meridion are artificially clean and bright. In the distance, the lights seem almost blinding, the height of the buildings looming in a menacing fashion. A sense of dread fills me, a terror of delights to imagine rooftop dancing in such a place, but I cannot help the soft tremor within. After being underground for nearly a year, my senses are almost too keen. To head in that direction right now might be enough to send me into madness. Like an ocean, I would have to enter it slowly, a toe at a time.

"How much farther is it?" I shiver.

"Just past the next block." Lucian's voice trembles slightly, as though he can't quite believe he's here.

We turn up another street, this one lined with trees taller than the houses themselves, their great leaves swaying in the wind. The brilliance of their colors makes me want to weep as I imagine the soft velvet of their skin, the warmth of the threaded bark.

"This one," Ghost says suddenly, pointing toward a thick clump of decorative bushes flourishing with red and violet leaves. Just beyond them stands the house of Madeline d'Arc.

Like the other homes in this part of Meridion, it has a quaint feel to it, as though it belongs in some other city altogether. In fact, judging by the pale stone walls overgrown with vines and copper shingles, it is downright primitive in comparison to the massive glass towers peering down on us from so far above.

It hasn't been occupied in quite some time; that much is obvious. Decayed greenery and moss overrun the slate steps, and a faint hint of mustiness emanates from the rotting wooden front door.

Ghost glances over at me with a sad smile on his face. "It probably isn't what you expected. We can take you to the more exciting parts of the city later, once we've figured out what condition the house is in."

I lower my hood, watching as the dragon launches from my shoulder to take a perch above the door, its copper snout rooting about the eaves with gusto. What it's looking for, I can't say, but if Madeline created it, then I suppose it is home, too.

Which leaves me the odd one out. As always.

"I don't know what I was expecting," I say finally. "It's a bit run-down, aye, but nicer than anything I ever lived in." My mouth twitches when I look at Lucian. "Except at the Conundrum, of course."

Lucian tips his head in self-deprecating agreement. "For a brothel, it had its charms. At least for a little while."

The three of us share a rueful smile at the memory of the building that had been our home for a time—much longer for the two brothers than for me. I couldn't help wondering about the fate of the proprietress, Molly Bell—who could say where she might be?—but the shark of BrightStone would always find a way to survive. Never mind that she betrayed us all in one way or another, playing her games and spinning intrigues.

I quell the thought, still uncertain of all the things that happened. "I suppose I thought it would be more like Madeline's lab beneath the Mother Clock."

Lucian mounts the steps, then runs his fingers over the door. "Mother had a sentimental streak. She didn't like bringing her work home to us if she could help it, and even with her reputation as the Architect, she thought it best if we lived simply... Or so we were led to believe," he amends. "The gods know she had her secrets." He fumbles at the panel beside the door. "Let's see if the family code still works, shall we?"

I take a step nearer, my clockwork heart thumping a little harder. "And if it doesn't, I'm sure I'll manage it, aye?"

"It will need some work," Ghost muses, eyeing the roof. "A thorough cleaning, if nothing else, but it looks manageable."

"The day our mother didn't create something sound enough to last the ages is the day she died," Lucian said, tapping a particular pattern on the panel. Meridian locks were all keyed to certain touch patterns, though I'd never quite understood the mechanism behind it.

He frowns when nothing happens and taps on it again. "Well, I suppose Fionula wasn't lying about that," he says wryly, gesturing to me. "I think we'll be needing your services after all. Our family code appears to have been overwritten."

I step toward him, and my fingers hover above the panel as I shut my eyes to listen to my heartbeat. The clockwork mechanism vibrates within my chest in a patten only I can feel. *Click, click, whir, whir, click.* The cadence is simple enough, and I tap out the matching beats on the panel.

The door shudders, pistons creaking behind the wall, but it opens smoothly enough for all that.

"There now," Lucian says with an air of satisfaction. "What did I tell you? It will need a bit of oil and a code reset, but otherwise, it's in perfect working condition. Thank you, Mags." He starts to step over the threshold. "Ready?"

I gesture at the dragon. "Come on, then." It puffs out a smoke ring and glides to my shoulder, its tail wrapping about my neck.

Ghost takes my hand again. "Welcome home."

The first thing I notice is the smell. Musty, yes, but there's a hint of something else that reminds me of the lab Ghost and I found beneath the Mother Clock in BrightStone. We're standing in the foyer—a stone floor covered by a threadbare rug of crimson silk. A bit of sunlight streams in through a series of small round windows nestled above us. One of the panes is cracked. Two passages split off from here on opposite sides, and there's a coiled metal stairway in front of us. Bits of paper line the floors, trash and peeling wall coverings.

Beside me, Lucian sniffs. "Lavender. Still here after all this time." He turns toward me. "She was very fond of the herb. Used it for everything."

"I remember. Ghost mentioned as much down below." My mind drifts to the darkness of Madeline d'Arc's underground lab. There was lavender stored there, as well, and I even found traces of its presence in the Pits.

"I used to wonder why she had so much of it about the house, but maybe it helped her forget the realities of her lab." His face grows tight. "Given what we know now about the Rot and how it came to be."

"I suppose it doesn't really matter," Ghost muses aloud, stooping to peer into a decorative crystalline vase that hasn't held flowers in quite some time.

A sigh escapes Lucian. "You'll forgive me if I take my leave for a few moments. I would prefer to revisit the house alone and take stock as I will within my memories." He shoves his glasses farther up the bridge of his nose and doesn't bother waiting for an answer before turning away and striding down a creaking hallway.

"Aye," I say to his retreating shadow.

Ghost smiles. "It's how he is. You know that. I'll give you the tour, though—or what I remember of it. Probably wouldn't hurt to make a list of things that need repairs."

He pulls a notebook and a charcoal stick out of his satchel and hands them to me with a grin. "Care to do the honors?"

"Me?"

His mouth curves with amusement. "It will be good writing practice for you."

I roll my eyes and shift the notebook so I can write on it. Inside, I'm secretly pleased. Even if I'm barely functionally literate, Ghost knows my discomfort at unfamiliar places, so him passing me the notebook is a chance to regain a little of my confidence. It's easier to hide if my hands are busy.

I walk behind Ghost as he ascends the stairs, his hand trailing lightly along the banister. The steps groan something fierce beneath my feet, and I wince at the sharpness of it. "No sneaking about in this house," I mutter.

"So far, any damage I've noticed is purely cosmetic. Though we'll need to make sure the pipes are in working order." Ghost smiles wryly. "After the last several weeks, I'll admit to looking forward to baths on a regular basis. You too, I expect."

I nod at him. After nearly a year of living underground, the idea of clean water whenever I want seems like a miracle, never mind the concept of bathing. He reaches out to run his fingers through my hair, an odd expression on his face, but he doesn't say anything.

There isn't anything to say. No one else on Meridion has any real understanding of what I went through except for Ghost. Not having to explain things to him is far more precious than anything else at the moment.

"Well," he mumbles and returns to climbing the stairs. He pauses to tap a crack in the wall. "Write this one down. There may be a leak somewhere. It looks as though the drywall is crumbling."

I scratch out a note on the parchment. It's a bit hard to read, but I can write it out later so it's clearer. In the Pits, I got some practice when I was studying the records of the Rotters. The bonewitch Georges let me borrow them in the hopes that we could find a pattern in the afflicted. This was before we knew it was the Meridians themselves who had distributed the plague as part of their quest for immortality, of course.

And now all those notes lie in the sunken remains of the Pits, months of my hard work no more than soaked parchment and blurry ink.

"Ah," Ghost says, pulling me from the dark recollection of my past. "Here, this was my room."

I peer through the first doorway at the end of the hall on the right. "It's a…nursery?"

And it is. There's a bed made for a boy, smaller-sized furniture, the rotting remains of some blankets, and what appears to be a rug made of sheep's wool. I snort, remembering Ghost's recitation of the old children's rhyme when we were in the Pits. *"Baa baa, black sheep,* aye?"

"Of course. I was young when we left, after all." His mouth purses. "Think I'll be needing some new furniture." He strides to the far size of the room and opens the window, a hazy breeze playfully lifting the tattered curtains. The dust stirs, making me sneeze.

"Should I write that down?"

He shrugs, something unreadable on his face. "Maybe. Maybe not."

I cock a brow at him. "Something I should know?"

"Let's look at the other rooms first." He turns abruptly and returns to the hallway, then opens the next few doors, craning his head into each one. "This one was Lucian's. It's going to need new linens, but he'll probably have a better idea of the rest, so we'll ask him about that later." He frowns. "I don't really want to go poking around his things anyway. And there don't appear to be any leaks or anything."

"Good enough. What's next?" I slip past him into an elegantly appointed bedroom, a large four-poster up against the far wall. Sunlight pours in from two immense circular windows, blinding me painfully enough that I'm forced to turn away despite my smoked lenses.

"Sorry!" Ghost ducks into the room and pulls the heavy drapes closed.

I blink away the hot rush of burning tears as my vision slowly returns. "Your mother's room, I take it?"

"Who else's? For all her love of simplicity, she certainly had her extravagant moments. But I suppose she earned it." He shoves a hand through his hair. "There's so much here I'm not sure about, either. I mean, all these little figures and the books… I'm surprised there's anything left at all. I would have figured the place would have been ransacked ages ago. They were so desperate to find her."

My dragon suddenly leaps from my shoulder to land upon the ornately carved fireplace mantle. "Making yourself home I see," I say dryly.

"Well, perhaps it's right," Ghosts says. "I suppose you could have it, if you wanted. You've done so much for us, the least we could do is give you the best room."

I suppress an inward shudder. "Maybe. Those windows open?"

"Of course you'd want to know that." He laughs. "They do but not in a way that you'd easily make your way out of. But we've a few others that might suit you better."

"It's just a little… *Oppressive* might be too strong a term," I say, walking toward the bed. "It's a lot to live up to, is all I'm saying. The bedroom of the scion of Meridion is a bit heavier than I like, aye?" I reach out to touch the bedpost. "It wouldn't ever really be mine anyway, and sleeping under shadows makes for poor dreams…"

My voice trails away as a sudden familiar whirring vibrates faintly in my chest. I frown, taking a step closer to the bed. "There's somewhat here." I trace my fingers over the headboard, changing my position and moving side to side, forward and back until I find the place where my heart beats hardest.

Ghost watches me curiously but doesn't say anything until I press what appears to be a hidden panel and it reveals a tiny keypad. He waves me on. "I doubt this will be the last such secret we find in this house. Given your ability to open locks, we may want to be cautious. I don't know if my mother was the sort to lay traps for would-be burglars, but it also wouldn't surprise me, given the circumstances."

I tap out the rhythm on the keypad, rewarded with a tiny snap as the headboard retreats from the wall. It slides down several feet to reveal yet another panel, this one obviously connected to what appears to be a safe.

"Layers upon layers," I say, going through the process again. I grunt when the safe makes an audible clank and the safe door pops open.

Ghost leans forward to peer within and pulls out a series of scrolls. He unrolls them hesitantly and then deflates. "It's in code, of course. It's similar to the one we found in the Mother Clock, but I don't really recognize it. We'll have to show it to Lucian. He might be able to read it." He tucks it into his satchel. "Shall we continue?"

I grunt at him. "All right, then. But I don't think I want to stay in here. Too many secrets." I shudder, imagining somehow unlocking the ceiling in my sleep and having it come crashing down on me.

"Fair enough." His mouth kicks up in a half smile. "I don't think there are any repairs needed, so at least note that. We'll sweep it again when Lucian is here in case there are any other secret cupboards lurking about."

I go to shut the safe and reach inside when something shiny catches my eye. "There's something else here."

"What is it?" Ghost peers over my shoulder while I retrieve a small silver tube with a series of tiny cogs imprinted on the top. He stills. "It's my mother's family crest stamp," he says. I hand it to him, and he rotates it for closer examination. "We're lucky it wasn't stolen. We'll have access to her account with this, and that means more bargaining power."

We retreat to the hallway and find another room, this one smaller than the others. "I think this was meant to be for guests, though we just used it for storage. I don't remember there being a bed here, anyway," Ghost says, inspecting the corners. He opens the window with a little effort, grimacing when it gets stuck partway. "Damp."

A slender breeze tickles its way inside, sweeping through the cobwebs to stir up the dust. "Probably not a bad idea to do this to all the rooms," I note. After so many months belowground, fresh air feels like a fever dream. To think I can have it whenever I want is a luxury beyond measure.

Ghost beckons to me and opens the window farther. "Here, come see the view." He makes room for me to poke my head outside. Squinting against the glare, I see a sprawling courtyard filled with trees and overgrown bushes—a tangled mess of vines and turned-over pots and what looks to be a dry fountain filled with leaves.

"Oh." I'm struck with a terrible wanting the more I study the courtyard, as though I might create a secret sanctuary of growing things to strip away the terrors of the Pits. Some small sound escapes me, and I'm not even sure I can vocalize this desire with words, only that I need it…and this room to overlook it, to hear the wind laughing in the branches of the large tree overshadowing this part of the house.

"Are you crying?" Ghost presses his lips against my forehead.

"No. Maybe. I've never really seen trees before we arrived here. Not like this. Not one I could climb or taste or touch..." I wipe away what must be tears.

"It's yours, if you want it," he says quietly. "I don't think Lucian will mind, and we'll be stuck here a while. Might be a nice distraction for you."

"I don't know the first thing about gardening." There's a bitterness to my words as I remember Joseph and his greenhouse down in the Pits, and my failed attempts at stealing the lights to grow food in the Rotter village. All those intentions, washed away as easily as the river flooding the Pits themselves.

Everything I tried to do down below is gone, and there's a small part of me that is deathly afraid of reaching out for this bit of greenery that Ghost dangles before me. Promises are so easily broken.

"I'll help you," he assures me. "There may even be some books downstairs that can explain some of the basics. Reading practice on top of it all."

"Aye, professor," I say dryly. "That settles it, then. I want this room, if I can? Mayhap we can move one of the other beds in here?"

He nudges the paper in my hand, then watches as I scrawl out my furniture request. "If you're going to stay in here, you'll definitely need more than just a bed. I think some darkening curtains, too, to make it easier on you during the day. And of course, clothes, aye?"

I glance up from the paper. "You did say you'd get me some new shoes a while ago, if I recall." I've only been out of the Pits a short while, and though the clothes I was given are serviceable enough, I want to find out what it feels like to be a real citizen and not simply gutter trash.

Not that I have any idea where to begin here. It's one more thing I'll have to rely on Lucian and Ghost for.

Best get used to it, Mags. You're sailing on new waters.

"So what's next?" I move along from my thoughts, not wanting to tarnish whatever new beginning we are trying to make.

"Mmm." Ghost gestures at me to follow. "There's one more bedroom up this way. It's more of a suite, really. I think my mother had an apprentice or two at one point, and they sometimes stayed overnight."

The last room is indeed quite large, with a privy of its own, several large dressers, a couple of moth-eaten carpets, and a pile of sagging mattresses. I open the windows on the far side to let some air in and wave away the dust.

"Looks like this room's been ransacked," Ghost says ruefully. "We'll have to get rid of what's left of those beds for sure."

I pace about the room slowly. "We should fix it up. Get it ready."

"Expecting a lot of visitors?" Ghost raises a brow. "Believe me. There's no one here on Meridion who will give us the time of day until we clear our name."

A scowl twists my lips as I study the cracks in the gilt mirror on the wall. "Like I'd put in any effort for Meridians. No, for my clan." I look up at him. "Our clan," I amend.

Confusion crosses his face. "Our clan? Oh, you mean the Moon Children from the Pits? Surely you can't mean to bring them here."

"Why not?" I lean against the wall, arms crossed. "They've earned it. I don't know if any of them will even come, but if they want to, they should be allowed." And the truth of it is, most of them probably would not come, but I can't help but think of Gloriana, who was studying to be a bonewitch under Georges's tutelage in the Pits, learning in the dark with trembling hands and cast-off tools.

She would jump at the opportunity for a formal education, to learn from real Meridian doctors. As for the others, well, it'd give them something they've never had: a choice.

"This is going to be hard enough with only the three of us, Mags. You know this." Ghost hesitates, but doesn't elaborate

I know what he means. And he's probably right, but that doesn't mean I agree with him. "I've danced to Meridion's tune all my life. Don't you think it's time we stopped?"

He thrusts his fingers through his hair. "You're never one to mince words, are you? All right. We'll talk it over with Lucian. If we can get permission, we'll do it."

"That's your first mistake, aye? Asking permission."

"So you've said before. Look where it got us last time." His words are sour, but there's a smile turning up the edges of his mouth. It splits into a wide grin as I return it, the two of us dissolving into fits of laughter at the absurdity of it all.

As plans go, it's not much. But it's a start.

Upstairs, downstairs, away I go,
Stripped of pride and pleasure,
With only myself to offer up,
To amuse you at your leisure.

— CHAPTER THREE —

So that's all of it, then?" Lucian flips through my chicken scratch notes, frowning at various points and holding the parchment up to his nose. My collective efforts with Ghost have revealed that the house was impeccably built, with a whimsical charm that belied d'Arc's mechanical genius. Or perhaps it was simply meant to be a safe haven for her family.

My fingers brush the edges of the heart-shaped panel on my breastbone, uneasy. After everything that was revealed in the Pits, it would be no wonder if she'd sought a refuge from the shadows that surely hung over her workspace.

One does not seek out immortality lightly, after all.

That said, while the house's structure is perfectly sound, many of its appointments were not so fortunate. As Ghost noted, the place was probably ransacked more than once and little care was made to preserve whatever was left behind.

But it's livable. And for the moment, that's all that matters.

"Too bad we didn't bring Copper Betty with us," I muse aloud. "We could have set her up to cleaning." I eye the windows in the great room with distaste, the musty curtains drawn against the afternoon sun. "And just who's going to climb up there to wipe the dust off those, I wonder?"

"I'm not sure bringing Molly Bell's automaton up here would have been the best idea." Lucian begins making notes on top of my notes. From over his shoulder, I can only make out a rapid set of computations involving numbers I don't really understand.

"Technically, she's *my* automaton now," I say. "Josephine said she'd watch over her for a while until we get settled, but I doubt she'll want that responsibility forever. I'm sure if you asked Lady Fionula to retrieve some of your supplies or books or whatever from BrightStone we could simply ensure she was part of the cargo." I waggle my fingers at him. "Airship magic, aye?"

"Mmmph," Lucian mumbles, noncommittal. "Maybe. In the meantime, we want to blend in among the people. And that means keeping quiet and clean and not making any fuss." He raises a gimlet brow at me before fixating on Ghost. "And I mean it about those rooftop outings, understand? We can't afford to attract attention. Not until we're fully reinstated," he adds, his expression going sour.

"The neighbors are going to talk anyway," I say, disappointed he is being so insistent about it. Moon Children clans live and die by the rooftops down in BrightStone. After trying to find my way to Meridion for so long, it seems somewhat cruel to take it away. Though, perhaps I should try to content myself with simply enjoying the sights of the floating city itself.

"Will we be staying the night here?" I ask, my stomach suddenly rumbling. Going through the house took us far longer than I expected. It's already late afternoon.

Ghost flashes me a guilty look. "I think food might be in order first. And I imagine we can purchase some basic bedding for tonight." He nudges his brother. "Oh, and we found these."

Lucian takes the scrolls from Ghost with a bemused stare. "How odd. Wherever were they?"

"Mags discovered them hidden in Mother's bedroom. Behind the headboard." Ghost's eyes grow intense. "Can you read what they say?"

Lucian unrolls them and turns them about. "It's not a code I recognize, to be honest."

Ghost pulls out Madeline's family crest stamp. "And we found this."

Relief flickers on Lucian's face as he takes it from his brother. "Oh, thank the gods. With this, I can visit the bank tomorrow, and with any luck, I'll be able to get our accounts sorted." Eyes dancing with amusement, he unfolds a series of ornate sheets of paper from his vest. "I also found these under a hearthstone in the kitchen fireplace. Lenders' notes. It seems our mother did quite a bit of lending in her own right over the years. There's enough here—with interest, mind—to set us up *quite* nicely, even if Mother's stamp doesn't pan out."

Ghost sighs. "Well that's one bit out of the way, then."

"We should hold off on trying to collect on these debts for a little while. Until we look...presentable." Lucian reaches out to tug on my ragged hair with an air of weariness. "Not that we don't love you as you are Mags, but I think we're going to need a professional who can arrange this into something more socially acceptable."

I pull away to sit on the floor with a yawn. "What does it matter? Between the eyes and the glowing hair, it's not like people aren't going to stare. If anything, we should make me stand out *more,* aye? A spectacle to distract from whatever the two of you are doing."

Lucian opens his mouth and then hesitates as though weighing my words. "You may be right," he admits. "If we enter you into high society, so to speak, you'll be the first Moon Child most of the citizens will ever see. You'll be considered an exotic oddity at best and a mongrel at worst. Could you handle that?"

A bark of laughter escapes me. "You've just described my entire life. It'll be exactly the same, except this time I'll be in fancy dress.

And maybe not be so hungry." I stretch out my arms and roll onto my back. "And who says I'll be the only one? I want to bring the others here, too."

"Out of the question," Lucian says immediately. "I understand where you're coming from, but I can't get bogged down running a boarding house for Moon Children."

"So, what?" I yawn again. "We're equals now, aye? I'm sure I can manage the day-to-day parts of it. We're not babes, you know?"

"No one's saying that, Mags." Ghost touches my shoulder with a careful hand.

"Maybe. But you were the one who said I needed to be the voice of the Moon Children. My people. *Your* people." I cock my head at him. "Or no?"

He looks away. "I don't know."

"Just so. And I did not just spend nearly nine months underground in the dark so you could simply do the same thing to me here. Metaphorically, anyway. Besides, I'm IronHeart. You need me." I crack a half smile at Lucian, but it's self-mocking more than anything else. I'd picked up the name after reemerging from the Pits, the common mythology of a dragon sleeping within the bowels of Meridion notwithstanding. The fact that there was a bit of a prophecy involving the fall of Meridion wrapped around the name was an irony I didn't mind accepting, even if no one really believed such a thing.

Lucian purses his mouth at the moniker. "Fair enough, Mags. We've got a lot of work to do. I think the kitchens are in good shape, but seeing as we don't have any food, it might serve us best to return to the hotel until we can get things livable. Or at least some better mattresses."

Ghost shrugs. "We're here now, aren't we? I say we just stick it out here."

I shake my head. "You two and your damnable pride. Only fools argue over not choosing a warm bed and a hot meal over what other people think. At least let's go find something to eat. I hate arguing on an empty stomach."

The three of us gather ourselves, but there's a tension now that seems to linger over the two brothers. I don't think it has anything to do with me so much as with whatever secret expectations they've been nurturing, as though rediscovering their family home would somehow instantly restore them to what they'd been.

Before, I might have left the two of them alone to figure things out—and if they asked me for space, I'd give it to them—but I'm past the point of dealing with this sort of nonsense.

"All right, you two." I step between them, flicking them both on the nose. They snap out of whatever inner monologues were holding their attention, both of them rewarding me with sheepish smiles. "That's better. Food first, sleeping arrangements later."

"Practical as always, Mags." Lucian sweeps past us toward the front door.

"Well one of us has to be," I retort, holding my hand out to Ghost. "Come on."

He squeezes my fingers tightly. "Aye."

Evening on Meridion doesn't simply creep over the edge of the horizon the way it does in BrightStone. It envelops the floating city in a cloak of everchanging hues, the sky illuminating with a brilliance I've never seen before, even if it is through my darkened lenses.

In BrightStone, a fog drapes itself over the city streets, even on the brightest of days, leaving everything in a dull haze that grays into three basic shades of brown and an occasional red. But here, tall glittering towers shoot up high above us like silver flower stems, their tips bursting into bloom in a riotous display of pinks and oranges, soft blues, and a hint of ebony-purple. If the gods designed such a place, I would not have been surprised.

Eventually I have to turn away from it. Even without the light piercing my eyes, staring up at the sky is a good way to get pick-pocketed, at least in my experience. Do they have petty crime on Meridion?

My time in the Pits taught me that, despite the pedestal the citizens of BrightStone put Meridians on, they were capable of such terrible cruelty. Sparrow had always wondered if they were born of angels, but if so, they must have fallen so very far.

A light breeze slides past us, blowing the hood of my cloak back to tickle its way through my ragged hair. Of course, the disadvantage to traveling about the city in the evening is that my hair's glow is much more obvious. Never mind that the streets we walk down are filled with people whose skin crackles with lightning. Instead of the gentle electric flickers that pulse along the highways of their veins, I'm lit up like a beacon, and the dragon perched on my shoulder doesn't help.

Once I take off my glasses, the difference becomes even more apparent, as do the murmurs coming from all around us.

My eyelids drop lazily, belying the flutter in my wrist when Ghost strokes the back of my hand. "Courage," he whispers. "They're only curious."

"For now," Lucian says, his tone ominous and resigned. "Let's get out of the street. Maybe we'll attract less attention that way."

We duck into a narrow alley, away from the prying eyes and gaping mouths. A sign hangs outside a simple door proclaiming food. At least, I assume it does, as we slip inside too quickly for me to really get a good look at it. It's not terribly crowded, but it smells divine, and I can't help my mouth from watering.

It's dimly lit, which makes me stand out the more, but it's easier on my eyes so that's a plus. We take a table in the corner. It's made of burnished wood highlighted with bronze leaves carved into the edges. Cracked glass lanterns hang from the walls, the golden light flickering in a cheerful way.

"Rustic," Lucian notes fondly, looking around. "Hasn't changed much since I was last here. Nearly the same decor, even."

"I don't remember it at all," says Ghost, sliding into a seat next to mine and flagging down a harried-looking waiter with an armful of dirty plates. His eyes widen when he sees us, but to his credit, he merely nods.

"A little before your time," Lucian says to Ghost with a small smile. "I would come here with Jeremiah after our philosophy classes..." He seems to shiver. "Ah, but that was so long ago now."

I study the hollowness of his eyes as he orders a round of drinks from the hapless waiter who has finally made it to our table. Ghost leans against me, resting his head on my shoulder as though struck by sudden weariness

Lucian looks up as the waiter arrives with our mugs of ale. "Do you still make the chowder? The one with the white sauce and the biscuits?"

"Of course," the waiter assures us smoothly. "An order of the chowder, then?"

"One for each of us," Lucian says, gesturing at me and Ghost. "Assuming that's all right with you. It was one of my favorites." The waiter whisks away as we nod our affirmatives. I catch Lucian looking at the two of us with an odd expression. "When did the two of you get so cozy?"

I stiffen, but Ghost doesn't let me pull away, leaning even harder against me. I flush despite myself, and for once, I have no answer. I'm not even sure there's really a word for what Ghost and I are. Certainly there's something between us, but how do I explain that to someone else? To have lived through what we did... It leaves a mark on a person.

Ghost and I are marked like that. All of the Moon Children from the Pits are. We all had our scars and nightmares, had saved one another and been saved in return. In the end, I merely glance away from Lucian, as though to talk about it would cheapen it.

"Shh, Brother." Whatever else Ghost's about to say is cut off at a sudden outburst across the restaurant. A bar on the far side is overrun with a small but lively crowd, arguing among themselves in tones that grow louder and more frantic by the moment.

"Ah. Students. It was hardly worth coming here if you couldn't be entertained by arguing the finer points of Meridian lore." He gestures over his shoulder. "There's a university a few blocks away."

"A university..." I echo, a sort of wonderment underlying my tone. I've never seen a university before. Most of the schools in BrightStone are in the Upper Tier. I didn't have access to those areas once I'd joined a clan, and foster mother or not, Mad Brianna hadn't put much stock in even basic education.

Given Moon Children were thieves and cutpurses mostly, our classrooms had been of a very different sort. Unless a Moon Child had been exposed to such things before their change, as Penny had, there wasn't much hope for learning it later. Why waste schooling on those doomed to die in the Pits anyway?

The thought of Penny sobers me. I miss my friend, but even so, memories of her always turn toward Bran and the rest of my clan. How are they doing down below? I have no doubt Bran is looking out for them, but I still want to do right by them. Whatever that means.

"Mags wants to see the other Moon Children educated, and I agree with her," Ghost says quietly. "And I think we should try to do it here. BrightStone is too tainted. After so many years of oppressing Moon Children, I hardly think the Upper Tier snobs are going to be too keen in letting them into the same classrooms as their precious children."

"It's a fair point," Lucian admits, turning toward me. "But it will take a lot of work, Mags."

"Please," I say fervently. "I know we have a lot of catching up to do, but I think those who want it—*really* want it—will make up for it. With no more Tithes, I don't know what our purpose as Moon Children is anymore, but if we aren't provided with some opportunities, we'll be doomed to being nothing more than gutter rats for the rest of our lives." My mouth purses. "Which could be for a very long time, aye? I mean, the Rot started as an attempted Meridion immortality serum...and we're children of Meridians who took it, so..."

"That's something else we'll have to figure out. Infertile or not, if it does turn out that you have an extended lifespan, I'm sure some of the inheritance laws might need changing." Lucian studies Ghost. "But that's neither here nor there at the moment. Ah, our soups have arrived."

It's an odd shift in the conversation, but I've discovered Lucian doesn't like talking about things he doesn't have an answer for, so I let it slide. Besides, I'm starving, and the chowder is warm. The three of us dig into our food without another word, our only conversation echoing within the clink of spoons and my own hasty swallows.

It's hard for me to eat slowly. In the Pits, food was so difficult to come by that we all gobbled it up as fast as we could. Even Ghost eats faster than he might usually, though he nudges me gently in the shoulder.

"It's all right, Mags," he says, his eyes flicking to my empty bowl. "You can have as much as you want."

I smile sheepishly and take a roll, polishing it off in a few quick bites. "Old habits."

"Well, we're going to have to work on that," Lucian points out. "While your table manners have a certain charm, not everyone is going to be so understanding. So let's see...Moon Children education, the restoration of our family name, the collection of debts, and Mags's entrance into Meridian society. Does that about cover our current goals?"

"And fixing up your family house," I add. "Oh, and Ghost said I could have the garden, so I'll be wanting somewhat to plant." I finish the last of my soup, letting the spoon fall with a noisy clank.

"Did he now?" Lucian and Ghost share a long look. "And a garden. Well then. Shall we see about—?"

The last of his words are muffled as the students at the bar all get up at once and start filing through the doors or drifting to other parts of the tavern, as though some hidden signal told them that *now* their conversations were completed. I breathe an inward sigh of relief, anticipating a rush of quiet that will be very welcome to my now ridiculously sensitive ears.

One of the students, a brash-seeming young man with glasses and a wild spike of dark hair, approaches us, head cocked quizzically. "Oy! Is that some sort of costume? Is there a performance in the park again this evening?"

"Not that I'm aware of," I say coolly, turning up my face so the full effect of my glowing eyes is revealed.

Lucian coughs a warning, but the student jumps back in surprise, the lightning in his skin flashing rapid patterns up and down his arms. "Oh! You've got one of those new gen-med procedures done! Did it hurt?" He leans in for a closer look. "I wanted to get something like that, but it hardly seemed worth it since it's so expensive and the effect doesn't last—"

"She's not a Meridian," Lucian says firmly, interrupting the young man before he can say anything else.

My gaze darts to Ghost, but he shrugs. So much for keeping things quiet. Oh well. It was nice while it lasted, I suppose.

"I'm a Moon Child," I say finally. The dragon on my shoulder suddenly moves, its wings flashing out wide behind me.

The dragon's effect is even greater than the one caused by my hair, evidenced by the wave of gasps from the remaining students clustered by the door. They rush toward us almost immediately, their faces alight with a multitude of expressions: eagerness, curiosity, interest. What I don't see is the usual repugnance, the hidden warning signs, the sniffs of disdain, or the sour stink of fear. It is so incredibly different from anything I've ever experienced, and I waver with emotion, making it hard to swallow past the lump in my throat.

An oddity, yes. But a person at the core of it.

"Uh, is there something I can help you with?" I ask, trying not to fall over at the onslaught of new faces. Beside me, Ghost shifts almost imperceptibly. It's subtle, but he's positioned himself just a bit in front of me.

"A Moon Child? Really? I've always wanted to meet one!" A bubbly girl with a delicate beauty pushes her way to the front with a smile, her golden curls framing a pointed chin and dancing blue eyes. "My name is Lottie, and this knucklehead is Christophe."

The student with the black hair tips his head toward us. "Sorry if I came on too strong there." He brightens. "Mind if we sit?"

"Of course. We were about to leave, but I think we can spare you a few minutes." Lucian gestures to them all, sly amusement twinkling in his eyes. "Pull up a chair. Drinks are on me." He holds his hand out to shake theirs in quick and neat order. "Lucian, at your service. This is my brother, Trystan, and of course, you now know Magpie."

They don't wait to be asked twice, and in an instant, at least ten of them are perched in various places around our table. The waiter shudders but does a quick drink order, dodging around them with brutal efficiency.

"Oh, I have so many questions," Lottie says, moving her chair a little closer to me. "Is it okay if I ask? I mean, Moon Children—I practically thought they were fairy tales the way the history books talk about them. But to think we actually have one *here*?"

It takes everything I have not to recoil from her closeness, the way her presence seems to fill my space. I stiffen beneath the directness of her gaze. "Ah. Yes. So it would seem. I'm not really sure where to begin." My eyes dart toward Lucian. How much did he want me to say?

"It's all right, Mags," says Lucian. "Why don't we start with the basics?"

I frown at him, not sure of his game, but in that moment, I realize he's pulling their strings nearly as much as he's pulling mine. And he never does anything without a very good reason.

"What the hell. I'll play." I reward Lottie with a cautious smile. "What do you want to know?"

A tisket, a tasket,
A poppet and a basket.
One to fill with all my things,
One to dance from pulling strings.

— CHAPTER FOUR —

So you really are from BrightStone, then? All of you?" Lottie pushes away her empty glass on the table, her eyes slightly glazed over. I've lost track of how many she's had, but her focus is still whip-smart. "I'd heard we recently reinstated contact, but they haven't really said why."

"To think we're already allowing visitors!" Christophe interjects. "Hey, do you think they'll allow us some field trips? I've always wanted to see what it was like."

"I'm not sure it's as open as all that," Lucian says thoughtfully. "We're a bit of a special case, as I am a Meridian."

Ghost smiles wanly. "It's a little confusing since we've been on BrightStone for so long. Our skin seems to have lost its electric pulses."

"Ah, skin-wasting." Christophe nods, peering at Lucian closer. "Shame, mate. I've not seen that before, either, but my understanding is that it's reversible once you're up here long enough." His own skin is fluttering with a steady beat. No longer the nervous excitement of before, this seems more routine. Comfortable.

My eyes dart to Lucian and then to my own arm. As a half-breed, there might be a chance I'll also get the electrical pulses in some fashion. How difficult will it be to hide my emotions then? It's an uneasy thought, and I immediately push it away, mostly because I'm too cowardly to want to examine myself that closely. Though by Lucian's reckoning, I can't keep my emotions in check even *without* such obvious indicators.

"So…Magpie, is it?" Lottie blinks at me. "Is it true what they say about Moon Children?"

Ghost nudges me, as though he can feel me bristling beside him. "Well, that depends on what they say," I retort smoothly, not in the mood to coddle them. "If they say we're half-breeds, then yes, that is true. If they say we are treated as third- or fourth-rate citizens, less than the rats the inhabit the sewers, then yes, that is true." My eyes narrow at her, her skin flashing in sudden panic. "If they say we are nothing more than scapegoats for a plague of Meridian origin, then yes. That is also true."

"Mags," Ghost hisses, frowning.

"Ah, no, that's not what I meant," Lottie says, looking away. "I only was hoping to find out if you were truly of Meridian lineage, or if that was a rumor made up by…well, whoever, I guess. There's been so much debate lately in the classrooms about Moon Children and what it might mean for our own families." Her mouth compresses into a tight line. "If I offended you, I'm sorry."

"I see." I suck down another mug of the ale, tossing my head back at the end and turning to expose the brand on my neck. There's a pause in the air around us as the students suddenly go silent. My own heartbeat is rattling along, but that's not anything they need to know just yet.

"What is that?" Christophe asks quietly. One hand reaches out as though he might touch it, but a shake of Ghost's head has him retreating.

"It's the mark of my clan," I say. "The symbol that indicates I'm allowed to be sacrificed within the Pits, the mines used to house plague victims." I lift my face toward them, my voice growing husky. "I spent almost a year underground. In the dark. Starving. Eating rats. Caring for the plague victims until they died."

Lucian leans forward before I can add anything else. "Magpie is a sort of liaison here in Meridion, a voice to speak for the other Moon Children in BrightStone. We'd like to bring more here, of course, but we wanted to make sure the situation was safe for them—prejudice being what it is, of course."

Lottie nods a little too vigorously, but there's a gleam of innocent righteousness beaming from her face. I don't look at Lucian. I suspect I know what he's doing, but I can hardly blame him. We do need allies. What better place to look for them than the students of the local university? Not that I would know much about that sort of thing, but looking at the eager faces all around us, I think I understand.

I soften my expression and catch Lottie's eyes. "I could use your help, you know. All of you." My mouth drifts into a smile. "I'm afraid I don't know much about your culture, and I want to be able to properly teach my brothers and sisters the right way to visit—perhaps even to stay."

"Stay? Really?" Lottie looks at me with rapt attention. "Where would they live? Could we bring them to classes? I think my humanities professor would just love to have you give a lecture on post-modern plague survival."

"One step at a time," says Ghost. "I'm sure we can arrange something, but we have slightly bigger problems at hand." He grimaces. "The first being a place to stay. We have a house, but it's a bit run-down. We need to fix it up before we can bring any of the others here."

I let my eyes widen, my face growing slack and innocent as I turn toward Christophe. "I don't suppose you'd know of anyone who might be able to help us out? I don't think there's anything structurally unsound with the place. It's mostly roof leaks, peeling paint, and whatnot."

The words hang from my lips, and I can see the calculations whirring in Christophe's mind, his face practically buzzing with beer and ideas. It's not a malicious thing, I don't think, but it reminds me very much of Lucian after he's made some sort of discovery. Like a cat who's found something pretty to play with, maybe. Something he'll want to show off later. And what a nice way of becoming indispensable to the strange new person in the city but to offer help?

"Oh, I'm sure I can round up some of this group to lend a hand," he says with a smile.

Lottie nods. "Of course! And maybe some of the vocational students could assist with the electrics. My arranged is in that school. I could talk to him, if you want."

I frown. "Arranged?"

"Arranged marriage partner," Lucian explains. "They often have them on Meridion as a way to keep the bloodlines and inheritance issues in check. Limited resources up here and all that."

"It's not final yet," Lottie says, staring at her mug with glazed eyes, her cheeks flushing hot. "I mean, he's nice enough and all that..." She jerks her head up. "Do they have arranged pairings in BrightStone?"

I stifle a laugh at the idea. "Not among Moon Children. Maybe in the Upper Tier, but that's not anything I really bothered with. Social niceties aren't for the likes of me, I'm afraid."

"Bet they could find someone up here for you. Those eyes of yours..." She yawns at Christophe. "As much as I'd like to stay and keep talking, I think it's about time to head out. I still have a paper due tomorrow."

"It's been fascinating, though. Really something," he says apologetically as he gets to his feet. "If you want to give me your address, I'll ask around and see how many are willing to help." A hint of mischief plays over his face. "I'm sure we wouldn't mind cutting a class or two. We can stop by in the morning, if you like?"

Lucian produces a pen from his vest pocket, writing something down on one of the napkins and hands it to him. "That will do nicely. And this isn't a charity, mind. We'll pay you for your work, if that helps with the undecided."

Christophe brightens. "I suspect it might. All right, then." He reaches out to help Lottie to her feet. "We'll see you tomorrow."

"Tomorrow," Lucian agrees, tipping his glass at the other man with a slight smile.

"Well that was...interesting." My feet lurch out from underneath me, and I let out a belch that rumbles out of my chest loudly enough that it should bring the buildings down around us. Or so it feels from the way it echoes down the alleyway.

Lucian stares at me, pinching the bridge of his nose as a cluster of people jerk their attention toward us. I suppose it makes sense. I've removed my cloak, a flushed heat radiating off my face in waves, and my hair and eyes are lit up like silver lightsticks.

I size up the closest building, my fingers suddenly twitching. "You think they'd notice if we took a little detour?"

"No, Mags. Not tonight." Ghost takes my hand firmly. "You don't know how to run on metals like this, and you're sure as hell not going to try it drunk."

"Drunk, skunk," I mumble, yawning. "So Lucian, was Ghost arranged too?" The ale has loosened my tongue, the question dropping out of me with all the grace of crumbling bricks.

Both Lucian and Ghost flinch. "I was six or seven when I left here Mags," Ghost says. "Even assuming I was, it's not like I have any recollection of it. I doubt anyone would want me now, given our current situation."

"Oh, I don't know," I slur. "You'd be a great catch, aye? The son of the great arch— *Mmmph.*" I frown, realizing he's cupped his hand over my mouth.

"That's quite enough." His nostrils flare, and I know he's annoyed, but it's all a haze and I'm not entirely sure how I'm supposed to react. "I don't need my potential matrimonial status blasted out to the neighbors quite yet. This is Meridion, not a stud ranch."

"All right, children." Lucian tugs on both our shoulders, pushing us in front of him as we turn onto the next street. "If you're going to fight, at least wait until we get home and you can have a proper row there. Although, that still begs the question about sleeping arrangements. My bed is still in reasonably good shape so it will suit well enough for tonight. But you two..."

"Not sleeping on your...on your mother's bed," I say, my voice still too loud. "I'll take the floor. Slept in worse places. The dead make for poor pillows." Staggering, I shuffle away to vomit noisily against the wall of the nearest building.

"Mags?" Ghost's concerned face wrinkles into resigned disgust, when I return, wiping my mouth with the back of my hand. "Keep that up and you're sleeping alone, either way."

"Not like I was expecting some sort of sexy shenanigans," I retort, my eyes watering.

"No shenanigans of any kind," Lucian says sharply. "Not while I'm around at least."

"I'll remind you of that later," Ghost says, something dark in his tone.

Lucian makes no sign that he heard him, and inwardly, I roll my eyes. Another brotherly spat, I suppose, weighted by history and memories I know nothing about. At the moment, my brain is swimming in pleasant confusion so I don't much care anyway. Sometimes the drama between the two of them is ridiculous, though if I'm honest enough, Moon Children are no better. Bran, Penny, and I certainly had our moments. But whether there's a deeper meaning to Lucian's words or he simply doesn't want to hear Ghost and I shagging, I don't really know.

Not that Ghost and I have shagged, either. Not even down in the Pits. I'm not entirely sure why. Before all this, it was just me and Sparrow fighting for survival on the rooftops of BrightStone. I might have had a casual dalliance here or there with other clan members, but it was never long-term, nothing more than a dropping of trousers and a quick press against a brick chimney.

There was never a need for it to be anything more. As I told Ghost so long ago, there's no room for love in the lives of Moon Children. The threat of the Pits hung over us like a pendulum made of knives, our deaths a certainty. To take the risk of truly binding yourself to someone was simply asking for heartbreak. I'm sure some of the others tried to make it work, but we all knew where that road led. And I'd always been more than content to walk it alone.

But I'm not alone now. Between the fragile clan I helped create in the Pits and Lucian and Ghost beside me, I have people to rely on, to care for. It's unnerving and new, and sometimes it feels as though if I breathe too hard, the delicate tendrils holding us all together will disintegrate like ashes beneath a hollow wind.

But no, that isn't quite right, either. Somewhere beneath it all are bonds forged in iron and smelted in blood, and no matter how stretched they might get, they will never break. Because some bonds are beyond mere mortality.

I glance sideways at Ghost. The two of us never really talked about whatever it was between us. There wasn't time before, but perhaps there is now.

"Ah, home sweet home," Lucian mumbles, and I realize we've reached the house. He runs his fingers over the panel. I'm standing close enough to it that my heart whirs in response, beating the pattern as he presses the buttons in time. It's different from earlier; he must have changed it before we left.

The three of us tumble into the foyer, the overhead chandelier flickering when I tap the switch to turn it on. Almost as one, we let out a collective sigh. Not that the place is any less dusty and empty than it was a few hours ago, but there is still something about it that feels like *home*.

Lucian lets out a yawn. "I think there might be some passible linens in the cedar closet. I don't know about you two, but I'm about ready to crash." He staggers up the stairs, running a hand through his hair.

"Well, he's tucked off," Ghost says. "Anything else you want to do?"

"Only if it involves a bed. Where are you sleeping?"

"Well, I suppose that's up to you. If you want your space, that's fine, but I wouldn't object to sharing. Not to do anything other than sleep," he says quickly. "But I…" His words drift away even as his fingers drift into mine.

"I understand." And I do. After so many months down in the Pits, I haven't slept alone in ages. Besides, the memories come pouring in at night, washing over me in a haze of death and rotting flesh.

Cowardly maybe, but Ghost had his own trials down there, including being captured and forced to sit blindfolded in a cage full of Rotters. I know he hasn't been sleeping particularly well, either. Yet, here in his family's home, it somehow feels more formal than anywhere we've slept before. And oddly enough, it doesn't bother me in the slightest. "Of course," I murmur. "Always."

He lets out a ragged breath, as though he'd been afraid I'd say no, and a small piece of my heart breaks a little that I still might be considered so faithless. Or maybe he's suffering from his time below more than I thought.

Together we mount the stairs and head down the hall to the room we decided would be mine. Ghost disappears momentarily and comes back with an armful of blankets and pillows that smell faintly of cedar but seem clean enough for all that. But then, I'm not one for niceties. I'd been lucky to have blankets of any sort growing up—and certainly had nothing so nice in the Pits. Such things are now the height of luxury, with or without a mattress to curl up on.

"So, one of you going to give me the details on this Lady Fionula business? I thought Lucian had a lover already. Jeremiah?" I mumble at him as we arrange the blankets into something satisfactory.

"Ah, that's a sore spot with him." Ghost toes off his boots, and I do the same, crawling into the blankets. "As you may have guessed based on this morning's breakfast conversation, Lucian wasn't arranged to be married to Jeremiah, but to his sister, Lady Fionula."

I nod. "Well that would explain her overall attitude, then. She seems a bit put out about the whole thing."

"Just so. It was quite the scandal at the time, and not only because of our exile. Casual relationships between the same sex aren't frowned up in Meridion—even if you're married, you can have a mistress or what have you—but a marriage is expected to result in children. By its very nature, it's meant to continue the bloodlines."

I'm trying to wrap my brain around the concept and not sure if I should be surprised or horrified or both. Or maybe it's all old hat to people like this, lost in their odd decadence and godlike sensibilities. Maybe that's why the scientists in the Pits were able to kill us so easily, our infertility. If a life is thought so little of, it's easy to end it without conscience.

"So your brother didn't want to marry her, despite that particular clause?" I frown.

"He's a stubborn thing, if you haven't noticed," he says wryly. "When it comes down to it, he wasn't willing to compromise. A lot of hurt feelings all around, really. He was actually very fond of her, as well. He just liked her brother that much more."

"*Mmmph.* How very romantic." And I suppose it is, though I hardly know a thing about romance.

"Isn't it?" Ghost's voice is suddenly husky and hot in my ear.

I shiver, shifting so we're lying face-to-face. The door's closed, and even though there aren't any lamps in the room, we're illuminated by my hair. There's no hiding in the shadows here. Just simple, naked emotions reflected back at each other in careless fashion.

It's the first time either of us have really looked at each other in a very long while. Before I was captured and forced into the Pits, we'd been too busy trying to solve the mystery of the origins of the Rot, to survive in a political game of cat and mouse that left very little space for anything else. Not that he hadn't tried a gentle overture at least once, but even he had been quick to acknowledge that the timing wasn't right and entanglements of that nature could not happen. Perhaps if it had been merely a physical act, it would have been simple enough, but nothing is ever simple when it comes to Ghost.

He wants more. I know it. I've always known it. But the Pits themselves became a nightmarish parade of death and sadness, and the need to escape had ridden us hard. And since finding our way topside, we've had almost no time to ourselves, either.

But now perhaps we could.

He brushes the hair out of my face with careful fingers, stroking the side of my cheek. I close my eyes, marveling at the simple grace of the gesture. The warmth of his hand, the scent of his skin, lavender and a hint of something else, lingering in his shirt as he pulls me closer.

There's an odd edge to his breath when he exhales, and he buries his face in my neck. A damp heat slides over my collarbone, and I swallow. He's crying.

I'd only seen him weep once before, when we found the remains of his mother in the Pits, surrounded by her lab equipment, empty and alone and anciently quiet in her repose. But that had been different—a grief hidden under years of hoping and wishing, the anguish of a little boy forced to lose her too soon.

This... This is different.

My own hands drift up over his neck and into his thatch of brown hair. "It's all right," I murmur. "We're here and alive, and I won't leave you again. I promise." The words babble out of me.

He clutches me even tighter as the last of his sobs fade. "I'm sorry," he whispers, pulling away so we're looking at each other again. His cheeks are flushed and damp, misery and regret mingling in the dark depths of his eyes. "I think I'm a bit overwhelmed," he says finally. "You. The house. Finally being here."

"It's a lot to take in. And I'm completely dependent on you and Lucian to guide me through everything. Why do you think I want to bring the rest of my clan?" A soft bark of laughter escapes me. "It's ridiculous and I know it, but for all my fine words to Lucian earlier, I'm a little afraid of how it's going to turn out. Having my clan... Well, it's a family, aye?"

"Aye." He leans forward to brush his lips against my eyelids, then moves slow and delicate over my cheekbones before finally reaching my mouth. The kiss is long and lingering and hot, and it's filled with quiet promise, echoed in the burning need threading beneath my skin.

"But don't forget our family, either." He pulls on my lower lip with his teeth, nipping me gently. "You and me, Mags. Sometimes I think I would be happiest if it was just the two of us." He rolls onto his back. "Just leave this behind. Meridion. BrightStone. All of it."

"And where would we go?" I raise a brow at him and worm my way over so I'm nestled in the crook of his arm.

"Anywhere. Nowhere. Someplace safe and quiet. Simple." He lets out a quiet chuckle. "Somewhere private."

I pause. "If it's a simple shag you want..."

"No, that's not it. Not all of it," he admits wryly. "We'll get to that part. Maybe when we're both a little less drunk. I don't know about you, but I'd like to remember that moment outside the haze of too much ale."

"You've more patience than I do," I grumble, debating if I should just take matters into my own hands.

"Oh, I'm not. Patient, that is." He nips my ear. "But I *am* tired. My dreams have been bad since we came back from the Pits. It's hard for me to shut my eyes without seeing…everything. Some of this other stuff feels as though it's a walking nightmare, even now. Like I'll wake up and I'll be back there in that cage and the smell… The smell, Mags, it's going to overwhelm me, and you…you won't be here at all. Because I've been waiting and waiting and looking for you, but no matter how fast I run, you're never there. It's always as though I've just missed you."

I've been so caught up in everything else going on that I've barely stopped to consider how the other two are really feeling. "You haven't mentioned any of this before. I didn't know." A hot flush of shame rolls through my belly. "I'm sorry."

"Didn't want to worry you." His voice is growing softer, drifting into something thick and heavy, and I realize he's falling asleep. "You did so much for us. I can't bear to ask you for anything more."

He goes silent then, and the rise and fall of his breathing slides over me, wrapping me in a quiet comfort. Back in the Pits, listening to my clanmates breathe in the darkness was one of my few anchors to remind me of our humanity, that despite what I had to do, what I'd been asked to do, we were still somehow connected and alive.

The difference now is that his breathing is only for me, connecting me to this room, this life, and I know I've escaped whatever fate was destined for me below in the Pits. In the BrightStone slums, I'd always been the one to protect Sparrow. It was an instinctual thing, born of many years of living on the streets, a bond deeper than even sisterhood might be. But Ghost and I were nearly equals in that respect. For all he's tried to protect me, I've done the same for him, both of us rescuing each other from ourselves again and again.

My fingers twine around his, and I pull the blankets up tighter. The breeze blows in through the window tasting cool and clean, and the leaves of the tree outside laugh in a fit of sighs, the creak of the boughs an odd lullaby.

When I dream, Ghost and I are on a ship, rocking upon the waves as we sail away into the horizon.

Pat-a-cake, pat-a-cake, baker's lass.
Where is your future and where is your past?
Wrapped in poison and sugared dough,
Sweet and sour and full of woe.

— CHAPTER FIVE —

Footsteps on the roof, my feet flying over copper shingles, moonlight hazy on Sparrow's hair, reflecting soft and silver. She laughs, her face turning toward me for an instant, but it's blurry. A lost memory fading from the recesses of my mind, her brown eyes sparkling as she smiles.

My heart shatters with a grief I've pushed away again and again, a loss I will never understand. "Wait!" I call, but my voice is nothing more than a raspy hiss, and she slides away into the fog.

I sprint after her, my coat sweeping behind me, but the bobbing form is gone. And then I'm barefoot in the dark, my toes slapping against the flat damp ground of the Pits, the air thick and hard in my lungs. I clutch my hammer in my hand, waiting for Rotters to shamble from the shadows, the cloying scent of death a perfume that will forever taint everything I touch.

When I reach the great waterfall, I see a Rotter kneeling there. My hammer has become a knife, the handle nestled in my palm. How many times did they beg me for death? How often did I grant it? My skin is flush with their black blood, staining me like acid.

"Please," the Rotter groans. "Please." Sparrow turns her face toward me, the flesh falling from her cheek, teeth spilling onto the ground as her tongue hangs loose as if it's barely attached.

The blade cuts her throat quickly, the hot blood sluggish as it drips, and yet she doesn't die. She falls into my arms, her fingers clutching my shoulders. "Your fault," she mutters. "Your fault…"

I jerk awake, clawing at my throat as I struggle to breathe. I've somehow become entangled in the sheets like some sort of deranged spider, the corner of one side smothering my face. Coughing, I roll to my side, twisting out of the linens so I'm lying on the hardwood floor, the cool air seeping over me from the window.

Ghost is still sleeping, and I don't have the heart to wake him, though my own chest is whirring in a frightful manner. Even my clockwork dragon remains motionless on the mantle, a puff of smoke escaping its nostrils. My feet urge me up, and before I realize it, I'm through the window, fleeing into the branches of the closest tree and sucking in huge gulps of air.

I shake off the memories of the Pits and the way they collapsed on us, the waterfall flooding the tunnels while Ghost and I tried to escape. We came so close to dying that day we could have kissed Death on the mouth.

But Sparrow was never in the Pits, never Tithed. The Inquestors killed her because of my foolishness, and I'll never forgive myself for it. My fingers find her necklace at my throat, the last connection I have to her—black leather, crystalline jade beads. The High Inquestor broke it once, and Ghost found every bead, digging in the filthy cobblestones to bring it to me when I had no hope of ever seeing him again, of ever being free of the underground maze of despair I'd become a part of.

Shivering, I focus on the feel of the bark beneath my hands, the rustle of the leaves. Foreign things to me, certainly, but no less soothing for all that. Right now, anything different is a distraction. I wince slightly at the moon peeking through the clouds now and then. She's like an old friend, and I take comfort in her, clinging to the branches until my breathing matches the sway of the tree and I doze off into a restless sleep.

"Mags?" Lucian's voice wafts up from the bedroom, pulling me from my respite. "Ah, there you are. Should have expected it I suppose." He peers out the window at where I'm perched in the tree and snorts. "And here I thought you'd be halfway up the Five Towers by now."

"I figured I'd start small, aye?" I say airily, the nightmares of the previous evening retreating to some dark corner of my mind. Not that I even knew what the Five Towers looked like, but it sounds exciting enough that I'm itching to see it. With any luck, I'll get a real tour of the city to put a sight to the name. "Never really climbed a tree before. I wanted to enjoy the moment."

I relax against the bend of one of the larger branches, the bark carving its presence into my skin. The roughness has a reality to it, even though simply being here is more of a fairy tale than anything I've ever known. From the peppery scent of the leaves to the ticklish march of tiny bugs parading up and down the branches, it seems almost obscene in its purity. The dawn's light has me closing my eyes against its brilliance, but for some reason I don't want to really go inside, blind or not.

"Did you want breakfast up there? Ghost's returned from the market with some basics, and I believe the students will be here shortly to start work on the house." He cocks a red-hued brow at me. "And not that I'm much of a fashion plate myself, but you might want to take a few minutes to wash up before they arrive. We're going to have to get you some clothes today, too. Perhaps that Lottie girl can help us out."

I stifle a groan. "If you remember, I killed a man the last time I wore a corset. I'm not entirely sure that was the corset's fault, but I don't want to take the chance."

He rolls his eyes. "Fair enough. But we'll still need to figure something out. Come on." He holds out a hand to me, but I slip down the branch easily enough and crouch on the windowsill, balancing on the balls of my feet.

My stomach rumbles loudly just as Ghost enters the room, a hamper of biscuits hanging from his arm. I sweep past Lucian, practically dancing to the basket, my toes wriggling as Ghost hands me a pastry.

I nibble on it carefully, trying to be mindful of whatever manners I've got, but I give up in the end, tearing into the buttered monstrosity and gulping it down. I follow it with two more. Ghost sets the hamper down, and I spot what looks like a cluster of sausages wrapped in wax paper.

The three of us set to it, polishing off the rest of the food in short order. My dragon launches itself to my shoulder, and I reward it with a bit of old coal I found in the kitchen stove yesterday. It munches happily enough, leaving tiny bits of black on my arm as it chews. I brush the crumbs of my own meal from my lap and lick the butter from my fingers. "This is really good."

"Well, we'll stock the larder as best we can," Lucian says. "Perhaps better table manners will come with a fuller belly."

I shoot him a sour look. "Aye, well."

"That's not particularly fair." Ghost pokes him hard in the arm.

"But he's right enough," I say. "As long as I get to eat my fill, I'll try to be civilized. After all, can't scare the locals into thinking a monster lives here. The horror."

"Somehow I think you'll manage." Lucian rubs his fingers over his chin. "I suspect I might do with a bit of a shave and a cleanup, as well." He glances over at his brother. "And you? Will you keep your hair dyed or let it grow white again once we've seen the Council?"

About to take a bite of another sausage, Ghost shuts his mouth and then shrugs. "I don't know," he admits. "It would be easier to assimilate if they think I'm still a normal Meridian, but..." His gaze flicks to mine, holding it for a moment. "But it feels dishonest. I'm not the same as I was. Or maybe I never was normal to begin with, depending on when Mother injected me with the serum."

I'm not sure what to tell him. I understand what it is to hide oneself for reasons of safety and political motivation, but I also know how tiresome a burden it is. The students who have offered to help us did so thinking me exotic, but I'm uncertain they'd be as enthusiastic if they discover that one of their own people has been turned into one of mine. If you can even call it that. I'm not sure if Ghost is truly a Moon Child or if he merely looks like one. What we had assumed was simply a genetic anomaly found in the progeny of Meridian and BrightStone's people turned out to be less about mating and more about who was injected with the serum. Or more specifically, the Inquestors who were given the serum and had a child with a BrightStone woman created a Moon Child. A BrightStone citizen who was injected got the Rot.

In the end, I'm not sure if it makes any difference, but I know Ghost is trying to spare my feelings. I reach out to squeeze his arm. "Retain the illusion a little longer, maybe. It will come out soon enough, and better to do it on terms of your own making, aye? Don't give the Council any reason to turn you down."

"Wise words, oh Magpie," intones Lucian with a smile. Whatever he's going to say next is cut off by a sudden knocking on the door. "That should be them." He brushes off his lap and heads out of the room, his feet tapping lightly down the wooden hallway. There's a distinctiveness to his step I haven't heard before, even when we lived at Molly Bell's. Perhaps it's confidence that this place is his, if nothing else.

"I suppose we ought to go join them." Ghost cracks his neck. "I'll be very happy to have a proper bed and a working kitchen."

"There you go again, putting on all those high-class Meridian airs." I slip on my boots and hold out a hand to help him up before snagging my glasses.

"What can I say? I'm just greedy, I guess." A little grin flits over his face, and he ducks in fast to steal a kiss.

"Bold fellow, to court a Moon Child." But he only grins wider at my expression, tugging my hand so I'm forced to follow him down the stairs. My dragon glides behind us, landing on my shoulder as we reach the foyer

Lucian has opened the door, revealing the wide-eyed stares of Lottie, Christophe, and a handful of others, their heads raised on straining necks as they attempt to peer inside.

"Oy," Christophe says, gaping at us. "When you said you needed help fixing up the place, I didn't know you meant the d'Arc mansion! I mean, you told us your names, but it didn't register... To think we met the scions of d'Arc in a pub! I thought this place was haunted for sure. I don't think anyone's been inside here for years."

Lucian's smile grows tight and thin. "Haunted by old memories, perhaps." He tips his hat at the group. "I'm going to head to the bank to determine our financial situation. If I can clear that up, I'll see about ordering us some additional furniture. I suggest you start on the plumbing first and then maybe the electrics. The roof after that and then we can focus on the internals—fading wallpaper and broken windows and the like." He hands a thin leather wallet to Ghost. "Some basic notes as to what I found in some of the other rooms, as well as some payment slips if you need to purchase supplies." And with that, he strides away, his hands shoved deep into his coat pockets.

Lottie is armed with a set of buckets and brushes and gives me a brassy smile as she shoves her way past Ghost. "Come on, you lot. Let's get started." She turns around as she studies the foyer. "Where do you want us?"

The other students pile in behind her, and Ghost gives a little bow. "Anyone here know pipes? I believe the bathtub upstairs is not working correctly."

"I think I can manage that much," Christophe says, hoisting his toolbox at me with a good-natured grin. He gestures at two of the other students and they mount the stairs, chattering like excited birds at a feeder.

Lottie smiles. "They've been wanting to try out their skills in a real environment for some time now, especially in an older building like this where everything isn't so cut-and-dried." She gives the house an appraising look. "The architecture is very interesting, did you know? No one builds houses like this anymore."

"I don't think anyone ever built them like this," Ghost says before turning toward me. "Shall we take a look at the roof, then?"

I frown at him. "I don't know anything about roofing."

He raises a brow at me, his eyes flicking sideways at Lottie, and I know what he wants. The other students watch me curiously, and inside, I cringe. But I had agreed to become a circus animal of sorts to help our cause, so here we are.

"Maybe. I can at least make the effort," I say, squatting to unlace my boots.

Ghost asks one of the students for a ladder, and I assume he's continuing his own charade for the sake of the act, and I leave him to it. I don't know the first thing about roofs except how to dance on them, but I suppose I can find a hole as well as anyone.

We head outside to the far side of the house where the brickwork seems most agreeable. Without hesitation, I dig my fingers into the stone, easily finding purchase in the grooves. After climbing my way up cave walls in the dark for so long, this is almost laughably simple.

I shimmy up past the first floor, resting briefly on the lintel of one of the larger windows.

"What is she doing?" Lottie whispers loudly. "Doesn't she know how dangerous that is?"

I can almost hear Ghost giggle as he drags one of the ladders to the other side of the window. "Ah, well, Moon Children are rather agile."

She seems to take this explanation at face value, making an appreciative noise as I sweep upward, edging away from the massive round window that must be the one in d'Arc's bedroom.

I give it a wide berth, not sure how solid the frame is. There are no shutters around it and no sill of any kind. Once I scramble over the drainpipe and lift myself onto the roof proper, it's easier to find my bearings.

I mockingly doff an invisible cap at the others when they applaud. I'm almost disappointed I didn't include any real acrobatics, but perhaps it's better to save that sort of thing for later. Besides, the copper roof is bright as the Hells. No sense in doing anything too stupid when I can't see. And speaking of copper, it might be early morning, but the roof is going to be plenty hot under the sun.

"Oy," I shout down to Ghost. "Bring up my shoes, aye? I don't fancy frying my toes off up here."

He salutes me and gathers my boots, tossing them over his shoulder by the laces and ascending the ladder in short order. He's followed by Lottie and several other students though I'm not sure if they're going to be helping with the repairs or tagging along, but it doesn't particularly matter. The roof is plenty big to hold all of us.

By the time they climb up, I've already found two small holes where the wood trim rotted away. I point them out before beelining to the far side of one of the chimneys. It's the larger of two, but aside from the moss growing over the bricks, it seems structurally sound enough.

Lottie's group has found another hole where the roof tiles aren't overlapping right. Ghost pokes his finger into it. "Might have some mice coming in and out of here," he says, blowing away what look like mouse droppings. Maybe we should get a cat."

"And here I thought Meridion was beyond such mundane things as pest infestations," I say dryly, ignoring Lottie's snigger.

"Well, we don't have too many pests in general, but this house hasn't been kept up, obviously. It's only natural, if you think about it." She studies my face, her nose wrinkling.

"What?" I ask, unsure of what she's about.

"I was just thinking you really ought to do something with your hair." Her tone sets my teeth on edge.

I touch my hair despite myself, despite never caring about what I look like, save that one time at the fete at Lord Balthazaar's. But back then, Lucian and Molly Bell had disguised me as a courtesan, primping me with cosmetics and a glorious wig—and an unfortunate corset, even. Of course, I'd never had access to such things before, but I hadn't had more than a few minutes to appreciate their affect. I'd been on a mission to save Ghost, after all.

I blink at her. "I didn't mean any offense," she offers quickly. "Just that watching you climb the wall and the way you move on the rooftop here—you're exceptionally graceful. I was just thinking maybe..."

My face flames, my cheeks burning, but I can't tell if it's shame or something else. I don't dare look at Ghost. He's never said anything about the way I look, even when at my worst in the Pits, coated in the blood of the undead, but I'm fairly certain I don't want him weighing in on it now.

"I...see," I manage finally. Would this be the start of it, then? To have such luxury of time as to actually be able to care about fashion? I pinch the bridge of my nose, and beside me, Ghost is utterly still. Is he laughing? I don't want to look.

Would dressing up help our cause? Hurt it? Am I playing the part of some sort of noble savage or pretending to dance for my betters like a trained monkey on a leash? Or would it make the higher courts more open to our presence as we grovel before them to beg for their assistance?

In the end, practicality wins out as Lucien's gentle prodding and Lady Fionula's comments about looking more civilized for the Council echo back at me. "All right," I say finally. "What did you have in mind?"

"There is a salon near the university. Though, I'm sure you'd make quite the stir if your hair starts...glowing." She chews on her lower lip. "Well, you're bound to be noticed sooner or later. Perhaps we'll pick up something a bit more fashionable for you to wear, as well."

She climbs down the ladder, presumably to let Christophe know of our little excursion, and Ghost gives me a nudge.

"Look at you, making friends and getting popular." There's a hint of laughter beneath the words, but it doesn't feel as though he's mocking me.

"Ah well," I mutter. "I can roll in the mud afterward, if you prefer it that way."

His mouth quirks. "Mud or muslin, Mags. I'd love you in both, but I'm rather intrigued by whatever she has in mind."

I humph at him, my cheeks still hot, and I slap them hard as though to take the sting out of it. Being so flustered is a new feeling and not one I'm sure I like.

But here we are.

"Go on," Ghost says, digging into the wallet to pull out the Meridian notes. "I don't know how much you'll need, but this should do to start." He counts out about ten of them and I quickly fold the stack into a back pocket. "If you need more, see if Lottie can help you open an account for the House of d'Arc. It might work."

"If not, I can always run," I say, smirking when he chuckles.

"Yes. You definitely can run." He nudges me toward the ladder when Lottie reappears from the house, her face supremely satisfied. "We can handle the work here, and Lucian should be back sometime in the afternoon anyway."

I shake the dragon off my shoulder. "You stay here," I tell it, watching as it leaps to Ghost. "No need to explain you on top of everything else."

It hisses at me.

"Just so," I agree, tugging on my hair with a frown. Sucking in a deep breath, I make my way to where Lottie stands.

"Are you ready?" She beams, her golden curls a halo around her heart-shaped face.

"Aye. I suppose so."

Butterflies pressed betwixt and between
The pages of a book unseen.
Rotting wings and broken eyes
Crumbling like your unspoken lies.

— CHAPTER SIX —

Snip. Snip. Snip.

I shut my eyes, trying not to flinch away from the sound of the shears.

"—have a style you'd prefer, Magpie?"

I startle from my thoughts, eyes snapping open at the question. I have no idea how to answer it.

"Whatever you think is best," I say faintly. "Though I wouldn't mind trying to keep it longer." Ever since the High Inquestor shaved my head as part of the Tithe procession, I've been rather sensitive to it. Body heat was a precious commodity down below in the caves, and the fact that my hair now nearly reached my shoulders was at least somewhat of a reward.

The woman cutting my hair frowns thoughtfully, tipping my chin up and turning my face this way and that. "The texture is so unusual. And this color... I think we might do best to even out the sides here. However, there is a lot of damage in the back. I will do the best I can."

I can only nod at her. Her own hair is piled high in a magical swirl of golden curls. It's a marvelous feat I surely would never be able to emulate, but perhaps she can work my hair into something suitable.

The salon we are in is bright and cheerful, and the rich colors remind me of Molly Bell's Conundrum in the exquisite designs of the patrons' outfits—silks, brocades, cuts of cloth I have no name for, save that they are beautiful. But the resemblance ends there. Molly's girls were always beautiful, but it was a hollow beauty, sadness leaking like water through a sieve in the quiet damp of their eyes.

Here, customers come and go, their conversations like chattering birds as they exchange pleasantries and quiet gossip. Hands, feet, hair—there are other services involving massages in the back, but I can barely stand to have anyone touch me for too long, let alone Meridian strangers.

Lottie sits across from me, her voice a comfortable cadence that reminds me a bit of Sparrow's raw enthusiasm. Someone who has not known true pain, perhaps, but there's something soothing about it, so I let her words roll over me, light like the pattering of spring rain.

"So are you promised to him?"

I frown. "Am I what to who?"

"Trystan. You know..." She leans in with a knowing wink. "The two of you seem awfully close. I'd hold on to that one if you are. When those two finally announce the restoration of the d'Arc name, they'll be inundated with betrothal requests, mark my words."

"Ah. I don't know anything about that," I say, trying to keep my face neutral. "Trystan doesn't seem particularly interested in arranged marriages, from what I can tell." My mouth purses. "Our relationship..."

How to describe it to someone who has no understanding of such things? Am I supposed to titter and blush? Make sly comments? There are too many pitfalls in such a discussion, and I don't know the rules.

"He found me in the darkest hour of my life and saved me," I say, not sure I like the way she's sizing me up. "And I did the same for him. Close doesn't begin to describe what we are."

Her face pales at whatever she sees glaring from behind my glasses, and she swallows hard. "Well then. Perhaps we'll just stick with simpler topics." Her smile grows slightly stiff. "Are there any that will do? I feel as though I'm walking into spiderwebs of electricity, to be honest. You're a prickly one, Magpie."

"I don't mean to be. I just don't like people knowing things... about me," I admit. "The more they know, the more it can be used against me." And it had. Again and again and again. I was always kept in the dark by those who knew better—or thought they did—and they would use what they knew of me to coax me to do their work.

"You said you were promised?" Might as well turn the conversation to her. I might learn more about the Meridian culture that way, at least.

"Oh yes." Her eyes dim the slightest bit. "It's an arranged thing—so many betrothals here are. What with all the limited resources here, it's almost always political in nature. My intended is nice enough, however. We make a good match in many ways. Of course, we're putting off actually registering the paperwork until I finish university. I don't want any distractions, and well, that sort of thing is a huge one."

"Sounds it," I say, again feeling somewhat distraught at the concept. I always assumed Meridians were free to do as they pleased. Lucian was betrothed, of course, though that particular web looked as though it would need a great deal of untangling. I'm not sure I want to inspect it too closely.

Bran often pointed out how I tend to ignore what I don't want to know or admit to myself. And relationships between others are nothing I've ever espoused myself, with one or two exceptions. Safer that way, I suppose.

But still. Imagining what it must be like to hold the weight of a family's hopes is dreadful, and I'm suddenly grateful that I have no part to play in such things.

"There now. I think that should about do it." The stylist quirks her mouth in a half smile. She hands me a mirror and turns me so I can get a closer look. My hair is still white, but it's been cleaned and combed smooth, so it nearly appears silver beneath the light. It's almost too bright for me to look at. The ragged bits have been evened out, the front curled so it curves like the crescent moon to rest gently against my shoulders, my right eye shadowed by an artfully combed bit of bang.

I reach up to touch it, wondering at the softness of it. Its fineness slips between my fingers like dandelion cirrus.

"Thank you," I say finally, glancing up at the stylist. "It's lovely."

"Well, yes," she agrees. "But of course, it would be. Though sometimes it is the canvas that makes the painter, if you know what I mean."

"If you say." I turn to Lottie, who is somehow beaming ever brighter at my transformation. "Now what? You said somewhat about clothes, aye?" I pause, unsure of what to ask for. "What would be a practical choice for the Council? We're supposed to make some sort of plea there, but I don't know what would make a good impression."

Lottie nods, tapping on her mouth. "There's a boutique around the corner that should do."

"No dresses, mind," I say, critically eying myself in the mirror again. "I need to be able to move. Dresses are too…constricting."

"Let's see what we can find that fits first, and then we'll take it from there." Lottie pays the stylist with a couple of quick strokes in an little booklet on the counter by the front. "I had them charge your household. If that doesn't work, Lucian will have to come here to settle accounts, but I don't think it will be a problem."

The stylist's eyes flicker over the booklet, brows rising at me before rewarding me with a smile. "Please don't hesitate to recommend our services. We're honored to serve those of the House of d'Arc."

"I'm—" I start to protest, but then really, what difference does it make? Technically, it's true. I'm of the d'Arc household, if not the House proper. "Thank you," I say finally, letting Lottie whisk me out the door.

I wince at the sudden burst of sunlight as she tugs me along to what I can only assume is a series of apparel stores. "Remember," I mumble at her. "No dre—"

"I know, I know. No dresses. Got it."

In the end, after what felt like countless hours of trying things on, we finally emerge into the relative darkness of early evening, our arms loaded with shopping bags. My mind whirls. I have almost no idea how much we've just spent, only that we sent the charges to the House of d'Arc for a great many things a great many times. I don't even want to imagine Lucian's face when he finds out, but he did say I needed to become a bit more civilized, didn't he?

Lottie turned out to be as brilliant at clothing as she was at hair, her expert eye quickly discerning whatever passes for fashion up here and how to best suit it to my slight figure. Although her eyes narrowed in the dressing room, she said nothing about the scars on my skin or the brand on my neck, now openly flashing like a badge of honor.

"Don't hide what happened to you," she told me, her face dark. "We need to know, to understand. Don't let us forget it, you know?"

I'm not sure I share her enthusiasm, but perhaps she has a point. And not only has she found me clothing to wear, she's loaded me up with toiletries and shoes, underwear and combs—all things that I've never owned before, nor cared to. Her brow rises when I continue to wear my hammer strapped to my hip, but that isn't really open to discussion. By now it is practically an extension of me.

But I have to admit I'm grateful for her help. The idea of shopping with Ghost or Lucian would have been more awkward than I care to think on.

I chuckle to myself. Odd that such things would make me uncomfortable now, given how much I've been through, but sometimes emotions can't be explained.

We trudge our way to the d'Arc house, my stomach rumbling at the thought of supper. "Do you think they've gotten very far?" I muse aloud, not terribly upset at having missed out on the roof repair.

"Guess we'll find out. Though the group Christophe and I assembled is pretty good." She hums to herself and then snaps her fingers. "Food. We'll go and order some, shall we? To be delivered? I'm sure they're all bound to be starving at this point."

She changes direction without waiting for an answer. Before long, we find ourselves in line at some sort of vendor, a vehicle with delicious smells emanating from it that damn near has me ready to pull the rear door off it. My stomach growls again, but Lottie is already speaking rapidly to the man at the cooking grill.

She waves me over a moment later. "All set," she says smoothly, gesturing to the burly man inside. "Just sign your name here on this card."

The man gives us a little bow and a nod. "We'll be at the address shortly, Miss. Glad to serve the House of d'Arc," he intones.

I frown at Lottie, carefully scratching out my name in my childish scrawl. "Are you sure that's okay? I don't know about the budget..." I shift the packages in my arms, uncomfortable with their weight.

"The cost of doing business," she says with a shrug. "Besides, Lucian said he would pay us for the work around the house, right? This is just a more direct route of doing so. Most of us are happy to help in exchange for a meal. It's not like we need the money anyway." Her lips purse. "Don't worry about it. If it ends up being too much, I'll cover the rest of the expense."

It's on the tip of my tongue to ask how, but something in her expression makes me swallow the question. Her eyes are bitter-sweet, the laughing chattiness gone, and I decide I don't want to know. At least not right now.

She brightens a moment later. "But I think the others will be so surprised at your new look, they probably wouldn't even notice if we bought half of Meridion." She nudges me with her elbow. "I can't wait to see their expressions."

"Ah," I say. "Yes." Though the truth is that I'm frightened. After trying to hide what I am in BrightStone for so long, such exposure goes against everything I've ever done.

We round the last corner of the street to where the house lays nestled. A rush of relief fills me when I see the trees from the garden rising above the roof as though they are waving me home. I push my glasses a little closer to my face. The sun is lowering in the sky, but it's really to hide my own expression as we see the others milling about the house. A huge pile of trash sits in front of the steps—rotting wood, old shingles, pieces of pipe, moth-eaten carpets. A large delivery wagon is also there, and a cluster of students is trying to wrestle what looks like a dresser through the front door.

I hesitate, letting Lottie take the lead. The Meridian woman strolls toward the group, her skin flashing in an excited manner. I resist the urge to hang back even farther, chastising myself for my cowardice. What would Bran and the other Moon Children say if they could see me cringing before a crowd?

It was only fashion, after all. And yet, inviting scrutiny seems to be the most terrifying thing I've ever done.

Perhaps I might sneak in the back way. I shiver. There are too many eyes about. Before I can come up with anything better, a copper mass bullets its way through the front door, arcing over the heads of the students and ignoring their sudden shouts.

My dragon, of course.

"Thanks," I say when it alights upon my shoulder. I can't help but give it a fond pat on the neck. When I realize nearly all eyes are on me, I can only wonder how ridiculous I must look, laden down with bags and these oddly fancy clothes.

Still, I stiffen my shoulders and head toward them, my fingers clutching the handles of the bags with a white-knuckled grip. The fact that I, who easily wielded a hammer to strike down the undead and the dying in shocking numbers, can be undone by shoes is an enigma.

Lottie has turned to face me, her smile broad. "Oh, and we've got a dinner wagon coming soon, too, courtesy of Magpie, of course."

Her words drown in a ripple of excited exclamations. At least I know where I stand now on the chain of interests. But then, I understand better than anyone how important food is.

"I'll just take my things inside," I say to Lottie, inclining my head at the rest of them. I want to ask where Ghost and Lucian are, but the urge to dash up the stairs and hide in my room wins out. I don't run, exactly. It's more a fast walk punctuated by these clunky shoes that seem to echo my presence through every room.

The house has changed somewhat in my short absence. I can see signs of the students' handiwork in the distinct lack of dust on the landing, so there's that much at least. I hurry toward the room where Ghost and I slept the night before, and I breathe a sigh of relief.

The silence is a blessing, surrounding me with quiet strength, and I suck in a deep pull of air as the bags drop from my hands. And then I blink.

And blink again.

Lucian has apparently made good on his word. My room has been transformed. The bed, with its massive four posters, is luxurious almost to the point of being obnoxious. The mattress looks so soft I could sink into it like water, and it's strewn with sheets of exquisite linen. But the bed nearly pales in comparison to the elaborate vanity in the corner with an enormous mirror and an armoire I might be able to live in, given half a chance and the need.

Black curtains hang from ornate curtain rods above the windows, drawn tight and shot through with silver threads and elegant embroidery of moons and stars. The fireplace mantle has been painted white, and the dragon lands upon it, its eyes sly and knowing as it curls into a ball as if to sleep. I nearly trip on the thick sheepskin rug as I stagger toward the bed, my fingers trailing along the carved wood with curious fingers.

"Do you like it?" Lucian's voice startles me, and I jerk my head toward him. He leans against the doorframe with a champagne gaze and a half smile tugging at the corners of his mouth. "It suits you. The hair, I mean."

I touch my hair, my mouth going dry. "It's too much," I say hoarsely. "The clothes, the room… It's too expensive…"

"Ghost and I discussed it, and we have the money. For something like this…" He gestures about the room almost shyly. "It's a very small price to pay for everything you've done for us, Mags. The princess in a fairy tale has to be granted her castle at some point, correct?"

"I've never thought of myself that way." I sink onto the bed, my head spinning.

"I know, but you deserve it—a real place to call home." His face grows softer. "For as long as it can be."

I'm not sure I understand the turn of his words, but I let out a quiet chuckle as I study the carvings again. "Well, you certainly have good taste, anyway."

"Of course." He glances over his shoulder. "And speaking of taste, Ghost should be back any moment. I think he went out to look for some dinner."

"Ah, well, Lottie arranged for a food wagon to show up." I wince beneath his suddenly narrowed eyes. "We charged the House, so, uh..."

"Did she now?" He tugs on his chin. "I suppose I'll call it a business expense. Let's hope they've got some good beer with them."

He extends a hand to me, and I take it, letting him pull me to my feet. He ushers me down the back stairs and into the kitchens, and though I've only been gone for the day, even I can see what a difference it made. They students have been busy, cleaning the rooms with brutal efficiency. Additional furniture gleams from corners and in hallways—fancy dining tables, cozy chairs, elegant carpets.

"We didn't replace all of it," Lucian points out. "Some things have extremely sentimental value, but we are the scions of d'Arc. I expect we'll be receiving many visitors in the upcoming weeks, and we have to act the part."

I repress a shudder. I'm still trying to adjust to even being here. I'm not sure I'm up to playing hostess just yet. But I smile at Lucian all the same and tip my head in a jaunty fashion. "I can amuse them with my more...interesting talents."

"Your presence alone will be enough." He stifles a snort. "But perhaps those dancing lessons we talked about so long ago wouldn't be a bad idea."

I roll my eyes, but we're already at the front of the house. The students are clustered around the food wagon, eagerly devouring small packages of fried potatoes and meat on sticks. Lottie sees me and rushes over with a handful of both, Christophe trailing behind her holding several foaming mugs of beer.

"Here, you must be starving!" Lottie thrusts a wax paper bag of potatoes at me before whirling back into the chattering fray. Christophe lowers his mouth to her ear, frowning when she shakes her head, the two of them clearly at odds about something. But that's less important to me now than my empty stomach.

The potatoes are hot and nicely salted, and I gobble them up carelessly, ignoring Lucian's side-eye at my lack of table manners. "One thing at a time," I say. It's not like anyone else is paying attention to me anyway. "Will we need them to return?"

Lucian snags a few of the potatoes from my bag. "I don't think so. The majority of the harder work has been done so there's no reason to keep them from their studies."

"What about the suite? How long will it be before that's ready for visitors?" I press the question on him. I'm still not sure how I'm going to set that up, but I can't help the guilty surge flaring in my gut. That I should be enjoying such frivolities while the rest of my clan remain below…

Even if I've supposedly earned it. We all did.

"We'll work on it," he promises me. "Let's get everything settled first and sort out some of the house paperwork. It won't do us much good to bring them up here if we end up getting kicked out for some petty reason. And there are some who will try to make that happen, Mags, have no doubts of that. Once it gets out that d'Arc's family has returned, they'll be looking for any excuse to bring us down. Some of them, anyway." He tsks. "Politics."

"Oh, come now. You used to be in the thick of the political riffraff, if I recall." A dark-skinned man emerges from the side-street shadows, lightning pulsing over his skin in a bright rush that nearly has me squinting. His hair is long and braided, hanging to the small of his back, and his suit glimmers with a precise neatness that screams money.

Behind him, Ghost trails, wincing apologetically at his brother.

Lucian startles, his head snapping toward the voice. "Jeremiah," he says hoarsely.

Jeremiah's expression softens, though something like hurt flickers in his eyes when he turns toward the house. "I'm on official business on behalf of my sister. Your Council hearing has been approved for the day after tomorrow. I thought I might stop by in person to relay the news, but I see you're rather busy." His mouth kicks up in a half-smile. "Or do you have a few minutes to spare?"

The question is pointed, layers upon layers of meaning I cannot begin to fathom, but Lucian's ears become quite red, indeed.

"I, uh… I wanted to fix it up before…well, you know. Get all odds and ends sorted out." Lucian's words falter into a thick mumble. Finally, he chuckles with a surprisingly warm timbre. "Do you want to see it, then? It's a bit rough for formal hospitality, but…"

A smile breaks across the other man's face. "I thought you'd never ask."

Before Ghost or I can say anything at all, the two of them mount the stairs. They don't touch exactly, but there's some sort of tension woven between them that feels as though it might unravel at any moment.

"That's a kettle of fish I'd rather not open, aye?" I turn toward Ghost with a wry grin. He blinks at me, as though seeing me for the first time, and I can't help but touch the odd cut of my hair. I forgot he hadn't seen me like this yet. "Is it…all right?"

He snaps out of whatever his thoughts are, eyes darting from my face to my hair to my clothes with an odd expression.

Lottie snickers and hands him a beer. "I'd say it's more than all right."

"I actually look like a person now. I suppose that might make all the difference." I squirm a little beneath his stare. It's not that I mind it, but I feel more naked before him now than I ever have, even when I *was* naked.

He absently takes the beer from Lottie, throwing it back in three large swallows. "That's not it," he says finally. "But we can discuss it later." His brows rise on the last of his words, and I bite down on my cheek to keep from laughing at this obviousness. "That said, it might be better to leave them alone for a bit," he agrees, tilting his head in the direction his brother and Jeremiah went. "I suspect they have a lot of...catching up to do."

Lottie takes a swig from her own bottle of beer, staring at the house. "One of the great Meridian tragedies," she says, a hint of longing in her voice.

"What is?" I frown, not following her line of thought.

She gestures to the house. "The two of them. There's barely a schoolgirl on Meridion who doesn't at least somewhat swoon at the romance between the Houses of d'Arc and Brasheen. The brother and sister sharing a lover, the failed betrothal, the very public declarations of love as the sons of d'Arc are forced into exile." Her gaze slides toward Ghost. "It's heavy stuff."

"I didn't realize they were both his lovers," I say, trying to puzzle it out. Lucian's apologetic nature toward Lady Fionula suddenly made a lot more sense.

"Ah, it's simple enough, according to Lucian." Ghost shifts uncomfortably. "The Brasheen House is very traditional. They were the ones who insisted on the marriage to begin with. When Mother disappeared, they wanted to break the betrothal agreement, but Fionula refused. It was her way of protecting Lucian, I think. She knows he loves her brother more—everyone does. And since she's technically head of the Brasheen House now and Lucian is the head of D'Arc House...well it's a private matter."

I frown. "But she can break it off now, can't she? I would have thought with your exile it wouldn't still stand."

"That's up to them," Ghost says. "I don't pretend to understand it all myself."

"It has to go through the court system," Lottie says, her voice distant. "At least my own betrothal did. There were all sorts of clauses about how and when and why, and the penalties for breaking it. Not every agreement is written that way, of course, but mine was. It's really rather convoluted."

"That's one way of putting it." I stare back at the thinning crowd of college students. As tired as I am, I surely don't want to interfere in Lucian's reunion with his lover, as awkward as it might be. "What now?"

"I suppose I could take you on a bit of a tour of some of the city? Or the university?" Lottie suggests. "Seeing as you're new here."

It is as good a plan as any, and it's not like I have anything better to do. I nudge Ghost. "Would you mind?"

"Maybe," he mumbles. "But not for the reasons you think." He catches my hand, running his fingers up the inside of my wrist, my pulse leaping beneath his touch. "Let's go take a look at the city then, shall we?"

The breath of wind, the salty sea
A rising tide and a setting moon
A ship is sinking upon the waves
The depths to take my lover soon

— CHAPTER SEVEN —

"Meridion itself is split between the Outer Spiral and the Inner Spiral. There's any number of ways between them—air taxis are typical, of course, but if you want to get the real flavor of the city, nothing is better than the subway," Lottie informs me enthusiastically as we hurtle through a tunnel, ensconced within a comfortable train car.

I shiver against the feeling that we've been swallowed by some mutant worm. It's not like I've ever been on one before. There was a train in BrightStone once before the tracks rusted into nothing, and I have a vague memory of standing beside it as it chugged away.

The Meridian equivalent was far sleeker and faster, moving with a ridiculous smoothness. If it weren't for the way the lights blurred past the windows as we rattled along, I wouldn't have known we were moving at all.

I glance at the map on the wall of the train. There's a sprawl of colored lines showing various routes that twist like snakes until I can't tell one end from the other. "People really ride this monstrosity by choice?"

"Cheaper than an air taxi," Ghost says, staring out the window. His leg presses against mine as though to quell my sudden burst of nervousness at our speed.

"Like an ambulatory coffin." I shudder, eager to change the subject to something more distracting. "So we're heading to the Inner Spiral?"

"Yes. That's where we go if we want to do anything amusing. The entertainment district is there, along with better shopping and restaurants than in the Outer Spiral. Almost anything you can think of. Most of the Meridian population lives there, as well, in high-rise apartment buildings." A rueful smile crosses Lottie's face. "And of course, the Five Towers..."

Her voice trails away, and I can't help but inwardly laugh. I shouldn't be surprised that there's a hierarchy. People always seem to have the need to subjugate. I keep my thoughts to myself, craning my head to get a better look at where she's pointing, but the brightness of the lights outside makes it hard for me to see the details. It's well into evening now, the sky a shadowy purple, and the halo of the illumination is nearly blinding.

Even with my hair glowing, I barely stand out at all. Meridians pile in and out of the train cars, swept up in gossip, flashing skin, and elegant coiffures decorated with metal or silk. Their outfits alone are a riotous swirl of color and fabric that overwhelm the subtlety of some bioluminescent hair. A woman sitting across from us is wrapped in something resembling sea foam, and she leaves a trail of floating bubbles about her every time she turns her head. When she stands to get off the subway, a series of lights winks in time with each step she takes, her silver shoes elevating her almost a foot off the floor. She waves at Lottie before the doors shut behind her.

"A friend?" My gaze lingers on the woman's form as we pull away.

"More of a celebrity, I guess. A singer. They call her the Heart of the Sea. She's probably on her way to her private club. It's a massive airship that sails around the Inner Spiral, broadcasting her music as she goes. I hear she sometimes likes to slum it on the trains before her shows. It attracts attention." Lottie shrugs, though her pulse flashes at the base of her throat, betraying her seemingly casual demeanor. "We shared a tutor when we were younger. We often had lessons together, but we were not exactly friends."

I purse my lips, slightly taken aback. Clearly Lottie's social circles ran very high, indeed.

"Does she have a real name?" Ghost wonders aloud.

"Trade secret," Lottie says. "Obviously I know it. She trusts me not to go blabbing it around. Though, of course, I have no reason to."

We get off at the next stop. My mind is mixed up enough by all the movement that I barely get myself oriented. Instinct would have me get to the rooftops so I could map out the city, but the buildings here are monoliths of glass and steel and higher than anything I've ever climbed before.

Ghost takes my hand as we mount the brightly lit stairs from the train station and emerge in a brilliant sweep of technological wonder. We're in a valley, the mountains made of sparkling metal surrounding us like the center of a great crystalline eye. Far above us, airships and wind balloons dart through the sky, gently merging into traffic patterns I can't quite follow.

Everything around us is made of light, from the enormous screens displayed on the largest building proclaiming the latest in beauty products, to the various automatons selling things to eager patrons, to the footsteps people leave behind them as they walk down the streets, each step outlined in a soft glow that fades a few moments later.

"Fancy, isn't it?" Lottie gestures at it with a nod. "Everything in the city is basically geared to collect energy—solar, wind, kinetic—even the trees. The leaves on some of them are genetically enhanced to maximize photosynthesis, increasing the amounts of oxygen in the air. And you can't really see it, but there's a sort of magnetic dome around us—it helps keep the atmosphere constant."

I eye the sky above us, dubious, but see nothing of the sort. "Better that than getting blown off a balcony from the wind," I mutter.

Lottie giggles. "Well, with our limited resources, we try not to pollute what we have. We find that clean energy is really the best solution." She smiles at Ghost, her golden hair shining in a wave of technicolor reflections. "And most of it is thanks to your mother, of course. Without her innovations, I doubt we would have anything close to what we're using today. Even if she didn't come up with all of it herself, she laid the groundwork with her brilliance. Truly, she was amazing."

She natters on at Ghost awhile longer, the two of them letting me soak in the wildly changing atmosphere. It's fascinating and horrifying all at once. The sheer amount of richness on display puts BrightStone to shame.

No one pays any attention to us here. Between the lightning of their skin and the clash of colors and fashions surrounding us, I'm no more than another passerby. Hairstyles blinking with lights, gowns made of fog, a man with a sentient beard that plucks cookies from a tin he carries to put the biscuit in his mouth—it's a fever dream from which I can't wake. It doesn't take long for the sounds to overtake me, either. The talking, the laughter, the mechanical humming music that seems to make the very air thrum in time...

Above us, one of the screens flickers and the face of the Heart of the Sea appears, interviewing a mechanical fish with rolling eyes and golden fins. She's singing, but I can't make out the words. Her fingers waggle and beckon, and for a moment, it seems as though her hand will emerge from the screen and squish us all beneath her palm.

"It's too much," I whisper, tears welling up in my eyes as I wrap my head in my arms, trying to drown out the noise. My senses are in overdrive, forced to drink from a cup that never empties until I'm choking on it. My heart whirs in reaction to the sudden heaviness of my breathing.

Lottie is still talking to Ghost, words I don't understand about things I've never heard of, and then it's like I've retreated into myself, the world slowing down around me until I can only manage the time between one breath and another. If I move from this place, I'll fall through the floor, swallowed up by the city. My head swirls, and I nearly vomit, collapsing to my knees.

And then Ghost is there, gathering me up to take me out of the light and into the shadows of one of the overhangs of the train station.

I focus on his mouth, the curve of his lips, the shape of his nose, the smattering of freckles that are nearly imperceptible over his dusky skin. I almost waver out of consciousness, but Lottie dashes over to a kiosk, returning with a cup of water.

It tastes vaguely sweet, and I suck on an ice cube, the sensations bringing me back to myself. "Thanks," I mumble at her, though my mouth slurs even this simple phrase.

"I think she's overwhelmed," Ghost tells her. "I've got a bit of a headache myself, honestly, but her senses, they're much more sensitive from being belowground for so long. I should have thought of that." He stands in front of me, blocking out as much of the immediate light as he can. "We should probably take her back. Maybe we can try this again after we've all had a bit of a rest."

Lottie almost pouts at his words. "Well, perhaps you might want to see the university on the way back? It won't take long, and it's in the Outer Spiral so it should be much quieter."

I wave her off. I'm not particularly interested in going anywhere other than my bedroom back at the d'Arc estate, but whichever lets me escape fastest. "Whatever you want. Just get me out of here, please."

Ghost is already moving, flagging down one of the smaller airships. It's a cab, I realize, albeit one that flies, but I let him bundle me into it as quickly as he can, sighing in relief when the door is shut and the sound lessens into something I can tolerate.

"Sorry," I say to Lottie after she gives the driver our destination. "I haven't had much to eat today, either."

"Oh, of course," she says, a hint of pity flashing over her face. "I never meant to cause you distress. I simply wanted to show you some of the nicer parts of Meridion. We'll take a quick tour through the campus and then get you home so you can rest. How does that sound?"

My head aches at the thought.

"Up to you," Ghost says. "We can come back here another time. Meridion isn't going anywhere." The look in his eyes is distant, as though he's reliving some of his own memories, though clearly he isn't as affected by the noise as I was.

"Maybe it wouldn't hurt to look at the university," I say slowly, thinking of Gloriana and the rest of my clan. "If I could find out what it might take to get some of my clanmates acceptance to attend…"

"Of course!" Lottie beams at me. "I think that would be a brilliant idea. And maybe Trystan, too?"

"I'm sure Lucian would be encouraged by the concept," he admits, surprising me. He's never mentioned anything to me before about wanting to attend a school. His education had all been at Lucian's discretion, and certainly the doctor knew quite well what he was about when it came to schooling his brother. It had never occurred to me to ask him, and a rush of shame floods through me. When had I ever asked him what he wanted?

I don't voice my thoughts as the taxi lifts into the evening sky. I've been selfish enough for one evening. I would let Ghost have this moment and try to enjoy it. Besides, Lottie was being awfully insistent, and she was good enough to help me today.

Before long, we're away from the center of town, and from up here, I get a better lay of the land. Lottie narrates various points of interest as we travel, and the names roll through my mind.

"What's that?" I gesture at a building with a beam of light rotating from its pinnacle, flaring off and on like a heartbeat.

"The LightHouse," Ghost says quietly. "The flight mechanism for Meridion is housed in there."

The silence grows awkward, then. I shiver at what my heart had really been meant for. Supposedly the part of the flight mechanism was stored within, though we didn't have true confirmation of that yet. From the way Lottie looks away, it's clear she knows the d'Arc history. Madeline is considered a traitor for what she'd done, and that Ghost was her son clearly didn't make it any easier to talk about.

As we round a corner, the LightHouse disappears from sight. I sag, leaning my face against the cold glass. Ghost laces his fingers through mine, leaving us in silence the rest of the way.

The university is bustling with students when we arrive, most of whom pay our little trio no mind at all. To be honest, many of them are so entwined in various books or heated discussions I could have strolled across the grounds without a stitch on and I doubt more than one or two would bat an eyelash.

There is something refreshing about it, if I'm honest with myself—that they could be so enraptured in a subject as to let the mundane things slide right by them. On the other hand, I remember my time with Buceph in the Pits all too well, and sometimes that level of concentration leads to the inability to see subjects as human. I can't help but wonder where the disconnect lies. When does the pursuit of research override compassion?

As ignorant as I am of such higher learning, perhaps it really is for the best that I remain so. And yet, I cannot deny that things would be much easier if I understood more. But even if I don't wish to pursue such endeavors, it isn't really up to me if others in my Moon Child clan are interested. The least I can do is investigate what our options might be.

The buildings here are all made of brick and stone—far more familiar to me than the leviathans of the Inner Spiral. It reminds me somewhat of BrightStone in its layout, and compared to the coldness of the Inner Spiral, the peaked roofs and stained-glass windows are quaintly cheerful. My relief at this is palpable.

Lottie stops in front of one of the larger buildings to pick up a couple of brochures from a kiosk.

"I believe you missed my Enhanced Magnetic Theory class today, didn't you, Ms. Tantaglio?" An imposing woman with thick black spectacles emerges from the doorway, her gimlet gaze raking over all three of us as though weighing and measuring everything she sees.

Lottie startles, her face going red as she ducks her head in apology. "Ah, yes, Proctor Ermegarde. I had some…family matters to take care of this morning."

Proctor Ermegarde snaps her head toward me and Ghost, frowning. "The aforementioned family, I take it? How unusual. And just where are you two from? Some backwater school down in BrightStone?"

"Ah…yes?" I say, shrugging. I'd never been to school.

Proctor Ermegarde sniffs. "What are the schools coming to, I wonder? Well, I'll expect that thesis outline from you next week, Ms. Tantaglio, family or no." She strides away through the courtyard without waiting for an answer.

"Yes, of course," Lottie calls back. She shivers once we're alone again. "I'm sorry about that. The proctor is...opinionated when it comes to these matters."

"If you say," I mutter, though to me it's now overly clear that the university might not be too keen to welcome anyone from outside Meridion.

Lottie coughs. "It's too late to talk to anyone about matriculation just now, but maybe these will help." She hands the brochures to Ghost. They're glossy and full of pictures of happy, industrious students. "I'm sure with your mother being who she is, any university here would be glad to accept you without too much fuss. But as for Mags, I don't really know what the protocol would be for Moon Children. Maybe as an exchange student?" She lets out an awkward little giggle, and a part of me bristles at it.

Inwardly, I know she doesn't mean anything by it, but something about the way she looks at me and that odd quirk of her lips makes me twitch. I let out a bark of laughter, and it's uglier than I intend. "Do you think they'll have a class on killing plague victims?"

She blanches, and Ghost steps in between us. "That's enough," he murmurs at me, but there's a sharpness to it, and it stings.

I mumble an apology to Lottie, but she waves it off. "Perhaps it's time we call it a night," she says. "It's been a long day, after all."

"Aye," I say. The new boots are beginning to pinch my toes. Even the clothing seems to constrict about me now, and for an instant, I think about shedding it all and clambering to the nearest rooftop, to sprint away from this sudden wave of...responsibility? With the darkening sky, my hair is glowing more obviously, my eyes lighting up the darkness. Stares slide over me, gripping my flesh like fingers, and my nostrils flare in panic.

"I want to go home." I nudge Ghost with my shoulder. "I need to get out of here."

Lottie reaches out as though to squeeze my arm. "Are you all right?" Her fingers grasp only empty air as I step away from her.

"She will be," Ghost assures her. "Mags is just a little tired."

I hate the dismissiveness of his words, though I know they're not really directed at me. A simple explanation for a complicated problem, but one she would understand. Though *tired* doesn't even begin to cover it.

I let the two of them take the lead, and I trail behind them, wrapped in my thoughts and a burning need to escape the rush of people around us. Still too much noise. Too many bodies. I'm struggling to breathe, my head tucked down.

"Oh, how fascinating!"

Fingers trace over my scalp, combing through my hair with careless intent, and something inside me snaps. Without a thought, I whirl on my would-be attacker, sweeping their legs out from under them in a single motion. Months upon months of struggling to survive make the movements automatic, my mind going to that dreadful blank place I retreat to when I have to kill someone.

"Do *not* touch me!" My hammer is already in my hand, my fingers gripping it with practiced ease, but even as I'm raising it, some part of me is screaming to stop. Yet the hammer swings down, down, down…

For a moment, it's as though I'm watching it happen from outside my body. The hapless young man scrabbles on the cobblestones, his mouth wide open and wailing, but the sound of his voice shatters through my already sensitive ears, and all I want to do is make it stop.

SLAM!

I'm thrown onto the ground, leaving me gasping as the wind rushes out of my lungs. Ghost is kneeling astride me, knees pinning my arms to my sides.

"Don't move," he hisses, quelling my sudden instinct to throw him off. My body goes limp, the fight draining out of me, and a flicker of relief flashes in his eyes. But he's turning his head over his shoulder, calling for Lottie. "Is he okay?"

A crowd has gathered around us now, skin flashing in distress as they pick him up and brush him off. His face darkens with anger when he sees Lottie. His hair is black, and his skin lights up like a candle, fluttering uncontrollably around the edges of his jaw. A small bruise purples the corner of his mouth where the hammer grazed him. "Is this the kind of company you're keeping? You were supposed to be meeting with my family right now."

Lottie pales. "Corbin, it's not what you think."

"Isn't it?" Corbin points at me. "What is she playing at? I only touched her hair."

Understanding turns Ghost's face cynical. Abruptly, he stands, tugging on my arms to pull me up, heedless of the brochures under his boots. He hands me my hammer without ceremony. "And do you usually touch people you don't know? Let alone foreign visitors?"

The other man gapes at us. "How was I to know? I didn't mean anything by it!"

Ghost clears his throat, anger making his words sharp. "You don't need to mean anything," he snaps. "But this woman has spent nearly a year underground, fighting creatures you can't possibly comprehend."

There's a low ripple of disbelief at this, and my face flames red. I know this isn't what he intended, but that doesn't mean I need my dirty laundry aired so publicly. I don't look at Ghost as I walk away. Of all the things he's made me feel, shame has never been one of them.

Until now.

"Hey, you can't just leave! What about what you did to his face?" someone jeers after me.

I swallow hard and turn to face the group. "Come and take your revenge, then," I say softly, not looking at Ghost. I whirl the hammer between my fingers, my teeth bared slightly. "I'll take on all of you."

"Mags," Ghost says hoarsely, but I wave him off. Lottie looks like she's about to cry.

My glasses have been knocked askew, and I carefully place them in my pocket, allowing the eerie blue glow of my eyes to illuminate the little courtyard.

Corbin spits at my feet. "Monster," he snarls before turning on his heel and striding away, a cluster of young women cooing behind him as they struggle to keep up. With him gone, the rest of the crowd seems to lose its edge, and they disperse quickly, leaving the three of us standing alone in the center of the courtyard.

"Who was that?" Ghost demands of Lottie, bristling with a finely tuned fury.

"Ah," Lottie says, her face pinched. "Corbin. My…arranged. I don't know what that was all about, but we should probably leave before campus authorities are called. I don't know what they'll do. Fighting here is strictly forbidden."

"But experimenting on people is just fine, right?" I'm already kicking off the heeled boots that make my ankles wobble. With my toes set free from their confines, I wiggle them in relief.

"What are you doing?" Lottie gathers up the shoes in confusion.

"Clearing my head." I still don't bother looking at Ghost, even when he reaches out a hand. I dodge away. "Don't follow me. I'll be home when I feel like it."

"But—"

Without waiting to hear what else he has to say, I sprint for the nearest building. It's stone and easy to climb. I'm on the roof in seconds, and then it's all I can do to stare out across an ocean of metal and silver and gleaming lights that seem to rise and fall with the movements of the very city.

But it's not enough. Ghost and Lottie still stand there watching me, and I know my hair will give my position away faster than anything. I tear the lower half of my shirt to wrap around my head, extinguishing the worst of it, and then give in to my urge to climb higher and higher.

The university campus is old architecture, like Madeline's house, and I skip across the rooftops easily enough until I reach a newer building that looks past the Oubliette River. Great towers of glass and metal rise in the distance, reaching toward the heavens like the antennae of some monstrous insect. Their smoothness will be difficult to climb, but rarely are surfaces without some sort of flaws.

I let out a mournful sort of whistle and turn in a different direction, heading for a cluster of shorter buildings that will at least be feasible. And when I reach the highest, loneliest place I can, I look out at the lights below as I lean against the cold concrete. I wrap my arms tightly around my legs, suddenly wishing I had wings like my dragon.

Where would I go? What would I do?

To fly away seems like a very grand thing, indeed.

But such ideas are fairy tales. Meridion is no more a paradise than BrightStone was. It just looks cleaner on the outside.

And so I sit and rock and think of Sparrow and her dreams of seeing this city. And I weep.

Hello? Hello? Hello, hello, hello…

The whistles pull me from a hazy sleep. I'd been dreaming of comfits, the kind Sparrow liked to get from the candy store in Market Square down in BrightStone. Not that we'd ever been able to buy them outright, but sometimes there would be stale leftovers in the trash. Though it spoke volumes about the store since sugar was often at such a premium. Usually even the leftovers were sold for at least a few pennies.

I could still remember the explosion of flavor on my tongue, heady and sweet.

Another round of frantic whistles sounds, this time much closer. It would be Ghost, of course. There are no other Moon Children here, and those rudimentary signals are the only ones he knows.

A guilty twinge lances through my gut. How long have I been up here, anyway?

I let out a piping trill in response. *Here, here…*

Hello? HELLO, HELLO, HELLO…

A rush of whistles then, relieved and loud, and I can't help but smile at it, my earlier sadness washing away.

THUMP.

Sharp prickles dance on my shoulder, and I wince as my clockwork dragon lands on it in inelegant fashion. "Oy, it's you, is it? Did you lead the way for him?"

The dragon huffs at me, its heartbeat speeding up to match mine as it lets out a series of hisses and clinking of teeth, wings puffed up indignantly. I've never been scolded by it before.

"Aye, well, I suppose I deserve that," I say softly.

"Yes, you do." Ghost materializes from the early-morning fog, his expression an odd mix of concern, anger, and relief, the emotions swirling all over his face like tiny tornados. As per his name, I didn't know he was right there. "Do you have *any* idea how worried I was when you didn't come home last night? How worried Lucian was?" He waves me off. "Lottie was terrified. Thought she'd done something wrong. I know you are a prickly pear, Mags, and I love you for it, but just once I'd wish you'd think through your actions. We can't afford to make any mistakes—not here, not now. We have a meeting with the Council today, or have you forgotten?"

I turn away from him, my hackles rising, but I bite my tongue. How to explain the daily hazy nightmare I seem to be living in… The shadows of my past emerge from the corner of my eyes to taunt me with their mocking, at who I am, at what I've become.

"I wish I could." I whisper at him, turning my face away to press it into the welcoming cold of the brick. "What do you know?"

He squats down beside me, the tension cording off him in an almost tangible fashion. "I know a lot, Mags. I was there. I saw what you saw. Saw what you did."

"One part of it," I admit. "But not all of it. Not all of it." A shiver runs through me like a swath of ice, numbing my bones.

A flush of warmth over my forehead, his fingers stroke lightly over my hair. "You're burning up," he says, touching his face to mine.

I startle at the sudden intrusion but let myself sag toward him, nesting within his open arms as he wraps them around me.

"It's all right," he murmurs as the tears roll down my cheeks. "Come on. Let's try to get home before the city really wakes up, and Lucian can take a look at you."

I don't really remember much after that. A long climb down the building, perhaps. My hands and feet moving in rote fashion until we reach the ground. The sun is just peeking over the edges of the city by then, and I'm forced to put on my smoked lenses. Ghost has taken off his coat and wrapped it around my shoulders, but I'm already trembling so hard I can barely walk. When the ground starts tilting sideways, I stumble, nearly colliding with a burly man in a brown coat that seems too small for him, the sleeves too short, the collar not quite right.

Not made for him. Stolen.

My streetwise brain points out these small details with alarming cheerfulness, even as I struggle to slur out an apology. Where is Ghost? My mind is spinning, spinning, spinning, but it's all wrong because Ghost is on the ground, lying there without moving, a dark bruise already forming around his eye socket.

Sluggish, I crawl toward him, but it's like running through water—everything in slow motion, my movements trailing behind whatever it is my mind wants me to do. Am I screaming? I should be screaming, shouting Ghost's name, but it's nothing more than a hoarse whisper that slides away in the breeze like a deranged butterfly.

"What's going on?" I finally croak out, my eyes darting between Ghost and the burly man with his weak chin and too wide grin.

"Night night," he says, tapping me on the forehead.

There's an electric pulse that seems to tap directly into my skull, and then nothing at all.

The grass on which I sit
Is green and full of pins
Pricking me upon my flesh
The bearer of my sins.

— CHAPTER EIGHT —

"I'm surprised she even lasted as long as she did. Maybe there really is something to all this half-breed blood nonsense." The words sluice through my mind, rolling away like fish in a stream as I try to comprehend them. The voice is male. Deep.

"Or maybe you just didn't make the poison strong enough." Another male voice, this one younger—not that it matters since I don't recognize either of them.

I don't dare open my eyes to look. I can tell without trying that the light is going to be too bright for me to bear, and besides, why give away that I'm at least somewhat conscious?

Still... Poison?

But how?

The last time I'd dealt with such things, I'd lost a clan member to it. Conal and Gloriana had both accidently consumed poisoned eggs. Conal had died a terrible and painful death, and Gloriana nearly so. She would most likely never recover from the aftereffects.

My mind stutters as I remember the attack.

Ghost!

Panic lances through me, and it takes everything I can muster not to sit up.

Think, Mags.

He was lying on the ground, one eye growing purple. So he'd been physically knocked out, perhaps? By whatever that electrical pulse was? It reminded me of one of those pig-stickers the Inquestors used in BrightStone, but this was faster and stronger than those prods. But why take me and not him? Surely the son of d'Arc would be worth a hefty ransom.

"Eh, maybe I didn't get enough on her head when I touched her. I didn't have much of a grasp on her hair, after all. I'm sorry." My ears prick at the man's words. And that timbre… Something about the voice niggles the back of my mind.

Then it hits me. *Corbin.*

Not an accident, then, but a setup. The timeline doesn't match up quite right for anything else, not even coming back for a quick revenge.

I force my breathing to stay calm and slow, passive. I've been on the receiving end of enough of these situations by now, and there's no sense in reacting until I know what's what. The best thing to do is to collect as much information as I can and escape secretly. Or so I tell myself. Easier said than done, perhaps.

I wiggle my toes and fingers experimentally. I don't appear to be tied up, which is good.

Visions of being bound in Buceph's medical lab assail me, the table of instruments, the sharp smell of blood and fear. *The tightness of the leather straps, cutting into my skin, the icepick device lying on the tray with the promise of a sharp butchering of my brain, the septic burn of chemical cleanliness, as though his work were somehow not tainted by the insanity driven by the need to find immortality…*

"Uncle, how did you know the poison would even work? I barely touched her scalp." The words snap me out of my delusions, the present in sharp relief as a struggle to remain perfectly still.

"I didn't, of course. But something about that glowing hair. I knew it might be something special, so I took the liberty of obtaining some from that hairdresser Lottie mentioned to your brother. She was eager enough to answer my questions. Moon Child hair seems different from ours. Almost as though it's made up of photoreceptors, you see? Like electrical conduits. I was merely running under the assumption that it might absorb such things faster than a normal Meridian. And of course, I hardly think she'd be a match for one of our pulse weapons, either." This voice I don't recognize at all, but it's overly confident. Not his first attempt at kidnapping, then.

But Lottie?

She was the only one who knew what hair salon we'd gone to, but that didn't mean she'd actually been involved. Sometimes the most harmless words can be turned into weapons, given the proper set of ears. And if Corbin was her betrothed? Who was this brother?

My suspicions flare hot beneath my skin, only to be distracted by the men's continuing conversation.

"And what of the other one?"

"The scion of d'Arc? Better to let that one go, of course. The Council has no desire to be confronted with a Moon Child anyway. They won't care if she disappears. But d'Arc's children are another matter. That would involve an investigation I'd rather not be a part of. No, we'll simply let them think she's dead. Hopefully they'll take it as a warning that Meridion doesn't want their kind here. A bit of blood, some torn clothing, whatever is left of that ridiculous little dragon... Shame about it, really."

I go cold, pinned like a butterfly on a piece of wood. My dragon? What in the hells happened to my dragon? And Ghost... If he thinks I'm dead... A shiver rolls down my spine, despite my best effort to remain still.

"Well, then, let's take care of it now, shall we, Uncle? The sooner they give up, the better it will be for us."

Then comes metallic clinking and the gathering of belongings. I imprint it all in my mind—the smell of leather, the odd shuddering breath of one of them, the heavier footfalls. My senses, honed from months living in the dark, take it in and squirrel it away for later when I have time to process it.

"What do we do with her?" Corbin again. He's persistent about the details, and there's an underlying current of fear running beneath his words. I suspect he hasn't done this sort of thing before. Kidnapping and murder tend to be a bit higher on the rungs than simple assault.

"Leave her for now. It's not like she has anywhere she could possibly go. Just be sure to pull the lock when we leave. If she dies in the interim, so much the better."

The door slams shut, a lock turns.

My eyes snap open. Betrayal on all sides again. The light burns hot and bright in my eyes, and it's all I can do to keep from retching against the intensity of it.

I grope for the lamp, pressing buttons desperately until it dims enough that I can crack open my eyelids. It's a small room, windowless and spartan. I'm on a raised cot, and there's a table next to me with a carafe of water on it.

My throat is sandpaper, but I don't dare trust anything before me. Who knows what other experimentation they plan to do? I can't manage to turn the lantern any lower, but I slam it against the ground, where it flickers once and goes dark.

Relief floods me as I can see unfettered once more. The details of where I am, the plainness of the room, tells me nothing specific. I don't know enough about Meridian architecture to imagine where I could be. Up in a tower? Underground? For all I know I'm in the slums, though it's certainly nicer than anything I ever stayed in when I lived in BrightStone.

I go to study the door and then stop as I realize I'm dragging something behind me. A chain? A rope? It's some sort of cord connected to a panel on the wall, and it's attached to me via a collar.

What in the hells?

I give it an exploratory tug, but aside from indicating its tensile strength, it tells me nothing. I attempt to unbuckle the collar and am rewarded with a stinging shock against my neck, hard enough to jolt my brain off-kilter.

I sag on the bed, feeling all around the collar with my fingers. Probes on the inside, perhaps, lined up against the jugular. Struggle enough and I'll probably knock myself unconscious.

How oddly primitive. Considering where I was, I'd envisioned something far more advanced. But this…

Beside me on the table, I catch the winking of what appear to be bits of metal. My glasses are there, the frames bent. I twist them until they sort of fit, pushing them onto my forehead.

But there is far more than just my glasses there. I swallow a sudden wave of sadness as I spot a bit of wing, a coil of the tail, some broken metal. The head has been bashed open, displaying whatever made up its clockwork mind, and I clutch it to my chest as though I might somehow will it back to life.

The dragon has been the catalyst for nearly everything that happened to me in the last few years, good or bad. It was a nearly constant companion before I was Tithed to the Pits; seeing one of the last links connecting me to my life with Sparrow destroyed hurts more than I can bear. Fury lances through me, but I have no choice but to ignore it for now, tracing the cord on my neck to the panel on the wall.

It's closed, of course, but…

As I approach the panel, my clockwork heart whirs in its telltale way, and I smile sourly. "I'm the goddamned key to Meridion. You think such petty bullshit is going to stop me now?"

Almost immediately, the panel slides up to reveal a series of buttons. I pause and close my eyes, listening to the way my heart responds. Two fast beats, three slow, one stuttering. I let it repeat twice more for good measure and then carefully tap out the pattern on the screen.

The panel shudders, the light inside going dark as the cord does the same.

"Easy peasy." I slip the collar off my neck with deft fingers. Another quick look around the room shows nothing of interest. I have no idea how long I've been here or what time it is, and I've no real way of checking, but I do know I don't want to be here when they get back. While I suspect my chances of fighting them off in a simple brawl are probably high, who knows what other gadgets they have at their disposal? And I don't have my hammer, I realize a moment later when I check absently at my hip.

Damn.

The only door out of this room is in the typical Meridian fashion—metal, with a panel. I lean my ear against the door. Have they left a guard? Meridian doors seem to only be either fully open or fully closed, so there's no real way to simply peek, and no keyhole, either.

Still, what are my options? I study the ceiling and the walls, the floor and every other space I can find until I come across a vent nestled within a closet. A closet is a shit place to put a vent, but in this case, it might buy me some time if they're not aware of it.

And it's small—no more than a foot in diameter and round. Well, I've certainly fit myself in tighter quarters below in the Pits. Ghost and I had somehow climbed through at least one during our escape. Still, I could get stuck, and the thought of starving to death in the inner workings of Meridion's vent system isn't particularly high on my list of ways to die. I tamp down a sudden pinprick of fear, wiping a cold sweat from my forehead.

Maybe if I simply hide in it, I will be able to learn more when they come back. Assuming they won't look for me here, and I would guess not, given the size. I give the cover an experimental tug. It takes a little work, but it pops off eventually. There's a fair amount of dusty crud lining the inside, and I sneeze despite myself, peering down the vent with careful eyes.

It runs the length of the room and then turns a corner and disappears to places unknown. If I'm in some sort of apartment complex, perhaps it would be as simple as escaping through another room with no one the wiser.

I freeze at muffled voices outside the door. I can't understand the words, but the tempo feels as though its nothing more than exchanging pleasantries. My captors? Someone else? No time to lose, then.

I snatch up the bits of my dragon and roll them into a scrap of cloth torn from the bedsheet. I knot the makeshift pouch on my belt before sliding feetfirst into the tunnel. I don't fancy going backward much, but I need to close the vent behind me to cover my tracks. The main door clicks open just as I'm shutting the vent, and I slowly ease my way back, chuckling to myself at the sudden wave of panicked voices.

"What the… Where the hells did she go?" Anger, then fear. Demanding answers of whoever had been guarding the door. Furniture being thrown over as the room is searched.

I wriggle away from the vent entrance. The glow of my eyes and hair will be a dead giveaway if they happen to look in the closet, which they are bound to.

"How did she get the collar off?"

"Maybe she shorted it out? There was some metal left over here…"

"There's no damage to the wires, so no, I don't think that's it. Did you check the vent?"

"Why would she go there? Everyone knows that's a death trap once the engines fire up. Who wants to be sucked out a trash vent anyhow?"

My eyes widen. Just what have I managed to get myself into?

"She might not know. Have they run yet today?"

The closet door opens, and I squirm back even farther, my heart sinking.

Wait…

I retreat around the corner just as a light shines down the passage, and I exhale sharply. It's gone a moment later, and I can no longer hear their voices at all. But I suspect I've got bigger things to worry about.

Trash vents, trash vents… Where did they end up? I swallow hard. The junkyard in BrightStone is where they end up, thousands of feet below.

Aye, Mags, but you're fucked now if you don't find a way out…

Quickly I try going forward to one of the side vents. If I can manage to get into another room, I should be okay. But I'm blocked again and again. Even when I reach one, there's no way to remove the vent cover. Whatever mild breeze is currently blowing through the vents is enough to create a suction to make it impossible to open it from this side.

Nothing to do, then, but keep going down the main tunnel. If I can find a bit of shelter for when the main fans do kick on, that will at least buy me some time.

I let out an experimental whistle, though it's unlikely anyone will hear it. Still, it makes me feel better so I do it anyway, trilling out my requests for help. But only the echo of my own voice comes back to me.

THRUM.

THRUM.

THRUMTHRUMTHRUMTHRUM…

I jerk awake, wiping away a bit of drool from my mouth. At some point along the way I must have fallen asleep. I don't know how many hours I was traveling, but eventually I just couldn't go any farther. I'm nestled up in this bit of piping, my mouth dry as parchment, my stomach rumbling. And the noise… A noise that shakes the pipes like an earthquake, rattling through my brain with all the finality of death, woke me up sure enough.

The trash vents are turned on.

My thoughts hover in panic, even as the wind starts up, a biting, angry bluster that rattles the pipe around me like a bucking horse. Papers, dust, scraps of clothing, whatever a Meridian deems no longer worthy come shooting down the tunnels like an army of inanimate leavings. I duck my head to protect my face. Dirt and grit cut into my skin, even as I press my hands against the sides of the pipe in an attempt to keep from hurling down along with the trash. A bucket tumbles toward me, catching me in the forehead. I let out a cry of pain, but the damage has already been done.

And like all the rest of Meridion's leavings, I am thrown away.

Of course, it's never really that simple. I claw at the sides of the tunnel to slow myself down, but apart from tearing up my nails, it does little to halt my passage. When the floor opens beneath me, I'm left with no strategy but to keep my head down to try to avoid knocking myself senseless as I'm battered along like a cat playing with a ball of yarn.

The tunnel starts to gently slope, and I find myself sliding. I kick out my legs on either side to find traction, pausing just enough to catch sight of a large fan. And past that is a bright light that disappears into nothing.

"End of the line," I mutter, trying not to think of getting obliterated by the merciless fan blades spinning through everything that runs into them. No wonder most of the trash in the junkyard is so damaged. I always thought Meridians just took poor care of their things, but if it's routinely being destroyed this way… Not that it really matters. Scrap heaps are scrap heaps. Though the irony of forcing Moon Children to pick through those leavings to find me in pieces leaves me with a bitter laugh.

But none of these thoughts helps me figure a way out of this mess.

I grab a handful of garbage, snagging what feels like a bit of pipe and the bucket that now seems to have attached itself to my foot. Timing will be everything and there is nowhere else to go, but that doesn't mean I have to allow myself to be torn to shreds, either. At least this way, most of my body will be recognizable when I hit the ground.

The fans spin, spin, spin—too fast for my eyes to keep up with. But I hold the bucket out on the end of the pipe in front of me. If I can hold the blades still long enough to slip through…

The bucket is shredded upon impact, blowing bits of metal into my face, but the pipe catches one fan blade for a few seconds, groaning beneath the force of it. No time, no time… I launch myself into the tiniest of gaps, amazed by the sudden silence of the whirring fan, and then it seems to snarl, the engine coming back to life as the pipe snaps like a twig.

"Oh shit!" I shriek as the bounce back hurls me over the edge into nothingness.

Even with my glasses on, everything is shades of white and blue and blurry red as the sunlight hits me smack in the face. I'm clawing at the air in a haphazard attempt at flight and failing utterly. The world seems to hover, frozen, and I catch glimpses of airships sailing far above and the city of BrightStone far below. The misty sea is spread out far beyond the massive rusted anchors keeping the floating city in place, and the underbelly of Meridion passes me by.

Or I suppose I am passing it by.

The bottom of Meridion isn't quite as smooth and streamlined as I had imagined. While it's relatively flat, there are a number of small crenellations and bulging bits of metal, so it's clear there's far more going on than I'd been aware of.

There's nothing to grab a hold of, though. At the speed I'm traveling, anything small is going to slice right through me. But I'm not too far away from the anchor chains mooring the city to the sea offshore BrightStone.

I angle myself sideways toward the chain. It's not going to be pretty, but better than splattering all over the ground.

The chain ribbons past me, larger than anything I could possibly get my hands around, but I snatch at it anyway, scrabbling past the heavy iron to cling on to the edge of a link. It's huge, and my hands burn as the metal slices into my palms. But I've stopped myself, and for now that is enough.

Breathing seems to be harder here without Meridion's domed atmosphere to take the edge off the altitude. The real question is if I go up or down. I'm closer to Meridion, but going down is usually easier.

More to the point, do I even want to go back to the floating city? Already it feels as though my bonds with Ghost and Lucian are beginning to fray. And while deep down I know that's not entirely true, the doubts drifting on the surface of my mind are more than willing to make an appearance.

If only I'd somehow been more...sophisticated, perhaps? Less of a savage and more of someone they could be proud to show off. But I'm just as trapped here by my ignorance as I was down in the Pits.

I don't cry exactly, but I do give in to a moment of wallowing self-pity at once again being stuck between worlds with no way to fit in on either of them. It's just a bit more obvious at the moment, metaphors notwithstanding.

A ragged sob escapes me and is whisked away on the breeze. Or really, it's a howling wind up here, but if I think about it too much I'll never figure out where I belong. As much as I long to see my other clanmates, even I know that to retreat now would be cowardice. Bran would smack the shit out of me for wasting this opportunity.

And he'd be right to.

After everything I've done to gain this chance, giving up now for what basically amounts to hurt feelings would cheapen everything that happened before, all the lives needlessly ended for nothing more than Meridian hubris.

I owe them to try again, don't I?

And, well, Ghost is still waiting for me. Possibly injured. Frantic.

I hurt him by running off the way I did. He must be beside himself by now.

Guilt worms its way through my guts. I'd broken my promise. Kidnapping aside, I'd been the one to leave him first. "All right. Let's go up, aye?"

My shoulders pop as I stretch up my arms. Though the metal is far warmer than I'd like beneath the sun, it is tolerable enough. But I need to get out of here before night falls. The temperatures will surely drop past my ability to survive.

And so I begin to climb. The metal is slick, but my hands and feet are used to climbing, and I angle myself carefully, taking each link one at a time. By the time I reach the top, I'm soaked with sweat, frequently having to wipe my palms on my shirt, my eyes stinging from the effort, and my glasses constantly trying to escape my face. My hands are on fire.

The links are attached to some sort of swiveling connector. I guess to allow for movement if the floating city is caught in a storm or some such. But beyond that, the bottom of the city is unyielding to my tentative attempts to find purchase.

It's so clean, and I don't know if that is because of the type of metal or if the citizens keep it that way, like popping barnacles off the keel of a ship. Perhaps it's both. The metal of the gates down in the Pits never rusted, either.

I clamber into the swivel where at least I can sit and rest for a bit without worrying about being blown into oblivion. Goose bumps roll over my skin as the sweat dries, and I rub my arms against it. Condensation drips from a giant screw above the swivel, and I open my mouth to let the water drip onto my tongue. The metallic flavor is definitely lacking, but I don't care. The hell with falling. I'll die of more mundane things if I don't find some real water soon.

"All right, Mags, what now?"

I crane my head for a closer look at the bottom of the city. Aside from the engines themselves—enormous fans that aren't actually moving—there isn't much besides what appear to be a series of small openings dotting the landscape, flanked by square shafts that hang a few feet from the surface.

Thrusters, maybe? I have no idea how the city manages to fly at all, or even how it is currently staying aloft. Meridian magic, perhaps. Or farts. Either one was just as plausible.

The engines don't look particularly inviting. They seem to be filled with an awful lot of moving parts and machinery. Getting stuck seems almost a certainty. But the shafts hold promise, even if most of that promise involves more climbing. At least it would get me out of the wind, and they aren't likely to be garbage chutes this time. Of course, that begs the question of just how I'm going to get to one. The nearest shaft looks to be about ten feet away from the top of the anchor swivel. It's open, from what I can tell, but unless I somehow grow wings to get there... And if I had wings, all this would be a moot point anyway.

I pat down my clothes, but with these new things Lottie picked out, even my rope belt is long gone. This useless scarf, however, may not be as useless as I thought. If it will bear my weight, it might do as a makeshift rope I can use to swing to the shaft.

I slide the scarf from around my neck and test its stretch. It won't hold my weight for too long so I'll need to move quickly, assuming I can throw it over to the shaft. A series of hooks dot the outside of the chute like little tentacles, but without something to weigh down the scarf, I don't have any chance of looping it over. And I have nothing.

Except Sparrow's necklace.

It's not much more than some leather and beadwork, but it might be heavy enough to do the trick. I kiss it for good luck. Hopefully I'll be able to retrieve it, but if I have to lose it again, somehow it's fitting that it would happen up here, among the dreams Sparrow and I once had about this place.

I tie the scarf into a loose lasso, the necklace on the loop end to help weigh it down. "All right, Sparrow. Let's do this."

I toss the scarf toward one of the hooks. It misses the first two times but catches the third. I give it a strong tug, watching carefully as it tightens around the hook, exhaling when it holds fast. I suck in a deep breath, keeping my head high so I'm not forced to look at the nothingness below me. No second chances if I fall again. At least, none I'm betting on.

"Fuck!"

I leap from the swivel with all my strength, the scarf tied loosely about my arms as I aim for the shaft. If I can snag one of the hooks, I might be able to swing myself up inside, or somehow find purchase for my feet, so I'm not left dangling.

I overshoot, swinging past the hooks and just beneath the shaft. I scuttle with whatever's left of my momentum, fingers digging into the edges of the opening. It's not enough. My arms tremble as my fingers begin to slip and the scarf unravels from the hook and flutters away into the void.

I kick uselessly in the air, unable to do much more than hang on, and then even my fingers fail me, and I slip, hurtling backward into the sky.

Summer comes hot and damp,
The breath of Fall might kill,
Winter coyly flirts with Spring,
And I remain here still.

— CHAPTER NINE —

Except I don't.

I blink rapidly, staring down as I realize I'm standing on something solid. A questioning whir hums beneath my toes. I'm on…an automaton? A rounded dome with spindly little legs and some sort of thrust mechanism keeping it aloft, it's a hair larger than my foot. Its engines spin wildly as it struggles, keeping me precariously balanced on one leg like an exotic bird. On closer inspection, I realize the bottom of Meridion is crawling with them, polishing and scraping, intent on their jobs.

One mystery solved, it would seem.

"Uh, I seem to have gotten stuck out here," I tell it.

Can it understand me? Is it sentient like my dragon was? Or is it connected to something Meridian-controlled inside? Perhaps they can see me through its sensors. It burbles something I don't understand, bobbling up and down with me on it like it wants to dump me off.

"Got it. Okay, just maybe push me up inside this tunnel, then, aye?" I don't know if it has the power to get me topside the long way anyhow, so this will have to do.

I reach out as it tries to rise, snagging Sparrow's necklace from where it still hangs on the hook. I clutch it to my chest as we slowly move toward the shaft. It is small, as expected, but large enough to fit me. I scan upward and find a platform of sorts about a hundred yards above.

I let out a whoop. "Up there," I tell the little robot. "Get me to the platform and you're free to go."

It lets out a disgruntled hum, shaking as it continues to do what I ask. We reach the platform, and it dumps me without fanfare. It buzzes around my face, letting out a series of scolding chirps, and then immediately flies down the shaft and disappears.

"Thanks, beastie!" I call after it, but it's already gone.

The platform is bare metal, and the shaft stretches up farther than I can see. I suppose if it comes to it, I can always climb back down and end it all, but for the moment, I'm out of the wind and that goes a long way to helping restore my senses.

I slip Sparrow's necklace on again and skim my fingers over the walls. Too smooth to climb, for sure, and too wide anyway. A panel perched on the railing of the platform looks promising, lit up with a series of colored buttons. My heart starts to whir as I approach it, and I click a blue button to reveal the control panel.

A confusing array of switches and buttons glows up at me, and for a moment I want to slam my fist down on all of them. Why couldn't it be simple like one of those elevator things that took Ghost and me out of the Mother Clock?

Ah, but there is a button with an arrow pointing up. I press it, and the control panel beeps plaintively at me, a series of letters rolling by on the screen. Another panel shifts to reveal a Meridian lock. I stare down at the letters, struggling to make them out. "*Auth…oriz…ation. Authorization Re… Required.* Aye, of course it is. Because there's so much down here that needs protection in a hells-be-damned empty tube," I snarl.

I lean in closer, and I smile in relief when my heart clicks out the pattern. I type it on the lock panel, rewarded when the control panel turns green. The platform shudders for half a second before rising swiftly. It's almost eerie how quiet it is. In BrightStone, nearly everything is rusted and old, so it unnerves me how efficiently everything runs here.

After a few minutes, the platform slows, docking at the edge of a large tunnel. It stretches out in both directions, but at least signs of humanity linger in the walking platforms and the railings. That could only mean that people came down this way at some point, right? And more importantly, there must be an exit to take me up to the main level of the city.

In the meantime, I've got no idea which way to go, so I decide to go to the right. The lighting down that way looks more promising, bright enough I need to put my glasses on. I trudge down the hall, wincing against a sudden rush of illumination from what looks like a mess hall—metal tables and benches, and a smattering of vending kiosks. My stomach rumbles loudly, and I tear into the room and flip on a sink, sucking in great pulls of water. My throat feels as though it will crack.

Gulping noisily as I finish up, I turn my attention to the kiosks. They're locked, of course, but my heart unlocks them easily, and I snatch a handful of items, ripping the wrappers off whatever they are. Some kind of fruit bars and a meat pie, maybe. I don't even bother heating them up and just shovel the food into my mouth as fast as I can, then stuff my pockets with a few more.

"Hey, what are you doing?" A tired-looking man emerges from a doorway on the far side of the room. In my rush for food, I hadn't even bothered paying attention to the extra doors. "You aren't supposed to be down here."

"And yet, here I am," I mutter. "I'll be on my way, then. Do you happen to know the fastest way to the surface?"

"I'm supposed to report any unauthorized persons. I don't know if this is some sort of a joke, or if your little group is hoping to sabotage the power grid again, but you need to come with me." He walks slowly, but he's edging for the door out of here, his finger on a button next to a device on his shirt. An alarm, perhaps?

For half a second, I debate it. Being captured might actually be the fastest way out of here. But I've been taken into custody too many times in BrightStone; having the Inquestors take you in means beatings or worse, and usually several days of sleeping in a cell. I have no desire to find out what the Meridian equivalent is.

I casually snag another meat pie and shake my head. "I'm sorry. Generous offer, but I'm afraid I have to refuse. Prior engagement and all that." My eyes narrow as I try to measure how close he is to me versus how close I am to the door and what my chances are of slipping out between his legs. He doesn't appear to have any weapons, but that hardly means anything. Though the idea of having to outrun an entire contingent of these guys in a tunnel I know nothing about doesn't fill me with confidence, either. This isn't the rooftops of BrightStone, I remind myself.

But still.

I walk toward the door, nibbling on the meat pie as if I have no worries at all. "Have you tried these? They're really good."

He gives me a confused frown, his finger still hovering above the button. "I… What?"

"Here, try it." I whip the meat pie at his face, dodging as he instinctively tries to grab it, and beeline for the door.

"Hey, wait!" He lurches after me as I slip out into the tunnel, and I realize I'm probably an easy target, with my hair glowing as it is. Though as long as I can keep enough distance, maybe I can hide for a bit and then try to follow him to the exit.

An alarm blares behind me. He must have finally hit the button, and there's an answering howl in front of me as several more workers come out of hidden doorways. I immediately duck down a small access tunnel, but it ends with a grate too small for me to crawl through.

A rivulet of oily water slides through the gutter, and I immediately dunk my hair in it, ignoring the metallic filth oozing its way across my scalp. It dampens down the glow a bit, but it's obvious enough if anyone's really looking.

"What's going on?"

"Ecoterrorists again. This one stole a bunch of our food and ran down the drainage culvert." My original would-be captor pants his way up to the others, ignoring their sniggers.

"Are you sure it wasn't just your stomach?"

The man scowls. "I know a girl when I see one. She threw a meat pie at me..."

The group explodes in laughter.

"I'll bet she did, John. I'll just bet she did."

"B...but..." I almost feel sorry for John as he stammers back at them with his overalls and his thinning hair. Not my fault if his mates don't believe him.

"I think maybe we need to have a talk with the supe, John. There are too many rations gone missing on your shifts. If you can't keep your mouth shut one way or another, you'll have to find another position."

John frowns. "But that's not— I mean, I am telling the truth."

I suck on my lower lip in irritation, because despite my better judgment, I *do* feel sorry for him. What the hells.

Before the others can formulate another cruel response, I erupt from the tunnel, my eyes glowing wildly as I pelt them with the fruit bars I stuffed in my pockets. "The Pits, the Pits, gives you the shits!" I cackle at them.

They startle, scattering like leaves, and I bolt down the tunnel in the opposite direction. A momentary giggle of relief escapes me, until I immediately trip over something and take a digger straight to the face.

Ah yes, the graceful Moon Child in her natural habitat...

I roll to my side and wince as pain shoots up my calf. I appear to have sprained an ankle, but that's less important than the train of workers trundling their way up the tunnel behind me. I limp toward the side of the tunnel and gingerly start to climb, my fingers finding purchase in some rusted bricks that looked as though they'd been part of a larger platform once. If I can get beyond their field of vision in time, they may pass beneath me and miss me altogether.

I'm nearly upside down when they finally approach my position, their lightsticks blinding me as they scan the tunnel walls. I close my eyes against it as they move on, tears burning down my cheeks even as my fingers begin to cramp against the stone.

Buzz?

Something small bumps into my side, almost forcing me to lose my grip. I blink, realizing it's the little automaton drone from outside. It burbles at me in excitement.

"Shut up," I hiss at it as the men swivel toward the noise.

"It's a cleaner. What the hell's it doing in here?" One of them scans his light in our direction, shouting when I come into view. I grind my teeth in frustration, trying to scramble even higher. My bad foot loses traction, and I flail into the darkness, bracing myself for an impact that never comes.

I'm… floating? I open my eyes, shut tight against expected pain, and realize I'm hovering a few feet above the ground. Something hums beneath me, as the drone veers into my line of sight, beeping madly. I turn my head and snort. Hundreds of the little cleaners are holding me up, their rounded heads bobbing up and down like a sea of overly enthusiastic jellyfish as they shift to support my weight. I share a look with John and the other men, apprehension on their faces. I shrug as the first drone flies in front of me, its whirring somehow more impatient than before. Is it scolding me?

"I don't understand. What do you want me to do?"

In response, it moves closer to my chest, burbling when my heart starts beating out a matching rhythm. It lets out a single high-pitched chirp, and before I can even react, the entire wave of drones shoots me up toward the ceiling of the tunnel and over the men's heads.

"Later, boys!" I shout, unable to keep from making a little salute as I pass overhead. Old habits, I suppose. They gape at me, swallowed up by the darkness a moment later, their lightning skin flashing in confusion.

"So...not that I'm not grateful or anything," I tell the leader drone, "but where are we going?"

It doesn't respond except to dash ahead of the group, chirping in encouragement. My automaton carpet picks up speed, and before long, I'm hurling through the tunnels, sliding up and down in a maze so complex it would take me years to figure out where I was. Then I'm dropped down another chute with a rather unceremonious thump.

"The hells," I squeak, sliding face-first down the narrow passage and attempting not to slam my nose into a sudden turn.

I'm free-falling again, my brain trying to register where I am and what I'm seeing as I tumble in a heap into a pile of rags, the back of my head smacking on something hard. I groan, rubbing my scalp, relieved when I don't discover any blood. My foot throbs something awful, and my hair is a sticky mess, leaving oily trails on my fingers when I run my hand through it.

Whatever Lottie had done to it is long gone. If I had to guess, I'll be shaving what's left of my hair when I get topside, since it's probably ruined beyond help at this point. "Putting on airs, Mags?" I grumble at myself. "No one is going to care. Ragamuffin or princess, you're nothing more than a half-breed anyway."

"Oh, I don't know about that," intones a rich contralto of a voice, full of a certain dry amusement and melodic vibrato that sets my bones to aching.

I glance up at the source of the voice, then look away, and then look back again, suddenly feeling as though I'm melting into the floor.

"Welcome, Magpie," says the giant dragon, arching its serpentine neck as it cranes its massive head for a closer look at me. "I've been waiting for you for a very long time."

Ink stains, blood stains
Words of crimson rust
On yellowed pages crumbling
Upon the floor to dust

— CHAPTER TEN —

IronHeart..." The word tumbles out of my mouth before I can clamp it shut. All those stories and myths of a dragon living in the heart of the Meridion... Even Ghost laughed at me for believing it.

And yet, here it—she—is, a massive creature curled into a tight ball of scales and wings with a tail that twitches like a cat's. She's so big she nearly fills the entire cavernous room, a monstrous copy of the little dragon who'd been my companion for so long but polished to automaton perfection. She has winking eyelids, flaring nostrils, a mouth curling into a quiet grin, complete with sharp, shining teeth.

"Of course," the dragon says, her grin growing ever wider. "Who else would I be?" She gives an odd little tilt of the head, almost like a shrug. "The form is a rather quaint conceit, I'll admit, but vanity has ever been the bane of my existence. Though I must admit, I'm getting rather tired of the constraints. I would have designed all this much differently had I known how long I'd be stuck here."

I frown. "I don't understand. You make it sound like you designed...yourself. I thought Meridion was made by Madeline d'Arc. How are you even possible?"

The dragon's tail flicks in irritation. "Use your head, Magpie."

My jaw drops as I begin to process this new bit of information. "But we found her...you. Your body. Down in the Pits beneath the Mother Clock."

"Yes. What was left of my physical form, yes. I transferred all my research, all my memories, you see, into the form before you." She pauses. "I'm not completely Madeline, you understand. Just the parts of her that she deemed important enough to keep. And I have been waiting for you to bring me the very last piece I need."

I recoil from the intensity of her golden gaze. "My heart, you mean."

"Of course. It's going to free me from this place."

"And just how do you intend for me to do that?"

She laughs, throaty and deep. "I'm not going to reach down and pluck your heart from your chest, Magpie. Relax. That belongs to no one but yourself. But there may be a few components—programmatic ones—that I will require from you."

"Right now?" I am trying to keep up with this conversation and all the possible repercussions. Ghost and Lucian will be beside themselves. I have to tell them.

"We have some time," the dragon admits. "There are other things I have to plan for first, so there is no direct rush, except my own impatience. Something I've been trying to curtail for a very long time, mind." She lowers her head so I'm staring straight into one of her brilliant golden eyes. My clockwork heart whirs in response beneath its panel, and she tilts her head as though listening to it.

"Oh, it sounds like it's been tampered with. You didn't open it, did you?" Her eyes narrow.

"Ah, well, it kind of had to be opened. Someone tried to force it off my chest. I was going to die if Ghost didn't to get the water out of it." The words babble out of me, heedless. "And Lucian—I know he had to open it to fix it..."

My voice trails away as she raises a draconic brow at me. "I can see we have a lot of catching up to do. My spies are very clever, but they aren't omnipresent."

"Your spies? You mean the drones?" I gesture at the chute I'd fallen through.

"Well, the drones were just helping bring you to me. I can control nearly everything in this city in some fashion or other. But I mean the dragons. The little ones." She frowns. "Where is the one I sent you?"

"It's gone..." I choke out. "I was poisoned and when I woke up, my captors said they destroyed it." My heart aches, even as my mind tries to make sense of it. The dragon found with the dead Meridian architect on the streets of BrightStone. The way Sparrow and I had found my dragon in the slag heaps. The pieces of the dragon Josephine had tucked away in her forge, the basis for her wings. The prototypes Ghost and I saw in the Madeline's lab in the Pits.

We never truly knew what they were used for or how many of them there were. I say as much aloud, digging in my pockets for the few pieces of the dragon I have left. "This is all I found. I don't know if they were bluffing or not."

The dragon uncurls a clawed fist, and I place the pieces in her palm. She hums as she lowers her head. "It does look like one of mine," she admits. "But here, see that little piece there? The square one? Grab that and hold it out."

I do as she says, and she lets out a high-pitched whistle. Another drone emerges from a nearby pipe and flies to where I am, taking the chip from my fingers in a tiny, clawed hand. It beeps once, skittering off to a large panel full of buttons and controls I cannot begin to fathom. The chip is inserted into a slot, and with the press of a button, the screen above flickers to life.

Immediately images are projected upon it: me, Ghost, and Lucian. Molly Bell. The Conundrum. The streets of BrightStone.

"Everything my little dragons see and hear is recorded," IronHeart says. "Usually they return to me and upload the content as part of their programming, but your particular dragon hasn't checked in for a while. It happens sometimes."

My face goes red when the screen shows Ghost and me kissing on the steps of the Mother Clock. The shots before that had been of my fight on the gallows, my face bloodied, my hammer swinging. Of Bran and the High Inquestor. Memories of the terrible things I've done and were done to me.

I press my hands against my ears and turn away from the screen. I don't need to see all this again. I already know what a fuckup I am.

"Ah, my old house," the dragon says fondly. "I really enjoyed living there, even if the commute was awful. But my children, you know. I wanted them in a more natural environment. Not that it lasted very long. But see here… This is where I think you were attacked."

I turn back again, biting on my lip as I see one of my kidnappers come up behind Ghost and me, then see the electrical surges that drive us to the ground. I'm passed out, but somehow Ghost is still on his knees, crawling over to where I am. My dragon is hissing in fury, a gout of flame erupting across the screen as it hurtles toward one of my attackers. Everything spins about after that, the picture growing frantic and hazy until a hammer—my hammer—comes toward the lens and everything falls into darkness.

"Oh, that's so sad," I whisper. That they'd used my own weapon against it smacks of a betrayal the little beast didn't deserve. Spy or not, we'd been through so much together. And while I wasn't exactly thrilled it had been recording me all this time, I couldn't fault it for doing what it had been made to do.

"Mmmph," IronHeart says. "Well, it is disappointing. I had hoped it would do a better job of protecting you. It was an older model, however, so there were limitations. Would you like a new

one? One with a new body, I mean. Now that we have all its data uploaded, I can easily replicate its personality and interactions with you. It will be like it never left." She pauses. "With a few small enhancements, perhaps."

"Ah, I don't know." All of this feels a little too convenient for my taste. On the other hand, IronHeart is real and enormous and could quite clearly crush me like a bug. If her personality is anything like Madeline d'Arc's when she was alive, there is no doubt she's a formidable woman.

Maybe too formidable.

"The man I found with the parts of the dragon a year or two ago, the one who looked like he fell into BrightStone... He was murdered, wasn't he?" I already know the answer. He'd been knifed before he fell, but the question spills out of me, a part of the puzzle that has been bothering me since Sparrow and I came across the first of the clockwork dragons.

"Indeed," IronHeart says slyly. "He was becoming a problem, so I took matters into my own hands. Or claws, I suppose. I have my methods of communication, even if people aren't aware it's me—political games are practically a sport up here. It's not hard to arrange for a jilted lover to seek revenge in a rather final way."

Uneasy, I ponder this. As impressive as she is, IronHeart is an unknown, her motivations possibly suspect. She certainly admitted to murder a bit more quickly than I would've liked. And whether she means to let me keep my heart or not, I don't want to agree to anything without talking to Lucian and Ghost.

"So now what?" I ask. "I don't even know how long I've been gone for."

"That's easy enough. The date stamp on that last video was about five days ago. It would appear that poison made you rather ill." She frowns. "Pity your hair is so dirty. I would really like to get a sample of whatever it was they used. But no matter. I'll have my spies look for other clues."

"Five days!" I explode. "The others must be frantic by now! And Ghost was injured, wasn't he?"

The dragon pauses, her eyes rolling backward as though communicating with something I can't see. "Yes. But he is home and resting. Or...maybe not resting so much. That boy," she sighs. "Even when I left him at such a young age, I knew he would be a stubborn one."

"Maybe you shouldn't have left him at all," I snap. "He was devastated when we found your body. All this time with no communication at all. It's a wonder he doesn't despise you."

"Yes," IronHeart agrees softly. "And it wasn't my first choice of action, nor my second. But sometimes sacrifices are required for the greater good."

There's a hint of sadness in the dragon's voice, but I'm not entirely sure I buy it. Meridians by nature seem to be awfully good at manipulation. Buceph and Tanith were proof of that. And for all her genius, who's to say Madeline is any different?

"As to what's next, why, I'll send you back to my home, of course. For now. Eventually I'll need your services. With your heart there are some things only you can do, but I have preparations to make first."

"That sounds...ominous." I take a step away from her, though it doesn't really matter. I've got no place to run.

"You don't sound convinced."

"Ever since I found that little dragon, my life has been nothing but one big conspiracy after another. You'll forgive me if I don't exactly jump for joy at being rolled into another one." I shudder. Secrets make my skin itch, and this feels like a big one. "What do I tell Ghost about where I've been? I hardly think he's going to believe I was taking a holiday through the inner workings of the city, and I don't want to lie to him."

"Tell him the truth. Just not all of it," the dragon says airily. "You were kidnapped and poisoned, you escaped into the garbage chutes, were rescued by drones, and climbed your way back to the city to safety."

"He'll see through it. He always does," I point out.

"I'm sure you'll figure something out. You seem rather smart that way, from what I've seen over the years. But I don't think now is the time to reveal myself to either of my sons. Not yet."

"You could just not tell them it's you," I say, lip curling. "I mean, the legend of IronHeart should be big enough to override the possibility that you are also Madeline d'Arc."

"Oh no. Lucian would have me pegged in a hot moment. He's sharper than he looks and twice as crafty. I suspect he gets that from me." She arches her neck in a reptilian display of parental pride. "Besides, I think you need to figure out just why you were kidnapped at all. I would only be a distraction at this point. No, when the time is right, I'll reveal myself. Until then, keep doing what you have been doing."

I nod slowly, frowning. "What's your end game in all this? That's what I don't understand."

A sad smile crosses over her face. "Well, that's simple enough. I want to destroy Meridion." The dragon laughs as I gape at her. "Metaphorically, of course. As interesting as it might be to erupt from the bowels of the city in a flaming burst of fire or what have you, I'm not so cruel as that. There are innocent people here, and most are simply ignorant of the realities that make their existence possible. I merely wish to see them...educated."

Her words don't exactly comfort me, but I'll keep my mouth shut on my opinion for now. If I'm going to go against her request, I might as well do it when I'm well away from her.

I rub a dirty hand over my forehead. "I'll be honest. I need some rest. Can we have this conversation later? How do I get out of here? And more importantly, how do I get back? Because truthfully, the secret entrance is a right pain in the ass."

The dragon chuckles. "Of course. When I want you, I'll let you know. You'll recognize my helpers when you see them, I'm sure. As far as leaving, there is an elevator on the far side of the room. It will take you to the third level of the LightHouse. That's the center of the Meridian spire."

I have a vague memory of said spire from the air taxi and shudder, thinking of all the lights and the sounds. "So you're right smack in the center of the city and no one has ever found you?"

"Why would they?" she asks. "No one has really been looking. The best way to hide is to make it too obvious. Ever since the LightHouse was sabotaged, no one is allowed in or out—not without approval, anyway."

"And you make sure no one ever gets that," I say slowly.

"Smart girl. Everyone assumes someone else is keeping tabs on it, but truthfully, aside from a couple of guards for show, no one thinks about it at all. They certainly don't think *I'm* here. Fairy tales are supposed to be metaphors, after all."

"Well, I suppose I am talking to the creation of the woman who literally made her lab beneath the Mother Clock," I say dryly. "Old tricks are the best I guess."

"Just so. Most of the people here are simply content to be wrapped up in their various amusements and comfortable beds. Solving mysteries isn't something they aspire to." She gestures at me with a careful claw. "But *you* have a mystery or two to solve, I wager. Better get on that, yes?"

I'm not sure how far I'll get looking like something that crawled out of a privy, but I can already tell she's not going to give me anything else. "All right," I tell her. "Later, then." I steer myself in the direction she indicates with her tail, giving her a small nod when I enter the elevator.

The devices make me nervous, but I'm so tired right now, it could be filled with spiders and I wouldn't care. I just want to go home. I may have to trust she means what she says, but even I'm not so stupid as to take her words at face value.

The elevator whooshes shut, the cylinder door closing so I can't see outside it. It begins to move upward at a sleek pace, but my stomach still lurches a bit. "Like a damn coffin."

I press my hands to the sides when it slides to a stop. The door panel opens, and I have to turn away from the sudden wave of city lights twinkling. But at least it's night. I pull my glasses over my eyes, grateful that my hair is probably filthy enough to keep any intermittent glow from giving me away as I attempt to navigate home.

When I step onto a small metal staircase, the door shuts behind me and the panel recedes into the wall. My heart doesn't react when I touch it, which puzzles me, but I don't have the energy to figure it out now. Perhaps it's a one-way door that simply cannot be opened from the outside. It would make sense given that IronHeart would undoubtedly not want any accidental visitors.

There's an enormous platform high above me, probably the entrance to the LightHouse proper, but I get the feeling no one is really climbing this thing to get there. And why would they? With an airship, it would be easy to ascend to that level. The opposite of my problem, of course, but my little bit of space is more of an emergency exit, it seems. The staircase that wraps around it in either direction is at least a good place to start.

I start heading down, surprised by how my hands shake when I take the rail, though I probably shouldn't be. It has been a while since I got any decent rest, I was poisoned, and except for the kiosks in the mess hall, food hasn't exactly been throwing itself at me. So I concentrate on not tumbling down the curving staircase face-first, keeping my balance as best I can. The cuts on my palms burn, but the pain keeps me sharp so I don't try to quell it.

It's foggy out and there isn't much of a moon, but I don't have any problem seeing. I try to enjoy the clean night air, sucking in great gulps of it. For all the time I spent in the Pits below, I don't know that I'll ever really get used to crawling through the guts of a city like this. Not willingly anyway.

But I push those thoughts away. Better to process it all later, after a hot bath and a hotter meal. Ghost must be frantic by now. I'd actually welcome a scolding from Lucian for being so careless about my surroundings.

I've grown terribly complacent, depending on the two brothers to guard me up here, and this experience, as interesting as it has been, has really shown me how much I need to continue protecting myself. Admitting as much stings a bit, if I'm completely honest. After everything I've been through, surely I've earned at least someone who could have my back? And perhaps that is unfair of me to think, but sometimes even I need to wallow in self-pity. I don't even have my dragon anymore.

I've reached a landing that has a bit of space, so I stop here to look out across the cityscape, trying to get a sense of my direction. Below me, the obnoxious noise of the Inner Spiral bubbles up with its nonstop musical seduction. Nothing I want to subject myself to just yet, and I don't think I'll be able to find my way through the subway trains Lottie took us on before, either.

In the far distance, there is a flush of aqua light that seems to glitter—the Oubliette River. If I can head toward that, I'll at least be closer to the Outer Spiral, though it's a lot of walking. I feel around my pockets, but any jingle I had is long gone—and I doubt anyone would take me anywhere, looking the way I do.

I let out a long, mournful whistle. It's not a clan signal exactly, but it's the sort of thing Sparrow and I would have come up with, something soft and sarcastic and full of self-deprecating humor.

Where to? Where to? Which way is home when you have no home?

The sound echoes off the nearby buildings, and I whistle it twice more out of obstinance.

Home waits for you!

I nearly fall over at the reply, repeating over and over again for the span of a minute. It pauses, and I hesitate. *Which way?*

The whistle grows closer. *Here, here, here. Find me, find me.*

My heart whirs rapidly. Who could it be? Ghost doesn't know the Moon Child language, and as far as I know, I'm the only one here. I clatter down the rest of the stairs, continuing to call out my location as I descend the tower to a cluster of nearby buildings. Their roofs are flat and close together, and I easily make the leap onto them, pausing only long enough to get my bearings and whistle again.

Exhaustion sets my limbs to trembling, and I finally sink, unable to go any farther. I sit and pant, rubbing my swollen ankle. In my rush to follow the whistles, I forgot I was injured earlier, and the throbbing pulse jetting its way up my leg could mean nothing good. I need Lucian to look at it for sure.

I whistle a soft trill, putting my smoked lenses back on when the moon peeks from behind the clouds to bathe the rooftops in silver.

WHOMP.

I'm nearly pitched head over heels as a series of bodies piles half on top of me until I'm wrapped in a tangle of limbs and silver hair and glowing eyes. A burble of hysterical laughter ripples out of me as I recognize my clanmates one by one and hug them fiercely. Rosa with her copper skin and soft arms. Haru's shaved head and unabashed grin. Dafyyd's perpetually sad face and gentle demeanor. Gloriana with her watery blue eyes and shaking hands. All of them terribly thin and knowing far too much of death and fear than anyone has a right to.

Rosa wrinkles her nose. "Hells, Mags, but you stink. Where have you been hiding?"

"You wouldn't believe me if I told you," I mumble, swallowing back a thick lump in my throat. "How did you— Why are you here?"

"Ghost sent us a message by way of Josephine and Bran through the BrightStone Chancellor. Arrangements were made to send us up through that liaison lady, Fionula, I think her name is." Rosa smiles. "Apparently it's a bit of a diplomatic...incident? The first and only Moon Child to be granted access to Meridion suddenly disappearing isn't that great for inter-city relationships."

The others giggle at her words, and I suspect there's a bit more to the story than that, but explanations can wait. I look around at my clanmates again and frown. "Where's Bran?"

Haru shrugs. "Wouldn't come. Nothing to do with you, he said. He hopes you're okay and all that, though he seemed to think you'd manage whatever was going on."

"It's just...the Meridians. He hates them," Dafyyd adds a moment later, tugging on his hair. "I'm worried about him, to be honest. Since we got back topside, he's fallen apart a little. Not when he's needed—he's always managed to push himself to get a task done—but now..."

I nod. "There's too much free time to think of...things." We all give a bit of a shiver, memories washing over us. "And he was down there for three years," I add. "I wasn't in the Pits for nearly as long, and some days..."

Haru squeezes my hand when I don't finish, and I sag in response. I don't need to explain anything to them. They know. They *know*.

I wipe away a rush of tears, the others ignoring my sudden show of weakness. "How did you ever find me?"

A wry smile plays over Gloriana's lips. "We didn't exactly ask for a layout of the city, but Ghost told us where you'd last been seen and what happened to him. So we started there, and everyone took a different direction. We just fanned out, searching outward the last few nights. This place is amazing, by the way. The food alone... Anyway, Haru heard your whistles tonight so that led us to you easily enough."

"Small favors. Did Ghost mention if my kidnappers were caught?" I struggle to get to my feet, careful of my injured ankle.

"No, only that you were acting strangely before they electrified you." Rosa purses her lips. "He's very worried about you, Magpie. The only reason he's not out here looking for you is because he hit his head when he fell, and Lucian doesn't want him out and about on the rooftops until we know his balance hasn't been affected."

"And I agree," Gloriana says firmly. "Concussions are nothing to play around with. I'm sure he'll be all right, though. Lucian didn't seem overly concerned."

"Well, maybe he should be," I mutter. "I wasn't just attacked, you know. I was poisoned."

Their heads snap toward me, laughter washed away in remembered grimness. I don't look at Dafyyd, knowing he's still bitter about Conal's death. Gloriana fists her trembling hands to hide the way they shake.

"Are you sure?" Rosa asks, her eyes narrowing.

"Aye. The men who took me said as much, though they didn't know I was awake at the time. It knocked me out for a few days." I pause, wanting to tell them about IronHeart, but I don't want to muddy the waters. Not yet. Not here. "It seems to have worn off, but the sooner we get back home, the sooner Lucian can check me out."

The others look at me and nod. "Then let's go," Gloriana says, pulling me up.

She and Rosa keep me steady, the two boys helping me climb down the building without hurting my ankle any further. I sigh with relief when we make it to the street below, so very grateful they are here.

They hug me hard again when a soft sob escapes me, our foreheads pressed together, and I know I can do anything with my clan at my back. Anything at all.

The trip to the house doesn't take as long as I imagined it might. Of course, this is because Haru and Dafyyd run along in front of us to tell Lucian and Ghost I've been found. I don't know if they even have a chance to tell them anything else before Lucian arrives in one of those air taxis, hovering above the ground with an eerie lightness that belies the solidness of its metal doors.

He takes one look at me in my tattered rags and oily hair, the others holding me up as I limp beside the building, and his face shutters into something tight and angry. Without a word, he whisks me into the carriage, the others piling in the back.

"Just like old times, aye?" I mumble at him, rewarded by the curl of a lip and a flash of teeth, but otherwise he says nothing.

I don't pretend to know what's running through his head. I can probably guess, but a wave of exhaustion washes over me, adrenaline slipping away as my body realizes that its finally safe and among friends.

Almost immediately, my eyes close and I doze off, listening to the chatter of my clanmates as they point out various highlights of the city. It seems harmless enough, but we're Moon Children. If they're remembering landmarks, it's because they are expecting to have to travel by rooftops, and what better way to learn layout?

I take comfort in this, even if I wish things didn't already turn out this way. But my clan's here now, and that is good enough for me. With these thoughts pattering through my head, I fall asleep for real, drifting away on dreams of clockwork dragons and smoke and a cart full of old apples.

"Oh, she's awake. Fetch Lucian, aye?"

My eyes flutter open my vision blurry with sleep. Even in the near total darkness of the room, I recognize Rosa as the one who just spoke, and she smiles down on me. "Welcome back. You've been asleep for nearly a full day and a night."

I shift, my bones stiff and heavy. "I'm getting too old for this," I grumble.

"Growing old might not be such a bad thing," she says. "It's not like most of us have ever had that sort of fortune, anyway."

She's right. I know she is. But that doesn't stop me from wishing my joints weren't throbbing like the hells, either. *"Mmmph,"* I say intelligently. "I'm starving. Where's the food?"

"Lucian wants to check you," she says. "But he has some stew going downstairs. It's very good."

"Yes, it is." My voice grows wistful, remembering those quiet winter nights in the Conundrum reading with Ghost and supping on chicken soup. "Where is Ghost?"

"Right here." His gravelly voice electrifies me, and I shift to my side to see him lying on a cot beside my bed, his head still wrapped in bandages. "I asked to be set up here when you came in so I could watch over you."

I bite my lip at the haphazard earnestness staring at me from the depths of his eyes. "Aye," I say finally, unable to trust myself with anything else in front of the others.

"Lucian brought some medicine earlier," Rosa says. "We told him you were poisoned, and he took some blood samples, but I'm not sure he found anything useful."

"I don't know if he would. It was topical. They brushed it on my head." I turn back to Ghost, coughing slightly. He hands me a cup of water and I drink it quick, ignoring the way my stomach rumbles. "The boy…man…whatever he was—the one I attacked? He touched me a moment before. The poison was on his glove, and he spread it into my hair."

Ghost frowns, his eyes narrowing. "So this wasn't random."

"Nope. I was a target." I hesitate, wanting to bring up Lottie's possible involvement, but I decide to wait until Lucian joins us.

I stretch, watching eagerly as Haru trots into the room with a tray of bread rolls and a steaming bowl of soup. He sets the tray on the foot of the bed and tosses me a roll. Immediately I set to eating it, tearing it apart and wolfing it down in a matter of seconds. The others give the tray appraising looks of their own.

"It's really good," I mumble between bites. "You should go get some while it's still hot." Everyone but Ghost bolts out of the room, and I laugh. "We never change, do we?"

"When it comes to food? I don't think it's possible for Moon Children *to* change," Ghost agrees. He eases onto his back on the cot and stares up at the ceiling. "Though to be fair, food or no, I'm happy you are home."

He rolls onto his side, his hair parted rakishly. "Lucian is furious, you know. We were supposed to keep you safe. Meridion was supposed to show you the best that our people could be—the potential for a cultural exchange with BrightStone, the acceptance of Moon Children. And instead, it's more of the same."

"I tried to tell you and Lucian. It's not as simple as cutting my hair or putting me in fancy clothes. People see what they want to see. The trappings of what they consider civilized don't change what I am underneath. Even to Lottie and other students, I am nothing more than an exotic charity case."

Ghost actually flushes at this, something uncomfortable passing behind his eyes, though I'm not sure if it's because of my words, his own internalized guilt, or some combination of the two.

"It's not your fault," I tell him, then lift the bowl of soup to my lips and drain the last of the broth. "But now you see why I need the others here. That's what a clan is, aye? A family who won't betray you and will have your back utterly and without fail." I swallow against a hard lump in my throat. "I didn't realize how much I needed them until I didn't have them. And they need me, too."

"So do I, Mags," Ghost says hoarsely. "Don't forget that." His hand slips into mine, and he squeezes it with hot fingers.

"Never." I raise my arm to kiss his knuckles. It's bold of me, but I've never gotten anywhere wallflowering. He lets out a strangled sigh, his eyes dilating, and for the first time, I see the licks of lightning flashing beneath his skin. "Just remember...you belong to me. Even when those hordes of marriage invitations start pouring in."

He lets out a deeply unhappy chuckle. "They already have. Not all of them are serious, of course. Some are just poking their noses into the fray to see what the excitement is all about. At least two insist I was arranged before Lucian and I even left Meridion, but without my mother here, there's no way to prove anything one way or the other. I'm not entertaining any of them, if that's what you're thinking."

"I'm sure you think that," I agree. "But I also think Lucian is smart enough to make sure you keep them all dangling and guessing. To end the chase so quickly with such a blunt response will do nothing for your family name."

"I don't care," Ghost says stubbornly. "Let *him* entertain the concept if he's so bloody interested in dancing that way. I want nothing to do with it."

"Somehow I don't think you have much choice." I say it seriously with a tinge of regret. Society seems to require so much of even the simplest things, and almost none of it is fair.

He slides off the cot and wriggles into the bed next to me. He holds on to my waist as he buries his face against my shoulder. "Mine," he mumbles.

"Are you sure that's not the concussion talking?" I gently pat the bandage with careful fingers. "How bad were you injured, anyway?"

"I just clocked my head on the ground. Should be all right in a couple more days, according to Lucian, but I don't feel that bad right now." He squints as he prods the left side of the bandage. "There's a bit of swelling still, but I think it looks worse than it is." He pauses, the corner of his mouth quirking up. "You, on the other hand, look awful. Unless sewer-pipe chic was what you were going for."

I roll my eyes, though I can't quite help but touch the tangled, oily ruins of my hair. "Oh, but it's always done so well for me before." I think about the fancy clothes I was wearing and the time Lottie spent trying to fix me up. "What a waste of jingle."

I crane my head to look in the mirror and grind my jaw. I didn't realize just how bad it is. I've been dirty before, but this is on a whole new level.

"We tried to wipe you down real quick when Lucian brought you home, but until you woke up, he didn't want to mess with you too much." Ghost nudges me. "A bath, then?"

He doesn't really wait for my answer so much as pull me to my feet and gather some towels from the linen closet. "We've been keeping the hot-water heater going so there should be plenty of water to fill the tub."

I let him lead me toward the bathroom. It's down the hall past the larger bedroom, and a quick peek shows me the other Moon Children have claimed it, piles of blankets nested in various corners and a hammock hanging between two of the bunks. I can hear them arguing downstairs about whatever they're eating, and I can't help but smile at the cheerful squabble.

When we reach the bathroom, Ghost draws me a bath, barely waiting for the water to fill more than a couple of inches before dumping bath salts into it, the water foaming into a bubble-filled monstrosity. "Get in," he says, turning around for the sake of modesty.

I almost laugh at it, but I do as he says, stripping the shredded pants and filthy shirt from my body before easing into the tub. A squeak escapes me, unknown scrapes burning as I settle in. When the foam reaches the level of my chest panel, I shut the water off, still cagey about submerging it.

Ghost pulls up a stool and a basin, and gestures at me to turn my back to him. "I'll do your hair." I ease myself in his direction, tipping my head forward as he pours a basin full of water over my head, then applies a gentle sponge to my shoulders. "You're pretty bruised up here."

He leans over and presses a kiss to the nape of my neck, his mouth hovering by my ear, but he doesn't say anything. Instead, he rinses my hair again before drawing a comb through the worst of the tangles.

"Just where exactly did you end up? This is awful." He tsks at me.

"Down the garbage chute." I gesture airily.

The combing stops. "Did you now?" His voice is a strangled sound. "That was a truly stupendously bad idea, Mags. You could have ended up in the incinerator."

"In a manner of speaking, I did," I say. "But no, I ended up falling right off the edge of Meridion and onto one of the anchor chains. Climbed my way back up inside and found my way to a maintenance tunnel. I might have returned faster if I still had my dragon. They destroyed it when I was taken, the suck-tits." I pause, still unsure about bringing up IronHeart. "Took me a while to figure out how to get to the outside."

"Enough," Ghost says weakly. "That is horrifying and terrible, and if I think about it and how close you were to dying again..." He chuckles. "You're either the luckiest, or unluckiest, person in the world. I have no idea which."

"Makes for a hell of a story, either way," I agree, running my fingers through my now not-quite-as-oily hair. It will do, though I suspect any styling is long gone. I turn toward Ghost, expecting some sort of off-the-cuff comment only to have him capture my mouth in a greedy kiss.

His hands cup my face, pulling me closer until I'm half out of the tub and he's practically falling into it, but he doesn't let go, nipping at my lower lip with almost furious intent. When he finally retreats, he's breathing hard. A loud peal of laughter bubbles up the back staircase, hammering home that we are not, in fact, alone.

"I'll wait," he murmurs.

"Wait?" My own voice sounds oddly husky, reverberating off the steamed walls with a quiet certainty.

"Until Lucian declares you well. And then..." He exhales sharply. "And then we will finally acknowledge what is between us, yes?"

His fingers twine tightly around mine as I look up at him. "Aye," I breathe. "We will."

Darken my door with your shadow
Like the breath of the north wind blowing.
Your footsteps tread to cross
The threshold of my knowing.

— CHAPTER ELEVEN —

The prick of the needle pulls my attention away from the current conversation, and I snarl lightly at Lucian, who ignores me as efficiently as ever. "There now." He presses a small bandage to the insulting little wound and tapes it up with a swift motion. "Without knowing exactly what it is they poisoned you with, treatment is a bit difficult."

"So what is this, then?" I gesture at him with the arm.

"Vitamins. And an antibiotic, just to be on the safe side, given what you were climbing through." He puts the used syringe in a metal bowl and hands them to Gloriana. "Careful of the needle, my dear. Please take these to my office so we can autoclave them correctly."

Gloriana gives me a happy smile and does as he asks, picking up other loose bandages as she goes. She's beaming, and it makes my heart sing to see it, even if I can't help but notice the way her hands continue to shake. Her hope of becoming a bonewitch grows frailer by the day. No matter her enthusiasm or intelligence, no one wants someone with shaky hands holding a scalpel. With any luck, perhaps the Meridians, with their advanced technology, could assist her with a cure of some sort.

Lucian watches her leave with a little nod of approval. "I'd forgotten how useful it could be to have an assistant," he says. "A willing one," he amends a moment later, snorting at my eye roll. "Though you could have some promise, too, if you'd like to get back to your studies—especially if you truly entertain any thoughts of entering the university. Ghost told me that's where you were the night you were…taken."

I shrug. "I don't know if higher education is for me. I don't think I have the patience for it. I was only looking in case it was something the others might want to do. Making Moon Children self-sufficient is half the reason I'm here."

"Fair enough." The doctor eases into the chair beside the bed and takes a lock of my hair between his fingers and rubs them together. "I've never had a real chance to study the conductive properties of Moon Child hair," he says slowly. "I'd never even thought about it, given how preoccupied I was trying to solve the riddle of the Rot. But now…"

I thumb my hand at his medical bag. "I'm sure you've got some scissors in there somewhere. May as well take some now as opposed to sneaking it when I'm asleep or some such."

He has the courtesy to look mildly offended at my words, but he rifles through his bag all the same. He retrieves a small pair of curved shears and quickly snips off a bit, placing it on a nearby tray. "I'll want samples from all the others," he notes. "For comparison. If I can manage to determine what they used, we might be able to trace down the source of the poison."

Ghost pops his head around the doorframe. "There's a little more to it than that, if what Mags told me is true."

"Oh?" Lucian watches as Ghost sits beside me, puzzled.

"The men who captured me were related…and they know Lottie. One of them was Corbin—Lottie's promised," I say quietly.

Lucian gapes at me. "Are you sure?"

"She might not have been aware of it. I rather hope she wasn't—I was starting to like her." Ghost speaks slowly as though trying to piece together the events of that night.

"She might not," I agree. "But you might argue she was rather insistent about taking us to her university campus, even though she knew I wasn't feeling well." My mouth compresses, not particularly liking the picture that was emerging. "Trust is a bag of cats," I remind him. "More likely to scratch you for the petting than reward you with a purr, aye?"

Lucian exhales sharply. "That would definitely be a matter of interest for the Council, but we can't simply go around making accusations, not without some kind of proof."

My fingers tap absently on my leg. "I'm guessing my word as the victim wouldn't amount to much?"

"As a Moon Child and not even a citizen? Unlikely. I'd rather hoped Meridian politics wouldn't have reared its ugly head so soon," Lucian says, resigned. "But Lady Fionula did warn us. At any rate, we'll have to plan our next steps carefully."

"And Lottie?" I hesitate, not sure if I want to confront her about it.

"I think saying nothing for now would be best," Lucian muses. "Ghost said she was named a Tantaglio at the university? That's one of the Noble Houses. Even if she's part of one of the family offshoots, the main House is extremely powerful. They could make things even harder for us if we make a fuss too soon."

"Making a fuss or not—keeping quiet doesn't mean much if we're being poisoned," Ghost points out.

"Well, I know that and you know that, but we'll take what they care to give us and then play the game as best we can." Lucian's eyes slide sideways. "And with the sudden appearance of more Moon Children, I think we have some new pieces on the board that they aren't going to be able to control or predict."

"However did you persuade Lady Fionula to bring them here? I thought you were against it—or at least until we were settled." I fold my hands primly.

"Curious, isn't it?" he says, his face smooth as glass. "I simply sent word to the Chancellor to let her know of your disappearance. Apparently, she insisted on sending several boxes of supplies via airship."

"He wasn't this calm about it when we opened them and found most of your clan inside," Ghost says dryly. "At all."

"Yes, well." Lucian coughs into his fist. "That being said, they made themselves useful enough. I figured as long as they were here, they might as well try to find you. I simply asked that they stay out of the public eye and not draw attention to themselves."

"Despite their rowdiness, we can trust them. At least when it comes to you," Ghost mutters at his brother. "And right now, allies are rather scarce. Whatever the Chancellor's reasoning, I'm glad they're here."

I can't help the tiny swell of pride lifting in my chest. "Aye."

"Say what they will about Moon Children as a whole, but you're a tenacious and stubborn group, Mags. And your ability to surprise should never be underestimated." Lucian rubs the stubble on his chin, his mien thoughtful. "Perhaps it's time we try to utilize that."

The other Moon Children are lazing about the shared bedroom with contented mumbling. One of them appears to have absconded with a bottle of whisky from the kitchens, and they pass it around good-naturedly, their cheeks flushing with quiet laughter.

I wave them off when they attempt to toss it my way. "Doc says nothing for me until we know the poison's out of my system." I still give the bottle a longing look as it passes me by.

Rosa pouts but sucks down another swallow. "Your loss, I suppose. Too bad Bran isn't here to share it with us."

We all go silent at that, and there really isn't much else to say on the matter. Bran has his own demons, and he will work them out the way he feels is best for him, despite what we'd prefer.

Dafyyd wanders over to the window on the far side of the room. It's open, and the night breeze rolls in past us, full of unfamiliar scents and noises. It's almost seductive, beckoning us outside with the promise of rooftop dancing in a way we've never known.

Never mind that I just began recovering or that the others spent the last several days searching for me. This and that are two entirely different things, and the siren song of freedom beats heavy in my blood. Almost as one, we slip out the window to the roof of the house.

From here, the breeze grows even stronger, and we stare out at the Inner Spiral in the distance. All of us look at each other then, eyes lighting up. For a moment, I feel a twinge of guilt. Ghost remains holed up with Lucian, planning whatever strategies they think best, when he should be here with us. But my clan needs to run, too—a reaffirmation of our bond—and if I don't lead them, they'll go without me. I can see it on their faces.

I let out a soft whistle, a questioning, coaxing trill, as I walk to the edge of the rooftop...and sigh. "That's the one thing I kind of hate about this place," I say. "It's too far away from the rest of the city."

Rosa's mouth purses. "It does rather lose that romantic edge if you have to climb down and trot to the nearest tall building, doesn't it?"

I sag, sitting on the edge of the roof with my feet dangling. The others follow suit, stretching out beside me as we look up at the moon.

Gloriana dangles the whisky bottle between her knuckles. The alcohol seems to have stilled the tremor in her hands. "Wonder what the others are doing down below. How strange to think of them staring up at us and wondering what we are doing here."

"Aye. But that's what we're trying to change, isn't it?" I point out. "Though I don't know if we can undo so many years of being conditioned to live like...like we do." Not even my time in the Pits so much as the everyday burden of struggling for food, jingle, and a warm place to sleep.

I study my clan with an air of melancholy. So few of us here. So few of us left.

My fingers twitch, and Rosa tosses me a cigarillo from her pocket. She scratches a lucifer on the sole of her boot, and I light it quickly, taking a long drag. It tastes like shit—definitely a lower-grade tobacco than is my wont. But memories flood back all the same: Sitting on a roof with Sparrow in a time that feels like forever ago, staring up at the glittering skies of Meridian cutting through fog with razor sharpness that made our hearts bleed and our dreams wander.

Will there ever truly be a place for us? I wish I knew. In that moment, I would give anything to simply have an answer. But I don't, not even for myself.

So I sit and smoke the filthy BrightStone cigarillo, the others leaning up against me, clinging to one another as though we are tethered ships moored in the soft swells of a beginning storm.

We fall asleep there, of course. Despite the hardness of the roof and the odd city noises I can't quite get used to, something about the familiar rise and fall of the breath around me, the random assortment of limbs and nestling bodies wrapping me in a cocoon of warmth and safety, is something I'm loath to break away from.

It might be nearly dawn when I finally roll over to see Ghost sitting a little ways from us, his back against the side of the house as he watches us sleep. There is something wistful on his face. He never really knew the true inclusion of a clan, and while technically, he is now a member of this one, there was barely any time to really discover what that meant before he and Lucian whisked me away up here.

Even now, Ghost stands between both worlds, trying to cross a divide far deeper than my own. I raise my head to catch his attention, and his face swivels toward mine. I press a finger to my lips and gesture at him to come to us.

Slightly puzzled, he does so, his naked feet slipping over the copper roof, a cat in the fog. He kneels beside me, as though uncertain of what I'm asking, but I give him no time to really react, pulling him into my arms and into the pile of us.

He lets out a startled grunt, but I'm already curling around him, the others shifting with sleepy mumbles and slurred words. They make room, all of us somehow fitting around his presence like pieces of a puzzle.

I slip into a relaxed doze, my arm around his waist as he sags, his body melting into the group.

Together, we sleep.

"You can't just go about napping on roofs like some kind of jungle cats," Lucian snarls at us, thrusting his fingers through his hair in frustration.

"Can't you just imagine it?" I jest. "Roving bands of feral Moon Children peeking through windows at night, sleeping wherever, Meridian children leaving out bowls of milk and bread for us in the hope of luring us inside..." I exchange a glance with an amused Ghost. "Maybe it wouldn't be such a bad thing."

Lucian's nostrils flare wide. "I need a drink. And it's too early to drink." He frowns at the empty whisky bottle in Rosa's hand. "Who said you could take from my private stock?"

"There weren't no signs on it," Rosa says sagely. "Not that I can read anyway."

"Not that it would have stopped you, even if you could," Dafyyd adds with a grin.

"Well from now on there are ground rules. If you're going to live here, we need to establish some basic boundaries." Lucian takes the bottle from her, staring mournfully at the lack of alcohol.

"So what are they?" I ask, leaning up against the doorframe with a yawn as I ease a crick in my shoulder.

"I don't know yet!" he snaps. "No more drunken orgies or whatever it was you were doing. Especially *not* in public, is that understood?"

"What's an orgy?" Haru eyes the doctor uncertainly from where he crouches on the nearby sofa, his face puzzled.

"The Hells save me from Moon Children," Lucian swears and stomps out, punching Ghost lightly on the shoulder. "This is all your fault."

The other Moon Children giggle, and even I can't help but break a smile at his flustered visage. Despite everything that's happened over the last few days, it feels good to be able to tease him.

Ghost shakes his head. "Don't mind him. He's just got a lot on his mind, I think. Romance problems."

I raise a brow at this. "Trouble in paradise already?"

"You know it's not that simple, Mags. His betrothal to the Lady Fionula was never formally dissolved, even with her turning a blind eye to his love for her brother. I'm sure she'd rather move on—and it would have been better for her family if she had—but she chose to remain loyal to ours, in solidarity with her brother." His voice grows low. "She has sacrificed much for our cause, and Lucian cannot betray that."

I rub my forehead. "There's nothing simple when it comes to Meridians, is there?"

His mouth quirks up. "There's nothing simple about anything, if you haven't noticed."

"I'm sure if Bran were here, he'd argue the point," I say dryly. "Food, freedom, and fucking. That was the main thrust of his clan leadership. Although as themes go, it's not bad." I miss his simplistic take on life. In the Pits, there wasn't much else to work with, but here, I feel almost as caged.

"We need to scout out the buildings better," Haru says suddenly. "If you are taken again or if something else happens, we need a better understanding of the streets—the loose windows, or open sewer hatches. Everything here is so clean and even and straight."

"An advantage for some things," Dafyyd says, "but not so much for others. Hard to find good hiding places."

I chew on my lower lip. "What are our chances of contacting Josephine? Those wings of hers might come in handy. The city here is larger than anything like BrightStone. Having the ability to fly without needing to rely on airships would be a boon. Or hells, if we had our *own* airships here..."

Josephine had invented a set of self-propelling wings that allowed the wearer to glide from place to place. They are still a work in progress as far as I know, though they were used during our escape from the Pits when BrightStone rebelled against the Inquestors.

Haru brightens up at the prospect. "Josephine was training some of the other clans in how to use the wings. There aren't enough for everyone, and not everyone wants to learn to fly anyway, but maybe..."

"There's still nothing quite like putting feet to brick, though," Rosa points out. "If you want to learn the ins and outs of a city, you have to walk it. Doesn't mean we can't keep to certain areas, but I think if we're going to do this the right way, it has to be done with a purpose. We can't just run ragged all over the place."

"Look," I say finally, "the last time I was really seen by the public, I was at the university. We could go there to look for information, but I don't want to make the rest of you targets, either. It's great you're all here though I'm not sure making the presence of additional Moon Children known will work in our favor."

Gloriana steps forward, placing a hand upon my shoulder. "It's a chance we have to take, Mags. We need to step into the light sometime, don't we?"

Ghost says nothing to any of this, watching our conversation play out in the early-morning light. In the past, he might have said something encouraging, but since coming back from the Pits, that part of him feels…not broken, exactly, but weary. Certainly more cautious than before. My eyes meet his, and he nods.

"Anything to add?" I ask him, all the same. After all, he's clan. He should have a chance to weight in.

"I think she's right," he says. "But beyond that…I'm not going to sit here and promise you I'll be able to protect any of you or that you won't get hurt." He rubs his head ruefully. "Despite all my hopes, I've failed miserably on that account. So maybe it's time to follow your lead."

I nod slowly, eying his hair, still dyed a light brown. His skin has started to glow faintly with the electrical pulses declaring him a Meridian. "Who do you want to be?" I ask him softly. "A Moon Child or a Meridian?"

He grows pensive. "I know what I want, and I know what I should do. But they don't exactly line up at the moment, and for now, *this* is what I need to be. Ask me again later…"

His words are interrupted by my growling stomach. I ignore my clan's snickers. "Breakfast first, aye? Let's eat, and then we can figure it out."

We parade into the house through the window, the scent of freshly baked bread wafting through the hallways. Ghost lingers at the end and grabs my hand as the others tromp down the stairs before pushing me against the wall, his fingers running down my neck and across my collarbone.

His mouth presses hard upon mine, nipping frantically at my lips before he buries his face in my neck. I let myself go limp, my fingers twining in his hair. A ragged growl escapes him as Lucian calls for me from the hallway.

I bite at Ghost's ear, disappointment vibrating through my bones as I slip away from him, his hand grasped tightly in mine. I round the corner into the hallway, nearly bumping straight into Lucian's chest.

"Ah, there you are. Good. I want to do another blood draw before you eat." He waves Ghost on. "Go bring us a tray, would you? We'll be in my office."

Ghost looks as if he's about to object but simply exhales sharply before doing as his brother asks, leaving me to trail behind Lucian until we reach his office. It's been cleaned up since I was last here and it's beginning to look like a proper bonewitch's study now, complete with all sorts of instruments.

"I'm thinking of opening a practice later," Lucian notes as he draws a vial of blood. I look away from the needle, my memories in the Pits assaulting me until I feel as though I might vomit. But it's over a moment later, the sting of the wound fading quickly.

"You're really planning long-term, aren't you?" I press on the bandage.

"I have to," he asserts. "Drifting about won't help us. The best we can do is push forward into normalcy so that we can persuade the Council to grant us the restoration of our family House." His champagne eyes fix on me. "And I haven't been completely honest with you, Mags. There might be some things happening in the next few days you won't be happy with, but—"

"Teach me to suck eggs, why don't you?" I pace away from him, ignoring the chill shivering down my spine at his words. "When has anything we've ever plotted made me happy?"

"Point taken. But, Mags, this is probably going to be...painful. For you, in particular. I simply ask that you trust me." He pauses, his voice suddenly dead quiet. "And that you trust Ghost."

I don't remotely like the sound of whatever this is, and a flare of anger swells high, making my cheeks burn. "I'd have thought you learned your lesson by now, Lucian. Every time you two go off and make your little secret plans, everything goes to shit. And then I'm forced to rescue you. Is that what's going to happen again? Because I really think I'm done with this cloak-and-dagger, penny-dreadful garbage you seem to be using as a blueprint for your life."

He has the gall to flush, averting his eyes. "All right. That's fair. I've been hiding things for so long that I have trouble opening up and trusting—even you, and you're family now." He sucks in a deep breath, running his fingers in little circles on the desk. "Over the last few days, we've had a number of inquiries about Ghost. I didn't want to bring it up while you were healing. But there's one in particular... There's been a request that we honor an old betrothal contract—one made before the fall of our mother."

I raise my brow. "A betrothal contract? Made when Ghost was, what? Five? You've barely returned to Meridion and now some unknown person suddenly wants you to honor a promise made between children?"

"Betrothals aren't always made with the consent of the parties involved," Lucian points out. "Not up here." There's a sting of rebuke in his voice, but I don't think it's directed at me so much as some part of his past. And I suppose he would know if things between him and Jeremiah are still so messy.

"And she's not an unknown, as I was just now made aware of." Ghost materializes in the doorway, startling me with the sharpness of his voice. Anger crackles from him as he strides into the room, his eyes burning a hole in his brother's back. He turns to me, baring his teeth in frustration as he throws a piece of parchment on the Lucien's desk. "It's Lottie."

"Lottie!" I explode, this sudden revelation slamming into me with all the grace of a brick to the face. "Aye, that's rich. Why didn't you tell me before? And how could you possibly entertain such an agreement after my poisoning?"

"Well, to be fair, she was only a child when the betrothal was made, as well," Lucian says, flinching away as Ghost fumes at him. "And we only found out about her possible part in your poisoning yesterday. Obviously, had I known before, I wouldn't be entertaining this at all."

"Everything about this entire situation reeks of entitlement and opportunity, possibly set up the moment we arrived on Meridion," Ghost snarls. "Turn it down."

"Oh, come now," Lucian says. "I chose to go to that college pub the first night we arrived home. It was pure coincidence that she was there with the other students. How could she have known?"

I waver. Lottie had seemed nice enough. Certainly she had tried to become friends with me, showing me around, fixing up my appearance. But what if it was only calculated, feigned affection? A chance to get in good with the others around Ghost so that such a move like this might be met with approval? And with me out of the way... What could this be but a knowing manipulation? But then the thought strikes me. Why would Corbin help her?

"And what of the fact that she's already promised? She was quick enough to tell me about that when we met." I frown. Maybe too quick, if I think on it. What if she didn't want this betrothal, either?

"What difference does it make?" Ghost snaps. "I'm not going through with it. I'm not some...some prize to be won simply because it's convenient now."

"No one ever said we'd go through with it," Lucian says, tapping his fingers on the table. "It's a ruse, of course. A chance for Ghost to enter the inner circle of Meridian high society."

"For what purpose?" I gesture around the room. "We're restoring your name, aren't we? And what about BrightStone alliances and reclaiming rights for Moon Children? How is getting wrapped up in a possible marriage going to help with any of that?"

I exchange a heated look with Ghost. In this, at least, we're in agreement. "What's next?" Ghost reaches out to grasp my hand. It's shaking, whether with rage or fear I'm not sure. "Will you parade Mags about like some sort of brood mare to entice the others into thinking she'd be a good match?"

"If I have to," Lucian snaps back. "Our position here is more precarious than either of you know. This tightrope must be walked if we're to survive. If we pretend to go through with it, it buys us time and possible answers." He points at Ghost. "I know you're smart enough to see this. And you're more than capable of pulling off such a plan."

"I don't want to talk about it anymore," Ghost says, rubbing his eyes. "The answer is no."

"It would just be for a short time—weeks, a month at most. And given they will have to break her other arrangement, for the sake of propriety, we can press our advantage in the meanwhile." Lucian's lips compress tightly, a white line slashing into his face. "It's not ideal. I know that. But if Lottie truly was involved in this poisoning, then that may mean the Noble Houses are beginning to make their move."

"So what?" Ghost roars, whirling on his brother. "Don't you ever get tired of this? What difference does it make who is doing what?"

"And if they take away our right to be here? Would you have us kicked to the streets again after we have given up so much to reclaim our birthright? Because I will not, Trystan." Ghost startles at the use of his real name, something seeming to snap along his spine. Lucian presses on, his voice heavy. "I did not sacrifice so many years of my life running and scrounging along the streets of BrightStone, searching for cures, for solutions, for answers, simply to throw that effort away because we suddenly have a comfortable bed. Our mother would not have done so, either," he adds.

Ghost lets out a noncommittal grunt, pacing from the room. His usual silent footsteps are long gone, feet slamming into the hardwood like hammers to nails, every inch of him stiff with fury.

The other Moon Children peek from around the stairs at the end of hall, eyes wide, and I make a shooing motion at them.

"Lovers' quarrel?" Rosa winks at me, making a rude gesture with a bread roll she's been eating.

"Not exactly. But leave him alone for a bit until I have time to sort it out, aye?" I run my fingers through my hair, glaring at Lucian. "Suppose I'll go clean up your mess. Again." He flinches at my words, but I turn on my heel and stride after Ghost.

He's easy enough to find perched on the rooftop outside my room. I adjust my glasses against the light and stare at his back, hunched and angry.

He lets out a bitter laugh when I sit down next to him and dangle my legs over the edge. "Sometimes I really hate my brother," he says. "I get so tired of dealing with all these machinations and secrets and all the rest of it. I just wish I could fly away from all of it. BrightStone. Meridion. The Pits. Leave it all behind, start somewhere else."

"Sounds lonely. But I said the same thing to you once, didn't I? About escaping BrightStone. To let it deal with its own problems." My mouth curves into a wry smile. "I believe you mentioned something about honor or wanting to support Lucian or some such nonsense."

He slumps so his head rests on my shoulder. "Some days I think I should have taken you up on it."

"It would have made things easier," I agree, then press a kiss to his brow.

"It's not that I don't understand what Lucian's trying to do. I've always understood it, and why he's doing it, but still."

"Still. Sending a girl to the Pits to slaughter plague victims is one thing, but entering a sham marriage? Yes, I can see why you'd draw the line there." My tone is mocking and sharper than I intend it to be, giving rise to the fact that perhaps I am just as hurt at the concept as he is.

"That's not... Gods dammit, Mags." Before I can say another word, his mouth is on mine, frantic, impatient, and without a hint of the gentleness he always used before. He's breathing hard when we finally come up for air, his eyes darkening even as the lightning flashes beneath his skin in an almost seductive fashion.

His nostrils flare as he pulls me to my feet. "Come on," he says hoarsely, as though he can't quite figure out how to speak.

There isn't much else to say as we slip back into our room. Ghost locks the door with a savage twist as I draw the curtains, leaving us in near total darkness, save for my glowing hair and his electrified skin. There is something uncanny about it, the sudden silence of the room juxtaposed by our ragged breathing and punctuated by a bout of raucous laughter down the hall. Then Ghost is sucking the skin of my collarbone, and I stop thinking about anything at all.

He peels off his clothing, leaving him naked before me, the color in his cheeks high. He's all long limbs and wiry muscles, scars crossing over his abdomen like silver rivers beneath the lightning. There's nothing challenging in his face when he looks at me, just a simple presentation of what he is, who he is, his hair falling into his eyes as he tumbles us both into the bed. My own clothes flitter away in a matter of moments until there's nothing between us but our skin.

He's seen me naked before—most of the way, if not all of it. Not that it matters anyway. We're past that point of shyness, if we were ever there at all.

We don't bother with words. We're past that point, too, leaving us only with the same quiet language that guided us in the Pits.

A stroke of fingers here, a press of tongue there, soft questioning sounds and answering breaths.

There is something bold about his demeanor, yet supremely gentle, his mouth finding each scar upon my body and tracing the whip lines of where I'd been flogged. I shiver beneath his touch, my skin sensitive and aching.

"Each one of these marks… Each one a measure of what you gave up for us. For me." He nips the back of my neck and finds my ear as I squirm.

"Aye, well, save the sweet talk for later," I say, impatient.

He buries his face in my hair, his body shaking with sudden mirth as he turns me over so we're facing each other. "Oh, Mags. You will forever be my undoing."

"Best remember that," I grumble, darting in for a nip or two of my own, legs parting to grant him entry. And then there's no more room for talk at all, or thought, or much of anything else, save the rocking motion he's making and our echoing sighs of pleasure, entwined and quiet and perfect.

The night breeze rolls over my naked flesh many hours later, the curtains open wide enough to let in the moonlight. Everything about us glows in soft silver, my vision gauzy as I watch Ghost sleep. From this angle, his proud jaw is relaxed, his frowning brow unfurrowed. Even his chestnut hair seems lighter, making me wonder if the pale Moon Child color that is his legacy will eventually reveal itself to the other Meridians.

The light beneath his skin is calm, only an occasional flash pulsing with the quiet beat of his heart. He's sprawled on his back, arm thrown over his head, his breathing slow and even, as though it's the first time in quite a while that he's slept so peacefully.

Perhaps it is.

Demons are rooted deep within us, like rag dolls made of fear and shadows, given shape in the dark of the Pits. He'll carry his forever; most likely so will I.

My eyes drift toward the closed door of our bedroom. That we've been shut up in this room for the majority of the day is not so unusual. That both my clan and Lucian have left us undisturbed is fortunate. Whatever mischief they've managed to get themselves into is their business. At the moment, I don't care in the slightest.

Ghost murmurs something I can't quite make out and turns on his side to wrap me in his arms. But I can't quite get comfortable, and in the end, I slip away and toward the open window, taking solace in the tree branches. I feel as though I'm burning, an inferno beneath my skin that I can't seem to extinguish. Whatever Ghost and I are is anything but casual, but somehow this moment has opened something inside me that I've kept sewn shut for a very long time.

Sex within Moon Child clans is almost always spontaneous. Or at least as far as I always remember it. The Pits changed that in some ways—not so much for my views on it but in how the quiet of the darkness made us cling together out of necessity, to feel another's warmth in the bowels of the earth itself. That I didn't actively participate in anything more intimate than casual touches meant nothing. The offers were there, but I was so wrapped up in the horror of the place that I couldn't begin to allow myself to give in to such things. If I were down there much longer, perhaps I would have, pairing off with Bran or Gloriana.

So it still seems strange that I would hold out for so long for whatever Ghost had been offering. Yet, now that I've tasted it, I realize that I would protect it with everything I have in me.

The thought of betrothals fills me with fury. Lottie's involvement is troubling to say the least. I genuinely wanted to like the girl. And the gods know we need as many allies as we can get up here. The disappointment rolls around my guts for a bit, and I ponder on it. We could ask her outright, but if the situation is as delicate as Lucian seems to think, the last thing they need is a headstrong Moon Child mucking up the works.

Still, I'm not going to just sit here like some sort of prim-and-proper lady, either.

"There you are." Ghost leans out the window. He's not dressed, and the early-morning light plays over his skin, rippling over his muscles as he breathes. Much of his abdomen is dotted with small purple bruises, and I can't help but smile in satisfaction.

"Here I am," I agree, my gaze suddenly bold.

Mine…

Without a word, he scrambles into the tree beside me. "Well, I can't say I've ever done this before," he says dryly. "Not naked at least."

"Ah, and is there a list, then? Of things you've done naked?" My face grows serious. "The people have a right to know."

He snorts. "No, they don't. But if you're really that interested…"

"How long of a list can it be?" I say wryly.

He flushes. "Long enough. So, uh, now what?"

"We're sitting naked in a tree. Now what, what? There's a limit to even how flexible I am, Ghost."

"That's not what I mean." A scowl crosses his face. "I mean, what about us now? And this whole betrothal thing and Lottie and all the rest of it. I don't want to hide what I am anymore, what we are to each other, not even to do so simply for the sake of the family name."

"I don't know," I say slowly. "Moon Children don't get married, so this is new territory for me. At the most, we might exchange a token or two, but none of us really would expect it would last forever. Sooner or later, well, you know."

"I don't know how binding a marriage would be between us, anyway. At least on paper," he admits. "Even if we could manage it somehow, if Lottie's family can prove I was betrothed to her first, it might override anything we do now."

"And if they knew you were a Moon Child, in truth? That you're most likely sterile, the way the rest of us are? What is the point to marriage if not to produce children? That was the issue with Lucian and Jeremiah, wasn't it?" I shake my head. "Not that I've ever wanted children, mind. Even if I could have them, I probably wouldn't. It's too risky for everyone, and it's unfair to make a child for nothing other than selfish reasons."

His voice grows pensive. "I'm sure Lottie's family wouldn't want to pollute their precious bloodline, even if I'm d'Arc's son." He nudges me. "Or we could just skip all this and leave, you know. You and me. Right now."

The idea hovers between us, real and raw and aching, and a part of me burns to tell him yes. But I can't. My clan depends on me. The other Moon Children below depend on me. And somehow it would cheapen everything I've done up to now—the Pits, Sparrow's death, the Archivist's death, Penny's death. How many of them gave up their lives for me? To simply run away would diminish their sacrifices.

"No," I tell him, regret and sorrow making my voice ragged.

"Of course not," he says sadly. "Things have never been that simple between us. Why start now?"

"Don't be ridiculous." I squirm my way over so I'm next to him. "Things have *always* been simple between us. It's everything else that's a complicated mess, aye?" I poke at the love marks I left behind on his neck.

"When you say it like that..." His fingers run over my jaw to lightly turn my face to his, and he captures me in a long, lingering kiss. "No time," he complains after a moment. "Come on. I'm starting to get bug bites on my ass."

I laugh, wondering at the absurdity of watching his naked backside retreat from the tree to the window. I stand, enjoying the last bit of breeze against my skin, and follow. The two of us dress slowly, and I wonder if the others will be able to tell what sort of night we had. Who cares anyway? One look at my neck and the jig will be up. Let Lottie chew on that for a while.

A tap on the door has us exchanging sheepish grins. Ghost opens the door, stiffening when he sees Lucian in the hallway. "Now what?" he says sharply.

Lucian pokes his head in, brightening when he sees me. In his hand, he holds a slip of paper. "Oh good, you're both here. I need you to get changed into whatever finery you can manage. We're about to present our case before the Council."

Quick tongues and painted eyes
Words that glitter and gleam
Quiet truths wrapped in silver lies
Echoed in my silent scream.

— CHAPTER TWELVE —

The road winding to the air taxi station seems ridiculously short, though maybe it's just how my heart rattles that makes it feel that way. I would like to have my clan with me, but until the Council is aware of their presence, officially, there isn't much sense in rubbing it in their faces.

"I'm surprised they've given us such short notice," I say, sliding into a seat next to a window for a better view. I adjust my glasses against the glare.

"Well, given the circumstances, our docket has been moved to the High Council. Normally, we would have gone to one of the lower civil courts, but with your kidnapping and the possibility of betrothals between the Noble Houses and whatnot, there's too much going on. And this way we can attempt to rectify all sides of it to everyone's agreement." Lucian's eyes flick to Ghost, who remains stiff and unmoving beneath his brother's stare.

I kick both of them in the shins, my pointed boots scraping their ankles quite deliberately. "Both of you knock it off," I hiss. "If this is your idea of presenting a united front, you're doing a shitty job of it. At the very least, we still hold the ace card, aye? My heart trumps any sort of marriage proposal, I'd imagine, so we can let this ride and see how it plays out."

Ghost pinches the bridge of his nose. "And you would see me wed to another?"

"Of course not, idiot. But you can at least play nice until we know for sure, right?"

"And then what?" He gives me a sideways glance, one brow raised.

"And then...I don't know. We find the sleeping dragon in the heart of Meridion and bring the whole thing crashing down." I smile winsomely, skirting the urge to tell them the truth. "Why waste time with petty arguments when you can go straight for apocalyptic annihilation?"

"Sometimes you scare me, Mags," Lucian mutters. "But no, we'll hear them out and go through the proper channels as civilized folk do."

I frown, but say nothing, choosing to stare out the window instead. We rise on a bit of air, somehow riding on the currents, and come close to other balloons in a graceful dance that has us just out of reach of touching. It's dizzying and nauseating, and I end up having to turn away.

Lucian's grand ideas always seem to depend too much on expecting people to do the right thing. It's naive, but the fact that he keeps on with it, despite the failures, reminds me why I'm so fond of him. Even if it's infuriating sometimes. But perhaps it balances our little triangle out some since I nearly always assume the opposite. And I'm rarely disappointed, for all that.

Before long, we stop at the highest station. The platform is suspended above the city spire and attached to a set of steps mounting to what appears to be a floating path. We're not too far from the LightHouse and I feel a modicum of pleasure that I'm starting to recognize the layout of the city. There are rails on either side of the path, but it's only wide enough for us to walk one at a time—and so we do. Lucian in front, me in the middle, and Ghost bringing up the rear.

I look down only once, trying to swallow a wave of nausea. I'm not afraid of heights by any means, but something about the way this little path sways in the breeze sets my teeth on edge. It takes all I have to simply crab-claw the rails instead of hurtling my way through Lucian and onto firmer ground.

Lucian chuckles. "It's not usually this shaky. It looks as though they've been doing construction. When I was younger, the wind balloon station was closer."

"Delightful," I say icily, happy I didn't have enough time for breakfast. At this rate, I'll be puking before long. But we make it to the far end of the platform path and to the steps of the building proper.

A faint glow emanates from each step as we climb the stairs. It's not glass exactly—it's not nearly slippery enough for that—but it retains a crystalline polish even so. At the top of the stairs we are met by Jeremiah, Lady Fionula, a group of people I don't recognize, and...Lottie. Our eyes meet, and she has the grace to look away for the span of a few seconds before raising her head to stare at Ghost with such a fierce intensity that I fear he might ignite like paper.

Is it desire? Hatred? I can't be entirely sure. The fact that she might be using him infuriates me to no end, not to mention the possibility that she betrayed me. Or am I simply angry at myself for falling for it?

That thought twists inside me with a far more uncomfortable burn than I want to admit.

Despite my better instincts, I nudge Ghost, leaning my face toward his ear as though to whisper something sordid. Am I being protective? Jealous? Trying to spur her into giving away her hand? I can't answer that, and part of me hates that I can't.

"What are you on about?" He grinds out the question between lips that refuse to budge beyond anything other than a stiff grimace that I suspect is supposed to be a smile.

"Nothing exactly." My eyes slide toward the group, pleased to see Lottie's expression turn stony. I drape my hand over his shoulder. *Mine.*

It's petty. I know it is. And despite my words to Ghost to the contrary, just once I feel like I've earned the right to be petty. After all, I wasn't handed everything on a platter simply because of my birth. I clawed my way from the worst BrightStone has to offer. Ghost belongs to me and I to him. I will not be giving him up simply because of a promise allegedly made when they were children. That sort of garbage is for fairy tales.

Lucian shakes Jeremiah's hand, and the two of them exchange a look I don't quite understand. Something like fear flashes across Jeremiah's face, and my stomach sinks. Not a good sign. I'm already casually eyeing the doors and the height of the ceilings, as though I might somehow throw myself off the building if given the chance to run.

But I keep moving forward, concentrating on the careful placement of my boots. Ghost's hand drifts near mine, and we don't clasp fingers exactly, but our palms brush casually in a sort of lingering expression of comfort.

Lottie and what I assume is her family are in front of us, flanked by servants in gold and green livery. Jeremiah's sister follows us, murmuring something to Lucian that I can't hear. But I can tell from the wobble in her tone that she's worried.

The council room is at the end of a long hallway, great windows framing us on all sides to wash the marble in a pale sea of sunlight. I can only push my smoked lenses closer to my face, my head tilted slightly downward to help block the worst of it. Then we enter the round room of the High Council, and the doors shut swiftly behind us. I flinch at the way it sounds like it's locking, and even Lottie appears unhappy. Several rows of benches made of a light-colored wood line either side of an aisle, glittering in the light like old bones emerging from a sea of crimson tiles, which are neatly laid out in an easy path straight to the dais. Lottie and her family take a seat on the far side of the room, while our group finds a place on the opposite, a wide swath of cerulean carpeting dividing the two.

In front of us is a curved crescent of a table where seven Meridians sit, equally spaced—three men and four women. Their robes are various hues of blue, simple and stark as though the weight of their station is adornment enough. The robes cloak each person from neck to wrist, presumably to hide any emotional flashing of their skin—an illusion of neutrality maybe. Several wear gloves and at least one woman is veiled, her eyes glittering behind the gossamer strands of a spider's web.

Lucian leans over to whisper in my ear. "They are the High Council, Mags. Whatever you do, please don't anger them. Speak only when they ask you to and be as respectful as you can. These people have the power to destroy everything we've tried to do on a whim."

I chafe beneath his words, but I know he's right. Even if I want to revolt in some fashion, where would I go? I'm thousands of feet above BrightStone, several hundred or more at least above Meridion's main city itself. Short of simply hurling myself to my death outright, I am out of options.

What about IronHeart? I exhale sharply, pushing away any thoughts of the prophecy for now. Unleashing something I can't control is madness—and something tells me the dragon isn't one for being controlled.

So I sit and wait, my ears pricked like some wild thing about to be discovered in a nest of thorns.

"First order of business, we call Lucian d'Arc to stand before us. I am Madam Councilor Greta, and I will be supervising these hearings today." The woman at the center of the councilors is tall and imposing, all the more so for being raised above us, and her face and limbs seem impossibly long and narrow. Her eyes are dark and unyielding as Lucian gets up from the bench and takes his place to stand upon a star on the floor, which pulsates with a startling pattern in silver and gold that shimmers at his presence. It's as gaudy as anything else I've ever seen here, but I suppose if all you have is wealth, what else can you do but piss in gold privies?

Uncharitable of me maybe, but I've seen precious few examples of Meridians who aren't completely wrapped up in themselves. Maybe the students and a few others, but anyone with any power seems to be a right git.

But then, isn't that always the way of it?

"There are several matters to attend to this morning," the councilwoman intones. "The first of which is the restoration of your birthright to its fullest. I understand you wish to formally declare your place of abode to be your mother's summer house?"

Lucian bows slightly, just a nod of his head, but his back is ramrod straight. "Yes, Madam Councilor," he says, and I hear an edge of arrogance rippling through his voice to match hers. "With our limited funds, we are in the process of making several alterations and repairs."

"And what is your end goal?" Her eyes flick toward me for half a second. "Will you be opening a boarding house for guests? Taking a position at the local university? Opening your own practice?"

"Ideally, I'd like to open a practice. But until our name is fully restored, my options are limited," he admits. "Though I have submitted my notes on the BrightStone Rot to the Meridion Department of Medicine in the hopes that I might improve their understanding of the complications of the physical differences between BrightStone citizens and our own Meridian bloodlines."

His voice drones on as he explains some of the more esoteric minutia of the Rot, and I let my mind drift away. This part I don't understand so much, and I don't need to. I lived it, after all.

"—and what of your marriage plans?" The woman looks down at her notes and wrinkles her nose. "Were you not promised to

Lady Fionula before your subsequent exile? My understanding is that there was some confusion therein as far as your suitability to merge Houses."

Lucian flinches, and Lady Fionula takes to her feet to gracefully stand next to him. "The misunderstanding was all of ours, Madam Councilor. And though my own parents are no longer here to give their guidance, I am more than capable of making my own decision on this matter." She turns and gestures to Jeremiah. "It is no secret that my brother and Lucian love each other, no more than it has ever been such. Given that I love them both in their own fashion, I wish to rewrite the terms of our contract to allow the two of them to have whatever union they so desire." A glimmer of tears shines in her eyes. "I'm not so cruel as to deny them that. And I have additional prospects that I wish to explore, free from the bindings that currently hold me back."

The councilor scribbles something in a little book in front of her. "Noted. As this is agreed upon by all parties, we will allow it." Her face cricks up in a crooked smile. "No one can fault your intentions in having waited such a long time. We release you from your contract."

Lucian lets out a strangled sob. Jeremiah says nothing, biting down hard on his lip, but his eyes crinkle in sudden joy and even I stifle a smile, glad that at least one thing appears to be going well so far.

"As to whatever relationship you choose to bind your Houses, that is, of course, up to you. We cannot officially recognize it without children as part of the process, but to that end, you may do as you like." The councilwoman coughs, eyes fixed on Lucian. "As far as your work is concerned, you will be fully reinstated into the medical profession and may open your practice as you wish, within certain terms that I have outlined for you here."

"We thank you, Madam Councilor." Lucian bows deeply and retreats to the bench. Fionula sits down beside him, leaning to whisper something to her brother. Jeremiah blushes hotly, but he can't quite keep the smile off his face, either.

"And now that brings us to the next case. Trystan d'Arc, please come forward."

Ghost lets out a ragged breath and rigidly stands to take his place upon the star. The councilor stares at him critically and then nods. "You were very young when you left Meridion, were you not?"

"Yes, Madam Councilor. About five, from what I can remember." His voice is strong, his back straight as he answers. As though he were merely having a casual meal of tea and biscuits with an old friend. I marvel at his composure.

"And were you familiar with the contract made between your House and that of Lottie Tantaglio?"

He shakes his head. "Not at that time, no. I don't recollect much more than my toys and our leaving upon the airship to BrightStone."

The councilwoman cocks a brow at Lucian. "And you... Were you aware of any such thing?"

Lucian frowns. "My mother entertained many offers, so I assumed it was nothing more than another request. To be honest, I thought the majority of offers were rescinded in the weeks before our exile, seeing as our mother had disappeared and left us in disgrace." His head swivels toward Lottie and her family, something unreadable on his face. "At any rate, we wish to cancel any sort of contract, given the current circumstances."

The councilwoman nods. "Do you have proof of the canceled agreement? Unfortunately, it was long enough ago that we really need some sort of written evidence." She holds up a piece of paper. "Caspian Tantaglio, head of Tantaglio House, was good enough to provide a copy of the original betrothal agreement from the Office of Records."

"I'm sure he was," I mutter, giving a sideways look at them. Lottie stares stonily ahead, her face pinched and pale, the lightning flashes of her skin covered by her clothing. I assumed her long, high-necked gown was some sort of matrimonial fashion statement, but now I wonder if it's more to hide whatever she's feeling. Even her hat seems to be artfully askew as though to prevent a good examination.

Her family appears much the same. Her mother has the same sort of dress on, her face covered by a veil. Her father... Well, it's hard to say exactly what's going on beneath his skin. His face appears to be carved from glass from this angle, for all that it's not moving a muscle. But perhaps he's learned how to school that electrical pulse to the point that it reveals nothing. Or maybe he's just that confident.

Lucian clears his throat. "You will have to give us time to produce such documentation. Our mother's estate is still in a bit of disarray, and we have not had sufficient access to go through all her records. She was rather secretive, if you remember," he adds wryly, "even from her own family."

"Indeed. It hardly seems to require an explanation." She taps on the desk in front of her, and then the group of councilors huddle together, whispering in voices I can't pick out.

At last, they turn about.

"Given the unusual timing of these requests, and given that the Tantaglio House has chosen to break off a separate betrothal contract with a different House to pursue this one, the situation has become rather difficult." She shuffles the neatly organized pile of parchment and makes a series of notes. "I see that the other party did not consent to the withdrawal. Is this correct?" Lottie squirms slightly beneath the clipped tone of the words, though her father shows no response at all. "We will allow the d'Arc House a week to produce any documentation proving the dissolution of the aforementioned betrothal contract."

Ghost breathes a visible sigh of relief, echoed by my own grateful nod, but then we both stiffen at the councilwoman's next words. "That being said, should no proof be found, you will be required to honor the original contract. Are the parties in agreement?"

I attempt to lurch to my feet, words of protest hovering from my lips, only to be jerked to my seat, Lucian's trembling hand gripping me like iron. "Do. Not. Move," he snaps, his voice colder than anything I've heard from him before.

I sink down, sliding away from him as a hot flush flares over my cheeks. In front of us, Ghost bows his head carefully toward the Council. "As you wish."

Lottie's father tips his head. "The terms are agreeable. However, we do have an additional request."

"Go on, Caspian," Madam Councilor Greta says sharply.

"Seeing as Trystan is so newly returned to Meridion, we would like to invite him to join our household during this time so we can assist him with reassimilation into Meridian society. Undoubtedly, he has been exposed to many untoward influences in BrightStone, through no direct fault of his own. It is an older Meridian custom, but one we feel is worth reestablishing in this situation."

My head snaps toward him, the pit of my stomach upending in dread at his words. *No. I do not allow it.* My mouth forms the word, but somehow I'm frozen, a mouse beneath the gaze of a cat.

"Father," Lottie hisses, turning away when he glares down at her.

The councilwoman frowns. "This is a bit unusual, and frankly, such things should be handled directly between Houses."

One of the other councilors, a man with a fat pudding of face says something to her, and they whisper among themselves for a moment.

I stare at Lottie's family, my stomach dropping with the gall of the request. "They can't seriously be considering this," I say to

Lucian, my heart breaking when Ghost remains steadfastly facing forward, his shoulders stiff.

"It *is* an older law," Jeremiah says quietly when Lucian remains silent, clenching his jaw. "Though not one commonly enacted."

"You can't object?" My nails cut into my palms. "Why are we just sitting here?"

"Because their House is allowed to make such a request," Lucian grinds out. "This isn't a trial. We can certainly protest it, but..."

Ghost finally turns toward us, carefully avoiding my gaze. "Don't protest it," he says, keeping his voice low.

My mouth drops. "What?"

"It will give us an inside edge, aye? I might be able to find out something about the poisoning. Maybe I can get Lottie to crack or find some kind of proof." His smile grows halfhearted but unwavering as he tugs on his hair. "We still have a trump card."

Madam Councilor Greta clears her throat, startling our attention back to her. "All right. We will grant the request upon further consideration. But only for the allotted week granted to provide any additional evidence disproving the betrothal is presented."

Ghost nods. "I will return to our estate and retrieve any necessary items first and present myself to the household gates first thing in the morning." He turns to Lottie's family, and I can't see the expression on his face, but I don't really need to. "Is this acceptable?"

"Yes," Caspian says, smiling at Ghost. "We look forward to having you stay with us." His eyes dip toward me. "Of course, we would prefer it if any additional guests were kept to a minimum. Distractions will only impede the forming of relationships."

Ghost nods again. "Of course."

"Very well," says the councilwoman. "We shall reconvene on this matter within the week, upon production of proof." She gestures at Ghost, indicating he should sit down.

Ghost stiffly walks to our bench, taking his seat beside me. He says nothing, staring straight ahead, but his hands are clenched together, lips pressed into a sad rictus of a smile. I want to say something, but I know better than to upset whatever balance he's holding on to. Later, I tell myself, half-ready to scream in frustration.

"Let's see, next on the docket." The councilwoman stares at me. "Ah, yes. The Moon Child. Please stand on the star."

I get to my feet, suddenly grateful my skin shows nothing of what I'm feeling, my eyes hidden behind my smoked lenses, carefully masking my gaze from the others. Inside, my heart begins to whir madly, and it takes everything I have not to press my hand against it. Surely they can hear it…

"Please take off your glasses while you stand before us," the pudding-faced councilor says coldly. "Don't you think it's rude for us not to be able to see your eyes?"

"If I do that, I will not be able to see you," I say simply, losing patience. "Wouldn't that be considered just as rude? Perhaps if you can cover the windows and dim the lights?"

There's a collective gasp at my words, but I ignore it. In the end, they are only people. They can be killed like anyone else.

"And if there are no lights, how would we see you, then?" the councilor snarks at me.

"Trust me. You won't have any problem." I slip off the scarf that's been fashionably covering up my hair, letting the silk puddle to the floor.

A moment later, they've done as I asked, lowering window coverings and dimming the ornate chandeliers, and even Lottie's family murmurs when I begin to glow. I remove my smoked lenses, tucking them into a pocket in my trousers, and turn toward the Council. The councilwoman recoils slightly, and I know she must see the way I glitter in the dark, not with the electrical thrum of the Meridians but with a soft haziness that belies all the sharp edges inside me, pushing against my skin.

Madam Councilor Greta recovers her composure. "We were not aware of this particular Moon Child…trait."

"Not all of us have it," I admit. "Only those few of us who managed to escape the Pits. But that's not really why I'm here." I lower my head. "I want to instate Moon Children as full heirs to the city, for them to be recognized as citizens who can take advantage of everything your society has to offer."

"Out of the question," the councilwoman says. "For one thing, we have no records available to us, so even if we accepted your proposal, we have no way of knowing to which families you belong. As to the other, the entire point behind our intricate family relationships is the creation of children. My understanding is that Moon Children, by their very nature, are sterile. Even if you should be granted access to a family name, you would be nothing but an anchor weighing them down, consuming their resources with no way to repay them. Why would we want to do such a thing?"

"Ah, well, I can see why that might be an issue. But while you may not have records, there is a chance that BrightStone might have them." I press my lips together. "There are a number of brothels that provided services to Inquestors. They would know if children resulted out of such unions…"

"That's even worse," the pudding councilor grumbles. "Inquestors were sent below because they were practically criminals as it was. What makes you think those families would want reminders of their shame lurking about?" He pauses, peering behind me to look at Lottie. "Ah, I see. You are hoping to make a betrothal claim to override theirs, is that it?"

I blink. "What?"

"Anyone can see you're rather attached to the sons of d'Arc, but I'm afraid marriages between…races really can't be allowed. Even if we acknowledged your claim to a family name, it wouldn't be enough to sanction a marriage into one of the highest caliber Houses in our history." His lips turn down. "Sorry."

"I see," I grind out, though I really don't give a fig for his answer so much as it pertains to me.

"Do you?" the councilman drawls. "How do we even know your story is true? The Pits, you say?" His mouth twitches in amusement, and it takes everything I have not to leap across the table at him, my arms trembling with a rage made of death and darkness, the shadows of fallen Moon Children filling my vision.

"Indeed, Councilor Tendou," Madam Councilor Greta proclaims. "I believe there were records of such things." She taps a scroll in front of her. "Lady Fionula did send her report to us, if you recall."

"Then where is the so-called solution from our illustrious Madeline d'Arc? That was what was promised—a cure to the plague we supposedly created. That was the crux of the Architect's little temper tantrum, was it not?" Councilman Tendou leans forward in his chair, staring at me hard enough to nail me to the floor. "Or was that merely another romanticized story that sprang up to try to keep her reputation intact? So far, I see nothing about solutions, real or imagined, save this ridiculous story presented by exiled family members and a Moon Child who wants a claim to our city."

"There is much more that needs explaining." Madam Councilor Greta's eyes fall on me again, dropping to my chest. "The report indicates you forced your way onto Lady Fionula's airship by... what was it? Something about your heart and the mechanism to turn on Meridion again? IronHeart, was it?"

"IronHeart?" Councilman Tendou sniggers, and I bite my lip hard enough to draw blood. "Enough of this," he says. "We have real work to do here. There's no time for fairy tales." He turns to the others. "I realize Lady Fionula pulled some strings to expedite their docket, but this is a waste of time. You should be grateful we even agreed to see you at all."

The councilwoman nods, scratching something out on a smooth piece of parchment in front of her, and the group of them huddle together in their robes, their voices muffled whispers as they argue over something we're not privy to.

And I no longer care. Without waiting for their secret conversation to end, I leave the star and its arbitrary boundaries, beginning to pace back and forth in front of the dais like a caged tiger. Cold rage at being dismissed rolls violently through my limbs.

"Grateful? I should be...*grateful*? What makes you think it's fair for you to spawn an entire subrace of people and then leave them in squalor, only to round them up to use for genetic experimentation to further the creation of a serum only for Meridion's benefit? One would think Meridians have no shame at all, really, so what would be the harm in including us in their family tree?" My hand twitches and I wish I had my hammer, but I can already tell I'm losing the battle. Their minds are made up.

The councilwoman stills. "And you have proof of all this? The experiments? The serums?"

"I lived it," I snap, turning to display the brand on my neck. I catch Ghost's horrified, desperate expression, and for a moment, I think about it, about telling his secret right here and now and stopping this entire farce of a hearing. But that would be a betrayal beyond measure and not one I would ever come back from.

"This is what the Inquestors did to keep track of us, marking us like cattle for their Tithes." I unbutton the top of my shirt, slipping out of it as though I merely removed my own skin. The shirt falls to the floor, leaving me in my smallclothes to cover the panel on my chest. I raise my arms so they stretch up and out, revealing every rib, my collarbone jutting from my neck, the nubs of my spine, the tent-peg hips peeking over the waistband of my trousers. "And this is what the city of BrightStone did—kept us starving and alone, forced to live like animals in the trash heaps for an immunity to a disease that you unleashed upon them."

I turn again, pointing to a series of tattoos in various locations upon my arms and my belly. "Bonewitch tattoos, the calling cards of every street doctor in the city, marking citizens and Moon Children alike." I chuckle angrily. "We were told it was to help the Inquestors keep track of citizens ill with the Rot, but in truth the Inquestors bribed the bonewitches to inject the serum into unsuspecting BrightStone citizens to cause a plague, simply to have more subjects to experiment on in the Pits." I resist the urge to spit on the floor, my upper lip curling.

I tug on my hair. "I spent over eight months in the dark, creeping underground, eating rats, watching friends be torn apart by a Rotter army trained by a Meridian scientist who dissected us, poisoned us, *murdered* us, used our bodies for experimental serum treatments and his own sadistic pleasure. *That* is the legacy you have left us. Left *me*."

There is silence for the span of a few breaths, but it draws out far too long. I almost feel like a statue, eternally standing with all my flaws on display. The tension grows uncomfortable, thick enough for me to climb, but still, I stand, my eyes locked on the Council.

Look at me. See me. See what you have helped create.

"Put your clothes back on, girl. You've made your point." A gruff older councilman gestures at my shirt.

"Have I? Of all the things I've mentioned, please enlighten me as to what part I should be most *grateful* for." I snatch up my shirt, savagely thrusting my arms into the sleeves and fastening the buttons. "There are hundreds of us down below, hundreds more sent to their deaths over a span of nearly twenty years, through no fault of our own. I demand justice for my people. The Inquestors you sent to BrightStone—you knew they were criminals, yet you let them run rampant on the city below with no supervision."

"That's not completely true," the veiled councilwoman points out as though she hadn't heard a word I'd said. "After all, our science division was down there, as well. They should have kept the Inquestors in line. They were in charge of the entire project dealing with that plague, and that would have included the force used to protect it. It was entirely their fault, I'm sure."

I let out a bark of laughter, hollow and disbelieving. Where to even begin with this one?

"Convenient," I say finally. "Since the entire science division you speak of ended up underground and are now dead beneath a cave-in—caused by your Inquestors, mind—it makes it hard to refute your words." I pause. Except Joseph. He had survived, as had Rinna. And even the High Inquestor had been taken into custody by the Chancellor of BrightStone. So perhaps...

I eye the Council again. Did they know this? Their skin remains calm and composed. Clearly they are masters at controlling their emotions. But still... What is it I'm looking for? Acknowledgment of the misdeeds prevailed upon Moon Children? Revenge? Or something else entirely?

"You stand there and listen to me speak, but you've already made up your minds about whatever it is I'm about to say. What will it take for you to actually hear me?"

"Well, records, of course. Those would be helpful. But also witnesses—those who aren't Moon Children themselves would be best. We'd prefer to talk to more reliable individuals who can corroborate your words." Madam Councilor Greta scratches something onto a piece of parchment in front of her. "It's a very fine story, but I cannot help but think it's a touch exaggerated."

I exhale slowly, wondering at how my hair hasn't actually exploded into flame as a wave of pure fury slams into me. "Proof, aye. I can get you that."

"Very good." She waves dismissively at me. "We'll expect that within the week, as well—same as the other proof needed for the d'Arc betrothal."

I turn on my heel without any of the proper bowing protocol, ignoring the disapproving tsks. If I'm to be considered nothing more than a barbarian anyway, why disappoint them with acts of civility?

I slip my smoked lenses onto my face, the better to hide what feels an awful lot like frustrated tears brimming. I don't have time for that sort of emotional nonsense. If this were the Pits, I could solve this issue with nothing more than my hammer and a couple of well-timed blows to someone's face, but that won't win me any favors here.

I sweep past the others and out into the glittering golden hallway, flinching despite the glasses.

"Mags!" Lottie's feet tap behind me. "Mags, I'm sorry. I'm so, so sorry. I didn't know. I swear it!"

I whirl on her. "Didn't know what, exactly? That you were previously betrothed to…to Trystan? That we 'accidentally' ran into you shortly after we arrived on Meridion? That you so nicely offered to help us out, fix me up, find me a spot at the university?" I lower my head my teeth bared. "That you deliberately made sure I'd be poisoned and kidnapped while innocently taking a walk with you?"

The blood drains from her face, and I know I've struck a nerve. "I would never—"

"Oh, I think you might. I can't prove it yet, but I will." I place my hand on her shoulder and give it a tight squeeze in warning. "Next time, make sure whoever you're working with actually finishes the job. I won't be nearly as nice about it if it happens again."

"I'm sorry, but you'll have to refrain from talking to our daughter." Lottie's father pushes me away with his cane. He's a tall man with broad shoulders, looming over me as he thrusts forward into my space. His face is smooth and polished, as though he spends a lot of time rubbing lotions into his skin, and his dark hair is slicked back and combed within an inch of its life. Yet, for all the handsome cut of his jaw and the line of his nose, he's wrapped in smugness like a fur coat. It drapes over him, ensnaring the very cadence in which he walks. "While I'm sorry your claim was refuted, that doesn't change the fact that you are not part of the upcoming discussion between Houses. You have no business here."

Behind him, I see Ghost and Lucian, the others trailing along. Ghost's face is ashen as he stares at Lottie, and I whistle a clan signal at him. He smiles faintly but makes no other response as Lucian takes my arm, leading me away and out of hearing.

"I'm sorry, Mags." He lowers his head to mine. "I'll do everything I can to set this right. I know we can find the information around that house somewhere."

"You'll be looking for it on your own, then," I say sharply. "I've got my own scavenger hunt to attend to down in BrightStone. There's files there as well—Molly Bell will at least know where to find them, I'm sure."

His expression turns pained. "Mags… They were mocking you. Records don't mean anything. If they really wanted to determine family bloodlines between Moon Children and Meridians, a simple blood test would tell us exactly who you're related to. Our own medical hall here keeps track of every Meridian's genetics to keep from inbreeding and whatnot."

I sag. "Of course. Of course they do."

"You couldn't have known." He reaches out to squeeze my shoulder, but I shrug him away.

"How could I? No one tells me anything." I frown, trying not to sulk about it, but given everything else that's happened, it's a bit hard seeing as I'm once again playing the game with no knowledge of the rules. "So what do I do?"

"Head back to the house for now," Lucian says, his mouth a grim line. "The Tantaglios have asked us to lunch to…well, I don't know why. Rub it in our faces? Pretend to celebrate? We'll have to play nice, but it's probably better that you're not there. We'll figure something out when we get home." He pauses. "Damn. We never did mention the other Moon Children."

"Why bother? They probably couldn't tell one of us from the other," I say savagely as I move away from him. "We're nothing but subhuman mongrels, aye?"

"Mags!"

I wave him off and head toward the steps to the station where the airship is moored. Since it appears I'll be making the return trip alone, there doesn't seem to be any point in waiting while the families exchange their greetings.

I've barely made it to the midway point of the stairs when someone slams into me, nearly sending me tumbling the rest of the way. I struggle before I realize it's Ghost, his arms wrapped so tightly around me I feel as though I might stop breathing. My heart whirs in response, and I place a hand on his arm as he buries his face against my neck. Unlike his brother, he doesn't make any promises about fixing the situation. He simply murmurs my name into my ear, and everything he's left unsaid swells deeper and deeper until my blood is singing with it.

"I'll come for you," he whispers. "You won't have to wait too long."

"Not if I come for you first," I retort lightly. "Besides, we've been through worse. An inconvenient marriage pales in comparison to having you pull my heart out in truth, aye?"

He turns me about in his arms so he can look directly at my face. "Trouble darkens your doorstep no matter where you live. It only seems logical that I would be the cause of some of that."

"You know the easy fix to that, don't you?" I pull away from him slightly, his hand lingering in mine. "Not to live in a house."

"Talk to me once all this finished," he agrees. "I think there might be something to that."

I shiver at his words. There's a ring of truth to them, and for a moment I wonder what it might be like to simply travel the world, feckless and free. And then he's gone, retreating toward whatever horrors the afternoon is likely to have in store for him.

I watch him leave, his shoulders drooping in a defeated resignation and then finish my own descent to the airship, boarding it without delay. Its engines thrum soothingly as I wait for it to unmoor and begin the flight to the main station in the heart of Meridion. I will continue my journey to discover the truth, the way I've always done it.

Alone.

Ebon wings and crimson quills
Feathers made of silken blades
Sharp to write and quick to kill
Curses, cuts, or accolades

— CHAPTER THIRTEEN —

Well maybe not entirely alone.

Lady Fionula slides into the airship beside me and motions at the driver to takes us below. The cool blue of her dress enhances the darkness of her skin, the lightning quiet. "What a travesty." She reaches into a glittering purse to pull out a cigarillo. My fingers twitch but I don't ask for one, merely wait for her to light it up, the rich scent of the tobacco reminding me of warm afternoons on BrightStone rooftops. "Well, that was exciting, wasn't it?"

"I'm not sure that's the word I would use." I wipe at my suddenly burning eyes. I hadn't thought I would cry, but even I have my limits.

She watches me carefully. "I think you are very brave, Mags—Moon Child or not."

"You'd be the only Meridian in there to think so," I say. "I could have barked like a dog for all the interest they showed."

She laughs, and it's a beautiful, sophisticated sound that fills the carriage with a ripple of amusement. "The High Council can be merciful, but they're also rather self-absorbed. You're an enigma, and an uncomfortable one at that. They simply want you to go away." She puffs on the cigarillo. "Don't give them the satisfaction."

Frustration rolls through me, setting my teeth on edge. "That's easy enough for you to say," I retort. "I'm sort of out of options if you haven't noticed."

"Lucian would probably say otherwise," she says, one brow raised. "He's waxed long and poetic over you and your resourcefulness to me and Jeremiah. I'd like to see some of that for myself."

I snort and decide to change the subject. "Why did you wait until now to dissolve the betrothal agreement? Surely you and your brother could have moved on when Lucian was gone?"

"An interesting question." She takes another long drag of the cigarillo. "I was an awful lot like that Tantaglio girl, you know. Eldest child in my House. The fate of our family on my shoulders. My parents were very traditional. They were the ones who insisted on the betrothal in the first place." She rolls her eyes. "The usual inheritance garbage."

"I wouldn't know," I say.

"Of course you wouldn't." Her smile grows brittle, a flash of lightning at the pulse point of her throat displaying her irritation. "You've been running wild and fancy-free all your life. For all your misguided hopes about Meridion, I wouldn't be at all surprised that Lottie wishes she were you some days."

Now I laugh, and it's sharp and biting. "Please. If any of you really understood what my life has been, you'd throw yourself right off this city in despair."

"And if you were in my shoes, you might very well do the same." She flicks the stub of her cigarillo out the window. "I'm not here to play Who Has the Shittiest Life with you. I'm simply saying that not everyone up here has it as easy as you think. As for the answer to your question? Because it suited me to remain betrothed to a man who wasn't here."

I blink, slowly understanding. "It gave you freedom."

"Just so. Plenty of pity, to be sure. To be betrothed to the son of the woman who betrayed Meridion? It takes no small amount of backbone. People here can be ridiculously petty. But yes. It kept my parents out of my hair until they died, and that left me in charge of our family estate. I was free to pursue my own academic and professional endeavors without a constant stream of would-be suitors. You have *no* idea how tiresome all that is."

"No, I don't," I say, still unsure of why she's telling me all this. It's helpful information—another piece of the puzzle I didn't know—but I'm still not inclined to be particularly sympathetic to Lottie just yet. "But now that Lucian is back..."

"I certainly have no wish to wed him. And this way my brother is happy, Lucian is happy, and I am at least free to find a new suitor more to my own liking. In the meantime, I'm self-sufficient and I've got nothing to prove to anyone. There's freedom in that, too, you know."

"Do you have someone in mind?" I don't know why I even ask it. It certainly has no bearing on me what she does, but perhaps I'm still so reeling from what happened at the Council that I simply want to hear her talk in the hopes of drowning out my own thoughts.

"Perhaps. Perhaps not. I'll be taking my sweet time making a decision." She hesitates. "As far as Trystan goes, you have your own freedoms here, as well. You're not technically a citizen, and if you break our more common traditions or taboos... Well, you're not from here so people may overlook them. That said, what will you do?"

I want to trust her. Surely Lucian would have said something to the contrary if she wasn't trustworthy, but it's hard. "I don't know," I finally confess. "I thought about going to BrightStone. I know Lucian said they were mocking me, but real physical proof might make a difference. That and one of the original Meridian scientists is still down there, and I think I might be able to persuade him to bring his evidence here."

I have no idea if Joseph will even entertain the idea, but he's probably the best option I have. He remained behind on BrightStone, agreeing to testify against the High Inquestor and Lord Balthazaar for their crimes against BrightStone and their role in spreading the Rot.

While I might be able to gather some information from Madeline d'Arc's copious notes that we found in her lab, Joseph would make a formidable ally in this case, even if I have to drag him up to the floating city myself. Surely the High Council would take his word as far more credible than mine.

"It might not be a bad idea," she admits. "I'm sure if Lucian and my brother would stop making cow eyes at each other long enough to come to their senses, they would say the same. I could arrange a message to be sent to Chancellor Davis, if you like? That certainly seemed to work before and it might save you some time."

"It would be easier," I admit, "but if he says no, I want to go through some of those records myself. A messenger won't be able to do that. There are a few others who might be worth talking to, as well."

I think on Molly Bell and shudder. The Shark of BrightStone would be even less likely to respond to a remote request from me than an in-person one. But when it comes to intrigues and schemes, there's no one better. And she keeps a tight trade on secrets. Who knows what sordid information she'd be willing to sell me? Or what favors she might demand in return?

I grimace, frustration making me want to clench my teeth. "But I have no way of going there—or getting back."

"You're right about that. We don't have the ships open in both directions yet. Eventually the Council would like to loosen the restrictions—for tourism at the very least—but right now, until we're satisfied that the Rot is completely gone, we aren't allowing regular BrightStone citizens passage to Meridion or the reverse. That said…" She chews on her lower lip. "I think I know a way."

She sits up and rattles off an address to the driver. He complies, shifting direction abruptly. When we dock at a station near the edge of the Inner Spiral, Fionula gets out. "I'll meet you at the d'Arc house shortly. Pack up anything you think you might need for your trip, but don't do anything rash until you hear from me."

"But…" My protests are lost as she dashes off, her heels clicking rhythmically on the walkway that edges the platform, leading in the city proper. The airship rumbles away, leaving me to my own thoughts as we sail through the city.

"I smell a rat," Rosa declares upon my explanation of Ghost's sudden betrothal. "This reeks of a setup. Maybe next time there's a Council hearing we should all go."

"Not sure that would really help." I snag one of the luggage bags out of Lucian's closet and shove some of the better pieces of clothing from my wardrobe into it. Not that they will do me much good for rooftop dancing, but perhaps I'll earn a few points for at least looking presentable. "I do think we should all go to BrightStone. I don't know exactly what I'll find down there, but I'll definitely need your assistance. That and I'd rather keep you safe. If someone else decides poison is the best way to deal with us or plots some other attack…" I let the words drift away. They know what I mean.

Haru's eyes are very bright as he watches me throw some toiletries into a satchel. "Given the timeframe, it makes sense to split up to find this information, anyway."

"Aye. We know the Inquestors have some of it. Every one of us Tithed went into that damn book of theirs. Our names. Our clan marks. Molly Bell might have records, too, assuming we can trust her to give them to us. And maybe the Chancellor of BrightStone can help. After all, the High Inquestor is still under her charge. If there was an admission of guilt, that might be enough to tip the scales in our favor. At the very least the High Inquestor might have kept some from his communications with Buceph."

My words sound far more cheerful than I feel. I recognized the looks the High Council gave me—pure and utter disdain that I should be thrust into their presence, that I should ask anything of them at all. You'd think I'd be used to it, but it stings more now. Maybe because I began to hope that it could be different.

"Do you think this will help make us citizens?" Gloriana's question is plaintive. "I really want to enroll in the university. There's so much to learn." She hides a trembling fist behind her back.

"I don't know," I admit. "But I can't simply wait up here and do nothing. We've got no real say in anything, but if we can find proof, at least we can try."

Rosa shivers beside me. "Who'd have thought we'd ever be working with BrightStone."

"I'll not deny it," I agree. "Necessity makes for strange bedfellows and all that."

"Speaking of bedfellows..."

My eyes narrow, Ghost's absence a tad too sharp for my liking, and Rosa closes her mouth immediately.

"Sorry," she mumbles.

"It's fine." I finish with the last of the bags and sling them over my shoulder. I know leaving Ghost behind without saying goodbye is a rotten thing to do but waiting for him to leave tomorrow will be just as painful and won't get me answers any faster. I pull out a notebook from under the bed.

What was there to say?

I'll come for you.

I scrawl the words in my haphazard fashion with the stick of charcoal, then leave the note on the pillow where he'll be sure to find it.

Dafyyd taps on the doorframe before popping his head inside. "There's a Meridian lady waiting for you in the foyer, aye?" His voice is serious and quiet, the way it always is, as though he can't quite shake the cloak of tragedy that's settled on his shoulders.

"All right. Help me carry these downstairs." I toss him one of the bags, and we head to the foyer. The others are there waiting, staring in open curiosity at Lady Fionula. To her credit, the Meridian seems nonplussed, a hint of wry bemusement in her expression as she digs through the leather-bound satchel on her shoulder.

"Ah, Magpie. I feel a bit like an exhibit at the zoo," she says. "I wasn't expecting additional company."

"Sure. But who's watching who?" I drop the bag on the ground. "This is my Moon Child clan. The Chancellor sent them up when I was…missing."

She frowns. "Are they all going with you?"

"Yes. I don't want to leave them here. I don't know what Lucian's plans will be, but the fewer distractions he has the better. Plus, they know BrightStone. They'll be able to help me gather information much faster than I could do alone. Is that a problem?"

"Hopefully not." She waves me off, pulling out an official-looking scroll bound by a blue ribbon from the satchel. "Here. Present this at the airship dock, the one you used when you first landed here."

I take it from her, surprised. "This is…"

"The best I can do, given the short notice," she says. "I am the liaison to BrightStone, am I not? Might as well use what little power I have. It provides passage for you and your…guests to BrightStone and one trip back within the week. It does expire, so see that you return before the date listed." She eyes me critically. "If you *want* to come back."

"Thanks." I tuck the scroll into my own shoulder bag. "Would you blame me if I didn't?"

"No. We have not been particularly kind to you. But then, have we ever been kind?" She raises a brow at me. "It might be better if you don't return, to be honest. This bridging of cultures you're trying to do… As honorable as it is, I suspect it will lead to nothing but trouble."

I give a mocking little bow. "Oh aye. Haven't you heard? Trouble is what I'm best at." I pause. What was I forgetting? Ah. Money. "Actually, I find myself a little strapped for jingle, aye? Care to donate to the cause?"

Her face grows slightly sour, if not surprised. Reaching into her satchel, she digs out a small purse. "Several weeks ago, you stood before me at the base of the Mother Clock and threatened to bash your own chest in to force me to allow you to come to Meridion," she says. "That level of commitment to your cause? I'd really like to see it again. Don't disappoint me, Magpie."

"I'll do my best." I take the purse from her, discretely weighing it in my palm. "This will help." I whistle at the others.

Follow, follow…

"Farewell, Magpie. Should circumstances change, I will send correspondence your way via the BrightStone Chancellor. You may do the same, and I will do the best I can to coordinate a response." Lady Fionula inclines her head at the group of us and then takes her leave, gliding out the foyer and into a waiting hover-carriage.

We troop out the front door, and I lock it behind us, the Meridian mechanism whirring as it seals shut. The other Moon Children pull their hats over their heads and their smoked glasses over their eyes, and for a moment, I feel almost as though we're going through a different sort of Tithe altogether, but I shake that off. No sense in courting trouble. It finds me fast enough on its own.

"All right, then. Let's go."

Only a few passengers get on board with us when we reach the airship docks. They look like soldiers, and they load what appears to be some sort of construction equipment onto the airship. The Meridians offered to assist with the cleanup of BrightStone from the riots and the Rotters, so that's probably what it's for. I can only imagine how far along they've gotten since I left, but hopefully the worst of it has been removed by now.

The group of us wander toward the center of the airship. I throw my bags in the rack above the seats, and the group of us sit in a cluster beneath it.

When everyone on board is settled, the airship engines thrum into action, and we descend swiftly toward BrightStone. It's almost dizzyingly fast—significantly faster than it was when flying up to Meridion—and I find myself looking away from the window as my stomach lurches suddenly.

A few minutes later, we're moored above Market Square. They lower the gangplank, as there hasn't been a chance to build a proper station like the ones above yet. We collect our things and follow the soldiers onto the raised platform and then onto the streets of BrightStone proper.

We've descended into my old home surrounded by the usual fog and mist, the salt air burning my skin. Even though I was only in Meridion for several weeks, the dampness here somehow feels more cloying than the Pits. But there's something comforting about it, too. It is home, after all.

It's odd somehow, to be here again and in this way. Before, we would have scattered into the shadows, away from the people strolling about the square. But here I am in Meridian clothing, equal to anything found in the Upper Tier, flanked by what must look like Moon Child manservants. It's surreal, and a part of me is violently shaking with how wrong it feels, even if it is an act.

Haru jogs up beside me. "What do you want us to do?"

"Well, the first we'll do is flag down a cab." My shoes are comfortable enough, but we're beginning to draw a bit of a crowd. Besides, something tells me Meridians don't walk around much down here.

Rosa points to the cab stand across the square and I snort. I'd nearly forgotten about the stand, as though my time in Meridion was already wiping away the footprint of BrightStone from my thoughts. Memories tumble about my head like crisp leaves, brittle and uncertain. For a moment it feels like I am a stranger here, and it hurts more than it should.

Rosa and Dafyyd glance at each other. "We'll go find Bran for you. Where will you be?"

"I suppose I'll start with the Chancellor's office. At the very least, I can update her as to what's going on. She may have access to some of the records that wouldn't be available to us otherwise." I pause. The BrightStone Museum had been a treasure trove of hidden information and likely to have the information I needed, but it burned down, set on fire by the Inquestors to cover their tracks, killing the Archivist in the process.

A twinge of sorrow runs through me. Archivist Chaunders did not deserve such a fate. And there's no denying we could have used her wisdom now. But we'll just have to do the best we can with what we can find.

Rosa and Dafyyd disappear into the crowd, and the rest of us pile into the vehicle. It's a tight squeeze with all my bags in the small horseless steam cab, but we manage. I slip the driver one of the chits from the purse Fionula gave me. It's entirely too much for the basic fare, but with a little extra in his pocket, perhaps he'll be discreet about the whole thing. And then we're off, weaving our way through the narrow roads of BrightStone.

If the cab driver has any doubts about his passengers, he doesn't show it, taking us through the main thoroughfares without delay.

We pass Prospero's Park and cross the Blessing Bridge, the Mother Clock bonging out the hour. My head whirls, and I wish Ghost were here to throw some ideas at, but there's no sense in hoping for what I don't have.

The taxi halts, and I realize we've stopped outside Town Hall. Situated in the Merchant Quarter, the building is imposing enough in its own way, but after the massive structures of Meridion, its dual columns and marble steps seem somehow quaint.

We emerge from the carriage and ascend the steps, drawing a few curious stares but not much else. Apparently dressing like someone who belongs here goes a lot further than I thought. I try to ignore the blister forming on my big toe as I approach the entrance, trying to figure out what to do next. Do I knock? Just walk in?

I hesitate and then move forward again, only to be interrupted by Gloriana. "Bran actually comes here once in a while. He's got a special knock that they know. Here, let me."

She reaches out and taps the knocker several times, smirking when the door swings wide. An elderly doorman bows to us as we sweep past him, though his brow furrows in confusion.

"The Chancellor was not expecting Moon Children today, I don't believe," says a secretary at a desk just inside. "It wasn't on the schedule."

"I'm afraid I don't have an appointment, but I think if you tell her Magpie is here, I'm sure she will see me."

The secretary sniffs faintly "Ah, yes. I'll inform her. Wait here please." She shuffles down a hallway and through another door, leaving us to cool our heels.

"Perhaps I should have seen to Bran instead," I say dryly after about fifteen minutes without any additional response.

"Damn straight you should have," a familiar voice snarls from behind us.

I whirl, half laughing when I see Bran standing there, his arms crossed petulantly with Rosa and Dafyyd behind him.

"We found him just up the road, aye?" Rosa pipes up helpfully.

"So I see." My mouth curves in a half smirk as my eyes meet Bran's, and for the merest second, I see him pounding my hammer toward the face of the High Inquestor, pulling back at the last second when the Mother Clock begins to sing.

"What the hells are you wearing, Mags? You look like a damn street clown."

Spell broken, I smile sourly. "The height of Meridian fashion. They take me more seriously when I'm not dressed like a ragamuffin, even if I'm still treated like a sideshow attraction at a carnival."

"Those shoes are ridiculous enough to be one." He smirks.

"You're one to talk." I tug on his shirt. "Look at you. New clothes, a bath, and some food and you're actually pretending you're a person. How dare you?"

He stares at me a moment longer, and then we both laugh, tumbling into each other's arms, the other Moon Children pressed up around us. After spending so much time together in the Pits for so long, even a short separation feels like an eternity.

"Not to put too fine a point on it, but why are you here? Surely things can't have gone wrong *that* quickly?" He pulls back to look at my face, something sad rolling over his own. "Ah, so they can."

"I guess that depends on how you define 'bad.'" I pause when I hear the door behind us open. "We can talk about some of that later."

His eyes narrow. "All right, then. It seems the Chancellor is ready now." He thrusts his chin in the secretary's direction, and I turn to see a pair of guards emerge, flanking a prisoner in chains.

I don't think much on it until they pass us and I get a better look at the man's face. It takes me half a breath to recognize him without the crimson robes I'd last seen him in, and I startle despite myself.

The High Inquestor.

He's dressed in a prisoner's garb, drab and gray with a red armband on either side. His face is tired and worn, hair slick with oily sweat. Clearly, they haven't exactly been giving him the creature comforts he's accustomed to. I remember the bottles of wine and the cartons of cigarillos he'd been sending to Buceph below in the Pits, expensive amenities of Meridian origin.

A part of me wants to vomit, the bile building in the back of my throat like a floodgate of angry bees. The urge to spit at him rises, and I swallow it down like the poison it is.

Bran nearly killed him during our confrontation after we'd escaped the Pits, and I truly wish he had, the hammer splitting the Meridian's head apart like rotten fruit. But in a nearly heroic effort to try to bring the man to justice, Bran didn't.

And now here we are.

I stare at him from behind my dark lenses, keeping my face as smooth as possible. Yet his eyes flick sideways as he passes, mouth curling up in the faintest hint of a smirk. Bran stiffens beside me but otherwise remains perfectly still, perhaps also imagining what would have been if he had killed the man that day.

I ache to reach out to Bran but doing so would be a sign of weakness, and that is the last thing we need to show in front of the High Inquestor. Prisoner or not, he would use everything to his advantage. He had not run the darker side of BrightStone for nearly twenty years because he was a fool.

And then he's gone, passing through the foyer and down the hallway. "Back to the cells," Bran sneers at the man's back, his upper lip curling. "Too good for him, if you ask me."

"I didn't," Chancellor Davis says from the doorway of her office. She beckons us inside.

I hesitate and then wave at the others to follow me into the office. The Chancellor sighs but seems unsurprised when Bran joins us. The office itself is well-appointed with thick carpets and leather seats. A decorative chandelier made of colored glass picks up the light from the nearby window, splashing us all in soft rainbow hues.

It seems frivolous maybe, but there's something relaxing about it. Perhaps she's as desperate for color as the rest of us. The hells know BrightStone is gloomy even on its best days.

The Chancellor takes the seat behind her desk, pushing aside some papers as she looks at us. "That was a bit more awkward than I anticipated. There's a reason I try to only invite Moon Children here on certain days. I'll thank you to remember that."

"He's a waste of space," Bran snaps. "He should be hanged."

"Justice has to be fair on all accounts," she says mildly. "And that includes him, waste of space or otherwise. He still has access to a great deal of information, and we will be trying him as soon as we can clear the docket." She rubs her forehead, her eyes weary. "There are many issues at hand, not mentioning reparations for victims of the Rot."

"As you say," he mutters.

Ignoring him, she turns to me. "Are you here to report the goings on in Meridion? Because I have to say, information has been rather scarce overall." She raises a brow. "Lucian has not exactly been keeping his end of the bargain in making sure we're informed."

I flush slightly. "It's a bit complicated."

"Everything is," she retorts, unimpressed. "But it's not an excuse. Now please, elucidate the matter, if you would."

Quickly, I lay out the basics of our arrival in the floating city: the house, the university, my being poisoned.

Chancellor Davis pauses in her note-taking and nods. "Ah yes. That would explain the request I got from Lucian insisting your little crew here be allowed passage to Meridian. I denied it, of course." Her gaze darkens as it sweeps over my clan. "But I see they managed anyway."

"It's what we're good at," I say. "But more to the point, I need access to BrightStone records now, if we want a chance to prove that we've a claim to Meridion, as well."

Bran coughs. "And why would you? They've already tried to kill you once, Mags. They clearly don't want us there. Why force the issue?"

"Because it is our right," I snap. "So much has been stripped away from us. We have nothing. Even now, we're just living on the edges of BrightStone fighting for scraps. Don't you want a chance to be something more? To have a family or at least the beginnings of one?"

"I already have one," he says shortly. "I don't need a clown with shit hair and shittier shoes to pretend there's more to offer than that. So you can count me out of this whole debacle."

The Chancellor raises her brow at that. "That may be your opinion, but surely the rest of your clan should have the opportunity if they want it, yes? And even so, what's the harm in trying to at least track down this information? You have my permission to search for whatever records you need. I imagine the Inquestors will have some of them." She snaps her fingers. "And Joseph, of course, has been in the Mother Clock cataloging Madeline d'Arc's legacy. I suspect he would be able to help you more."

I nod slowly. "All right. Where do I find him now?"

"He's actually set up an office in the Mother Clock itself. Says it's easier if he doesn't have to leave too often. I think it's...personal."

"He knew her," I say. "He helped her build the Mother Clock, so I assume there's a lot of history involved." I pause. "And what of the High Inquestor?"

"Off-limits," the Chancellor says flatly. "He's far too dangerous for the likes of you, even behind bars. Start with Joseph. I'll have my people go through the records here to see what else we can find. I'm assuming there's a time limit on this?"

"No more than a week." I exhale sharply. "It's an impossibility, I'm sure."

"Perhaps. Perhaps not," she says. "It is still good to hear that some progress is being made, even if it's not quite what we hoped for."

I want to ask about the other Moon Children, but I hold my tongue for the moment. I'll get a more truthful answer from Bran anyway—or at least one that will lay out how things *really* are as opposed to how a politician wishes to see them.

She smiles at me. "Keep your chin up, Magpie. We'll figure it all out. It just may take more time than we hoped."

I thank her and take my leave, Bran at my side and others trailing behind us. "So where to now?" Bran side-eyes me doubtfully. "And will you be wearing those…*clothes* for the duration of your stay?"

I snort at his suddenly polite tone. Politely mocking, maybe. "For a little while, yes. At least until I settle a few things with some of the record-searching." I nudge him. "Even you have to admit people take you a little more seriously when you're not dressed like a vagabond, aye?"

He scowls. "Maybe."

"But we'll need lodging. Where are we crashing these days?"

"Some Moon Children just stay where they always have—in the outskirts or in what's left of the Warrens. Which isn't much," Bran admits. "I suspect at some point it's going to be collapse completely. It's definitely not safe to stay there long-term. I've done my best to persuade them to join Josephine and me over at the Brass Button Theatre, but those Moon Children… They're feral even by my standards."

Before my time in the Pits, BrightStone had three different Moon Child clans, often fighting among themselves for territory and resources. After the Pits had collapsed and the Rotters had been released, the clans were forced to work together for survival, but not all Moon Children wanted to be a part of it.

"Rory was their clan leader," I point out. "He had a tendency to beat the shit out of them on a regular basis. Having no leader at all is probably a blessing, aye? Plus, you and Josephine are from different clans. It's hard to simply change allegiance overnight."

"You could go talk to them, though. You and Haru? Aren't you both from there?"

I nod slowly, trying to determine if I truly have the time for such things. "I'll do what I can," I say finally. "But first, I want to see Josephine."

The Brass Button Theatre is still a burned-out husk, though I can see signs of some basic reinforcement techniques around the edges. Enough to keep what's left of the walls from falling in, anyway.

I half expected to see crowds of Moon Children lazing about, but everyone is hurrying around on a series of errands—carrying boxes, tools, weapons, or other random items.

"She runs a tight ship, I see," I murmur.

Bran winces. "You have no idea."

"Oh, I think she does," Josephine drawls from above us. She's leaning over the rail of one of her captured Interceptor ships, which once belonged to the Inquestors, hovering silently on its mooring line. She drops a ladder off the side of the ship and shimmies down with a smooth flourish. "Oh, I love doing that."

"If your head gets any bigger you won't be able to wear those fancy hats you proclaim to hate," Bran retorts, though there isn't any real malice in it.

"Fair cop," she says with a smirk, doffing her feathered cap at him mockingly. "It's hard being a captain, you know." She turns toward me then, eyes narrowed critically. "And just what have you done with your hair?"

"Latest Meridian fashion," I mumble, getting tired of talking about it. "But that has nothing to do with why I'm here."

"Oh, I'm sure. All that trouble to steal you lot up to Meridion and now you've brought them back. What a complete waste of bribes." She curls her upper lip in disgust. "Hope you all had fun."

"You're just jealous," Rosa says, rolling her eyes.

"Damn straight I am." Josephine smiles at me sourly. "But something tells me this isn't a simple social call."

"No. But it might be easier to talk it over on a full stomach. I'm starving." I didn't pay much attention to eating after the debacle with the High Council, and I need a moment to compose my thoughts. Food will help with that.

Josephine points up at her ship. "Let's take it upstairs. I suspect we'll have more quiet that way. Kitchen's well stocked, too. Don't know how well you'll manage in those shoes, though."

"I'm sure I'll figure it out."

And I do, albeit with a couple of near misses and a torn trouser hem. But in the end, I'm on deck and Josephine has fired up the engines and takes us higher through the mist, barking out orders to various Moon Children crew, who hop about like crickets in a salt storm, leaping from line to line with hardly a care.

The rest of my clan takes advantage of the opportunity to drum up a little mischief of their own, mainly of the edible variety, and they head directly for the food stations Josephine has set up on one of the lower levels. I can smell whatever's cooking from here, and it makes my stomach rumble.

"If I thought this thing could fly high enough, I'd launch us straight to Meridion," Josephine says when the ship finally slows down and is coasting on the mist. Bran hands me a loaf of bread he's picked up from somewhere below deck, and I eat it quickly. "What's it like up there, really?"

"Better than any of the tales have ever mentioned," I say. "And worse. Riches beyond measure, food fit for kings, technology that escapes my understanding. The people there… Some are nice, I guess. Some aren't. There's a hollowness to many of them, I think. For all the material things they have, it feels like it's never really enough. Or maybe with resources uncountable, all they have is to worry about things like fashion and betrothal laws." Inwardly, I flinch, thinking of Ghost.

"Sounds like envy to me," Bran says.

I shrug. "Some of it probably is. I don't know if we'll ever be accepted there, to be honest. I went before their High Council, but they've sent me on a wild goose chase for 'evidence' that doesn't come from me. That's why I'm here, you know. To try to prove who we really are."

"And why can't those two fools you chased up there help you with that?" Josephine cranes her head back and forth. "I can't help but notice they aren't here with you. Too busy living it up now that they're back home to help out a friend?"

"Ghost's got himself wrapped up in a political marriage contract that was made when he was a child. At this point, I'm not entirely sure he'll be able to get out of it in a…satisfactory fashion." I glance at Josephine and let out a self-deprecating chuckle. "I don't suppose you'd let me borrow a pair of those wings of yours?"

Bran lets out a bark of laughter from where he stands on the prow. Josephine and I both ignore him, but her eyes narrow. "Planning to just swoop in and fly away with him during the ceremony?"

"If I have to. I'd rather not, because that sort of thing is bound to sour our relationships with the other Houses…" My voice trails away as I realize Josephine is frowning at me. "What?"

Bran curls his upper lip. "Listen to you. 'Sour our relationships with the other Houses,'" he mimics, his voice dripping with mockery. "It doesn't take you long, does it? Maybe you really are a magpie, then—simply repeating what everyone around you says."

Stung, I draw myself up. "And you're so much better, then? You wouldn't even go up there to help me when you heard I'd been poisoned. Some clanmate you are, coward."

His head snaps back as though I've slapped him, and I regret the words as soon as they've left my mouth. "And *you* left us," he hisses. "You abandoned your clan the moment something better came along, and for what? To leash yourself like a dog to prove you can be held up to standards that aren't yours?"

"I just wanted a better life for us."

"For who? *Us* or *you*?"

He's moving on me now, and I find myself crouching into a defensive stance almost on instinct. Rory used to beat me and Sparrow simply for disagreeing with him, and while Bran and I might have had our share of squabbles, he's never made a move to actually attack me.

Splash!

Cold liquid slaps me in the face, leaving me sputtering as I cough up a mouthful of water. From the corner of my eye, I see Bran's face squinch up, both of us turning on Josephine at the same time.

The Moon Child leader gives us both a biting look. "Fucking or fighting. Neither is allowed onboard my ships. If you've an inclination to do one—or both—take it somewhere else, aye?"

Bran frowns at me. "I don't really want to do either."

"That makes two of us, then," I retort. "Maybe you could back off a little. All I'm doing now is asking for your help. If you don't want to give it, that's fine, but you don't have to treat me like I'm some sort of criminal." I reach out to squeeze his shoulder. "You and I, all of us, we've been through too much together to be driven apart by whatever this is."

His face softens, and he looks away. "'M'sorry," he finally mumbles.

Josephine raises a brow at me. "What is it you really want, Mags? To rescue Ghost from a would-be marriage? To insert yourself into

Meridian society? Because to be honest, I'm not sure you're going to be able to do both. And from the way you're talking, I don't think you really want to."

"I don't know," I admit. "Ghost comes first for me, of course. But should he? If I have the chance to raise us up as a whole, shouldn't I take it? Shouldn't *we*? They aren't going to really be sorry for what they've done until they see us as people who were wronged. Why should they get away with that?"

"They shouldn't," Bran says. "Why do you think I never wanted to go up there in the first place? You're the one whose head's been full of rainbows and bullshit. A few of them treat you like some sort of exotic animal and suddenly you want to forgive them all and work in harmony?"

"That's not it," I say lamely. "Not really." I slump against the rail until I'm sitting with my feet hanging over the edge, tapping on the metal. "I just… I don't know. Expected they might actually hear what I have to say. But it's all rules up there—propriety and bloodlines and Houses. Not to mention IronHeart herself."

Josephine startles. "I thought that's what you were calling yourself." She passes me a bottle of something amber colored. I uncork it and take a swig, coughing as liquid fire rolls down into my guts.

"Oh no. There's a gods-damned dragon up there all right. A real one. Only no one knows about it but me." Blood fills my mouth as I bite down hard on my lip. "I'm probably not supposed to tell you about it, either, but I feel like no one would believe me even if I shouted it in the streets. They'd think I was as insane as Mad Brianna and her mumblings."

Bran takes a seat next to me. "Aye, well, it does seem a bit far-fetched. Not that I don't believe you," he adds hastily. "The gods know I've seen shit that most people wouldn't be able to comprehend."

"Oh, well, it gets better." I take another swig from the bottle, my head beginning to feel lighter and lighter. "It's got a chip or something in it…with Madeline d'Arc's memories. It can fucking talk, aye? And it specifically *told* me not to mention it to Lucian or Ghost. But, I mean, how am I supposed to tell them their mother is inside a deranged mechanical dragon living at the heart of their floating city? And oh yeah, I think she might want to blow up the whole place."

"Introduce us," Bran croons, taking the bottle from me.

I nearly spit as Josephine chortles, coughing so hard she has to pound my back. "I forgot your delightful sense of humor," I croak. "And I'm pretty sure introducing you would be a bad idea. Though maybe the Meridians would listen to us if we showed up at their door with a dragon. She told me my heart wasn't quite right since it was rebuilt, by the way."

"Bullshit." Josephine glares at me. "We followed her notes to the letter. There was nothing wrong with that heart of yours once we were done."

"Maybe. I had a hard time understanding what she meant half the time. I still don't know exactly what it is that she wants, just that she will be in touch with me when she wants to see me again." I ignore a sudden rush of goose bumps on my arms.

Bran polishes off the last of the bottle with a couple of deep swallows. "Eh, who cares what she wants? If it's that far beyond our understanding, maybe focus on what you can change, aye?" A half smile kicks up the corners of his mouth. "Moon Children aren't cut out for civility, if you haven't noticed. At least, not for long. All those fancy trappings on you and it looks like you found your mama's fur coat in her wardrobe and you're playing pretend. No one will buy it if they look at you for longer than two seconds."

I turn away. "I'm trying."

"You can't play a game when they're the ones making up the rules as they go," he points out. "That's what you taught me down in the Pits, that's when we finally managed to try to make a difference. Well, until the Inquestors collapsed the mines on us and the roving army of Rotters, but at least we tried, right? We tried."

"What's the plan?" Josephine nudges me with her foot. "Is this a rescue mission or an espionage thing? Are we gonna try to assimilate, or are we going to just burn it all down? Because from where I'm standing, that's really the main issue. We have to figure out a specific goal. What's our end game?"

"I thought by becoming Meridians we might be able to have better lives, and maybe we should still fight for that." I rub away the beginnings of a spectacular headache, my fingers pressing on my temples. "But to be honest, right now, I think maybe I just want to go somewhere else and start over. Not that I'm one for running away exactly, but..."

"Speak for yourself." Bran grunts. "Running away is a heathy instinct. It's worked for me so far."

I glance over him, trying to determine if he's mocking me. I don't think he is, but he certainly isn't giving himself enough credit, either. He managed to survive three years underground without losing his sanity, trying to protect the other Moon Children as best he could. Can I do any less now, when things don't seem particularly easy?

I'm not sure what I was expecting when I arrived on Meridion. That the people there would simply open their arms as though we were long-lost relatives dearly missed? Expectations are simply excuses for disappointment. I should know that by now.

"I'll find the paperwork first, I guess," I say finally. "Whatever records to show that at least we are deserving of recognition. Even if they won't accept us as such, just to simply have a voice, maybe that would be enough of a start. Maybe Joseph will come back with us. As far as I know, he's our only real link between both places, and I suspect his word will be taken at face value far before ours will. And failing that..."

Bran raises a brow at me. "Time to crash a wedding?"

"Oh, we'll crash it all right." I struggle with words as a nervous wave of energy ripples through me. "Right through the stained-glass windows of those fucking towers they're so proud of. Are you in?"

"Like you even have to ask," Josephine muses. "I've been wanting to put some of my other devices to a test or two."

Relief floods into me so hard I actually begin to shake, tipping my head forward into my hands. I'm not crying exactly, but Bran makes an alarmed sound all the same and I wipe hastily at my eyes with my shirt. "Sorry. I had been thinking of how I'd do it if I was alone so it's a bit of a shock to me—"

"That we actually have your back? Silly thing. What did you think clans were for? We're all in this together. Though I have to be honest, I really just want to steal some more ships. Just think of it—an entire armada of Moon Children sailing into the great unknown." Josephine's voice grows wistful. "It's a pipe dream, of course, and I have no idea where we'd go or what we'd do, but..."

I nod. "I understand."

It's true, too. When I was younger, all I'd ever wanted was to get to Meridion. Sparrow and I had dreamed of it so wholly we could taste it, as though the floating city contained all the answers to our problems. If we could just get there, everything would be okay. But it was not that simple. And the price we'd paid for such dreams was much more than a pound of flesh. Somehow simply moving on and finding a new place for ourselves doesn't seem so far-fetched.

"Even if we did manage such a thing, we'd be no better off than the Meridians are, though—sterile and all. No babies, no long-term investments." Bran's cool line of logic shatters the crystalline softeners of my vision like a wall to the face.

Josephine smirks. "Eh, I was never a fan of babies to begin with." And then her face grows more serious. "But Mags, for all your talk of crashing weddings and whatnot, you realize there's a chance that Ghost won't want to come with you, with us. What will you do, then?"

"He will," I snap, my voice fierce, though inwardly there's a tendril of doubt uncurling to snag its way into my guts with tiny pricking thorns. "He doesn't want this. He's told me as much."

Her lips press together. "I hope you're right."

I stare out at the drifting fog swirling below my feet. "I hope I am, too."

Secrets fall from lips unbidden.
Light now shines on what was hidden.
Upon my face, upon the sand,
To cup the dawn within my hand.

— CHAPTER FOURTEEN —

The ship slices through the mist, engines thrumming in time. Josephine left us long ago, going belowdecks to do whatever a captain does, leaving Bran and me alone.

"I am sorry," he says after a while. "For not coming up to Meridion with the others when you were in trouble."

I shrug. "It's all right. They said you were having difficulty with the nightmares and everything."

A thin bead of sweat appears on his forehead, and he leans forward to rest his face on the cool metal of the rail. "Every night, Mags. Every night. I'm back in the Pits and I'm watching her fall… I'm so afraid. So afraid…"

Her. Penny.

They were lovers in the Pits, though I don't know if it was truly a soul match or merely fondness sprung from the need to not be alone in the dark. Not that it matters anyway. Penny was lost in the mine collapse, shaken from the wall into a writhing mass of Rotters who tore her apart before our eyes.

I swallow hard, suddenly very aware that I tucked such terrible memories away as deep as they would go, trying to forget everything about that place. But Bran's eyes burn with such self-loathing I suspect he will never forgive himself.

I scoot closer to him, turning as if to offer him my shoulder. He wraps his arms about my waist almost immediately, burying his face against my abdomen, his head resting on my lap. I don't offer any words of comfort and he doesn't ask for any. What is there to say? Murmuring platitudes now is useless. We both know what happened is not our fault, but there's no way to explain the guilt we feel that we are here and alive and she is not.

When his shoulders start shaking, I gently run my fingers through the glowing hair, leaning forward until I'm partially curled around him, the two of us clinging together as he sobs. My own tears slip down my cheeks, and I sigh raggedly against it. I'm so close to a breakdown myself, but I still can't seem to allow myself that freedom.

Not yet.

When I finally sit up, Bran's eyes are closed, his breathing even and deep. I stroke the furrows of his brow, watching as they unfold to smoothness. In all this time, I've never really noticed all the little details of his face. In the Pits, we were all filthy and the light was fleeting, even with the glow of our eyes. And to be honest, I don't think any of us really wanted to look at one another too hard. Or maybe it was just me who didn't, using distance as yet another shield from our reality.

But Bran has had it harder than most—his sister's torture at Buceph's hand, the death of Penny, the anguish of not being able to help all the Moon Children sent below. It's aged him, I think, though I don't know exactly how old he is. But all of it is written in the crow's feet about his eyes and the worry lines tracking brutally across his forehead.

What can I do except offer him a place to retreat to?

I don't know how long we sat there, only that I must have dozed off because I'm awakened abruptly by a gentle nudge behind me.

"So he finally managed to fall asleep?"

Josephine, returned from wherever she'd gone.

"I suppose." I realize the ship isn't moving. We've moored off the Mother Clock, but Bran still sleeps like a baby, his mouth wide open in a quiet snore. "I don't think I've ever seen him like this. In the Pits, none of us could fully relax, you know? Always an ear listening, an eye open. Waiting, waiting... For what I don't know, but we all did it."

"He's been a bit of a mess, to be perfectly honest." Her face softens. "I don't think he lets that outer shell of his down very often. It's good you're here right now, even if you're not staying. Sometimes there are things only clan leaders can share, and that's what you are now, for better or worse." She thrusts her chin at me. "And what of you? Do you sleep at all?"

"Only when I can't help it," I mutter. "But it's hard to get comfortable, even up in those cozy beds up there. I don't like sleeping alone."

"None of you do, from what I can tell. The others from the Pits are exactly the same. We had to put them in a separate room, too, because they tend to wake up screaming. It was actually a relief to send them up to you."

I tug on my hair. "Even among outsiders we're outsiders."

"Eh, we'll manage. It will just take a little time, I think. The younger ones, like Haru, have actually been doing quite well."

The Mother Clock bongs out the hour, and both of us wince away from it. Bran startles from my lap, his eyes wild as he rolls away.

Josephine grabs his arm, shouting something at him that I can't hear beneath the bells, but he stills, shivering until the metallic echo fades away.

"Sorry," he mumbles, rubbing his eyes furiously. "I... Sorry." Before I can say anything else, he stumbles belowdecks.

"Maybe docking here wasn't the smartest thing," Josephine says, grimacing. "That's my fault. Sometimes I forget how broken he is. And he *is* broken, Mags."

"We all are." I tear myself away from the spot where he was, trying to clamp down on my own sense of dread. That the leader I depended on for so long belowground has fallen apart like this...

"How long do you think you'll need?" Josephine nods at the clock. "I don't know what kind of hours that Joseph fellow keeps, but he should be there. I don't think he has anywhere else to stay."

"I'll be back as soon as I can." I pause. "Will Bran be okay, do you think?"

Josephine kicks down the rope ladder that will lead me to the ground. "As good as any other night. He'll probably drink himself to sleep again. That's what he usually does. I'll wait for an hour or so, and then I'll go back to the theatre."

My mouth compresses, but I fail to find any words as I start to climb down. "I know where to find you," I say finally. She salutes me mockingly when I reach the ground, and I mount the stairs to the front doors of the Mother Clock.

I suck in a deep breath and knock, rapping against the ornately carved metal with a decisive pattern.

There's no answer, but I'm not sure I expect there to be. If Joseph's down below in d'Arc's lab, there isn't any way he'd be able to hear me. The door itself is locked, but my heart whirs in time as I approach the Meridian lock on the side, and I easily tap out the code.

The door clicks open, and I quickly slip inside, pausing as it closes behind me. If he wanted it locked, he has a reason for it, and I don't want anyone else hearing what is most likely going to be a very private conversation.

"Hello?" Above me, the inner workings of the clock grind away like they always do, seemingly without end. I pop up the stairs to the upper landing, but aside from a few books on the control panel Ghost and I discovered last time we were here, there are no signs of the Meridian scientist.

So that means finding the secret elevator passage from the side room on the main floor. My heart whirs out the code for this one, as well, and the door shunts open, albeit stiffly. Swallowing hard, I enter the elevator. It's really not much more than a narrow tube and far smaller than I like.

The fact that I'm here and descending below seems like madness, and I'm suddenly very glad I didn't ask Bran to join me. Even if he has the right to see it, I don't think he would be able to manage it.

A startled Joseph meets me at the bottom, his floppy hat replaced by nothing more than a pair of glasses and thinning white hair. His face breaks into a smile when he sees me. "Ah, Magpie, is it? I wasn't expecting visitors, so I was a little concerned when the elevator started moving on its own."

I lightly tap the panel on my chest. "Comes in handy."

"I'd nearly forgotten all about it." He gestures at me. "Well, I'll make us some tea if you want to find a place to sit. I'm afraid it's a bit of a mess."

I wave him off and snag a stool from one of the tables. I'm hit by a wave of memories—Ghost and I stumbling on this place by chance, giving us a moment to rest and escape back into BrightStone. Even with my cut feet and broken heart, at least we'd had a bit of a respite.

My head snaps toward the corner where we'd found Madeline d'Arc's body, but of course, everything is gone. The rotting mattress, the moth-eaten blankets, the bones of the woman who created so much of Meridion and had left it in search for a cure to a plague the Meridians had unleashed on an unsuspecting populace.

"I took the liberty of neatening things up," Joseph says quietly, handing me a cup of steaming tea. "She never could abide a messy workspace. I suspect that's true even in death." He gestures at a plain box sitting on the bench beside a pile of her notebooks.

A frown turns down my mouth. "Is that…?"

He nods. "I had her remains cremated. Normally she would be interred in Meridion, but I've been a little afraid to go back."

"Maybe this is more fitting," I say, shifting on my stool. "This way her sons can make the final decision. I honestly don't know what the right answer is."

Something painful flits across his face as he sips at his own cup. "And how are her children? Lucian and…Trystan, is it?" The name seems to ripple over his tongue in an almost unfamiliar way, tripping him up, and he tries to hide it by taking another sip of tea.

"Ah, well, that's a bit of a long story," I say, eyeing him curiously. His reactions never made much sense to me. I mean, I always figured he knows more than he lets on, but I've never called him out on it. My lips purse. "I don't suppose you know how to get out of a Meridian marriage contract? Apparently, a betrothal was made with the House of Tantaglio."

"Marriage?" Joseph's face takes on a scandalized mien. "With the Tantaglio family? Why, that's preposterous! Madeline would never have allowed it. In fact, I'm sure she refused such an offer shortly before she left."

An inkling of an idea takes root in my head as I watch him fuss with the teakettle. "That's an awfully intimate piece of knowledge for a simple coworker to have, don't you think?"

"Yes, well, perhaps I was a bit more 'intimate' with her than I mentioned," he says dryly. "A fact I'm sure you've figured out by now."

"You did say you helped her build this place. Considering she was on the run, it doesn't take a genius to determine you were probably more than simply coworkers or even good friends." I weigh my next words carefully, half guessing at some long-held suspicions, but I'm fairly sure I'm right. "Do they know?"

"Does who know what?" He dances around the question. "What are you getting at?"

"You're Lucian and Trystan's father," I say bluntly. "Do they know? I'm sort of leaning against it since neither one seemed to show much interest in you when you met them during our escape from the Pits." My gaze softens. "But I saw your expression when Lucian was on those gallows. For someone you'd only just met, you seemed awfully desperate."

Joseph stills. "You're rather perceptive, Magpie. I didn't think it would be so obvious."

"I spent too many nights watching Lucian pace around the Conundrum not to be familiar with the way he moves. I remember thinking you walked like him even back in the Pits. It wasn't a priority for me at the time, aye? But looking at you now, there's no doubt he's nearly a perfect copy of you. The shape of your hands, the curve of your chin, it's all there. I don't know about Trystan, though. Maybe he takes after his mother more."

"Meridian bloodlines are tricky things," he says slowly. "I may very well be Lucian's father, but as for Trystan, I don't think so. D'Arc kept many secrets, even from me, and she didn't want to be tied down to my House. Her children would stand upon her name only. But I think she did it to protect both me and the boys." His face grows grim. "She knew there would be repercussions for her sabotage of the city, and while she was very outspoken about her beliefs, she didn't want me to bear the burden of them once she left."

"How very noble," I say, unimpressed. Given I met a version of the woman in Meridion, she didn't seem that self-sacrificing to me, but then again, I've never been trapped inside a metal body, either, so it's a fair cop either way.

"I'm not sure nobility has anything to do with it. Practical woman, Madeline. And she didn't suffer fools lightly. It didn't exactly make her a particularly popular person, even among other Meridians. Still, I have my regrets. After Lucian was born, we drifted apart. By the time he was two or three, I was out of her life and she was out of mine."

I frown. "But what of Trystan? If you're not his father..."

"I don't know. We never spoke about it, even when she came to ask me for help. At that point, Lucian was a young man with a promising medical career. I didn't want to create any additional confusion for him. I thought maybe after he finished his schooling I might approach him then, but that's when Madeline left and he was forced into exile with Trystan." He rubs his temples absently. "And by then I was already wrapped up in the Rot business and we ended up in the Pits—as you know," he adds wryly.

"Don't you think you might owe him a bit of an explanation now?" I prod. "I think he has the right to know. And even if Trystan doesn't get any answers out of it, I think just being aware that they have at least some family out there... That's probably what I would want, anyway."

"You could be right," he admits. "And to be honest, it's time I returned to Meridion for a while. I've given the Chancellor the information she needs to prosecute the High Inquestor. Once I'm done cataloging everything here, I will be going back. There's far too much information in these notebooks of hers to simply leave. Much of it is very dangerous. If I were smart, I'd dump it all down the shunt there or burn it."

"I think you should let Lucian make that decision, though I suspect he'll agree with you. But in either case, that's not really why I'm here."

"I didn't think you'd be paying me a social visit. What is it?" His brow furrows.

I drum my feet on the stool. "Well, for one thing, I need a way to stop the marriage. I thought maybe you would be able to help with that. But more importantly, I'm looking for a way to legitimize Moon Child claims to Meridian Houses, and I can't do it alone. I need proof of what families we belong to."

He whistles. "That's a tall order, Magpie. Most of our notes were destroyed when the Pits collapsed, not to mention that I'm the only survivor. Except for Rinna, but she wasn't involved in the research side of things. I think she could corroborate some of the information, but I don't know if the Council would simply take my word for it."

"You owe me," I snap. "You owe me and every other Moon Child sacrificed to Meridian selfishness. I'm not asking for miracles, Joseph. Just an attempt at helping us. It really is the least you could do. You were there, you knew what they were doing to Moon Children, even if you didn't take part in the...research directly. Notes or not, your word will be taken at higher value than mine."

"You're right." He draws a ragged breath. "And I am sorry. The Council that is there now is much different from the one that was there when I was sent down below. No, I think I would be better served if I continue my work here. And so will you."

"I think you're still a coward. It's just as well Lucian never knew you. At least he stands up for what he believes." I slide off the stool. "Keep wallowing in your lab and your memories, and pretty soon that's all you'll have left."

"You can't lose what you never had," he says stiffly. "Maybe it's better for everyone if I don't get involved. If Madeline had wanted me to be in Lucian's life, she would have seen to it."

I purse my lips, weighing my options. *What the hells.* "We could just ask her, you know."

"I... What?" He blinks at me in confusion. "If that's supposed to be a joke, it's not very amusing."

"I would never joke about something like this. But if you come back to Meridion with me, I'll show you something that's going to make you rethink your life choices a bit." I'm partially bluffing since I don't know how I'd actually get him to IronHeart—and I have no idea how receptive she'll be to the idea.

But I need allies in Meridion, people who know how the political situation works, people with contacts, even if they're ones that haven't been used in a while. Besides, IronHeart said not to tell Lucian and Ghost. She didn't say a damn thing about not telling anyone else. Of course, arguing the point with something that could eat you in a hot second is not the wisest thing, but then I've never staked a claim against my wisdom so why start now?

"I've been rethinking those choices since I met you," he mutters. "I wonder why?" He takes a deep breath. "All right. When is your hearing?"

"In less than a week, the same time Trystan's betrothal will be made official, assuming they can't find the paperwork declaring the contract void."

He grunts. "I should get these papers out of here and properly archived anyway. I'll use that as an excuse to make a visit to the house. The pretense of returning lost property to the d'Arc estate should be enough. I will testify what I know of the operations conducted in the Pits to the Council, if that is your wish. As to your issue with the Moon Children lineage, I'm afraid I haven't run across anything like that in these notes. Buceph kept genetic records of what he was doing, but those are gone. You're on your own there."

"Best I can hope for—for now. I'll keep looking in the meantime, but I will be returning to Meridion in a few days or so, if I can't find the information I need here." I glance around at the pile. "Will you need assistance hauling this up? I've got a few extra Moon Children from the Pits who remember you and might be willing to help."

An uncomfortable grimace is his only reply, and I shake my head. Perhaps it would be a tad too forward for both sides to suddenly be thrown together. Joseph helped our group down in the Pits when he could, but the others might not feel particularly altruistic about it.

"Copper Betty," I say suddenly, snapping my fingers. I'd nearly forgotten I'd left the automaton behind with Josephine. "I'll send her down. She'll be perfect for the job."

"Copper Betty?" he parrots. "How will I know her?"

"Oh, you'll know," I say, smiling. "But if I have time, maybe I can help sort through some of this too. Would that be all right?"

Joseph sighs. "Yes. For whatever it's worth."

"Hopefully, a very great deal," I say as I step into the elevator. "A very great deal, indeed."

Of course, finding the others is a bit of a mess. Josephine's ship is long gone by the time I exit the Mother Clock, and I find myself trudging through the BrightStone streets, my new boots giving me tremendous blisters. It's late evening now, and while I'm not particularly concerned for my safety, I am a bit peckish, so I stop at a street vendor to buy a bag of meat dumplings.

"I almost mistook you for a respectable citizen, Raggy Maggy."

The slow drawl prickles over my shoulders. I stiffen, nearly dropping the bag of dumplings, but somehow compose myself enough to neatly tuck them under my arm. I turn around and see Molly Bell standing before me, her magenta dress as neatly trimmed as ever, her teeth just as pointed when she smiles. For the briefest of moments, I imagine her face cracking open beneath my hammer, those jagged teeth sprinkling on the cobblestones like flower petals.

She cat-grins up at me. With my shoes, I'm taller than she is. Or maybe it's just that she's diminished in some way. "How very... kind of you," I manage to grit out.

Her laughter is ash falling all around me, paper-thin and useless. "You're not a very good liar, Magpie. But then, you never were." She tugs on my sleeve. "Found yourself a nice nest up there on the floating city, eh? New feathers, new shinies, you weren't hard to spot."

"It's not like I was trying to hide," I retort. "What do you want?"

"Oh, a little of this and a little of that. Perhaps I simply wanted to see how you were doing. Last I saw you, you were in the High Inquestor's keeping. I did try to get you out, you know."

"Oh aye. You tried very hard, I'm sure. One hand on the lock of my door, one on the High Inquestor's cock."

"Walking the line of power is a very fine line. It requires a delicate touch. But no, I hear you are seeking information. As the premier broker of such things, I chose to find you. Call it a good faith gesture if you prefer."

A bark of laughter escapes me. "I hardly think anything you do is in good faith."

"Fair enough." She peers over my shoulder. "I don't see your shadow anywhere. Stayed at home, did he?"

I stare at her, stone-faced. She's testing me, barbing her words to gauge my reaction. I've seen her do it nearly all my life, always answering questions with questions, trying to glean every bit of information she can. It's her trade so I suppose I can't really blame her. I doubt she could stop even if she wanted to. That doesn't mean I'm going to simply spill everything to her. She does owe me, and if she wants information from me now, she's going to have to work for it.

Molly laughs at my expression. "For all those fancy clothes, you still can't hide a thing you're feeling, can you? Your emotions play across your face like words in a dictionary, my dear, and it doesn't take a genius to read them." Her smile grows broad, teeth glinting in a dangerous fashion.

"I know you were breeding Moon Children for Buceph. I learned as much in the Pits." I step toward her, her face growing slightly pale. "I learned a great deal below. Perhaps you'd care to share your side of the story?"

She flinches beneath whatever she sees in my face now, and I allow myself a twinge of satisfaction. It's been a rough couple of weeks, and to find myself with the upper hand in a conversation is a bit heady.

"If you kill me, you'll never get your answers," she says suddenly, dropping all the mincing flutters and saccharine sweetness of our previous conversations. Her mask removed, I see her clearly for the first time in a while—the dark circles, the pinched mouth, her robustness somehow a ghost of its former self. "Follow me."

"To where? I'm not simply going to trot along behind you because you say so."

"Then don't. Up to you. I have some of what you're looking for, though, so perhaps you might want to see it before you make up your mind." She flounces away, not looking back, leaving me to decide for myself.

Is it a trap? Maybe. Probably. But one I have no choice but to enter. I follow her, my shoes tapping on the cobblestones in sharp report.

The Conundrum has been refurbished since I was last there. Not surprising really, given how long it has been. Although the girls still have the same sort of luminous looks to them, their eyes just as hollow.

The great room is much as I remember it—new trappings and a slightly nicer stage maybe. It's not as full as I would have thought, given the time of day. There are only a few clusters of men nursing their drinks and smoking cigarillos as they watch one of the girls parade around the stage in something that's meant to be a dance in the way that a skeleton resembles a person.

"It's a little slow, isn't it?" I say it aloud, but if Molly hears me, she pays no heed. For a moment I am transported to that night of Sparrow's death, the two of us following Molly into her personal office in the back, Martika nodding at us from her perch in front of the doorway. Lucian in drag, I learned later, though as disguises go, it had been pretty good. It took me quite a while to suspect him and longer yet to call him out on it.

A smile creeps over my face despite myself, but it flattens when I end up in Molly's study. Being dragged out by Inquestors to be stabbed in the back alley is not a memory I particularly feel like revisiting, and realizing that I am now fully alone within the shark's domain only hammers home how vulnerable I still am.

"Don't fret, girl. I'm not after you." Molly waves her hand dismissively at me. "Just by entering my establishment, you'll increase my business tenfold by the end of the week, especially if I can get you to buy a drink at the bar. The mighty IronHeart herself, returned from the underworld, granted passage to Meridion, favored by the sons of d'Arc. Why, you're practically a goddess."

"We remember things much differently," I retort. It takes all my effort not to turn around to check the doors behind me. Any show of hesitation or fear on my part will instantly lower me in status, and I don't have time for that.

"What do you think of the improvements? Half the place burned down when the Rotters flooded the streets, but thanks to a number of patrons and some savings I squirreled away, well, we're practically brand-new." She frowns. "You were right about it being a bit slower, though. Since the Inquestors have been mostly disbanded, they aren't exactly breaking down my door to get laid. Lack of jingle will do that."

"Let me be the first to offer you my condolences," I say pleasantly, without a hint of sorrow. "I can't say I don't bear you any ill will, but you did offer me shelter for a time, so I won't be actively trying to have you shut down."

Her brow rises. "As if you could. Your influence might be growing, my dear, but never underestimate the power of a woman's legs on the psyche of a man. Whether she's walking away from him or spreading them wide, it tends to leave an impression."

"I doubt Chancellor Davis sees it that way."

"You'd be surprised." Molly chortles at me. "And chancellor or no, she understands why my business is a necessary evil. Compared to the monstrosity you unearthed with the Inquestors and the Meridians, my little shop here is very small pickings." Her smile grows broader. "I'm rather grateful to you for that part, as well."

"Anything I can do to help the cause," I say airily, waving my hand at her.

"Indeed. So what sort of information do you need from me?" She slides into her chair, her hands idle.

I stare at her a moment more. Despite her assurances to the contrary, she looks tired. Not exactly defeated, but the powder on her face seems of a lesser quality than I remember, the curls upon her head not as tight. But that doesn't particularly concern me anymore, and I don't have time for games.

"Records," I tell her bluntly. "All the records you have of Inquestor-brothel relationships that ended with Moon Child births." I lean forward to lean upon the table. "I know you have them."

She pauses. Whatever she thought I wanted, this clearly isn't it. I've surprised her, and that is no small feat. If I can use it to my advantage...

"I might have had such things in the past," she says slowly, "but after the collapse of the Pits and the removal of the Inquestors, there was no need to keep them."

"Bullshit," I snap.

"No, no, it's entirely true." Her eyes narrow at me. "I may deal in information, but that doesn't mean I'm going to keep it around if it's going to implicate me. Something like that, well... Rumors are one thing. Explicit records indicating my role in the subjugation of the city is something else entirely."

My upper lip curls at her, even as my stomach turns over in disgust. "You have no shame at all, do you?"

"Shame is an emotion for the weak," she says, pulling out a long-stemmed pipe. She rummages around in her pockets for a packet of tobacco. It's sweet-smelling stuff, almost cloying, but I ignore it as she lights it up and takes a long puff. "And I've got a business to run and girls to manage. Besides, I already gave you all the information you're asking for. Not my fault you're too stupid to realize it."

Whatever I'm about to say is cut off by her last words. "What?"

"You heard me. I didn't say I destroyed it. I said I won't keep it around. And I haven't. I gave it to you."

"I think I would have known if you gave me something like that," I say dryly. "Unless there are boxes of paper lying about my old room that I wasn't aware of, I think you're full of shit. And I don't have time for this kind of nonsense."

"Gods, but you're dense. I always told Lucian it was a waste trying to teach you anything. A trained dog could have figured it out by now." She smirks. "After all the risks I've taken, here you've got that information wandering around the city so carelessly. It almost hurts me to think you're so helpless. Although, to be fair, I don't think Lucian has discovered it, either. If he had, he certainly wouldn't have sent you down here on a goose chase."

"He didn't send me," I snap, getting to my feet. "And if you're going to just talk in riddles like you always do, then I'm going to—" IronHeart. The drones. My dragon. Always watching. Always recording. Madeline d'Arc. The answer smacks me right in the face.

"You're going to what?" she asks sweetly.

"Copper Betty," I breathe. "Copper Betty has all the information. That's why she can't speak. You had her silenced so she couldn't share what she knew."

"Huzzah!" Molly claps enthusiastically, the way one would praise a poodle for not taking a shit on the carpet. "Oh, your face! Your face! I wish I could have it photographed." Tears of mirth run down her cheeks. "All this time," she wheezes. "All this time and you had everything you needed right at your fingertips. I even gave her to you when I figured you'd be heading up to Meridion, and then you…you left her here."

I flush, my face going hot and then cold and then hot again. I fight the urge to sit back down and cradle my head in my hands. There's no time to lose. I left Copper Betty with the other Moon Children. Josephine would know where she was now.

"Of course, seeing as she can't speak, I suppose you might have issues actually getting the information out of her, but that's your problem." Molly takes another long drag and offers the pipe to me.

I wave her off. "Even if I can't fully understand her, I know someone who does."

And I do. IronHeart herself would be able to extract the information, assuming I even trust the dragon to give it to me. But what choice do I have?

"Well, I wish you good luck," she says. "Remember your Molly Bell when you finally succeed in whatever plot you've found yourself wrapped in. After all, without me, you'd have nothing at all."

I roll my eyes, but I cannot argue her point. For all the betrayals and lies, she is right, in her own way. "I'll keep that in mind," I say, giving her a rude salute as I leave. Her cackling laughter chases me from her office, into the hall, and out of the Conundrum, echoing through my mind like the haunting cry of a half-mad banshee.

Flying is nothing more
Than gravity giving chase.
But only birds know the secrets
Of falling with grace.

— CHAPTER FIFTEEN —

Of course, the thing about Moon Children is that we're nearly impossible to find if we don't wish to be seen. After traipsing about the finer points of Market Square for the better part of the hour without a wisp of pale hair to be found, I decide to take matters into my own hands.

Or feet, as it were.

My boots are wholly impractical for this sort of thing, so I remove them and tie the laces to my belt. I wiggle my toes experimentally and then scramble up the closest building to the rooftop. It's achingly familiar and foreign to me all at once, as though I'm seeing a different city altogether. But the one below my feet tells me all I need to know with the slap of my soles on the copper shingles to the crumbling brickwork as I launch myself toward the next building and then the next, skimming the edges, twisting between crevices.

For all Meridion is such a deadly, pale beauty, its smooth edges seem to eliminate any true character of the city itself. It's less a breathing creature in its own right than a crystalline skeleton, unchanging and unyielding. Or maybe that's just my recollection. Here, at least, the fog welcomes me, enveloping me in a quiet comfort I hadn't appreciated until I no longer had it guarding me from the sun. After being confined for so long, being able to stretch my legs in true Moon Child fashion is more freeing than I thought it would be.

I'd missed it. And even so, I am alone. Yet I can almost feel Sparrow's shadow beside me, spurring me along, though Ghost's absence is brutally piercing. I allow that sadness to urge me forward, and before long, I'm perched upon the Salt Temple staring down at the Merchant Quarter.

It's much as I remember it, back when Lucian and I forced our way past the Inquestors to be there when Archivist Chaunders died. And the museum, as well, burned down to its foundation on the High Inquestor's orders. The loss of all that information is more keenly felt now than ever before, but there is nothing left of that building and no one else from there I could talk to.

A sudden movement below distracts me from my wallowing, glowing hair coming into view.

Bran.

I frown. During the Tithes, Rotters were often cared for by salt priests before being rounded up by the Inquestors. Religious or not, most people who go to the Salt Temple for help these days are either very ill or dying. But surely Bran isn't one of those? I whistle at him, worried.

He barely looks up, whistling back. *Come on, then.*

I pick my way down the rusty fire escape and then rub the flakes from my hand. The white rocks and shells of the path to the Salt Temple entrance crunch under our feet as we approach the bronze doors. No Inquestors this time, I note thankfully.

Bran taps lightly at the door, gesturing at me when one of the salt priests appears. An acolyte, really, judging from her apparent youth. "We need to see the old man."

Her face sours as she stands back to let us through. "You know he doesn't like being called that."

Bran shrugs. "It's true enough, isn't it?"

The acolyte shakes her head at me as we pass by. "Good friends of yours?" I look at Bran, surprised. "Never took you for the religious sort, aye?"

He grunts. "Been coming here off and on since you left. Needed someone to talk to that wasn't…a Moon Child."

I didn't press further because the tension that suddenly radiates off him reminds me very much of one of those rats I tried so desperately to catch in the Pits. I have no desire to be bitten by this particular rat. But I can understand it. His time in the Pits was much longer than mine, his losses more than awful. Perhaps talking with someone unrelated is the only way he has to work through it. It forces the realization that I've been so wrapped up with Meridion and the issues above, I've neglected my clan. That Bran was my co-leader wasn't much of an excuse, and a wave of shame runs through me.

I reach out to take his hand and give it a gentle squeeze. He squeezes back once before wriggling free and continuing down the hallway, with its myriad sea creatures entrapped in the pale walls. They glitter in the torchlight, just as oppressive and awful as I remember, but maybe Bran finds solace within them in a way that I cannot.

The acolyte sweeps past us, her blue robes swirling like mist about her. "You'll need to wait in his antechamber. He's at prayer right now." She points to an offshoot that leads to an austere alcove with half-moon benches nestled beside the window.

There are no cushions, and I sag onto the bench, the cold marble sending a chill straight into my bones. Bran takes a seat on the oppose one, his arms crossed, his head down. I shiver.

"It's like having an icicle shoved up my arse," I complain to Bran.

"That's to keep my fellow worshippers awake, I'm afraid," a raspy voice answers me with a hint of sarcasm. "I find the gods tend to listen to prayers better when they aren't being mumbled half-asleep."

I flush as the priest emerges from whatever room he was secreted away in, recognizing him from when the Archivist died. His brows lift when he sees me. "Ah, yes. I know you. I would not have thought we would cross paths again, but the gods work in mysterious ways."

"Aye." I shift uncomfortably beneath his milky gaze before it falls on Bran. The priest's eyes light up when he sees the Moon Child sitting there. "And what I can do for you, my son? Have you come for another session?"

There's no censure in his words, but there's still something about it that makes my skin crawl. Maybe it's just my aversion to all things religious, but I would give just about anything right now not to be anywhere near here.

Bran bows his head for a brief moment. "My apologies, Father. Things have been a bit hectic." I struggle to keep my jaw from dropping as he appears to humble himself before a salt priest, of all things. "Do you need more?"

The priest scratches his chin. "More would always help, yes. Do you have time?"

"Time for what?" I hiss at Bran, but he ignores me.

"I have some," he says softly, side-eyeing me when I grunt my displeasure.

"Ah, very good, then. I'll get things set up." The old man tugs at his beard. "Wait here a moment. I'll send someone when we're ready." He totters down the hall, his cane echoing back to us like a soft metronome.

I nudge Bran. "Just what is it that we're here for?"

He looks away, the light in his eyes dimming. "It's complicated. Easier to just show you." We wait in silence after that, my heels drumming lightly on the floor as the minutes tick by. The Mother Clock bongs out the hour in the distance. Even within these walls I can feel the vibration of it through my skin. Or perhaps it's merely my heart matching time with it. I have no idea anymore. It's as if my body is a singular living vessel for another one of Madeline d'Arc's mad inventions, as though I was only ever created for that. It's a small, mind-eating worm of a thought, and while I know I was mostly only ever a victim of circumstance, I still can't help but feel a little bitter about it.

Within a half hour, the acolyte finally comes to retrieve us. She leads us down a series of twisted hallways that take us into a basement. I pause before following, Bran nudging me along. "Keep your mouth shut while we're in there, aye?" he says as we enter a sick room.

It's not like the short-term ones I'm familiar with. When the Rot ran through people as it did, there really was only time to try to make them comfortable before they died or were Tithed. But this room was clearly set up as an actual medical dormitory of sorts. Real carpets and wall draping, soft maroon in color, with blue-and-silver blankets heaped upon a bed, and a pile of toys in one corner.

Toys?

I halt, realizing that there are signs of children everywhere here: drawings scrawled on paper, stuffed dolls, little mechanical wind-up insects that remind me of my dragon.

My head snaps toward Bran. "Something I should know?" It's not a serious question. Even if he *had* had time to impregnate someone since we'd emerged from the Pits, Moon Children are sterile.

"Shut your trap," he murmurs pleasantly as a soft sigh comes from the bed.

The priest is there, gently shaking someone under the blankets. "Alora," he says. "You've a visitor."

Alora wriggles out from beneath the covers with a small smile as she spots Bran. She can't be more than ten, but it's hard to tell. Living in BrightStone ages you, but to my eyes, she is young. I can't imagine she's lived on the streets for very long.

Her hair is a mousy brown and her eyes a curious blue. Her lips are dry and pale, as if she hasn't had enough water. For her to be ensconced within the Salt Temple is not a particularly good sign.

"Did you bring me anything this time?" She asks it plaintively, her voice hoarse. When she moves to stand next to him, I freeze.

The girl's a Rotter. I can tell from the way she moves, the joints too stiff, the telltale mottling of color beneath her skin like a permanent bruise, as if the blood has simply decided to stop moving beyond a sluggish speed. And then it hits me in the nose, that familiar odor of flesh starting to turn, sickly sweet and terrible. I bite back a retching sound, trying to keep from puking on the floor.

Bran makes no noticeable effort, simply bending to squat to her level. "I did," he says solemnly, producing a glass ball from one of his pockets. He clicks a button on the side of it, and it flares to life with a soft violet illumination.

She makes a little cooing sound of delight, taking the orb from him to roll it around in her palm. The light emanating from it gives her an almost ethereal mien, as though she truly walks the line between life and death.

I think of Sparrow with a twinge. Something about the unabashed curiosity on Alora's face reminds me of my friend, and I've missed it dearly. The girl scampers back to the bed, still making enthusiastic giggles.

"No improvement since last time, it seems," Bran says to the priest, a questioning bent in the lilt of his voice.

"No worse, either," the priest says. "She seems to have reached a steady state, but I think with another infusion, things might get a bit better. It's so hard to tell, given her age."

I stare at Bran, and he holds up a hand to me. "Not now. We'll discuss it when I'm done here." He strides over to a table with a reclining chair.

The girl perks up when she finally sees me. "Who are you?" she demands fiercely. "Did you bring me something, too?"

I make an awkward sound at Bran, who rolls his eyes. The priest acolyte has set up a series of tubes and bottles nearby, and she starts prepping his arm for a blood draw. I shudder and turn away. I can hardly bear the idea of a needle again after what Buceph attempted in the Pits.

My back to them, I approach the girl quietly. "I'm sorry," I say. "I didn't know I would be coming here. But I'm very glad to meet you."

She pouts for a brief moment and gestures at my glasses. "Can I try them on?"

I hesitate, wondering if my glowing eyes might frighten her, but then I suppress an unhappy laugh. The poor thing is trapped in a living nightmare. She's seen Bran anyway—she will hardly be afraid of me. I tug them off, wincing at the sharpness of the light.

She gives a slight pause when she sees my face but is immediately distracted by the glasses, sliding them off and on her nose as she raises her head to keep them on her ears. "These are funny," she says. "Bran won't let me borrow his."

"They're rather important to us," I admit to her. "Replacing them would be hard right now, and if we can't see well, we get lost." That wasn't it exactly, but how to explain to her the ins and outs of rooftop dancing without our vision? She seems a sheltered thing. "Where are you from?"

"None of your business," Bran says from his chair. "Ouch! Are we done yet?"

"Yes," the acolyte says softly. "We got all we need from you for now." Bowing once, she gathers everything and makes for the hallway, humming what might a lullaby beneath her breath. Bran gestures at me to join him on the far side of the room, and I do so, leaving Alora to play with my glasses.

"Where did you find her?" I frown slightly. Bran's altruism has never run past the few members of our clan and certainly not to random Rotters, children or no. The fact that he willingly donates his blood to her, binding himself to the girl in a half cure that seemed so repugnant when we learned of it…

"I found her wandering around the Cheaps after the uprising, or whatever you want to call it. She wasn't so far gone, but I knew what she was the moment I saw her." His voice grows small and grim. "I would have walked on by. I meant to. But she reached out and simply asked if I'd seen her brother."

I nod to myself. Of course. Bran lost his sister in the Pits after a long and terrible time of searching for her for years. I found what was left of her in Buceph's laboratory, half-alive, kept in pieces, part machine. She begged me to release her, and I did it—to her and every Moon Child kept within the confines there, nothing more than walking corpses themselves.

Something in him clearly broke at Alora's request. It is more than understandable. She represents a second chance at saving an innocent life. Who am I to gainsay him the attempt?

"I'm sorry. I didn't realize." My mouth compresses grimly.

He snorts. "Why would you? You've got your own problems to deal with, even if they're ridiculous and will never work."

"Makes two of us," I mutter, eying Alora. Her eyes flutter slightly, sleepy. I gently tug my glasses from one of her hands and replace them on my face. "So now what?"

"They'll prepare my blood and give it to her. Maybe it buys her a little more time. However long that is," Bran says grimly. "You can go now. I just wanted to show you."

"Are you sure? I can wait."

"I want you to go," he says finally, nudging me toward the door. "This is private."

I hesitate in the hallway, watching as he presses a gentle kiss on the girl's forehead, an unreadable expression on his face. I take my leave then, the image of his slumping shoulders as he sits beside her bed burning its way into my memory.

My sheep are strong and soft and stout
And playful when they turn about.
The coats so thick, the smiles so sharp
To hide the wolves within their heart

— CHAPTER SIXTEEN —

The sky is lighter when I emerge from the Salt Temple, false dawn making its way through the fog. I yawn, tired. I still need to find Copper Betty and get some sleep, but given the time constraints, I've managed to discover far more than I thought I would. Joseph's testimony. Copper Betty's secrets. There's only one thing left to confront, and that would be the High Inquestor himself.

The Chancellor has him locked away, as she noted—the man is far too dangerous to simply be available to the public—and she said he's off-limits to me, but surely there is a way to gather some of his notes, assuming he didn't just burn them all when the city was overrun. But I think not. Arrogant men have a tendency to feel they are above such shallow things as consequences. It's entirely possible he still has them.

Or not.

My head swims with potential outcomes. Has Lucian had any luck up in Meridion? Is Ghost safe from Lottie's petty indulgences? My mouth purses. As caged as I feel half the time, being trapped in the family home of someone you're being forced to wed is surely more brutal, even if that cage is gilded.

I think back on Josephine's words about her ships. What if we truly do leave? Would the two cities even notice? I don't think so, and that makes me far sadder than I have any right to be. Is there any reason for me to be doing this at all? Still, my heart whirs when I think of Meridion. It's as though some invisible force pulls me there, a longing I can't quite describe. I've had it for as long as I can remember, this burning need to get to the floating city, regardless of how its people have treated me. But then what?

A whistle in the dark attracts my attention. It sounds like it's a few houses away, and it's plaintive and mourning and achingly familiar. How often did I sit at the entrance to the Pits calling out for help? Can I ignore someone else now?

I let out my own reply, soft and trilling. It isn't meant to be a real answer. Just a bit of solidarity in the dark. I don't know if this person even wants any company, but perhaps it wouldn't be bad to reach out to the Moon Children who didn't escape the Pits with me.

Heading for the nearest set of rowhouses, I scale the drainpipe easily to the rooftops, whistling again to announce my presence. Not that it matters, but it at least gives them the opportunity to avoid me if they want to. I'm hardly one to intrude upon someone's private grief.

When I find them, the Moon Child in question is curled up against a gable, head tipped back into the shadows as I alight on the roof above them.

"Ah. It's you. Come to gloat, have you?"

I stiffen at the tone, my former clan leader's voice a wretched reminder of everything that happened.

"Rory," I say, forcing the tremor out of my own voice. Knowing he can't hurt me now is one thing, but years of living beneath his thumb still has me instinctively cowering. "And I'm not one for gloating...much."

I suppose it doesn't surprise me that Josephine and Bran didn't exactly invite him into their clan leader meetings. Rory was a coward who put himself above his clan, and he ruled with his fists, his motivation nothing more than his own survival. But it has been over a year since I last saw him, and clearly, it has not been a particularly good one. I can tell from the way he's sitting that one of his legs isn't quite right, his left hand twisted into a position that shouldn't be possible.

"What happened?" I finally ask. The gods know I don't owe him anything, except maybe a good beatdown, and yet, for the moment, I can't find it in myself to truly hate him. Pity, maybe.

"When the Pits caved in, the Warrens collapsed. My left side was trapped in the rubble, and I couldn't get out." Rory lifts his face to mine, and I can see the scars that crisscross over his cheek and neck. "And no one came for me." His mouth curves up in a crooked smile. "Reaped what I've sown, I suppose."

"Yes." Would I have helped him? He's part of the reason Sparrow died. He abandoned us when we needed the clan's protection. He sent Penny to the Pits in recompense to the Inquestors. He lied and stole and kept us starving while he fed himself.

So, no, on thinking about it, I wouldn't have. I say as much to him, and he laughs again, but it's full of bitterness.

"Fair enough. I have no excuse, no reasons behind what I've done except to survive. And now I can barely do that." He holds up his gnarled arm. "Too much damage. I couldn't find a bonewitch when I did manage to escape, or not one I could afford, anyway. Too late to do anything with it at this point. I've been told it's permanent."

I suppose it's possible someone in Meridion might be able to fix it. Lucian would be a better judge of that than I am, but I don't bother dangling the possibility in front of Rory. "You know what else is permanent? Sparrow's death. Penny's death. I watched her die, did you know that? Watched a perfectly loyal clan member—your second-in-command—be completely ripped apart by Rotters." I let out a half sob I didn't realize I'd been holding in. "There wasn't anything left of her but her hair."

He winces and averts his eyes. "I'm sorry," he mumbles. "I didn't want her to die. I didn't want any of you to die."

"Of course you didn't," I say pleasantly. "You just decided your own comfort was worth more." My hands ball into fists as anger rockets through me hard enough to set me to shaking. Inwardly, I know the true blame for our issues should be placed squarely on the Meridians, on the Inquestors, on the people of BrightStone. But it's so easy to grind out this hatred upon the man cowering before me, to make him the face of everything that's ever gone wrong.

So easy to simply hurt him the way he hurt me. But I can't. I don't.

How many people did I kill down in the Pits? How many death rattles haunt my sleep? Can I add another in cold blood?

His eyes catch mine, and I can't tell if they're pleading for mercy or release, but it doesn't matter. I won't grant him, either. And if I can't forgive him, I can certainly forget him. In the end, I lower my hands, my nostrils flaring wide as I clamp down on my emotions once again.

We stare at each other a moment longer until he waves me off. "Live a good life, Raggy Maggy. Do great things. Whatever nonsense you and Sparrow used to spout. One of these days maybe I'll even believe you."

"I don't care what you believe, Rory." I turn away, more than ready to move on. "And I don't think we'll meet again."

"No." He drops his head, stretching out his bad leg so it hangs off the edge of the roof. It seems as if he might just throw himself off, but he simply starts up that sad, odd whistling again.

And so I leave.

I trot across the rooftops, albeit with a bit more caution this time, my thirst for socialization more than quenched. If anything, I feel slightly sick about the whole thing, wondering if I should have taken revenge after all.

But letting him live with his memories, trapped within a broken body, perhaps there is a sort of justice in that, too. In any case, he is not my responsibility. He made his choices. Now he has to live with them, just like the rest of us.

The Brass Button Theatre is swarming when I finally get there. Josephine's ship is moored and a fairly massive crowd of Moon Children mill about. From the smell of it, I'm guessing it's breakfast time, but how Josephine is managing to feed everyone is beyond me.

My own stomach growls, and I don't bother to slip my boots on when I climb to the ground. My fine clothes have managed to tear in at least three places anyway, and I've got no one here to impress.

The other Moon Children hardly pass me more than an interested glance. Food for their bellies is a far more pressing issue than IronHeart. And that's probably how it should be.

At least they aren't fighting one another. Even if there are pockets of tension in places, there is clearly a defined truce about the watering hole.

I snag a bowl of whatever's being served from one of the large barrels, and I sip from the rim. It's a broth of some sort, dubious pieces of chicken or fish floating about. Not great, but it will do.

The barrel is being heated by captured steam underneath, the trapped air warming the contents. I haven't seen one used quite like that before, but it seems to work well.

I suck down the rest of the bowl and toss it in a pile with the rest. A few hapless Moon Children are already scrubbing them down while others serve drinks. I spot Josephine over on the far wall, close to her ship. Her eyes are scanning the crowd with brutal efficiency, and even though she doesn't appear to have any weapons on her, there's something rather dangerous about her all the same. Whatever it is, it's enough to keep everyone in line.

She spots me and waves me over, her face never wavering from its stony visage.

"Are you their warden?" I ask dryly.

She snorts. "Frankly, that might be easier. But no. Until we can manage to get it through everyone's thick skulls that they don't have to like one another, they just can't be killing one another, it'll be like this."

"I guess I hoped that after the Pits collapsed, we would all somehow work together."

"Eh. It will happen. Or it won't," she admits. "Most of them have never had to think beyond where their next meal is coming from and how to outrun the Inquestors. Suddenly realizing they have the ability to make choices and decide how their lives should go..."

I sigh. "It's never easy, is it?"

"You picked the wrong line of work if that's what you were looking for." Something pained slips over her features. "While the rest of BrightStone is grateful that you and the others seem to have overthrown Meridian rule, at least for now, they are still a very long way from accepting us." Her expression grows grim. "We've had a few Moon Children try to reunite with their mothers, if they knew who they were, and it's not pretty. Two of them actually killed themselves afterward."

The breath whooshes out of me. "I didn't realize it was that bad."

"How could you? You're up there, fighting the good fight. Rubbing shoulders with the elite. Getting poisoned. Kidnapped. The usual. Becoming a hero or whatever it is you're doing." Her eyes meet mine, and they're far more troubled than I've ever seen. "Upsetting the balance of a city isn't easy, but if things don't straighten out soon, we're going to fall back into our old ways simply because it's what we know."

"But we can't. After everything we've gone through, everything we've tried to do…" A wave of despondency sweeps over me.

"We may not have a choice," she points out. "Change is slow and painful, and sometimes it doesn't happen, no matter how much we want it to. I don't know. Maybe your idea of picking up and leaving isn't a bad one. We would be able to start fresh in a new place. We have the power to do that now, and that's no small thing."

"It sounds so romantic until you're forced to eat one another because none of us know how to farm or hunt." I shiver. Bran and I had managed not to let things get that bad in the Pits, but that didn't mean I wanted to go through it again.

"But is that really what you want?" Josephine presses the issue. "Simply getting by isn't exactly a winning slogan." She gestures at the thinning crowd of Moon Children. "*This* is getting by. Trying to get the BrightStone populace to pay us for honest work is a nightmare. With the Warrens in shambles, we don't even have that much to work with when it comes to finding housing. And to have you sitting there fretting about Ghost's marriage arrangements… Well, to be honest, Mags? I'm sympathetic, but I don't care much."

Her words strike me hard in the gut, and the truth of them is like a needle pricking my skin over and over.

"I never asked for this," I tell her softly. "To be used for the ends of others. Thrown into the Pits to merely survive. To become a murdering mercy killer. When do I get to think of what I want? Sure, maybe my ideas are too lofty, but why should we stop dreaming simply because we're too wrapped up in our own traditions to look past our noses at what change could bring?"

"Change is good, aye. But I don't know if they're quite ready for a full-on merge of societies. The gods know the BrightStonians aren't, and I suspect the Meridians are paying you lip service. It's all well and good to spout off about saving us, but we need a real plan, not just sympathy."

"It's not like I've got a finger on the pulse of Meridion," I snap back. "Half the reason I'm down here is to find undeniable proof to rub in their faces."

"Proof that they should either already have or could discover easily enough *if* they were so inclined," she points out. "People are very good at denying what's in front of them if it's something they don't want to see."

I sag, defeated. "I don't know. I suppose I hoped family meant something. But if we're so easily discarded due to something that's no fault of our own, how will it be when we don't fit their preconceived notions of what a Moon Child is supposed to be?"

"And that's why we have clans," Josephine says. "If there is no family to go back to, we make one of our own. Now we just have to learn to get along instead of killing one another."

"Is that all? Should be a snap." I look out at the crowd. It's mostly dispersed by now, the breakfast rush over. Those that haven't disappeared to places unknown lounge about in small groups.

"I saw Rory today," I tell her suddenly.

Her face shutters. "He is not welcome here and he knows it. When things got worse for us while you were in the Pits, he did nothing to help and everything he could to keep us from coming together. Whatever game he was playing, it would have ended once his creature comforts stopped coming in. And he was being bribed by the Inquestors, which I'm sure you're aware of," she adds, looking over at me.

"Yes. Sparrow and I usually just tried to stay out of his way, and you know how well that worked out." I reach up to rub my cheek, memories of being punched upside the head still potent enough to make me wince. "He didn't seem particularly well."

Josephine smiles coldly. "No one is *particularly* interested in helping him. I'm certainly not. The other clan leaders understood what was at stake and our need to try for peace. Rory's out for himself, as he always has been."

"Enough about him," I say, not wanting to give it more thought. "I have to find Copper Betty. Joseph needs her assistance to pull up some of those records and things. He's agreed to help me with some of the Meridian red tape, for whatever that's worth." I yawn. "And I could use some sleep."

"I can help you with both. There are still cots in the basement of the theatre. You should be somewhat familiar with those. As to the whereabouts of Copper Betty, she's down there, as well. I've got her doing metal sculptures in my forge. She seems to like it, oddly enough." Josephine frowns. "For a nonorganic thing, she's pretty opinionated."

My brow arches. "I thought you said she was an 'it.'"

"Eh. Change. Slow, but it happens." Josephine whistles, and a smile cracks my face as Tin Tin emerges from some shadow behind her.

"Oy, Raggy Maggy!" he shouts, a broad grin splitting his mouth.

He's a younger Moon Child, probably close to Haru's age, but he's helped me in the past, both with spying on the High Inquestor and in the Pits. He was the final Moon Child to be Tithed in the days before the whole thing came crashing down.

Josephine gestures toward the theatre with her chin. "If you would be so kind as to escort Ms. Magpie down below? See that she's given a place to rest, and if you wouldn't mind finding Copper Betty?"

Tin Tin gives her a hasty salute before grabbing my sleeve and pulling me behind him. Bemused, I look back at Josephine. The clan leader shrugs and turns away, barking orders at another Moon Child.

Good enough, then. I follow Tin Tin below, through the mazelike halls and rooms, the metallic scene of Josephine's forge thick in the air. "How's the flying going?" I ask him.

He chuckles. "We're not really supposed to use the wings. The Chancellor said it makes the BrightStone citizens nervous."

"But that hasn't stopped you, I'm sure," I say, amused at the way his eyes dart furtively away from mine.

"Not really. But I only do it at night," he insists. "And I practice out by the Warrens. There's no one out there anymore now so I have the place mostly to myself." He puffs out his chest. "I'm getting pretty good, you know."

"I have no doubt of that," I say slowly. "Up on Meridion, there are flying ships everywhere. Rooftop dancing is hard because the buildings are all so tall. It's difficult to get to the tops, and even then, some of the heights are nothing more than death drops. But if we had wings, nothing would be off-limits…"

"Sounds like an excuse to visit, aye?" He elbows me in hopeful jest.

"We'll see. I'm working on it," I tell him as we arrive at Josephine's forge.

The room is hot enough that I break into a sweat almost immediately, the air thick in my throat. Tin Tin points to the far corner where Copper Betty stands, her back to us as she works, her arms slamming the hammer mechanically on whatever she's making. *Plink, plink, plink.*

Before I was Tithed to the Pits, she'd been polished and smooth, but now she is worn in places, with deep scratches along the metallic curves of her body, though she is no less beautiful for it. Her clothes are simple, no longer the short skirt and revealing top she wore at the brothel as she served customers their drinks. Josephine dressed her in something practical for forge work. Thick leather and protective gear, though it is not needed perhaps. She doesn't exactly have any flesh to burn off, but I suppose it cuts down on potential charring.

I clear my throat, uncertain of how to interrupt her. In the past, she's been more of a servant, doing whatever Molly Bell asked her. She'd been a waitress, a maid, an errand runner, and apparently, a spy. "It's been a while," I start. "Sorry for leaving you down here."

The automaton plunges the metal spike into the water, her head turning toward me. Her electric-blue eyes fixate on me in a friendly manner, but with the same emptiness they always had.

I never really knew how cognizant the automaton was or what her actual programming was. Ever since I met her, her communication skills have been limited to nonverbal motions, though there have been times when I thought she really did understand me. But I wasn't concerned enough about it at the time to delve into it.

"Can you talk? Molly Bell said you have information I need." I know what the answer will be, but no harm in asking in case that is a ruse, as well.

Copper Betty stares at me and then slowly taps her metallic fingers over her mouth. Then she swivels her head, taps the back of her neck, and brushes away a cluster of coils that are meant to be her hair.

A chill ripples over my skin when I see the symbol etched there: a familiar set of three dots, like the ones that made up the signature of Madeline d'Arc on the metal plate covering my heart.

"Son of a bitch! She really did make you," I say aloud, as my stomach twists in excitement. "Can you help me? The information that you have, I will need to get it from you. I think I know a way, but you'll have to come with me up to Meridion."

Copper Betty's blue eyes glint as though she's genuinely considering the offer. Another shiver surges through me. When did she become so self-aware? She always seemed so mechanical before, but there are signs of a personality behind that metal mask that feel an awful lot like my little dragon. And then she nods.

"Thank you," I say, unsure of the manners protocol. Molly indicated that the automaton belongs to me now, but it feels more like Copper Betty is simply allowing me to tag along with her.

"We'll leave a bit later," I say to Tin Tin, who has been watching the entirety of this little drama unfold with a confused expression.

"I need to crash for a few hours. At the rate I'm going, I'll be passing out before I can even start sorting through Joseph's files."

Copper Betty cocks her head at me, and I explain the situation. She nods again and then picks up her tools and begins putting them away. She stokes the fire once more before removing her apron.

"What are you working on?" I ask, craning my head to get a better look, but she places a finger against her lips before shooing me out of the room. I frown at her secret, but my eyes are burning and in the end it's easier to let Tin Tin show me to one of the back storage rooms.

There are a few cots in there with basic blankets and pillows, and I crawl into one and pass out almost instantly. I dream of hammers attending a wedding, each one smashing into my chest with an odd rhythm until my heart bursts apart.

Twelve wooden soldiers standing in a row,
A rusted sword and a broken bow.
My hero came but far too late.
Who else to guard my would-be fate?

— CHAPTER SEVENTEEN —

"Is that the last of them, then?" I hand one of the notebooks to Copper Betty, who squeezes it into the box with precision.

Joseph looks over his ledger, crossing out a line or two as he counts. "I believe so. Thanks for your help. It turned out to be more than I thought. I still don't know how we're going to manage getting it all up to Meridion, though. We'll have to rent a carriage once we're there, I suspect. These boxes are far too heavy to simply cart over to…the house." He stumbles over the words, glancing at the box that holds d'Arc's ashes.

"We should take that, too," I say quietly.

"Of course." He carefully wraps it in a silk cloth, tying the ends tightly before placing it in a satchel. "No chance of that coming undone."

We carry the boxes up the elevator to the main lobby of the Mother Clock, but it takes a few more trips to get all the files. "Not sure how we're going to explain all this to the airship captain." I pull out the scroll Fionula gave me. "This is supposed to grant me passage, but I don't think it says anything about automatons or baggage…or other Meridians," I add with a rueful smile.

"Are you sure you don't want to bring the Mother Clock, too?" Josephine drawls from the doorway of the clock tower. "Figured

I'd come get a look at what all the fuss is about. It certainly seems like a lot." Despite her words, she sounds unimpressed. "Here. I brought you something."

She tosses a bag at me, and I half stumble to catch it, wincing at the weight of whatever it is. I cock a brow at her, but she only smirks as I open it to reveal a new hammer, shining and heavy, an elegant dragon design etched into the shaft. I swing it experimentally. "The balance is perfect, aye?"

"Yes, well, I saw you were missing yours. Rosa mentioned you lost it when you were poisoned." Her lips curl. "Figure we owe you at least this much."

My smile grows broad as I tuck it into my belt, the weight of it a familiar friend. I've felt almost naked without it. A hammer is both a weapon and a tool, as am I it would seem. The metaphor isn't lost on me.

I nudge the pile of boxes with my foot. "I think this is about it, though. We'll probably need to take a few trips to get it all to the port. Unless you can give us a ride to the Cheaps directly?"

Joseph tugs on his floppy hat. "Why not take her ship all the way to Meridion? That Interceptor of hers is large enough. I'm fairly certain we could find a place to offload a little closer to the house without having the guard get into our business."

"They don't fly that high, for one," Josephine points out. "Not to mention I don't know where I'd even go once I got up there."

"Sure they do," Joseph insists. "How do you think we got the ships down here to begin with?"

Josephine stares at him. "You mean we could have simply flown up to Meridion anytime we wanted?"

His mouth purses as he thinks it over. "I seem to recall we put a governor on the engines after we settled down here. The Council didn't want the Inquestors to be able to fly home, you see. They were criminals, after all."

I swallow the rude words on the tip of my tongue about the ironies of *that* particular statement, but Josephine's eyes have lit up with an almost monstrous longing. "Do tell," she croons. "And just *how* do we remove this governor? Can you do it?"

"Ah, most likely not." He points to Copper Betty. "But that automaton can. She'll have the strength for it, and Magpie's heart can open the mechanism."

Josephine makes a questioning sound, but it's less of an inquiry and more of a command. I know better than to gainsay the sly look upon her face. "Done." I nod. The implications of having transportation between the two cities unlocked and unsupervised is dizzying. I'd be able to bring the other Moon Children to Meridion without permission. We'd be able to leave if we want.

The freedom would put us on par with citizens from both cities. I rub the head of the hammer where it sits on my belt, imagining the possibilities. I turn to Joseph, hungrily desperate. "Show us," I breathe.

Of course, showing and doing are two very different things. Joseph might be a keen biologist, but his technological knowledge of airships leaves a lot to be desired. I can see Josephine's frustration eating her alive as he stumbles about the engine room searching for various buttons or settings.

"Crank shaft, crank shaft," he mutters.

Josephine's eyes narrow. "I can find that for you if you just—" Her fingers clench into fists, and she lets out a silent scream into her arm when something pops, a hint of smoke filling the tiny space.

Even Copper Betty looks frazzled as she watches with her emotionless face. She gestures at me, pointing at my heart. As her metallic fingers brush over my chest panel, there's an answering whir, similar to how it used to react with my dragon.

I frown. For a moment it's as though I can actually understand what she's saying. "Joseph, check by the air valve. The one over there." Copper Betty nods at me in approval.

Josephine's eyes narrow, darting back and forth between me and the automaton, but she says nothing.

"Ah, here's what I was looking for." Joseph lets out a grunt, wiping the sweat away from his brow and leaving a small smear of oil. He half smiles at me. "I think we'll need you for this part. The plate is locked."

"My cue." I duck past him to where he's pointing. Sure enough, there's a panel half-hidden by a handful of dangling wires. I'm fairly certain they weren't pulled out this way before, but I'll let Josephine handle that part.

Kneeling beside the panel, I touch it gently. My heart whirs, and the panel pops open to reveal the keypad. I make quick work of the lock, and a moment later, there's a loud grinding as though a gear is shifting.

Joseph hums thoughtfully, his eyes distant as though trying to remember something. His expression is a replica of Lucian's when he's trying to solve a problem, from the faraway look to the tilt of his head.

How is Lucian now, I wonder? And Ghost?

The thoughts are chased away from me as Joseph smiles. "Ah, yes. There was a tool we used to adjust the throttle, but we obviously don't have one now. Here." He gestures at Copper Betty. "You'll have to do it, I think. Your fingers look like they'll be strong enough to manage. There's a switch inside the hole under the panel. Go ahead and flip it up."

The automaton switches places with me, and her fingers delve beneath the panel. It's a tight fit, and by the end, she's contorted herself into a ball to get the leverage she needs, her blue eyes flashing furiously. There's a low rumble and another pop from below. She removes her hand swiftly, mechanic fingers tapping on the floor.

Josephine pushes past her to look into the hole. "That's done it," she says with satisfaction before glancing at Joseph. "Hasn't it?"

"That should be it," he agrees. "Now it will let you rise higher. It should be enough to get you all the way to the city."

"Excellent. All right. I have some plans to make so everyone out of the engine room, please." She shoos us out and closes the door behind us.

"Hey!" I bang on the door. "What about helping us taking all this stuff up there?"

"Of course, of course," she calls back. "Go ahead and get it loaded, aye? I have to fix these wires."

"Aye, Captain." I salute the door with a rude gesture, eying Copper Betty and Joseph. "Go ahead and wait on deck," I tell Joseph. "Copper Betty and I will handle the rest." The Meridian looks relieved and retreats above deck. I incline my head at the automaton. "Come on, then."

Haru and Rosa are helping to load the last box onboard. I'm stretching, my thoughts turning over and over as I try to determine my next steps. I've collected what I can down here, and I'm running out of time. With any luck the Chancellor will have found something from the High Inquestor we can use.

I count on my fingers. I've been here three days. Has Lucian found anything disputing the marriage contract yet? Am I missing anything?

Agitated, I pace back and forth inside the foyer of the Mother Clock. I've locked the elevator that leads to d'Arc's lab. There isn't anything of any real value left, but that doesn't mean I want random people squatting down there, either. It's a piece of the past that maybe should be left alone for now.

"Oy! Magpie? Are you inside?" Tin Tin's shout pulls me from my thoughts.

"Aye," I call back, heading outside and locking the door to the Mother Clock. "Time to go?" The airship is moored off the clock tower, and I go to climb the ladder.

"Wait. This arrived for you." Tin Tin clutches a piece of wrapped parchment delicately tied together with a bit of silk ribbon, the d'Arc crest stamped upon the back, along with a small sketch of a salmon. "Can't read," he complains. "But a messenger near Market Square gave this to me. Said it's from the Chancellor."

I grunt, undoing the bow with a snap of my fingers. "I'm not exactly expecting anything, but it looks like Lucian sent it." I lift my shirt where a matching salmon is tattooed upon my side. "It's his bonewitch mark."

Unsealing the parchment, I scan it multiple times, struggling to comprehend the floral script.

You are cordially invited to the wedding between the Houses of d'Arc and Tantaglio. Given the short notice, gifts are neither needed nor requested; however, there will be a masked ball the night before, held at the Tantaglio estate in the Third Tower. We look forward to your attendance.

Beneath this, Lucian has scribbled an additional note:

Perhaps you wouldn't mind forwarding this along to a certain mutual friend who is most likely interested in attending?

Your servant,
Lucian d'Arc

I read it again and then crumple it into my pocket.

"What is it?" Josephine calls from the top of the ladder. She clambers down gracefully, her crimson leather boots shining smartly in the sun.

"Wedding invitation. My own problem, I know. You don't really want to hear about it." I bite down on the inside of my cheek.

"That's pretty ballsy—to send it to you here. Surely there must be something else to it?" She pulls the note from my pocket and unfolds it. "Does it say who it's from? Oh…Lucian? Why would he send you this?"

"He sent it to Chancellor Davis. She sent it on to me, obviously. There wasn't supposed to be a marriage yet," I fume. "They gave me a week to find evidence, and same with Lucian and Ghost to find proof that there wasn't even a legitimate contract. Maybe they're trying to move up the timetable. And what is this nonsense about a masked ball?" I try to remember exactly what the Council said, but I don't think there was anything about that.

"They're probably being watched," she says. "This may have been the only way of letting you know how things are going. Anything else was sure to be intercepted, especially coming down here." Our eyes meet. "I think this is your sign to get your ass back up to Meridion."

"I thought you said you didn't care about this stuff?" I cross my arms, unconvinced by her sudden burst of altruism.

"I don't, technically. But you do." She snorts. "Plus, this gives me another excuse to go with you and check things out for myself. That's really my main motivation."

I pinch the bridge of my nose. For half a heartbeat I thought I might be able to do this without having everything implode around me. "There are no rooftops to sneak in on. I've never even been to any of the Five Towers, either, let alone that particular estate." I take the invite back from her. "And it's a pretty good bet they won't let me in, even if I *have* one of these."

"Sounds like you're giving up," Bran rumbles from behind me.

I startle at the sound of his voice, whirling to see him heading toward us, the rest of our little clan in tow. "I'm not giving up. I'm trying to figure out the best way to go about it is all. And where have you been all this time?"

I don't ask him about Alora, and he shakes his head at me when I open my mouth again. "Out," he says finally.

Josephine doesn't bat an eye, rubbing her chin. "Seems to me you've been in this position before," she points out. "Or was that story about sneaking into Balthazaar's estate dressed like a whore merely made up? At this rate, rescuing your lover is becoming a bit of a pattern."

I scowl at her. "That wasn't even my plan. That was all Molly Bell. And he's not asking me to rescue him. But that doesn't mean I want to sit here and do nothing. What about your wings? Tin Tin's been using them, I hear… Assuming you have a set to spare?"

She ponders this. "I might. I might not. I'm constantly refining them, but they're dodgy. Given the tightness of your schedule, I'm not sure you're going to have the time you need for more than a quick lesson. And up there? If you fall, there's no coming back."

"Already done that," I say. "But I see your point."

Josephine nods. "And I don't mind smuggling, Mags. People or products. But until I get a real feel for navigating up there, I won't be much help. The last thing I want to do is fly blind." She arches a brow at me. "That's how people get caught, you know."

"They don't seem to have much petty crime," I say. "They're like overstuffed sheep: they don't even know what a wolf looks like, let alone how to run from it. I suspect if we move fast enough, they won't know how to deal with it. And by then, we'll be—"

I pause. Where would we be? Even if I did manage to snag Ghost, where would we go? I let out a groan of desperate frustration. I'm running out of time.

"It *is* okay to ask for help, you know," Bran says.

Behind him, my other clanmates nod, and my heart stutters. "I didn't think you'd be interested," I say, unsure of his offer after everything we talked about. "I figured the last thing you'd want is to go up to Meridion."

"Maybe I need to confront some things." His smile grows crooked. "I may need you to…help me. I'm not much good with heights."

"And why wouldn't we help Ghost? He's one of us, aye? He came down to the Pits to help free us. The least we can do is free him." Gloriana's voice is trembling, and I wipe away a sudden rush of tears.

"Besides," Rosa adds, smirking, "he can do so much better."

The group of us erupts into giggles at that, a soft, pattering laughter that we instinctively keep low. Voices echoed in the Pits so we learned quickly to keep sound to a minimum, though I look forward to the day when we might shout freely.

"Is this a costume party or what?" My little clan and I are camped out on the rooftops near Market Square, watching the hustle and bustle of the BrightStone townsfolk making their way about their business. Josephine said she'd wait to hear the plan before determining what she would do, promising to look into the wings in the meantime. Flying or not, I needed to keep all my options open.

I shrug at Haru. "That's what the invitation says, but it's not exactly like we're really invited. I mean, yes, I have the invitation, but…"

"Well, if we all wear masks, it will be harder for them to spot us," he says.

"Except for the glowing hair and eyes," I point out. "Besides, we don't have the lightning skin of Meridians. They'll figure it out pretty quick, I'm guessing." My fingers tap restlessly on my leg as I puzzle it out.

"I hope they have good wine," Bran says plaintively. "At the very least."

"It will be the best you've ever tasted," I assure him. "I don't even know what counts as a good vintage up there, but everything I've had is miles beyond the pig swill we stole from Buceph."

He grunts. "So what do we do, then?"

"Maybe we don't try to hide ourselves at all. I mean, they're going to know what we are as soon as we show up. Maybe we'll simply be our own costumes." I chew on the inside of my cheek. "That's what Molly Bell had me do when we went to Balthazaar's estate to rescue Ghost. She hid me as part of a group of her whores, all of us dressed like Moon Children."

"I'm not fucking anyone for money," Bran snarls.

I wave him off. "That's not what I mean. Though I'm sure some of the ladies up there would find you an exotic enough conquest. But Molly owes me. If anyone is going to be able to help us pull this off quickly, it will be her." High fashion aside, the woman knows how to hide things. Her girls are masters at it—weapons, sleeping powder, ways to escape situations that would be most unpleasant, even given the circumstances of their chosen line of work. There isn't any reason she can't help us do the same.

"We're going in disguise?" Dafydd asks, frowning.

"Not exactly." I chew on my lower lip. "Meridians don't know Moon Child history well—they've certainly heard of the Tithes but knowing and seeing one are two very different things. We'll go as a Tithe."

The group of them still, frozen for a moment as they mull it over. "It makes sense," Gloriana says, her voice trembling. "Masks, cloaks, bells…"

"We'd be covered up," Dafydd agrees. "And if we had to escape, they'd be less likely to know who was who. Might buy us some time if we have to take Ghost with us."

"And then what, oh intelligent one? Run through the streets with him? It's not exactly like they don't know where he lives," Rosa points out. "It's a giant floating city. They'd be bound to catch us sooner or later."

"I'll bet on later. I was gone for what, several days? No one found me until you lot came looking. That doesn't speak too well of their surveillance abilities." I pause, thinking of IronHeart deep within the city, the beginnings of a plan starting to take shape. The dragon and her drones have a bead on the pulse of the city—surely she might be convinced to use them in an effort to protect her son? At the very least, we could take refuge beneath the LightHouse—I have no doubt she would do anything to keep her lair secret.

"Sure, we rescue him from the terrors of marriage and whatnot, but Mags, if we do this, you can kiss all that work you've done goodbye. They're not exactly going to welcome us for it." Gloriana stares up at Meridion and sighs.

I lean against the chimney, my eyes closing briefly. "Or maybe we'll draw attention to our situation. So far, the Council seems content to simply sweep me under the rug. If we make a big enough stink so that the citizens see us? *Really* see us? Maybe we'll be able to get some support from them."

"Maybe," she says, clearly unconvinced.

I understand her hesitation. I've been walking on eggshells in Meridion simply to try to fit in, to keep from messing up things for Lucian and Ghost. But how long will I continue to twist in the wind without making decisions for myself? I'm still angry about being shut out of whatever shady conversation Lucian had with Lottie's family. I'm sure he did it to protect me, and perhaps this way it's easier for me to move about. After all, if he is so dismissive of me, why would they pay me any mind at all?

But it still hurts.

"This dance isn't ours," I say aloud. "It never was. BrightStone and Meridion have seen to that. And I'm not sure we'll be able to learn the steps."

"Then we change the tune," Dafyyd says softly.

"Aye." I nod. "And we'll do it our way."

Although surprised to see me back so soon, the shark's grin becomes wide enough to gobble me up when I throw a handful of Meridian chits on her desk.

"We'll have to work fast. You'll need the basics of suits and dresses for beneath the cloaks, to start with," Molly Bell says, her eyes darting about the lot of us, lingering on Bran and Dafyyd. "And I'm not sure what I have that might fit the boys, especially the little one there." She points at Haru. To his credit, he doesn't flinch before her focus, but I suppose after living in the Pits filled with Rotters, it's hard to be afraid of the living.

"I don't care. I'm paying you more than enough. Hire additional seamstresses if you have to, but the sooner this is done, the better. It doesn't have to be completely perfect, aye?"

"Of course it does," she insists. "If you're going to do this, you need to do it right." She looks at us critically. "And the first thing you each need is a damn bath. I'll have your measurements taken after, so head down to my bathhouse." She frowns, looking at Bran's hair. "I suppose a haircut wouldn't be amiss, either."

He steps away from her. "The hells I'm going to let the Shark of BrightStone near me with scissors."

She grins, her laughter bubbling around us in dark delight. "Oh, it won't be me, dear. I'll send the hairdresser down to assist with that. Now if you'll excuse me, I've got some other business to attend to. You remember where the baths are?"

"Aye." I'd taken several there during my previous stay—not always willingly—but I trust her to know what she is about with this particular task, and the group of us troops down the back stairwell to the bathhouse.

It's as large as I remember, with benches and steam rooms, piles of towels and bars of scented soap. If there were any of her working girls here before, there aren't any now, and I can only hope that we won't be disturbed. Not that any of us care about being seen naked, but I don't want to be gawked at any more than I already am.

We strip easily enough, clothing lying wherever it's dropped. Haru and Dafyyd dive straight in, the rest of us taking our time to enter carefully. I avoid submerging my heart panel, choosing to sit on the steps, relaxing into the swirling waters. Rosa is washing Gloriana's hair, Haru and Dafyyd splashing in a sort of unmitigated glee.

And Bran sits on a bench, a towel wrapped around his waist. In the Pits, fresh water was at a premium and usually saved for drinking. The waterfall was there if you wanted to splash your face or soak your clothes, but it was bitterly cold and certainly not something to routinely bathe in. The lake by the Rotter village stank, and we rarely went there, anyway. To now enjoy the luxury of a large bathing area where we could take care of one another as a clan, as something close to normal, well I suppose that is overwhelming enough by itself.

I beckon to him, drawing him into the tub beside Rosa. He removes his towel, and the scars rivering over his body tell a tragic story that echoes mine. We all have them. He soaps up and crosses to the other side where the boys are, throwing the bar in their direction.

Rosa giggles, even as I pour a bucket of water atop my own head. The heat sinks into my bones, past the sting of old hurts, the pink tone of scars. Sometimes it's hard not to look at them and be transported to that time, each mark, each tattoo a piece of my story.

Rosa snickers at me. "You've got some mosquito bites on your shoulder, aye?"

I cough. Evidence of Ghost and his enthusiasm the other night, for sure. I'm certain there are more, but I don't dignify her laughter with a response. A twinge of melancholy hits me all the same, and I wonder what Ghost is doing now.

"I hate this." I became so used to having him with me the last month or so that to be separated over such ridiculous things irritates me to no end.

"You're allowed," Gloriana says airily. "But we'll get him back, aye?"

My jaw sets. "We better."

The fitting room Molly has set up is a monstrosity of dresses, cloth, mirrors, and people. Most of the other Moon Children are leaning up against the wall, either waiting for to be measured or being seen to by the house beautician.

In this case, it's Bran's turn. He stares at his own reflection sourly as the stylist snips his tangled hair with practiced ease. After she struggled to get a comb through it, it was agreed by everyone that a simple cut would be best.

Everyone but Bran, that is.

He looks down at the swiftly growing pile of hair mournfully, but even he admits he looks better. Freshly trimmed and shaved, his hair has a tousled look, cut so short it barely scrapes the nape of his neck.

He turns his head back and forth as though trying to get used to the difference in weight, rubbing the back of his neck self-consciously. "Now what?"

"Now we wait until they've had time to sew our costumes," I remind him. "And we'll have masks made, too. They won't be perfect, but I think they'll do well enough, given the time constraints. We don't have the capacity to match the sort of clothes the Meridians deem fashionable. They think us savages anyway—it won't matter what we do, in that respect."

"If you say so," he mutters. "But I always thought we *were* savages. At least a little."

"That's the costume part." I waggle my brows at him.

He says nothing else, just snags a bottle of whisky from the liquor cabinet on the far wall and retreats to where Haru and Dafyyd are getting their own haircuts.

In the end, we've cleaned up nicely, our ragged hair smooth and gleaming, the dirt wiped off our faces. My fingers are still somehow permanently hard, the nails worn down to the quick, but that comes with the territory of living underground, I suppose.

Molly Bell sweeps in once or twice to see how things are going, making biting remarks and quick adjustments to the clothing. At one point she sends up a tray of biscuits, which we all devour quickly.

After that, there's nothing left to do but wait, and I find myself in a pile with the others in a corner. Bran is snoring quietly, his head in Rosa's lap as she leans against Gloriana. Haru is half-curled into my side, and Dafyyd's sprawled carelessly in front of us, his arms and legs stretched out as though he's flying.

I watch the seamstresses bustle about, lulled by the hypnotic pull of the thread through the cloth, the snips, the chalk scent, and the soft chattering of their voices as they worked. How long has it been since Lucian, disguised as Martika, did the same for me?

It feels like ages, though it was only a little over a year. Whatever I thought life would be like at this point, this isn't it. Restless, I carefully extricate myself from the others and slip out of the room and into the hall. From below I can hear the sounds of merrymaking. Memories of another time flood back to me, leaving me melancholy.

I hesitate and then head up the back stairs to the upper landing. Molly's personal quarters are down below, if I recall, but my room was here, as well as Ghost's room and Lucian's secret lab where he'd been growing Rot in rats to search for a cure.

I haven't been back here since I was Tithed, I realize, and the thought strikes me through the gut as every little creak in the stairs rings hollow and familiar all at once. I find myself swallowing a deep lump in my throat. How much have I given up from here? How much have I gained? Do I even want to revisit this place at all?

Shadows upon shadows of memories. Ghost teaching me to read. Lucien scolding me for stealing his whisky again. Molly Bell dying my hair. Copper Betty serving us soup. Even the stale scent of the worn carpets and the tapestries on the walls mock me.

The one that hid Lucien's room is gone, the door standing openly. I pause outside it but head toward Ghost's room instead. The door is unlocked, and I pop my head in, looking at the single bed and the old bookshelf.

How many hours had I spent in here, crouched over a book with Ghost helping me to sound out the words? How many times had he talked me down from my fights with Lucian? Encouraged me to think past the immediacy of my own situation?

The bookshelf is bare, as though Molly simply emptied everything that would indicate anyone had lived there. I turn away and head to my own room, though I'm honestly not sure I want to see it at all. That part of my life is closed, and going back to look at it is simply a way to reopen old hurts. Perhaps the truth of it is that I am angry, that I've been eating the poison of a great deal of repressed fury.

Despair at the loss of Sparrow, at being forced into positions not of my choosing again and again until I was forced to sacrifice myself without truly understanding the loss of any innocence I'd had left. It's a type of grief, maybe. One that might never be healed, no matter what else I am asked to do or where I might go.

Yet, I press into the room anyway. My own bed is still there, as is the chair Lucian often sat in, the scuffmark on part of the hardwood where I stabbed a pencil in frustration, and the fireplace with its ornate mantle. My dragon perched there most nights, watching everything.

It seems less romantic now, realizing that IronHeart was essentially spying on us, but still. I cross the room in an instant, opening the window so that the cool breeze blows in. It stinks of rusty fog, but I don't care.

I still, as though somehow I might retreat to that simpler time. A hint of movement catches in the corner of my vision, a bit of parchment blowing in the draft from the window. It's half-trapped beneath a stone on the hearth of the fireplace.

I kneel to gently pull it away, rubbing off a bit of soot from the back of the folded-up scrap of paper. I turn it over to get a better look at it, and I let out a soft sound when I open it.

It's a charcoal sketch…of me.

My edges are soft and blurry, and I'm sitting on the overstuffed chair, my legs curled beneath me, eyes drawn to the window with a wistful expression, the dragon on my shoulder. *Magpie's Lament,* reads the inscription at the top in large scrawling letters. And then, far beneath that, in Ghost's elegant hand, are the simple words, *I miss you.*

I close my eyes as something breaks inside me, a wailing loss that I can't hold back anymore. I let out a sob, sinking to my knees, and I weep, huge ugly tears that half roll into my mouth. For who I was, for what I've become, for who I am now. For what I've been forced to give up. For what I won. For what I lost. For what I found.

My body shakes with it, and I can't help making a silent scream into my shoulder, though what I truly want is to shout it out to the world. But my grief isn't for anyone else. Not yet. So I bend my head, the quivering wave crashes over me again and again until a hazy calm reaches me. My eyes are burning and my vision blurs, but I don't mind.

An awkward scuff behind me has me whirling. It's Bran, and his alarmed expression at whatever I look like makes me laugh despite myself. "Ah, you seem busy," he mumbles. "I woke up and you were missing so I thought I'd come look. I can go."

"It's all right." I stand up, carefully refolding the parchment and pocketing it. I don't offer to show it to him. It's a private message from Ghost to me, and that's as far as it needs to go for now. "I needed to be alone."

"Understood." He glances at the window. "Come on. I want to show you something." Without really waiting for me, he squeezes through the opening and up the brickwork. I follow suit, curious.

"What are we doing?" I ask when we reach the roof. As tired as I am, the siren song of the night air coaxes me forward to run over the rooftops, making mischief wherever I can find it.

The breeze sweeps past me, cooling and fresh. I've shed the fancy clothes and shoes like a snake sheds its skin, and my eyes glitter as we stare over the lights of BrightStone, winking like stars in the mist.

"You'll see." He scans the buildings as though trying to find directions. The quiet of the city hits me then, in the predawn hours when there's no one around at all. "This way."

He takes off, not as fast as me nor as quiet as Ghost, but he maneuvers over the roofs with a smooth and graceful strength. In the Pits, there wasn't any room to really open up like this, but we do now, the roof tiles blurring beneath our feet. I nearly laugh aloud at it, but I'm dodging chimneys and window dormers, pipes and wires and clotheslines strung like the damp webs of deranged spiders. When we reach what's left of the Warrens and its ocean of crumbling buildings, I'm out of breath, the toll of the last few days finally catching up to me.

Bran seems no worse for wear, his stamina continuing to be a thing of impressive beauty.

I frown at him. "So why are we here? It's mostly empty, isn't it?"

"Precisely." He shuffles around a pile of broken beams and fallen bricks until he pulls out a large burlap sack. Undoing the drawstring, he pulls away the cloth to reveal a pair of Josephine's wings. He tosses the harness at me. "Shall we fly?"

"Head down, arms out," Bran warns me. "Watch your balance when you take off. These new sets have been adjusted for greater weights, but they're still not particularly stable. That ground comes up awful fast when you're hurtling toward it."

"How long have you been using these?" I ask him, shifting beneath the weight of the wings. They're stiff, as though they're meant more for gliding than actual flying, but I can't keep the grin off my face all the same.

"Not long." He slides into another pair. "This was the original set. You've got the one Josephine modified. Should be easier for you."

"You're an expert, then, aye?"

Now it's his turn to smile. "Well, I haven't died yet, so that's good enough. You ready?"

I crouch, my legs bunched beneath me as I suck in a deep breath, leaning over the edge of the building. The ground seems to wobble, or maybe that's just me. "One… Two…"

"Three!" Bran shouts, pushing me over as he leaps beside me.

I let out a partial shriek, swallowing it hard as I plummet. I find the handles of the wings, grasping tightly as they even out, catching the breeze as I suddenly launch up, flattening into a smooth glide.

"You're an arse," I snap, trying not to puke as he levels out beside me.

He laughs. "Of course I am. But now the worst part is over. You won't hesitate next time. Better to get it out of the way."

"Assuming there will ever be a next time," I mutter. "Where are we going?"

"Anywhere as long as you stay in the air. Maybe head back toward the Conundrum. We'll have to be there soon anyway," he points out. "But practice a little first."

"Such wise words." I bank suddenly as a building emerges from the shadows. Inside, my stomach rolls and flips as I rise up and then down, learning how to maneuver. The wings are masterpieces of beauty. However Josephine figured out the physics of the things, the intricately carved feathers, the little engine in the back to give me thrust…

"I could stay up here forever," I shout at Bran.

He rolls his eyes. "You say that now. Just wait until you accidentally fly into a storm or a gust of wind. The ground isn't that forgiving."

"Speaking of which, where do we land?" I scan the buildings below us.

"Anyplace with a flat enough roof. The ground if you have to, but it's a pain to climb in these." He grunts. "Just try not to land in the water. You'll probably die of dysentery if you get any in your mouth."

I shudder, well aware of this fact. I avoided any bodies of water in BrightStone as much as possible when I was living here. It isn't water so much as a living sewer sludge, full of oil and shite and rusted filth.

"How do we slow down?" My body is rolling back and forth as I try to keep upright, the Mother Clock sweeping into view like some great and terrible eye watching us, watching me. A hysterical giggle threatens to erupt from my mouth because it did, didn't it? In its own way, always watching, always…

"Pay attention, idiot!" Bran nearly slams into me as I suddenly rise, caught on an updraft. His wings scrape against mine and send me into a spiral until his hand snatches at my ankle. "Steady yourself," he calls.

I veer off, wobbling for a moment before finding my balance. I would have liked to enjoy my moment of flight—or controlled falling or whatever it is we are doing—for longer, but then the Conundrum is below us. We bank sharply as I attempt to figure out how to land.

"Put your legs down," Bran snaps. "You can slow down on the rooftops as you run. Otherwise, you'll destroy the wings and break your hips. And that's before Josephine gets a hold of you."

I do as he says, letting the drag slow me down a pinch, my feet reaching for the shingles as gingerly as I might. I laugh as I make contact, pumping my calves as I leap from one roof to the other. Rooftop dancing in truth, but eventually, even the wings slow down enough that I make proper contact. I'm panting, the soles of my feet burning as I stretch my legs and shift within the harness. It's digging into my hips, and I wriggle back and forth.

Bran lands nearby, wiping sweat from his brow with the back of his hand. "You're ridiculous, you know that? Did you listen to *anything* I said up there before we launched?"

"Clearly not," I say, finally getting the wings to fold in properly so they aren't sticking out.

He lets out an exasperated grumble. "You need your brain examined. That's always been your problem, Mags. You're never in the moment, always daydreaming about some point in the future. It's going to get you killed one day, never mind your erstwhile lover up there."

I flush. "I'm sorry."

"Don't be. You did well. Well enough for an escape or two," he notes. His eyes track skyward toward the floating city.

I nod slowly, understanding his meaning. "Hopefully no one will realize what they are when I'm wearing them."

"Just another bit of our costume, aye?" He half smiles before something grim takes hold of his mouth. "Mags. I've got a favor to ask of you. You're not going to like it."

"That doesn't sound suspicious at all." The hairs on the back of my neck stand at attention, and I poke my finger at him. "One clan leader to another, don't bullshit me."

He sighs. "Not a clan leader thing. And I don't need you to do it now. I don't know when it will be. Soon. But please. Promise me."

It's on the tip of my tongue to say no. I should say no. But I can count on one hand the number of times Bran has ever asked me for something. That he's doing so now can only mean it's important. And one look at his face shows me a miserable anguish that he even has to reach out to me for help at all.

"If it's within my ability," I say. "But Bran—"

He holds up his hand. "Consider the wings as payment. Josephine owes me, so now they're yours." I'm more confused than before, but I can tell he's not going to give me any more information right now. Instead, we climb down, the wings folded neatly on our backs.

They're too large to fit in the window so we go all the way to the alley, and I lead him in the back door. It's the spot where Sparrow was shot, but I don't allow myself to dwell on that.

Another day, perhaps.

We creep up the back stairs to the room where the seamstresses are finishing up their work. The rest of our clan is still fast asleep. I join them a moment later, watching them as though I might keep them safe. Leadership is full of such worries, it seems, but I don't mind. Beyond all expectations, we are here and we are alive and I hold to that, ignoring the river of worry that ripples beneath my pride.

Before long, I start to nod off myself, drifting away beneath a blanket of soft murmurs and quiet hope.

A mask of silk and a face of stone,
Mine to wear upon a throne.
But which is real and which is fake?
The truth is in the choice I make.

— CHAPTER EIGHTEEN —

Dawn is barely creeping over the skyline when the tired women finish, their eyes weary and watering. Molly clucks in satisfaction when she sees the completed work, tugging at hems as she ensures everything fits properly.

Black silk. Crimson lace. A smattering of bells upon a velvet string. The porcelain masks of plain white. A part of me shudders, looking at them. I'd worn the real thing once when I was Tithed. We all had, leading the Rotters to the Pits in their cloaks of white.

To wear them to a costume party feels like we're mocking our past, but from a practical standpoint, they will be useful. If we need to run away, no one will know which one of us to chase. Beneath the robes are simple, well-made dresses and suits—nothing that would compete with the Meridians, of course, but enough to be presentable.

"There now. That will make a proper sort of entrance." Molly runs a finger over the shoulders of Haru's costume, and her mouth widens in pleasure. "I wish I could be there to see it."

"You'll be there in spirit," I say, rolling my eyes.

She lets out a burbling laugh that runs down my spine. "Do make sure to give Lucian and Ghost my best, won't you?"

I make a noncommittal noise as we pack up the costumes, the masks, and the makeup Molly has given us. Not that I know much about how to put it on, but Rosa seems to have that part well under control, and I'm just as happy to leave it to her.

Rubbing my eyes, I gesture at the others, and we slip out the back door of the brothel and down the alleyways. We stick to the shadows for now, the bags hanging heavy on our shoulders.

"There are probably worse fates than being wed to a rich Meridian," Bran points out carefully as we walk. "It's not too late to change your mind."

"If it's what Ghost wanted, what he *truly* wanted, I wouldn't be doing any of this," I say, trying to believe my own words and failing utterly. "I'd be sad, of course, and confused. But it's not. He came down to the Pits to rescue me, even after everyone else assumed all hope was lost. This is the absolute least I can do."

He nods, his eyes dropping to where my hammer sits at my waist. "I just wanted to be sure. And if things should…escalate?" The word hangs in a distasteful way, though I know what he's asking.

"I suspect violence would not help our cause. We should avoid it, if we can—but I'm not going to let them take us, either, so we do what we have to." My fingers trace the edge of the hammer at my hip thoughtfully.

"All right, then. As long as you're sure, I'm with you." He shifts his shoulders, fists raised as though imagining punching someone.

"Mags!" Josephine whistles to us from her airship, which is currently docked in the Meridian port at the Cheaps. Although the Cheaps is more like a bay-facing shanty town, it was the most logical place to set up an actual airship dock, as well. The Meridian soldiers who have been coming to and fro to help BrightStone with the cleanup are using it almost exclusively, even if outright tourism is currently forbidden.

Seeing Meridian airships isn't unusual—the Inquestors had them, after all—but how long will it take before the soldiers realize it's being manned by Moon Children?

I still have Fionula's scroll tucked away in my shoulder bag, though in this case, I'm not sure what the protocol will be if we're taking our own airship. Josephine and I argued about it, of course. And on one hand, I agreed that sneaking up under cover of darkness might have been the more prudent option—but I didn't know Meridian laws. What if they shot us down?

I shiver. No. We would at least try the legitimate channels first. If that fails, we'll do it more covertly. The group of us climb the gangplank to Josephine's Interceptor. Copper Betty and Joseph are already here.

I've barely put set foot on the deck before the Meridian soldiers wave us down. "You don't have permission to dock here. Official Meridian ships only."

I head back down the gangplank, digging Fionula's scroll from my shoulder bag. With any luck this would be enough. "By order of Lady Fionula, Meridian liaison to BrightStone. It grants me the right of passage to and from Meridion." I'm half bluffing as I hand it to the guard at the main port kiosk, and I can tell by his expression it's not going to be enough. The scroll gives me permission to fly back to Meridion as needed, but it doesn't apply to other Moon Children, old Meridians, or sentient automatons, he points out, and it sure as hell doesn't apply to stolen Inquestor airships with tampered engines.

The guard keeps looking at the scroll and shaking his head, even when I slide a healthy number of Meridian chits over to him. His eyes bug out for half a moment, and he stares at me. He's trying to place who I am and if I'm someone important, but he can't quite do it.

"I'm sorry," he says at last, refusing the chits. "But rules are rules, and I can't simply—"

"Excuse me, is there a problem here?" Chancellor Davis strides toward us, flanked by a number of BrightStone guards and valets, her sensible face clearly indicating that she expects an answer. She's dressed smartly in an exquisite emerald suit that shimmers when she walks, her hair perfectly curled beneath a fancy feathered hat.

The guard gapes. "I'm sorry, ma'am, but they're seeking passage to Meridion. It's against regulations."

"Ahem." Chancellor David glares at me. "Why didn't you tell him you're part of my retinue, you stupid girl?" My head snaps back as though she's slapped me, but she presses forward, displaying a copy of the wedding invitation I was given yesterday. "As you can see, I've been personally invited to attend the nuptial celebration of Trystan d'Arc and the House of Tantaglio."

The Meridion lets out a curious cough as though he isn't quite sure what to make of it.

"The children of d'Arc and I have worked together for many years." The Chancellor's lips compress, and she gestures to Josephine's ship. "I chartered this ship to ensure that the entirety of my retinue may safely travel between cities with minimum disruption to your schedule."

The guard blinks. "Ah, I see. But this is very unusual, Madam Chancellor. I wasn't told about any of this."

The Chancellor smiles broadly, in a manner that very much reminds me of Molly Bell's sharp-toothed grin. "And why would you be, my good man? This is clearly an event for the elite. And as I've already mentioned, this lout was supposed to have told you up front. My apologies for the confusion."

I swallow a sneer and bow my head. "Aye, Madam Chancellor."

The guard hesitates. "Well, she did have a scroll from Lady Fionula," he admits. "I'll let it slide this once, but in the future, please try to remain within the proper protocols. The rules are made to protect everyone..."

I take the moment to retreat back to the airship, leaving the Chancellor to deal with the niceties of the situation. I'd feel guilty about it, but her little play act leaves me more than certain she can handle this on her own.

Joseph is on the prow, watching the goings on with a bemused air. "Odd to think I'll be going home today," he says finally, pulling the brim of his hat down like a turtle hiding in its shell.

Bran is side-eying the Meridian with disdain, but he says nothing. It's not something I want to get between. There is far too much history there, and whether Joseph was responsible or not, he certainly had been part of the awfulness down in the Pits. I can't hold it against Bran to feel as he does. As the others do. All I can do is try to hold them together as best I can.

Still, I'll be a bit more relieved once we reach the comparative roominess of the airship, if only so I can distance myself from the powder keg I'm sitting on. But for now, I'll bite my tongue and stare out at the scenery.

Chancellor Davis strolls up the gangplank with her retinue trailing behind her. "Permission to come aboard?"

Josephine emerges from belowdecks, her gaze darting between the Chancellor and me. "Something I should know?"

"My paperwork didn't pan out. The Chancellor is why we're being allowed to leave," I say. "I suggest we let her board before the Meridians get wise to the whole thing, aye?"

"In the future, you might want to run this sort of thing by way of the ship's captain before allowing passengers. Airships are tricky, and I need to make sure the weight is evenly distributed." She tips her hat at the Chancellor with a tight grimace. "Permission granted."

"Thank you," the Chancellor says as she and her people file into the ship. "I wasn't actually looking forward to being forced to utilize the Meridian ships." She smiles, glancing around. "This should do nicely."

"I wasn't aware we were available for charter," Josephine says bluntly.

"Of course you are," Chancellor Davis says, her pleasant smile growing stiff. "I'll ensure Moon Children have a seat at the next BrightStone council meeting with a proposal to make it permanent. Plus, this will give you an excuse to be up in Meridion. I suspect they won't look so kindly on Moon Children flying about in stolen property."

Josephine pulls out a pipe and a lucifer. She lights it and takes a drag as she mulls it over. I can't tell how seriously she's taking the offer, but she nods, puffing out a ring of smoke. "Agreed. Now can we get this carnival moving? I'd like to see Meridion before I'm dead of old age."

We make for an odd caravan on the trip back to the d'Arc residence. Seven Moon Children with pale hair and dark glasses, an automaton pulling a little cart full of papers, and an old Meridian who hasn't been to the floating city in nearly twenty years.

Josephine left with the Chancellor once she dropped us off at the main docking station to the city, presumably to take her to whatever quarters she would be staying in. But I know from the faraway expression in Josephine's eyes that she'll be taking notice of how everything in this city runs.

"Looks like we may have lost our ride to the ball," I murmur as the airship drifts away. Pure rapture shines on Josephine's face as she shouts orders to the other Moon Children she has on as crew.

"At least the removal of the governor worked," Joseph notes. "To be honest, I wasn't completely sure if we had gotten the right component. It would have been rather unfortunate to have the engine seize up partway here." I cough abruptly, and he chuckles. "I jest, Magpie."

Despite his amusement, a hint of melancholy lingers about him as we walk toward the d'Arc house. How much has the city changed, I wonder, since he was sent down below with the other Meridian scientists, eager and bright and set to fix the problem of the Rot?

And now, he is the only one left.

Even knowing he has returned, I'm not sure he will ever fit back in with the rest of his people. The Pits leave scars that can't always been seen, and he was weighed down by more secrets than anyone had any right to bear. But he says nothing and simply drifts along as part of the group, still wearing that ridiculous floppy hat and wrapped in his own silent thoughts.

Bran's expression wavers between awe and panic, and occasionally a bit of terror. The others have already been here, and they surely find the city less imposing this time.

"Do people always stare like that?" He shivers.

"Yes, they do. I don't think they see a lot of things that are 'different' up here. Anything that falls outside their rigid standards is automatically something to gawk at. It's not much different from BrightStone, really, but with less hatred. Or at least, less *open* hatred," I amend.

"Yeah, I'm sure getting poisoned was a step down for you," he says dryly.

"Point taken. I don't know. It's mostly harmless, from what I can tell. Ignore it."

"We should use it to our advantage," Rosa says, sniffing. "These people have no idea what we are or why we're here. We could turn things about. Imagine the rumors we could stir up!"

"Your willingness to control the narrative is admirable, but I suggest you focus on the task at hand. You'll do yourselves no favors now if what you desire is recognition by the Council." Joseph smiles faintly. "However intriguing your ideas are."

She huffs at him but says nothing after that, and we travel in silence until we reach d'Arc's house. *My home,* I think. But is it really?

The door locks are still engaged, so I quickly unlock them and usher everyone into the house as quickly as I can. The other Moon Children take Bran upstairs for a few minutes, and based on their giggles, they flee down to the kitchen after that, undoubtedly to raid the pantry.

There is no sign of Lucian, but a quick perusal through my room shows that my note to Ghost is missing so at least he got that. I poke my head into Lucian's room next. He's not here, but given the clothes strewn across his bed, I can only assume he's already left for the festivities at the Tantaglio estate. It's a bittersweet moment, but perhaps it is for the best that I don't see him until then.

Copper Betty and Joseph are still waiting in the foyer when I return downstairs.

I look at Copper Betty, wondering what she makes of all this. "Best to unload the information. Put it in Madeline's room for now. It's on the upper floor, the second door on the left. We'll sift through it later."

The automaton makes a sound that reminds me of a sigh but quickly sets about following my orders, dutifully hauling the boxes of evidence up the stairs.

Joseph eyes me uncertainly. "I should probably get out of your hair."

"Of course... You don't mind if we keep your research here? I mean, technically, it belonged to her, but..." I look at him, his eyes darting away miserably, and I let out a bitter chuckle. "It's Lucian, isn't it?" I ask softly. "You don't want to be here when he gets home."

"Not particularly, no," he admits. "This place holds a lot of memories for me, and many of them aren't good, especially the ones at the end."

"You're going to have to face him sooner or later," I point out. "I don't think Lucian will be overly concerned. He's rather pragmatic about this sort of thing."

Joseph looks doubtful. "I still need to take care of some business first. If I have any hopes of returning here permanently, there are things that need to be set in motion. Papers filed, that sort of thing. I need to see if I still have access to my family estate. To be honest, I'm not entirely sure I want to return so much. But maybe things on the Council have changed since I left."

I doubted that. Politics is politics, after all. Doesn't matter what side you're on, it's all shit and it all smells. It simply depends on how far away from the arsehole you are. Still, I don't voice any of this. "We'll be getting dressed shortly, and then the ball is a bit later so..."

"I'm certainly not attending that," he says, scandalized. "It definitely wouldn't be appropriate, given the circumstances. No, I'll be back in the morning after I've done what I need to do, and I'll organize those papers into something you can present to the Council to make your case." He rewards me with a half-smile.

"How can I reach you in case something comes up?" I frown as Copper Betty clanks down the stairs again, her blue eyes staring blankly at me.

Joseph pulls a notepad from his trouser pocket and quickly scratches out an address with a bit of charcoal. "This is the address to my family's apartments—the Trinity estate. Most likely you'll be able to reach me there, but the place is sure to be a bit of a mess. I doubt anyone's checked up on it in years. I was the last one, you see," he adds sadly.

He seems somehow frail when he says it, as though the weight of his years have crashed down on him all at once. I take the address from him, squinting at the writing. "I can send Copper Betty with you, if you like. She could maybe help with some basic cleaning or if you need something moved." I smile at her. "She's pretty strong, you know."

"I couldn't," he starts and then chuckles. "Well, maybe I could. I'm rather tired of dust, if you must know. Would it be all right?"

"I wouldn't have offered otherwise. This way I'll know she's safe with you and you're getting the help you need." I reach out to squeeze his shoulder. "I know things are strained between us—Moon Children's memories go back a ways—but you helped me when I needed it so the least I can do is the same."

Something softens in his face. "Then we'll be return in the morning, ready to go. The rest will be up to you."

"Is this on right?" I turn and turn, trying to gauge the way the corset is tied in the back, the ribbons trailing almost to my thighs. "I think it's wrong."

Rosa comes up behind me to make the adjustments, pulling it even tighter. I thank her and continue trying to wiggle my way into a set of hose. I've never liked the things. Hells, I've never liked any of these sorts of fashionable pieces.

"I feel like a sausage trapped in a casing," I say when I finally look at myself in the mirror, though I admit the effect is nice. Rosa's tied the ribbons into a series of artful bows that hang like a silk waterfall. Molly's ladies outdid themselves, especially given their limited time, the corset fitting snugly against me but not so tightly that I can't breathe.

And then, of course, there are the wings. Bran and I brought the set I'd practiced with. For now, I merely wear the harness as part of my dress. The wings are partially folded in, and whatever's left looks decorative and far too small for even a gliding flight. They remain a last resort, if there is no other way, though for now they'll be hidden beneath the crimson Tithe cloak.

A secret thrill runs through me all the same. But I have my clan at my back, and I can trust they will not betray me, armed with the knowledge that we will come up with a solution. There are too many unknowns to have a concrete plan in place—not until we get there and scope out the lay of the land, anyway.

The reality of such things is that plans never go as hoped, hence the contingency of my wings. Aside from that, if things really do go south, the others are to find their way back to BrightStone immediately, either through Josephine or whatever way they can find. At least there they can hide more reasonably, and I… Well, I would just have to wait and see. The Meridians already know who I am—revealing myself at the party won't hurt the others if they need a distraction to get away.

"You think this is going to work?" Bran nudges me away from the mirror so he can get a better look at himself. He cut a nice figure in his suit—lean and wiry with a hint of elegance. His eyes aren't any softer, though, and it is just as well they'll be hidden behind the glasses most of the time. Every bit of disdain he possesses sparkles from within those dark depths. Even a blind Meridian would know he isn't particularly sympathetic toward them, and that would ruin the illusion entirely.

"I don't really have room to think otherwise," I tell him. "The minute we lose our nerve, the whole thing will come crashing down. This is new territory for me, too." In some ways, it's even worse than the Pits. At least there I knew my station and how to survive.

Killing is terrible and easy, in its own way. Prancing before Meridian nobility in heels is another thing altogether.

My fingers smooth my skirts in nervous fashion. "Hopefully Lucian will lend us some support once he knows we're here."

Haru shrugs. "We'll do the best we can, aye?"

"Aye." I look at my reflection, hardly recognizing myself at all. Rosa has done all our makeup, my eyes kohled and my cheeks rouged, my lashes thick and silver. My dress is cerulean blue and cut so that the panel of my heart is displayed prominently.

I've always hidden it before, like a secret to protect, though I never knew why. But now they might as well come to terms with it, even as I am. It's a heady thought, but for the first time it's my decision to bare it.

At last, we're finished, adjusting our finery as we line up at the door, ready and nervous. Haru's raided the kitchen, casually munching on a dinner roll.

I envy his lack of concern. I've been unable to eat much of anything since we arrived at the house, and now the mere thought of it makes me wonder if I wouldn't simply burst out of this costume. I hand out the Tithe robes, and we carefully drape them over our eveningwear, making sure everything is hidden and attaching the bells to our wrists so they jangle with each move.

Gloriana looks as though she might be ill but gives me an encouraging smile. "I think it's time we reclaim this part of us," she says softly.

My throat grows tight at the sound, making it hard to swallow, and I try to ignore it even as I clutch the porcelain mask and trip on my heels as I try to walk toward the door. My little shoulder bag spills out onto the floor, and I scrabble to gather it all up.

I glance at the invitation a last time before tucking it neatly into the top of my bodice.

"This is on one of the Five Towers," I say. "We'll have to catch an airship. No chance at infiltrating the place directly."

"Ah well, we'll arrive in style and act like we belong." Gloriana frowns. "Hopefully they'll actually let us in."

"Aye," I agree. "It will be best if Ghost can make it plain enough that whatever this is, it's not going to happen. But if not…"

"We'll steal him away in romantic fashion." Rosa gives me a sideways glance.

"Aye," I say softly. "We will."

A dress of weeds and a feathered cap,
Spiderweb stockings and shoes of grass.
Silver armor, crystal traps,
And a hidden dagger made of glass.

— CHAPTER NINETEEN —

We traipse to the nearest airship station, our boots tapping lightly upon the street. Between our fashion, our hair, and our apparent lack of concern about either, we attract a fair amount of attention, but I find it bothers me less than it might have at one point. In any case, attracting attention is just fine by me. The more people who see us, the less the Council will be able to deny that we exist.

The airship platform is crowded, filled with clusters of evening revelers, many in exquisite gowns and elegant hairstyles. It almost seems as though half the city got an invite, but if this is as big a deal as I think it is, it makes sense.

As overwhelmed as the airships are, it's easy enough to board one among a cluster of partygoers. The group of us stick together as close as we can, bodies pressed up around us in a wave of perfumed laughter.

"Hells," Bran mutters as the airship lifts off.

I give him a sharp look. A thin bead of sweat breaks out over his forehead, but otherwise he's stone-faced. "It's a bit much." He points out one of the windows. "All these lights so far below."

"Mesmerizing, aye?" Rosa says, her eyes gleaming.

He shudders. "You know, there's probably such as thing as being too high."

"You should try falling off of it," I say, nudging him. "Whole different perspective."

He swallows and looks away. "No thanks."

I chuckle under my breath, watching as the Inner Spiral lights up beneath us in all its technicolor glory. The flow of airship traffic swerves around the LightHouse, heading for the Five Towers on the far side of the Inner Spiral. Close up, I can see they're massive with various landing areas and multiple tiers littered with magnificent estates, sweeping trees, and sparkling lights. It's like something out of a fairy story. I reach up and touch Sparrow's necklace, wishing she were here to see it.

I crane my neck, wondering if Josephine is in this group somewhere, ferrying the Chancellor here, as well. We haven't seen her since she dropped us off, so I can only hope she is managing all right. I say as much aloud.

"I don't think the issue is whether or not she crashes into something so much as if she decides to pirate other airships." Bran's mouth curls up in a bitter smile. "If you haven't realized, that Interceptor of hers was made to be much faster. This thing?" He knocks on the side of the hull. "It's just for hauling passengers. I doubt it would have the speed to escape if she simply decided to overtake it."

"It definitely doesn't have the…weaponry," Gloriana says, her voice lowering. "I'm fairly certain she's modified the Interceptor some since she took it."

I say nothing to this. The last thing I want is some sort of airship battle. That certainly won't do us any favors.

The airship is slowing now, gently descending toward what appears to be an enormous flower garden with a flat, circular stone area in the center. The airship heads for it and shudders when it touches the ground.

Some of the other passengers seem impressed at this, and I can only wonder what sort of riches it takes to have your own private landing area in your backyard.

A massive airship, larger than any of the taxis and fitted with colored lights and silver streamers, is moored just to one side of the landing area. "Looks like a marriage yacht or something," Gloriana notes. "Is that a piano on the deck?"

"That's probably the family airship," I say, my jaw setting tightly. Marriage yacht, indeed.

We alight from the taxi behind the other masses of people, placing our masks over our faces. They are all the same, pale and featureless, our mouths turned up in perfect smiles, our glowing hair hidden by our dark hoods, our eyes by the masks. As a group, I'm hoping the effect will be unsettling, the plain design at odds with the highly contrasting ones around us.

Ribbons, satins, precious gems, and gold and silver filigree. Masks that light up. Bird faces. Beast muzzles. Feathers and fur. Skin flashing with each smile, each laugh. Automatons moving quietly and efficiently around, serving drinks and small plates of exquisite-smelling food. It's a parade of clashing colors and noise that has me wincing beneath my mask, even as my mouth waters when a tray of candied figs wanders past.

But the stares coming our way are both curious and uncomfortable, and the crowd parts for us as we slip through in single file. Our bells jingle-jangle to announce our presence, the sound filling the quiet spaces between each careless conversation. For right now, we are clearly nothing more than a momentary diversion. And yet, for all our odd little procession attracts attention, we're carefully sizing up the hedges, the walls, the shadows—any spot that might be used as a hiding place or a way in or out of a particular area.

Bran is directly behind me and taps me on the shoulder. "Do you even know where you're going?"

"Of course not," I hiss, my words muffled by the mask. "It's not like I've ever been here you know. But—"

"Excuse me. This party is by invitation only." A man in the Tantaglio family livery raises his hand at us when we try to enter the gardens, where the main part of the party appears to be in full swing. I don't recognize him so much as the color of the uniform, which is the same as those of the servants who attended Lottie's family during the initial hearing—gold and green, with hints of crimson.

I pull the invitation from my bodice and hand it to him. It's crumpled, and he eyes it with displeasure. "This doesn't say you can bring a group with you. Invitations are for you and a partner. And your costumes are extremely…distasteful."

"We're entertainment," I say quickly, my brain trying to come up with a better reason for all of us to be here. I ignore Bran's snort, biting back the urge to kick him. Time to drop names. "Lucian and Trystan d'Arc hired us to put on a bit of a show for Lottie. Since their return from exile, they thought a demonstration of BrightStone hospitality might be nice. You know, to celebrate the upcoming nuptials."

"You absolutely were *not* invited as entertainment," the servant says, his chin jutting out at me. "I don't know what kind of game you think you're playing, but the Heart of the Sea is performing tonight. Not…whatever *this* is." He sniffs. "Go back out to the public celebration. This part is only for actual *invited* guests."

My eyes narrow at him, but there's a line stacking up behind us impatiently. I don't need to make a fuss just yet, and so the group of us retreats. I remove my mask after snatching a glass of champagne from one of the wandering automaton servers. It tickles my throat as I swallow it down in two nervous gulps. "Now what? Sneak in?"

Bran shrugs. "Not sure we'll have much choice. There's a spot or two back where we came in that look promising enough if we time it right."

I watch the multitude of visitors swirling around us, pausing in recognition when I spot a miserable-seeming Christophe. He startles when he sees me and then leaves his place in line to work his way over to us.

"Magpie," he says weakly, "I didn't think to see you here." He does a double take when he sees Bran and the others in their matching costumes. "Are they...Moon Children, too?"

"My clan," I say by way of introduction. "But they didn't exactly all get an invitation to be here."

He barks out an ugly laugh. "Neither did I, more's the pity."

I frown. "But I thought you were friends with Lottie."

"I was. I am. Maybe." He exhales sharply. "My brother was her previous betrothed. That makes my presence awkward and most likely something to be avoided."

A sliver of icy shock slides down my spine, and I stiffen, suddenly wary. I whistle a low warning to the clan. *Be ready...* "Your brother? Corbin, was it?"

Something guilty flashes over his skin, the lightning illumination his face. "I'm so sorry."

"For which part?" I retort coolly. "Having me poisoned? Or not saying anything about it afterward?"

He flushes, his eyes focused on the tops of his boots. "I didn't know. Not until after it happened. By then, Lottie's family was attempting to break the arrangement. And then you were found and no one was talking about what happened to you. My family was already in disgrace with the broken betrothal. I was forbidden from even leaving the house."

My finger traces the edge of my hammer. Beside me, Bran tenses, the rest of my clan staring intently at Christophe. In the barest of instants, they would move on him if I but whistled the command.

But there was no reason for that. If he could be made to testify…

"I believe you," I say slowly. "But you have to understand your word isn't much good with me right now." He bites on his lower lip, eyes flicking to the rest of my clan and nods. "Did Lottie know?' I ask suddenly, hoping to catch him off guard enough to get a straight answer.

He hesitates. "I don't know. I don't think so. But I heard you accused her at the Council hearing, so she would at least be aware of it now."

"What difference does it make?" Bran snarls. "Even if she found out later, it's not like she isn't taking advantage of it, aye? We wouldn't be here if she wasn't."

My thoughts turn to Ghost, and I steel myself against my wavering urge to simply run inside the party and take him. "Would you be willing to testify to what you know? Even if nothing comes of it, simply getting the truth out would be helpful."

"I will do it if I can. But understand, Mags, my uncle is *on* the Council. Whatever game he's playing—for money or some other reason—I doubt he would even let me get within a hundred paces of the court."

I snarl as the shock of this bit of information rattles through my bones. "It didn't feel like a game to me when he was talking to your brother about making sure I died."

A grimace crosses his face. "I'm not sure it even registers to him that you're a person. I think he simply sees you as an obstacle."

The other members of my clan chuckle at this. "Aren't we always?" I say softly. "Well and good, then. I'll be sure to let our barrister know of your involvement, or lack thereof. He can determine the best way you can help." I'm not sure how Jeremiah would handle it, but I clearly don't have the ability to make the Council listen to me.

"All right. I think I'll leave. I don't particularly like lingering on the doorstep." Christophe snags another glass of champagne before turning away and walking back toward the airship taxis. Sadness seems to envelope him. Does he love Lottie, perhaps? Or is it simply the realization that his family isn't the bastion of comfort it's supposed to be?

"So now what?" Rosa interrupts my thoughts, bringing me back to the present issue.

"Well, I don't think we'll all be getting in." I pull my robe and mask off, revealing my more traditional party garb. I gesture at Bran to do the same. "The two of us will enter like this. The rest of you will remain here in the outer gardens for now. But listen for a signal from us in case we need you to create a distraction."

Without missing a beat, Bran removes his own costume and hands it to Dafyyd. I hand mine to Rosa, whistling a warning to the others. *Watch. Wait.* They immediately withdraw, scattering into the crowd behind us, their bells jingling.

This time, I simply hand the servant at the entrance to the inner gardens my invitation. Without the masks on, he doesn't recognize us and simply waves us in with a bored expression.

"That was easier than I thought," I say to Bran, my breath escaping me with a relieved whoosh. I didn't even realize I'd been holding it in.

"Aye." Bran cranes his neck as if he could somehow see over the enormous hedgerow. He whistles a cautious greeting. *Hello.*

Here, here. The reply is whistled back a moment later.

"Good," I say. "As long as we can communicate, we'll be okay..." My voice trails away as we emerge from the darker path and into the garden proper. It's lit up with soft lights and delicate decorations, crystalline balls floating about like jellyfish. They softly pulse in time with a string quartet playing gently in the far corner.

A half-naked woman strolls into view, her dress swirling about her like ocean water and foam. Her golden hair falls almost to her ankles, dozens of tiny fish bobbling through the wavy tresses.

"The Heart of the Sea," I murmur as Bran lets out a low whistle. "She's the performer. She and Lottie were childhood friends or shared a tutor or something. She's very popular in the Inner Spiral."

"I'll bet." He points to a grove of potted plants beside a balcony, his eyes still tracking the sway of her hips. "I'll meet you over by those tree things in twenty minutes, aye?" Before I can even protest, he's gone, slipping into the crowd after the Heart of the Sea, his own steps elegant and sharp. I whistle something rude at him, and he waves his hand at me without turning.

"That's that." Shifting beneath the weight of the wings strapped to my back, I move out of the shadow of the hedges. Even with my hair and eyes glowing, most of the guests pay me very little attention at all. They aren't here for me anyway, so that suits me well enough. I prance and bow my way silently about, keeping track of all of them. Which ones appear truly wealthy, which are maybe pretending, my ears picking up all sorts of gossip.

"Highly unusual..."

"Well, there's no accounting for..."

"And I heard they had to pay off the original groom's family, but it looks as though it wasn't any great hardship..."

"I can't imagine why they would even want to go through..."

"That d'Arc woman has been gone for too long. What's even the point?"

"The feral little creature they brought up from that dreadful city... It has white hair, can you imagine? I heard it attacked someone in the streets..."

I bite down on my lip and let the words roll away. They don't know me. They don't know anything about me. And it's foolish to get worked up over it when I have more important things to worry about. Like Ghost.

I haven't found him yet, and it seems as though the main announcement won't be happening for a little while. There is a large table set up beneath a series of swirling lights, though, plates and cups set in glittering array. Clearly dinners and toasts are a planned part of the evening's agenda.

The main house lights are on in full golden display, casting the stone walls in welcoming luminance. But there are no guards upon the rooftops, no airship patrols around the grounds. Nothing that would interfere with what I might do. So different from BrightStone.

I make my way over to the potted plants and stare down at the city below. The breeze cools my face, and I suck in a deep breath.

"See anything interesting out there?" a melodic voice asks.

I glance up in surprise as the Heart of the Sea swirls past me to lean over the balcony as well. "Only the lights," I say, trying to keep my voice as neutral and cheerful as possible. Just another well-wisher with nothing to hide.

"I never get tired of this view." Her eyes meet mine, and she smiles prettily. "Oh, you were with Lottie on the train that night, weren't you?"

"Yes," I say, surprised. "With...Trystan. She was showing us the city."

She airily waves a hand. "I never forget a face, hon. Especially not one like yours. That hair... Are you related to the big fellow lurking over there?"

Indeed, Bran is looming quietly beside an elegant gazebo, a drink in his hand as he decidedly studies his feet and is furiously *not* looking in our direction.

"Ah, in a manner of speaking," I agree. "Though not by blood. He's a good man. He's simply curious about you. How long have you known Lottie? She said you shared a tutor." I change the topic of conversation as quickly as I can. Bran's secrets are not for me share.

She laughs, but there's a darkness to it. "Is that what she told you? Oh, my dear Lottie. Always what you wished and never what truly was." The Heart of the Sea turns toward me, and her electric eyes seem to have tiny whirlpools in them. "She was the sister of my soul, it feels like. We were the best of friends until one day we weren't."

"That sounds…vague."

She chuckles again. "Straightforward. I like that." The lightning ripples over her skin as she takes a sip of her champagne. "It was simply a matter of priorities. She allowed her family to determine her destiny, and I left mine to become…me. We've barely spoken since."

I wonder at her words and whether Lottie is truly a good person inside. Could she have had me poisoned, like I suspect? Or is she simply being manipulated by her family to do what they want her to do? Does it matter at all? Her quiet desperation may be a reason for it, but I still don't buy it as an excuse.

"I'm sorry," I say, hating the suddenly awkward silence.

"Don't be. It happens." Her face brightens as one of her fish pops out of a bubble to kiss me on the nose. "Ah, damn. I have to go." And just like that, the Heart of the Sea ebbs away, pausing to give Bran a quick wave before heading for the stage.

Bemused, he stares after her before retreating to where I'm standing. "This place makes me itch," he grunts. "They're so careless here. Nothing good about it."

"Except her?" I chuckle when he blushes. But he's right. The Meridians here are soft, wrapped in their materialistic dreams and security. Nothing at all like the Meridians in the Pits or the Inquestors with their sadistic electric pig-stickers and Tithes. "Did you hear anything of interest over by the stage?"

"Only rumors. Good food, though," he says. "It's really almost too rich, to be honest."

"I think they're going to be making their announcement soon." I incline my head at the marble dance floor which is beginning to clear as the music changes into something more tense and dramatic. The Heart of the Sea is onstage, and she begins to sing, her voice swelling with an electronic beat, a melodic hum that fills the air and makes my heart whir in time.

"Here we go," Bran says. There is a sudden tinkling sound of tiny bells, and out of the house comes the wedding procession. Engagement procession. Whatever it is.

First Lottie's parents, smiling broadly and dressed in exquisite fashion. Their costumes are elegant and refined, glittering with jewels as if to show their worth upon the very fabric they wear. Behind them is Lucian, escorted by Jeremiah, though the two men are far more subdued in their choice of clothing. But even from here I can tell their costumes are extremely well-made. Couldn't have them upstaging the parents, I suppose.

A smattering of applause and smiles erupt from the crowd. Lottie's mother pours the four of them tall glasses of golden liquor from a crystal vase. The group raise them high as the rest of the crowd echoes the motion. I bite my cheek hard enough to draw blood.

"We welcome you all here tonight for the joining of our two Houses, the return of the sons of d'Arc, and their welcome acceptance into Meridian high society..." Lottie's father steps forward, his voice a booming roar that carries over the guests. It's a jovial speech, punctuated by jokes I don't understand, though the crowd around us laughs. Their voices hurt my ears, making me want to clasp my hands over my head and hide.

"And now let's welcome the happy couple and the union between our two great Houses..."

Whatever else he says is lost in a blur as Lottie and Ghost appear. Lottie's face radiates triumph, her gold hair upswept in ringlets that cascade over her shoulders, her pale-blue dress swirling around her legs as she walks, like sea foam rushing past her. In some ways it's a poor imitation of the Heart of the Sea. But aside from the sudden taste of bile that sweeps into my mouth at her appearance, I'm fixated on Ghost.

His suit is nearly as fine as Lottie's dress, matching in its sea-foam color with black trim. It does nothing for him style-wise at all, and his face has a rictus of a grin plastered on it as he escorts her across the marble and down the steps to where her parents are waiting. I suppose he's doing a decent enough job of hiding his emotions as he bows to Lottie's parents before taking Lottie's arm to sweep her into a dance as the music swells, the Heart of the Sea singing low and softly romantic. Other couples watch for a few moments before taking to the dance floor, as well.

My feet are frozen where I stand. When did he learn to dance so well?

"The fuck," Bran fumes beside me. "Aren't you going to do something about that?"

"What can I do?" I say, miserable as Lottie's mother coos over something Lucian shows her. "I was told to let this play out."

"That's hardly the Magpie I know," Bran says bluntly. "Why even be here if you're simply going to roll over? How will you ever persuade them to give you what you want when you're too afraid to take what's rightfully yours?"

My nostrils flare as a sudden righteous anger vibrates along my spine. My clockwork heart whirs in my chest, making it hard to breathe. Ghost looks up then, and I nearly shatter beneath the drooping misery displayed within his gaze and the utter heartbreak of it all.

"You're too easy to read, Magpie." I startle, realizing Chancellor Davis has approached us. She hands me a glass of champagne, a puff of yellow feathers fluttering from her wrist. "Drink. Smile. Pretend to be celebrating."

"But—" I drown my confusion in the alcohol, welcoming the distraction of it burning down my throat.

"I understand. I sympathize. But you need to be careful." The Chancellor stands beside me, wedging her way between Bran and me. "Use this moment to your advantage, but don't let your temper trip you into something you'll regret. For what it's worth, I fully support you, by the way."

"For what it's worth, I don't believe we asked," Bran snaps.

She ignores him. "I'm not saying to not do anything. I'm simply saying you need to make your mark in a fashion that indicates you mean business." She pauses, glancing over the edge of the balcony as she finishes off her drink. "Incidentally, Josephine is docked a short ways away. I wanted her close in case I felt like leaving early. Perhaps I should send a messenger to make sure she's standing by."

She strolls off then, trailed by her retinue as she heads over to where Caspian Tantaglio stands holding court among a group of Meridians, their skin flashing with rapid excitement. She gestures at one of her aides and leans down to whisper something to him. He trots off in the direction of the landing port.

"Interesting," I say. "Best not to waste this opportunity. I think we'll need that distraction."

Bran nods. "I'm on it. If we get separated, where do we meet up?"

I point at the LightHouse. "Meet me at the base of that building, but don't get caught."

"Teach me to suck eggs." Bran melts away into the crowd.

I swallow hard and plunge myself into the swirling mass of dancers, attempting to at least move in the same sort of rhythm. Ghost and Lottie continue to turn in time, Ghost oddly stiff, as though he's trying to keep her as far away as possible without looking like he's doing so.

Lucian and Jeremiah promenade together on the edge of the dance floor, enjoying a quiet moment. I'm loath to interrupt, but this isn't a social call. I slip behind them. Normally Lucian is far more alert, but he is completely enraptured by his paramour, the two men making eyes at each other with an intensity that borders on obsessive.

I exhale sharply and tap Jeremiah on the shoulder, sliding between the two of them. "May I cut in?"

Lucian gapes, but I've already started moving. "Mags?" His mouth drops open as he numbly spins me out.

"Dancing lessons," I mumble, trying not to trip. "Guess we should have done those, aye?"

He recovers quickly, pulling me in. "What in the hells are you doing?"

"You sent me the invite, aye? I figured this was the way to go." I cock my head at him. "Or was I mistaken?"

"But this..." He shakes his head as though trying to clear it.

"Old tricks are the best," I say. "I even had help from Molly Bell." He coughs hard, as though choking. "I found data, by the way. Lots of it. I don't know how much will be needed as far as what we have to prove, but at least we might have a chance. Assuming we can extract it, that is."

Lucian turns us sideways into a promenade. "You've been busy, it seems."

"Indeed. Have you?" I stare at him.

He ducks his head. "They forced our hand. Whatever's going on here, they are trying to rush this through. All we can do is play along a bit longer." His mouth compresses. "Ghost is about two sheets to the wind right now. I don't think he's stopped drinking since he got here."

"Then why haven't you helped him?" I hiss. "Call it off!"

"That boy is as stubborn as you ever were," he says. "I haven't been able to get a word in edgewise with him nearly this whole time. If that horrible family hasn't been manipulating his time, he's been avoiding me."

"And no wonder," I snap. "For letting it get this far at all."

Above us is a sudden clap of grinding metal punctuated by a series of shouts and what sounds like a very large piano being jettisoned off the side of an airship.

The Tantaglio family airship, in fact.

I swallow a chuckle. My clan has done their job it would seem. Might as well take advantage of it.

"What in the hells is that?" Lucian gapes upward with the rest of the guests as the shadow of the airship sails past us, a lone scream trailing behind like a flag made of sound as the ship roars away, nearly scraping the sides of the one of the towers.

"A distraction." I whistle out a command, whirling to see Ghost's head jerk up from where he's been staring blankly past Lottie's shoulder. I hurry over and snatch at Ghost's hands to pull them apart.

Lottie's face grows pale as sees me. She backs away from Ghost. "Trystan?"

The music cuts off as Lottie's mother descends from her perch next to one of the buffet tables. "What is going on with our ship?"

Caspian wades toward us, his boots heavy on the marble and his cheeks flushed with drink and anger. "What is the meaning of this?"

"I'm coming back to claim what is mine," I say. "For you have taken without asking, assumed without understanding. If Meridion truly cared about its children, they wouldn't have sent Lucian and Trystan d'Arc into exile to pay for their mother's crimes, or hold Trystan to a contract made when he was a child and without his consent. He should make his own decisions." I point at Lottie. "And so should she."

Lottie's mother sneers. "While I realize the unfortunate offspring of Meridion don't understand how things are done up here, I'm afraid these contracts cannot simply be broken on a whim. Our very futures depend on it. Children and bloodlines are terribly important. I would hardly expect you to understand."

"Then there really isn't any point to this," Ghost says softly. "I'm a Moon Child."

Lottie's eyes fill with tears. "But you're a d'Arc... You're from Meridion. I don't understand."

"Mother needed a subject for her genetic experiments, and I was available." Ghost reaches out to take Lottie's hand. "I'm sorry, but this really would be a terrible mistake."

"But she's a half-breed. She doesn't know the first thing about life here... Savage..." The words fall out of Lottie's mouth like stones, but I barely notice the barbs.

Ghost's mouth twists into a half smile. "You'll never be able to understand. None of you will. She has killed for me, and I would die for her." His eyes roam the crowd. "Can any of you say the same?"

Lucian makes a strangled noise, but it actually sounds like he's choking back a ridiculous bout of hysterical laughter. And perhaps he is. After all, everything he hoped to do with this just came crashing down.

"This is a breach of contract, and we will not allow it," Lottie's father snaps. "To humiliate us in this way—"

"The way you tried to humiliate Mags?" Ghost thrusts out his jaw. "These last few days have been hell, but if you thought I would simply bow my head to your wishes because of my family... No, I think not."

Caspian draws himself up. "You and that damned mother of yours. Always so smug. Always so sure she had all the answers. Thank the gods we managed to get rid of her when we did. Exile was hardly a fitting punishment, but it was the best we could do."

Ghost freezes. "What did you say?"

I place my hand on his shoulder and squeeze a warning. "This is a setup. He wants you to attack him." Ghost trembles beneath my touch, his rage flaring to life in a crackling electricity under his skin. He takes a step back a moment later, his eyes narrowing at Lottie.

Lottie's mother gestures, and a rush of guards, both mechanical and otherwise, immediately emerge from the shadows, blocking the way through the main gates of the house. "The Council will hear of this! I don't know why you think we'll allow—"

"Wasn't really planning on asking for permission," I say pleasantly, tugging Ghost toward me. "Come on." He raises a brow at me, but to his credit, he doesn't ask what I have in mind. The crowd parts for us as we retreat to the garden walls and peer down below.

"What now? Surely you won't simply jump. There's nowhere for you to go." Lottie's voice cracks.

"That's the problem with you Meridians these days," I say. "All your thinking is done for you, so how could you possibly come up with anything else? I would rather die than be caged, but you relish it. All of you. And that's the saddest part of all."

I shift in my corset, reaching behind me to release the mechanism. The wings snap out from my sides. "Better hold on," I say to Ghost.

His mouth quirks up into a real smile. "I could hardly do anything else."

With our combined weight, there's little option but to simply tip backward, rolling off the wall in a blur of golden feathers with a thrum from the little thrusters.

A chorus of screams echoes past us, perhaps a rush to look down, but we are already hurtling toward the city of Meridion, its lights calling to us in a rushing glitter.

Tripping along the river's edge
Skipping stones of steel,
Hiding pennies beneath the hedge
Like wishes soon made real.

— CHAPTER TWENTY —

Of course, in hindsight, this sort of thing sounds very romantic. The reality is that physics is not particularly forgiving, and I didn't have much time to practice. There is no chance of us ascending in the damn things. I weigh too much for that, and double so with Ghost clinging to my waist, his legs trailing down. But we can fall gracefully, and that's what I focus on.

"Fuck me," Ghost mumbled. "What the hell are we doing?"

"Escaping. I think." I shift beneath the wings, trying to angle us so we are a little more level.

"Death is an escape, I suppose," he says dryly.

"Need a ride?" Josephine's voice rings out from below us.

I let out a relieved sobbing burble, turning us in a loose spiral to try to slow our descent to the Interceptor's deck. I have limited success, and we end up tumbling into a heap on the prow, my shaking legs collapsing.

"Nice of you to show up." I struggle beneath Ghost's weight.

"I would have been here sooner, but I had to get the ship undocked. Too many partygoers makes for rough waters, so to speak," Josephine says.

"Good flying there, Magpie," Bran drawls, something like a laugh floating out of him.

Ghost slips away from me, dry heaving. "Remind me never to let you pilot anything ever again," he says, wiping at his mouth.

I stick my tongue out at him. "Beggars and choosers." Bran helps me to my feet, unbuckling the harness with the wings. "Where are the others?"

"Joyriding through the Inner Spiral, I believe. They'll dump the airship somewhere obvious before abandoning it." Bran grunts. "That was the plan."

"And here I thought you would have taken it over," I say to Josephine.

She's scanning the skies above us with a practiced eye, her mouth compressed. "The last thing I need is to draw that kind of attention," she says. "Besides, it's big and pretty, but it's slow."

I crack my neck. "No one appears to have followed us. That's something."

Ghost blinks at Josephine as though suddenly realizing where he is. "The calvary, I presume?" His gaze sweeps over the ship. "I don't think I even want to know how you managed to get this thing up here."

"Long story," Bran grumbles.

Josephine gives me a wan smile. "Aye, well, we're not free and clear yet. I don't think that girl's parents are graceful losers." She turns a crank where she stands at the helm, and the ship turns swiftly toward a low-lying place beneath a series of skyscrapers.

"No. No, they're not," Ghost says. "I actually felt bad for Lottie. Everything I saw in the last few days showed that they're exactly the sort of Meridians Mother hated—wrapped up in the minutiae of their social standing and wealth. There is so little else in their lives." Regret floods his face. "If we had managed to bring her, too, I think that wouldn't have been a bad thing."

I fight back a sudden wave of jealousy. "You're free to go back up and get her," I grind out, ignoring Bran's smirk. "But I think we've got more important things to do."

Ghost slumps against a barrel. "Thank you," he says awkwardly. "For getting me out of there."

Bran rolls his eyes. "Oh aye. Shagging a girl that probably smells like sugar and roses, a fate worse than death, that."

"It was never about that," he snarls. "I know you don't understand it, but up here, everything is driven by family lineage, and arranged marriages are all a part of that." He points skyward, his eyes darting toward me. "Just look at my brother! You think the Council really wanted him to give up that arrangement with Lady Fionula? No. And they used me as the sacrificial lamb. I'm merely taking his place, and in return, he can get out of his own forced nuptials for the love of his life." His lips press together, and I realize he is deeply hurt at being used that way, even if his brother deserves a bit of happiness.

"Lucian said he wouldn't have let it go that far," I remind him. "I don't think he would have simply traded you like that. I imagine he's walking a pretty thin tightrope himself."

Bran shrugs. "But what does it matter now? You can do as you please. There *are* advantages to living on the fringes of society, aye?"

"And we ought to get to those fringes now before they send the Inquestors or whatever they have up here," Josephine mutters.

Ghost lets out a frustrated grunt. On one hand, I understood his anger. He has been a pawn his entire life, same as the rest of us, and he has always been on the outside—not Meridian, not Moon Child. Not until he finally threw in with the rest of us and was accepted into our little clan of Pit survivors. I am sure he's feeling betrayed by Lucian, and that is also fair. But there are bigger things afoot.

We wait a short while longer, hidden beneath an awning between two of the towers. But no guards come, no sirens blare out. "Do they truly care so little about their belongings that they'd let their ship be stolen?" My heart whirs nervously.

"People like that don't like being embarrassed," Josephine says. "In my experience, they don't always move for direct confrontation. They'll be more subtle about it."

"Poison," I say, snorting.

"Let's get moving," Bran says. "Where to from here?"

"The base of the LightHouse. But maybe it would be better if we made our way there on foot. I don't want to draw any more attention to us." I glance at Josephine.

"Agreed," she says. "I need to return to get the Chancellor anyway. I'm still under contract and all. I've been chartered to take her back to BrightStone, as well. I'll return as soon as it's safe to do so. Might need to lie low for a bit."

"What strange bedfellows we've become." Ghost rubs his temples. "Why the LightHouse?"

"Ah," I hedge. "I have something to show you. I think." And truthfully, I have no real idea if IronHeart will let me in, let alone the group of us. But now is the time. I can feel it in my bones.

"That sounds so reassuring." Bran curls his upper lip at Josephine. "You gonna make us climb all the way down there on our own?"

She rolls her eyes. "Aye, aye, sir." The ship descends again, finally dropping to an easy rooftop. Bran, Ghost, and I clamber down the rope ladder. "Until next time." She doffs her feathered cap at us, the ship rising again and disappearing into the stream of other airships darting to and fro among the buildings.

The three of us climb down a fire escape. We are still dressed in our fancy clothes, but it's convenient as we slip into the massive stream of Meridian citizens strolling through the Inner Spiral, blending among the populace and the twinkling lights.

This time I'm too distracted by my mission to let the noise upset me overmuch, though Bran is looking a little pale. But he sets his jaw and lets us lead him past the shops and the enormous screens, the food vendors and the music.

"Ah," Ghost says faintly as we approach a crowd of people surrounding the stolen airship. Smoke rises from the far side of it, but I'm not sure it's caught fire so much as committed some sort of vehicular suicide.

Great splashes of paint smear the sides, a childish scrawl reading, *Meridian Suck-Tits!* over the name of the ship. "I'm sure *that's* going to make a good impression." But as far as distractions go, I can't fault it.

By the time we reach the base of the LightHouse, Bran's nearly shaking with the overload, and we stop give him a chance to catch his breath. The flashing lights are pulsing in time with the headache arcing across my forehead, and I wince against it. I whistle sharply, relief sinking through my bones when it's answered and the rest of our clan appears from the shadows of a nearby building.

Rosa waves at Ghost. "Glad to see you made it, aye?"

"Aye," he says with a sad smile.

Bran vomits noisily beside the base of the LightHouse. "Now what?" His voice is a hoarse croak, and he wipes his mouth with the back of his hand.

I look up at the LightHouse with its winding stair that leads halfway up to IronHeart's hidden door. Climbing all the way up there to find no way in doesn't exactly appeal to me. Besides, I'm fairly sure she's watching.

"Anytime you're ready," I say aloud, unsurprised when one of those cleaning drones flits its way out of a sewer grate. It buzzes around my face and then zips back down.

Ghost frowns. "What is that doing up here? I thought they were bottom cleaners."

"You'll see." I stare at the sewer grate before reaching down to flip it open, my heart rattling out the keycode to the sewer pipes, making quick work of the lock.

"Really?" Rosa mutters. The others groan, none of them particularly wanting to reenter the underground in any circumstance.

Bran pales. "Do we have to?"

"Why go down there at all?" Ghost asks, his eyes dull.

"Well, there's someone I think you should meet. And then we can make some decisions." I suck in a deep breath, and one by one, we enter the grate, Bran yanking it shut behind us.

"These are cleanest damn sewers I have *ever* seen," Dafyyd muses. "Dry. Tall. Hells, we could just move in here."

"Speak for yourself." Bran shudders, his glowing eyes lighting up the passageway.

"Maintenance cleans the sewers regularly," Ghost says absently, his fingers tracing the wall for half a moment. "There's only so much room on a floating city, and the people here don't care for smells."

"Aye, we know," I say, my tone brusque as I remember my time with Sparrow in the junk heaps outside BrightStone. "They dump everything they don't like on us down below."

"How much farther is it?" Bran's voice holds a tremor that he can't quite seem to control.

"I'm not entirely sure," I admit. "Last time I pretty much just fell into it, which I don't really recommend. But I'm fairly sure there are some platforms or elevators that can take us part of the way." A drone hovers in front of me as I pause. It makes a steaming whistle and leads us down a series of passages before stopping at a door.

This one only has a keypad and a warning indicating we shouldn't enter. But my heart makes swift work of it, and we find ourselves at a metal staircase that swirls down into the darkness.

"Oh, that's so much better." Bran lets me move toward the front.

"Shouldn't be too much farther. This looks like it will be a straighter shot than before," I say, hopeful it's the truth.

"Straight shot to where, exactly?" Ghost's question is coated in a healthy dose of skepticism. He and I have always had rather different opinions on just what lies in the center of Meridion, but now I'll be able to show him. The concept makes me more nervous than I like to admit, but the time for secrets is long gone.

At last, the echo around us changes, the air growing warmer and more humid. The stairs stop at another hallway, but I recognize where we are now, and we slip down the passage, our feet silent on the concrete.

The drone whizzes through the doorway, and we follow into the antechamber of IronHeart herself. The dragon's enormous body curls all around the room, her eyes glittering expectantly as we approach.

"Well," she drawls. "Welcome, children."

Bran lets out a gasp and takes a step back almost behind me, even as the others hesitate. But not Ghost. His voice grows husky as he steps into the light of her golden gaze.

"Mother?" he croaks, and for a moment I can see him as that little boy, abandoned all those years ago by the one who made him.

"Yes," she says, her own mien suddenly gentle. "Or really, the pieces of her that she left behind." The dragon's head lowers as though to take a closer look at him. "You've grown up so well."

"No thanks to you," he erupts, his nostrils flaring. I catch the barest hint of lightning beneath his skin, flashing in a tiny maelstrom, his Meridian heritage coming to the forefront. He points at his paling hair, fingers shaking. "You did this to me. To her. To them! And for what? For *what*?"

The dragon stares back mildly beneath the onslaught of his words, but if she feels any remorse within that mechanical body of hers, I can't see it. The other Moon Children are restless. This moment between Ghost and his mother isn't really meant for us.

Fury flushes over Ghost's cheeks, and I hesitate. Maybe it is.

Moving next to him, I take his hand and gesture at the others to join us. "I know you are nothing more than an automaton. I don't know if you're capable of true emotions, but if there are any words Madeline left for her children—for all of us—then we might like to hear them."

Ghost sags, but his eyes never once flicker my way.

The dragon sighs, something melancholy taking shape in the draconian face. "I'm afraid I cannot give you the words you want to hear. I know that she disliked the path her cohorts were taking, but even with her place in politics and the power she wielded as the Architect, there were things she could not stop."

"And yet she allowed her children to be exiled, abandoned down below without ever a word in all that time." Tears well up in Ghost's eyes. "I found your body in the Mother Clock, down below in the Pits. I know you had access to the outside world. Would it have been so horrible to have taken us in?"

"It was far too dangerous to do that—for you and for me. I did what I could from the shadows, and I made my helpers to keep in touch with a few chosen individuals." A puff of smoke rushes from her nostrils as she exhales sharply. "I've been keeping an eye on you and your brother for a very long time, Trystan. I always knew where you were, and I was always so very proud of you."

Ghost turns away, his mouth compressed tightly. I step in front of him as though to block him from her sight, though it's a futile gesture. After all, she merely has to raise her head to see everything in the room.

"I don't understand. Mags says you're an automaton, but you speak to Ghost as though you are truly his mother," Gloriana points out. "So which is it?"

"Moon Children are such perceptive things," IronHeart rumbles with a hint of amusement. "In truth, there are times when I myself do not really know. Initially I was merely a repository for information, later developed into a weapon if the worst should come to pass. But Madeline was gone from Meridion for so long, and at some point, the reports she sent me were less fact and more emotional." Her golden gaze washes over Ghost, softening. "She had many regrets, and I am a creature of those as well."

When Ghost doesn't respond, she doesn't push the issue, turning toward the rest of the Moon Children. "And what of the rest of you? Where do you hail from?"

Bran, who has been uncharacteristically silent during the exchange, sneers at her. "Oh no, you don't get to ask that. You haven't remotely earned the right, aye?"

The dragon turns toward the screen at the far end of the room. It flickers to life at some unheard command. "I was only making small talk," she complains.

The screen flickers again and then shows images of Bran at various stages of childhood. "Bran Murphy. Spriggan clan. Moon Child eruption at the age of thirteen. Father unknown, mother deceased. Biological sister Tithed, presumed deceased. Leader of the Spriggan clan from age eighteen to twenty-three. Tithed at the age of twenty-four, in apparent hopes of rescuing his sister."

Images of Bran's sister splash across the screen. She's small and lively with dark eyes and a laughing mouth. I shudder. I saw her before, but in Buceph's lab she was nothing more than a pile of tubes and wires keeping her alive, though she'd been vivisected, limbs amputated, as she begged me to turn off the machines that kept her and our other Moon Children brethren alive.

Bran snatches the hammer from my waist and throws it at the screen with a scream from the depths of his very soul, as though all his fury erupted in that single rash act.

"You absolute cunt!" he roars, the screen shattering beneath my hammer. "Where in the hells do you get off? She is NOT for you!"

"Bran..." I reach out to him, terrified that something had truly broken inside the man.

"Don't touch me," he snaps, brushing past the others as though he might climb the walls to escape. But there is no such escape here.

"That was wrong of you," I say to IronHeart, the dragon looking abashed, if such a thing is possible. "All of this is wrong. We're not your subjects, and we aren't your enemy. If you want our help with something, asking might be the easiest way about it. I don't think we need displays of power to rub it in our faces how weak we are."

Rosa lets out an ugly little laugh. "We can always leave, after all," she adds. "It's not like we really *need* Meridion."

"For all its wonders, I don't know that I find the people all that attractive. Though I'd still like to go to the medical college here." Gloriana wiggles her trembling fingers. "Or perhaps there might be a way to fix these."

"In my more human days, I could undoubtedly have figured something out that would help you, but I'm a bit...lacking in hands at the moment." The dragon sniffs at the shattered screen. "It will take a while to get that repaired, I think."

"To what end? We're not your entertainment." I sift through the broken glass of the screen to retrieve my hammer and replace it on my belt. "How about you find some information that we *can* use? Something we can take before the Council..." My voice trails away as I suddenly remember Copper Betty. "I have an automaton, given to me by Molly Bell—you might remember her. She said she'd had some dealings with you a long time ago."

"Ah yes. We know her. And the automaton... What of it?" IronHeart looks at me shrewdly.

"Molly said it contained all the information we'd need, all of its observations over the years and...whatever else it had access to. If we wanted direct information on how the Inquestors were bedding BrightStone whores to create Moon Children for Meridion experiments…" I purse my mouth.

Ghost shakes his head. "The Council wouldn't even take our word for it, Mags, and we were *in* the Pits. We lived it, were scarred by it. They don't give a shit as long as they're insulated up here in this bubble of theirs. They have no reason to believe it."

The dragon taps her clawed digits on the floor, like rain falling on a roof. "All right. Bring this Copper Betty here. We'll see what can be done with her and if we can extract the information into a format the Council will listen to. Short of having me there in this form, anyway."

Bran curls his upper lip at her. "And what keeps you from doing that? Why wouldn't you simply show yourself and declare what you are and who you were?"

The dragon shrugs. "I wasn't programmed that way. Madeline d'Arc wasn't stupid, you know. She wanted to make sure that if I was found, I couldn't be corrupted and made to do something… regrettable."

The word hangs there like a flag in the wind, insinuating total and terrible destruction. I swallow hard, resisting the urge to touch the panel on my chest. The fail-safe. That's what Madeline's notes called it, the part that was supposed to make Meridion fly again. But how?

I exhale sharply. "All right. We'll bring Copper Betty. At this point, anything we have will be helpful."

Ghost nods slowly, the color returning to his cheeks as our eyes met briefly. "I don't know if anything we do will be enough, but we have to try, don't we?" His words echo hard and sharp, taking me back to that moment in the Pits when I discovered he had come after me, getting captured and, in turn, tortured and trapped.

My nostrils flare. "Yes. I think we do"

"Here." IronHeart's body ripples, her tail curling up toward the lower half of her body as her scales shake.

The tail uncurls a moment later, coming toward me, a small silver egg wrapped in the last coils. And by small, I mean larger than the size of my fists together—just small relative to her, I suppose. I open my hands as she dumps the egg into my waiting arms.

"So what now? I sit on it like a chicken, aye?" I say, studying the egg. It's beautifully crafted with intricate carvings all around it. Scales, I realize.

IronHeart laughs, her booming chuckle nearly shaking the room. "Of course not. Look on the base. There's a button there. I want to see if you can open it."

I stifle my frustration. Always another test, another way to prove I'm worthy of whatever others deem necessary. I flip the egg over as she directs, running my fingers over the base until I find the button she's talking about. It's small and unassuming, really not much more than a slightly raised scale itself. I give it a quick press.

Nothing happens, so I press it again, glancing up at IronHeart. "Now what?" The dragon just hums at me but doesn't answer, her eyes alight with wicked amusement.

For a moment, I wish I could just smash it with my hammer, though what she'd do if I suddenly pounded the hells out of her egg with it is probably something I don't really want to know. Robotic babies or not, she seems a bit unhinged.

I pull the egg closer to my chest, perking up when my heart whirs in response. Another Meridian lock, of course. But here there isn't a panel where I can tap out a rhythm.

Oh, but there is a rhythmic vibration coming from the egg itself...

My heart stutters and whirs in an almost questioning fashion, only for the egg to shudder again. When I press the button a third time, the egg unfolds so quickly I almost drop it. It's like a metallic flower unfurling into a silver…dragon.

Of course.

It looks nearly identical to my old one, except the metal glitters in a way that almost seems alive, the same sort of electrical pulses as Meridian skin rippling beneath its scales. The metal feels harder somehow, some other alloy than the original's brass and bronze, without the glass belly and the steam. This dragon is sleek and slim, and stares at me with appraising eyes and a cool demeanor.

"Doesn't seem to like me much, does it?" I give it a sour look as it launches into the air with a swift flap of its wings.

"It just doesn't know you yet," IronHeart admits. She chirps at her drone, who retrieves a chip from the control panel—the one I'd brought with me before. The new dragon has landed on a nearby table and waits patiently as the drone fusses with the chip. The dragon's chest scales slide away to reveal a similar slot to the old dragon, and the drone swaps out its chip for mine.

Immediately, the dragon launches into the air, clawing and biting at something only it can see. IronHeart lets out a hum, and the dragon sinks onto the table.

"Its memories need to catch up to the present," IronHeart says. "Give it a moment to go through the booting process, and it should recognize you well enough after that."

I slump onto the floor as I wait, suddenly exhausted. Dragons, crazy architects, or no, I need a real meal and a bed and to clean up. And some time to process everything that has happened.

I glance back up at IronHeart, who is crooning something soothing at the little dragon. It lets out a scolding hiss at her, part chatter and part anger, before finding its usual perch with its tail curled around my neck.

"My, my. Such loyalty is unusual," IronHeart murmurs. "But perhaps that's just what we need these days. Well done."

"Charmed, I'm sure." I snort ruefully, though I feel uneasy at the idea of it watching us, now knowing everything we do will get back to IronHeart. But how to tell my clan? Or Ghost? Or any of them? Because the fact of the matter is that IronHeart is already plugged into this place in ways I will never understand. If not this dragon, then something else—cameras, drones, who knows?

"Now go and bring me Copper Betty, and we'll see what we can do about the information she has." She shoos me away, her head sprawled upon her claws as though she is about to take a nap.

Ghost takes my hand, but as we turn away, the dragon's eyes open once more. "And Trystan? You've done well. So very far beyond my expectations. I just wanted you to know."

Ghost sucks in a deep breath, but in the end the two of us flee down the corridor, the others trailing behind us.

A brush of darkness
Along my garden gate
To turn my path
And twist my fate.

— CHAPTER TWENTY-ONE —

That was just…awful," Rosa says as we clamber topside from the sewers, taking refuge in the trees in a small park nearby. At least the leaves give us a bit of cover, and I've rarely seen the Meridians looking up at the stars. Why did they need to, after all? They're too busy looking down on everyone else.

"That was not what I expected," Bran says, his voice small, and I knew he was trapped in those memories of his sister.

I exhale slowly, trying to block out the memories of what I'd seen in Buceph's lab. "It would not have helped you to know how she died, Bran. Believe me when I say that."

"Aye." He says nothing else, staring off into the distance, and I turn to Ghost, nudging him out of his own thoughts.

"Sorry," he mumbles. "That was surreal in a way that I hope never to experience again. She was my mother, but then she wasn't. My memories of her are hazy, but her voice and her mannerisms were unmistakable, even in the body of a mechanical dragon." His eyes grow sad. "And you say you met her before?"

I nod. "By accident, when I fell off of Meridion. I ended up in there, but she didn't want me to tell you or Lucian yet. I'm sorry. I didn't mean to keep secrets, but with everything else going on, I didn't even know where to begin without sounding like I was half-mad." I give him a rueful poke. "You've been rather clear in never believing the legend, after all."

He snorts. "Fair enough. So what now? Do we go to BrightStone to find Copper Betty?"

"Ah, no," I say, realizing I hadn't yet told Ghost all that had happened. Quickly, we fill him in, his eyes widening when we got to the part about Molly Bell.

"You've been busy," he says hoarsely. "I wish I could tell you the same, but Lottie's family was ridiculously tight-lipped about their plans for me or her previous marriage partner. Aside from a countless number of lessons on etiquette that they insisted I learn in preparation for the masked ball, I was left alone in my room."

"Sounds dreadful," Rosa says snidely. "Food, a warm bed, what could be worse?"

He scowls at her. "Believe me, if you had to practice how to lift your fork for two hours a day, you'd be half-ready to throw yourself off the city, too. I know you think she betrayed you, Mags, but I don't think she did it on purpose."

"Even a fox will gnaw off its own foot to get out of a trap." Gloriana hides her trembling hands in her sleeves, her pale-blue eyes soft.

"I'm not responsible for her or her decisions," I say bluntly. "My clan is what concerns me. Moon Children as a people concern me. Not the inner mechanisms of political marriage." I look at Ghost. "Did she ask you to help her get free of it? Pour her soul of misery upon you?"

"Not exactly. We didn't spend much time together. I suspect she's very lonely, to be honest." A half smile curves his lips. "No clans for Meridians, it would seem."

"More's the pity for them, then." Dafyyd scuffs his foot on the ground. "Any chance we can get out of these suits? They itch."

I hesitate. My own feet are aching in the heeled boots. Roof dancing or not, I'm not sure I want to go traipsing around in my finery any longer. On the other hand, we have to get Copper Betty from Joseph, and I want to avoid going back to the d'Arc estate until we know it's safe. The last thing we need is to get tossed into Meridian jail, if there even is such a thing. Still, we'd move faster if we had more casual clothing, and judging by Haru's hungry eyes, a bit of food wouldn't be amiss, either.

I dig into my purse, looking for the address Joseph wrote down and coming up empty. "Damn." I upend the contents onto my skirt, sifting through what little is there. Except for a handful of Meridian chits, it's empty. "Now I have no idea where to go."

"Where are we trying to get to?" Ghost asks. "There's an information booth in the Inner Spiral. We should be able to look up the address there if you know the House name."

"Is it safe to go there?" Rosa hesitates. "We had our masks on the entire time so I don't think anyone would have recognized us…"

I shut my eyes, trying to remember the address. As it comes to me, I snap my fingers. "Trinity is the House name. Joseph Trinity. The Meridian who helped us in the Pits."

Ghost slides out of the tree, looking at the bedraggled state of our little clan. "I think if you weren't spotted, we should be all right. We can stop at one of the clothing shops, and buy some hats or something, which will help."

Bran stretches, removes his suit coat, and throws it over his shoulder. He pokes Ghost with a finger. "All right, then. Lead the way."

The crowds in the Inner Spiral are noticeably thinner than the time I visited with Ghost and Lottie, but it's no less obnoxious with its flashing lights and giant screens as I emerge with Ghost from one of the clothing boutiques. I split up the Meridian chits among the group, Rosa and Gloriana heading in one direction and the boys in the other.

A noodle café across the street is our meeting place. Haru and Dafyyd are sitting at the bar slurping down pasta as fast as they can. Gloriana and Rosa sip drinks, smiles flashing as they tease Bran with some little metallic toy they picked up. It strikes me at how much better we blend in with loose trousers and soft leather boots. Colorful shirts and each one of us wearing a hat or a scarf to cover our glowing hair, the dark glasses hiding our eyes.

Ghost and I slide into seats to place our own orders with the squat automaton manning the bar, and I imagine another life, another time. I wonder if the others around me can see it—what it would've been like if we had been born up here, loved, accepted. Running wild through the streets of the Inner Spiral, lost in waves of music and lights, every luxury at our fingertips for the taking. Laughing eyes and plump cheeks, clean clothes and soft hair.

The concept is painful, churning a sharpness within my gut at what we could have had but for the chance of our birth, our genetic misfortune. Hollow eyes nesting in the bones of faces long bereft of innocence is the legacy of Moon Children. And yet, if anything Ghost said about Lottie is true, is she any less empty inside? Maybe the Meridians are simply better at hiding it.

"Well, that's not good." Ghost gestures at one of the giant screens across the street. The group of us freeze as an image of the Tantaglio family airship sails across the screen, crashing hard into one of the giant fountain sculptures on the far side of the Inner Spiral. The clan, still in their Tithe costumes, scatter before anyone can react, heading into the shadows with a swiftness only a Moon Child could manage.

Inwardly, I breathe a sigh of relief. With the costumes, there is no way to identify them, and now that we are essentially hiding in plain sight, we'll be that much harder to find. Or so I hope.

I crane my neck, trying to hear past the all the jingles and noise to listen to whatever the woman on the screen is saying. "—And the youngest son of the Slinter House, Christophe, has been taken into custody as a suspect for vandalism and felony theft." A picture of Christophe talking to me in the garden appears, but my back is to whatever is taking the footage, and even though my mask is off, my face can't be seen. "As the brother of the formerly promised groom, Corbin, it is believed that Christophe attempted to sabotage the party to prevent—"

Whatever else she says is lost as an airship sounds a horn, passing in front of the screen. I slink down into my seat and finish up my meal, though my appetite is gone.

Ghost frowns. "But that doesn't make any sense. There's not even a mention of what happened with me."

"No. I think it's easier for the Tantaglio family to say their party was ruined by vandals than admit what truly happened. But still..." I set down my bowl as Ghost asks for the bill. "He told me he would testify for us, that he knew what his brother did. He didn't think Lottie knew it was going to happen, but—"

Dafyyd whistles. "What if this isn't simply a case of mistaken identity? What if they're doing this to shut him up so he can't testify at all?"

I shudder. "Remind me to never get involved in Meridian politics."

"Bit late for that," Ghost retorts gently before pulling his own hat down a little tighter over his head. He jogs over to a nearby kiosk manned by a patient-looking aged automaton. A few minutes later, he's back. "I've got the address. There was only one that matched that House name. Come on. We'll take the train across the river. It will be faster that way."

"Thank the gods," Gloriana says, stretching. "My feet are killing me."

Faster and less likely to be tracked, I think to myself. Taking a taxi straight to Joseph's might be more comfortable, but the last thing I want is to drag trouble straight to his front door. As we make our way through the streets to the nearest underground train station, the Heart of the Sea's airship glides overhead, fake waves rolling beneath it.

"Does she ever sleep?" I wonder aloud. Her face appears on the screen, a soft melody behind her voice as she sings, though I'm more focused on getting to the station.

Ghost pauses at the stairs that lead belowground, frowning. "Where's Bran?"

Rosa grins, poking Gloriana in the side, and points to the Heart of the Sea's airship. Bran is standing to the side of the stairway, his mouth half-open as an image of him at the party blurs across the screen, even as the music grows louder, the lyrics clear:

Lonely boy…
I'm looking for you…
Moon Child, running wild…
Do you think of me, too?

"That's a trap," Dafyyd says dryly.

Bran flushes red to the tops of his ears. "Aye, it is." He watches the airship roll past regretfully before following us to the train, his face pensive. To their credit, the rest of the clan doesn't tease him too badly, but then, all of us know how hard he took Penny's death. Every scant moment of happiness is precious, even if it isn't completely real.

We pile onto the train car, taking seats next to the windows and watching the city whiz by in a flash of speeding lights and blurred faces. We ignore and are ignored in turn by the other passengers in a refreshing moment of normalcy, which always seemed so out of reach in BrightStone.

By the time we find Joseph's apartment, it's the middle of the night and we're all struggling to stay awake. There's a code to enter the building, of course, but that's not an issue for me, and from there, Ghost finds a sign on the wall with a list of apartments and suites.

"Trinity, Trinity... Ah, here it is. 707. Shall we head up?" he asks.

I shiver at the idea of the elevator, but to their credit, my entire clan manages it without a fuss. I knock on the door to the apartment, wondering if Joseph is even awake. If I planned it better, maybe we would have found a hotel to sleep in and done this in the morning. But here we are.

A moment later, I hear the turn of the lock, my heart whirring in response. The door slides open to reveal an exhausted Lucian, his eyes red rimmed with a tired fury. "About time you lot showed up."

"Wait... What?" I peer into the apartment as though I might somehow comprehend if I am in some sort of fever dream.

Lucian digs into his waistcoat to pull out the paper with Joseph's address scrawled on it, waving it at me. "Someone was sloppy with their secrets," he slurs. "Found it by the front door when I went home."

"You're drunk." Ghost stares at him. "And you went home? Is it safe?"

"Of course it's safe," Lucian snarls. "We're not savages, you know. Jeremiah spent an hour trying to calm Caspian down. We're going to have to go before the Council anyway. He's seeking compensation for their family's humiliation." He hiccups loudly. "Will cost us a damn fortune if he wins."

I flinch. "We're here to see Joseph. Is he inside?"

"He's here," Lucian says, his voice growing high and tight with barely checked anger, an unrecognizable expression turning down his mouth. "We've been having an absolutely *fascinating* conversation about all sorts of things, in fact. Do you know what you've done? What you've started?"

"Not really," I retort. "And I never started anything. I simply finished it." I nudge Ghost. "Or he did, really."

My clan shifts behind us, uncomfortable. Then Joseph shuffles up, weary resignation echoed in his face. "Would you mind either taking this argument inside or outside? It's bad manners to linger in the doorway." He gives me a tight-lipped smile. "I don't want to upset my neighbors just yet. I only arrived this afternoon."

He waves us into the main part of the apartment. It's dusty in places, the furniture smelling as if it hasn't been used in a very long time, but I can see evidence of Copper Betty's handiwork in a newly mopped floor and a clean kitchen area.

"We're only here to collect Copper Betty," I tell him as the rest of my clan find places to sit on the sheet-draped couches. Their exhaustion makes them quiet, their usual banter replaced with soft yawns. "We can't stay long."

"Of course," Joseph says. "Sounds like I missed a hell of a party."

"You could say that." Lucian sags onto one of the larger chairs. "If you thought we had a mess before..."

Ghost moves beside me, taking my hand. "I'm sorry your plots untwisted so badly, Brother. But this was one sacrifice I wasn't willing to make. And neither was she."

Lucian sweeps his hand through his hair, pressing his palm to his forehead. "I never had any intentions of seeing you wed to Lottie, Trystan. It was all a ruse until we could get the evidence needed to prove our case. I just hoped you might have understood that better."

"And what of Lottie?" I ask quietly. "Was she in on this little plan, too? Or were you simply manipulating her and her family out of selfishness?"

"They came to *me*," he snaps. "Why not take advantage of them?"

"Because that's not the type of person you are," Ghost snarls back. "We're not on BrightStone anymore. You don't have to protect me or Mags. We're not children!"

Lucian gapes at us, flashes of guilt, anger, and some other nameless emotion crackling over his face. Lightning dances beneath his skin in an echo of Ghost's, tiny storms seeming to take shape before swirling away.

The two of them have clashed before, over me and over other things, but even I can see that both of them are on their last nerves of strained anger, like a wire pulled taut between them. In a moment it will snap, and then where will we be?

I force my way between them, pushing both brothers back with a hard shove so each is forced to stumble for balance. "Enough," I say. "*Enough.* We have so many things to worry about now, and I don't even know where to begin." I pause. "And you're not the only one who's been keeping secrets."

"Do tell," Lucian drawls, crossing his arms. "Does this have anything to do with a certain automaton currently cleaning up Joseph's bathroom? I realize you were down in BrightStone, Mags, but I hardly thought you'd be so concerned about household chores that you'd bring her with you."

"Aye, well, turns out she's more important than any of us thought," I say, trying to decide the best way to explain it to him and failing utterly. "Ah. It might be better if I just show you," I look to Joseph. "Can you get her?"

"Show me what?" Lucian frowns, his brow furrowed so deeply I could have hidden in the creases.

"You'll see. Come on." The three of us follow Joseph down the hallway to what I assume is his master bathroom. The automaton is dutifully scrubbing the sink, her blue eyes winking in an almost questioning fashion when she sees us. I nod at her. "It's time."

Copper Betty swivels her head and then taps the back of her neck. "There," I say. "Do you recognize that?"

Both Ghost and Lucian move in closer, Ghost letting out a low whistle. "Damn. I never noticed that before."

"It's not like either of us had any need to go poking around her hairline," Lucian grumbles, lowering his glasses as he stares at the back of her neck. "It appears real enough," he concedes. "Molly might have known Madeline's symbol, though. A lot of people did at the time. But I'm not sure she would have had known the exact order in which to put them."

"Copper Betty wasn't just a simple servant automaton," I explain. "Your mother gave her to Molly Bell for a reason."

"Oh, I'm sure," he retorts. "There's always a reason."

Joseph coughs slightly. "Yes, well, she was an interesting woman, your mother. I can't always pretend to understand her motivations, but she almost never did anything without a purpose."

"It's very fascinating, but I'm not convinced it was worth you trotting all the way over here in the middle of night," Lucian says.

"There's a bit more to it than that." I yawn, rubbing at my eyes.

"Will that be all for tonight, then? I've had a rather long day, and though my visitors have all been extremely interesting, I think it's about time I call it an evening." Joseph hesitates but doesn't press the issue. Has he told Lucian about their relationship? I cannot imagine that he has, but it's not my place to mention it.

"Of course. So sorry to have troubled you." Lucian bows slightly, and the gesture when he lowers his head is so similar to Joseph's that I might have thought them twins for half a moment, overlaying one face over the other.

"It's quite fine," Joseph assures him, walking us toward the front door, Copper Betty following. "I owe Magpie a debt I will never be able to repay."

"Our Mags has a way of collecting favors, it would seem," Lucian muses, his expression far calmer than it had been previously. "And you will be able to testify on our behalf to the Council?"

"It's why I'm here. I don't know how much weight my word will have, but if it's within my power to do so, I will try to convince them of the veracity of your statements." He reaches up to adjust the floppy hat he normally wears, but stops, as though realizing he no longer has it on. "I left the majority of my research and notes at your house. You may want some time to go through it before working on your defense."

"We'll take that under consideration." Lucian shakes his hand as we say our goodbyes. "It was very good to meet you, sir. I look forward to working together. My barrister, Jeremiah Brasheen, will be calling on you on the morrow."

We pass through the sitting room where my clan waits—or sleeps, really. They lean against one another, mouths open and snoring slightly. Bran cracks an eye at us as we stop and closes it again a moment later.

I hesitate, not really wanting to wake them up. "I don't suppose they can stay here for a few hours?" I ask Joseph. "I wouldn't normally suggest it, but they've had a long night."

The older man nods. "As long as they're quiet, I think we'll get along just fine here."

My dragon hisses in my ear, and I shrug my shoulders. "Stay with them," I say. "If anything goes wrong, come find me." The dragon makes a whirring noise of disapproval but does as I ask, landing on the edge of the couch above Haru's head and curling its tail around its feet like a cat.

Lucian stares at it as though suddenly realizing it's even there. "I thought your dragon was destroyed when you…disappeared?" He frowns and then waves me off. "Never mind. A mystery that can wait until morning."

Joseph murmurs his agreement as I gesture to Copper Betty. Ghost takes my hand as the four of us leave Joseph's apartment, the door closing behind us with a quiet click. For a moment I regret not asking Joseph to come with us—after all I had promised to show him IronHeart as well—but given the lateness of the hour, it could wait. He hadn't looked particularly interested in anything but finding a bed, and I could hardly blame him for that. Given the choice, I'd be doing the same.

Lucian yawns as we emerge from the apartment building. "That was a good idea, Mags, bringing Joseph up here. Testimony and notes aside, as one of the actual scientists sent down below, they'll have to listen to him."

"That's my hope," I agree, though I'm still rather dubious about the results. "At this point I'm assuming the Council has already made up their minds, though, regardless of what we say or do. I'm not sure there's any winning."

"The litigation of Moon Child acceptance into Meridian society could take years. Hopefully, it won't, but it's a complicated situation." I bristle at him, but he ignores me. "The wheels of bureaucracy move slowly at times. And speaking of slow, what now? We head home?"

The night is full upon us, and as tempting as it is to go straight to the house and get into bed, we can't risk Copper Betty falling into the wrong hands. Ghost exchanges a look with me and shakes his head. "Not just yet—there's something else we need to show you."

"That doesn't sound ominous or anything." Lucian cocks a brow at me. "Fine, then. Lead on."

Slippy rocks, chilly river,
Feet to follow my laughing song.
Falling heart, freezing shiver,
Blood that ripples, hot and strong.

— CHAPTER TWENTY-TWO —

"So what exactly is so fascinating in the sewers that you have to bring us here?" Lucian wrinkles his nose. "It's like we're back in BrightStone."

"Not hardly." I wait for Copper Betty to catch up to us. She isn't the fastest of automatons. "It's something I found when I fell through the trash chutes."

He shudders. "We aren't going near those, are we?"

"No. Just up ahead here," Ghost says, his voice low. I have to admit, he is taking most of today in remarkably good spirits, especially given the circumstances of the evening and the whirlwind of craziness that enveloped us.

But I know that will come crashing down at some point. Judging by the bags beneath Lucian's eyes, all three of us have been awake far longer than is wise, and it seems as though that won't be remedied anytime soon.

As we approach the doorway to IronHeart's lair, Copper Betty seems to hum. Or perhaps it's just a wavering vibration that emanates from her metallic skin. In fact, the automaton pushes past us as I reach for the door to unlock it, and she beats me to it, popping the door open with the merest touch.

"What is this?" Lucian asks, yawning again. "Running around the sewers with an automaton and a couple of Moon Children feels like we're entering penny-dreadful levels of nonsense."

"Oh, it's nonsense," I drawl. "Just not the sort you're probably expecting."

"Indeed," intones IronHeart in her dulcet tones, the sound reverberating through my chest. "Not the sort anyone expects, I imagine."

Lucian gapes as we enter the dragon's lair, her enormous face grinning in amusement. "Hello, my dear. It has been a long time, hasn't it?"

"Hells." Lucian promptly collapses into Ghost's arms, his eyes rolling into the back of his head.

"Is he coming to?" I wave my hand in front of Lucian's face as Ghost carefully lays him upon the tiles.

"I was rather hoping he might be made of sterner stuff," IronHeart says, her tone mournful.

"He's been through a lot," I retort, gently blotting at his mouth.

Lucian groans, and we back away as he sits up, his brow furrowing. "I just had the weirdest dream. That we somehow found the center of Meridion and there…there was a dragon…" A chuckle escapes him, but it's the sort of hysterical laugh someone lets loose when they're afraid they're going mad, and it's not at all reassuring.

"Stranger things have happened," I mutter. "Probably. Lucian, IronHeart. IronHeart…well, you know."

Lucian swallows hard, his gaze finally drawn to the majestic curve of the dragon's neck. "Wait, what?"

"You seem a bit slow today. Are you all right?" IronHeart's golden eyes gleam as a puff of smoke curls from her nostrils.

"I don't...understand." He turns to me and then to Ghost, then back to the dragon.

"Explain it to him, will you?" She gestures to Ghost who emits a rapid-fire series of sentences that leaves Lucian gaping even wider than he was before.

"This...this is crazy. And the Council..." Lucian's head jerks up, eyes alight. "Surely they'll have to believe us now with Madeline's own living work before them. And your research—it's all saved."

"Ah, well, that's the thing. The research from my time up here, yes. But aside from some snippets that I could access via my messengers, not everything from when I...that is, your mother, was on BrightStone was necessarily retrieved." Her eyes rest on me for a brief moment, but I'm not sure what she wants, so I keep quiet.

"But still." Relief plays upon Lucian's face. "However you've done it, it's safe. You're safe... But why didn't you tell us sooner?"

"Well, for one thing, I can't leave." The dragon's tail twitches. "It's part of the fail-safe mechanism. All well and good to have a dragon in the middle of the city, but really, I'm a self-destruct." She arches her neck smugly. "I'm nothing if not a bit of a showstopper, you know?"

"That makes no sense. You already stopped the city from moving. What more is there?" Ghost demands, anger flashing beneath his skin.

"Quite a bit," the dragon says. "If I let out the right series of electromagnetic pulses, everything that keeps this city floating will fail and we'll go crashing into the sea." She sniffs. "I suppose that's better than blowing it up."

Lucian sinks as though his knees are about to give out, his chin in his hands. "Madeline d'Arc was not like that," he insists. "She loved creating things. Why would she ever build something like this?"

"Maybe not all knowledge is worth saving," I say quietly, rubbing my arm over my various scars. "I think sometimes there comes a time where maybe it's better to just start over, aye?" I stare at the dragon without really seeing her, my memories of the Pits below and the horrors that had awaited us there etched into my retinas in a waking nightmare I've tried so hard to forget.

Lucian flushes. "Maybe not. But I'm not sure I would want to drag the Council down here, either, to let them know the realities of IronHeart... Undoubtedly, they would look for a way to shut you down," he tells the dragon. "If not outright destroy you."

"Indeed. I know secrets," she says. "Many of them." Her eyes are drawn to Copper Betty, who has been standing at attention this whole time, her body motionless. "But perhaps there is another way."

"We brought her because she has the other information we need from BrightStone," I explain to Lucian. "Molly Bell's breeding program with the Inquestors, whatever other things she may have observed, it's all inside." I look at IronHeart. "Can you remove the data and put it into some format we can present to the Council?"

"I can do better than that," the dragon says, gesturing at the automaton with a clawed finger. "Come here, child."

Copper Betty hesitates, and I nod at her. "It's okay." I'm not even sure what I'm reassuring her about, but it can't hurt. Still, I can't help the nervousness that clenches at the base of my throat.

The automaton shuffles forward to the dragon, the two bronze mechanicals seeming to stare each other down. The dragon lets out a ticking noise, and Copper Betty does the same, then presses a button on the back of her neck. Her mouth opens, her head tipping backward to reveal the metal tongue that has remained silent for as long as I've known her. She lifts her tongue to reveal a slot beneath it, nestled within her jaw. Her eyes shutter, and a small square chip emerges from the slot.

"Take it, Magpie," IronHeart commands. "Carefully."

Holding my breath, I reach for it, my fingers scraping over the metal as I retrieve the chip. Copper Betty closes her mouth, blinking rapidly as I show it to IronHeart. "Now what?" I ask.

"Put it in here. The same slot we used for your messenger dragon. I won't be able to fix the larger screen for a while, but this should suit." She gestures at the control panel with its confusing buttons and gears, a wave of sounds that clink in my head and make my heart whir in return.

I place the chip in the same slot as before, the smaller screen above flickering to life. Images, words whispered and furtive, sounds of pleasure, babies crying into the silence—it plays back in a whirlwind, and I blink in dizzy recognition. Inquestors, whores, Molly Bell, a young Ghost, a younger Lucian, me. I even catch a glimpse of Sparrow from the fateful night the Inquestors killed her. I nearly turn away, but she's gone a moment later.

The pictures go backward until we see an image of Molly Bell from years ago, young and without the pointed teeth. She's gesturing as us. "Are you sure this will do what I need it to?" Molly says.

"Of course. I built it, didn't I?" The picture grows fuzzy and then clear. Based on the sudden gasp of both Ghost and Lucian, the woman who comes into view can only be Madeline d'Arc. The real one.

She radiates impatience, supremely confident in her power and her creations. Her hair is the color of honey and rum, her eyes the same warm champagne as Lucian's. Beneath her skin flickers the lightning, but it's faded, indicating she's been on BrightStone for at least a while. Her face is bare, save a splash of oil on her cheek and grease in her hair. There's an exhausted bent to her expression, as though she's gone weeks without sleep.

"It's not ideal, but with the parts I've modified, she'll run damn near forever, I suspect. No voice box, as requested. Or at least not one that can be turned on by normal means." Her face grows grim. "And in return, you'll do as I ask, yes?"

Molly waves her off. "Yes, yes. Of course. I'll watch out for them and do the best I can to make sure they don't get themselves killed."

"Well enough, then. Copper Betty is her name, and I will loan her out to you under the condition that when the time comes, you return her to me. It may not be me in this form, mind, but you'll know." Her voice drops. "When IronHeart roars, Meridion falls."

"My only wish," Molly Bells says fervently. "And yes, anything."

Madeline nods, stretching her arms up to crack her shoulders. "Farewell, Ms. Bell. May your fishing be successful and your whispers take shape."

"May Meridion slip into the sea and drown itself," Molly retorts, turning back to admire Copper Betty, her face taking on a pleased mien that I recognize all too well. Undoubtedly, she was looking for a way to get something else out of the scion, but when she turns around, Madeline is sauntering away through the alleyways whispering a tune I recognize from Ghost's own such serenades.

The screen shuts off with a blip, and the dragon grins. "Well, isn't that interesting?"

Lucian has sunk back down so he's sitting on the floor, his legs half sprawled out before him. "The hells," he says over and over.

"It is rather a lot to take in," the dragon admits. "Even for me. Getting to see my original form again..."

"Do you actually have affection for her?" Ghost asks, glancing over at Copper Betty, who is running her fingers over her metallic lips in a fashion I've never seen before.

"In as much as I might for anything, I suppose. Knowing that someone has made you into a living thing—or a sentient thing, perhaps," the dragon amends. "One cannot ever quite get over the awe of that, regardless of the reason for your creation. Whatever my original purpose, it's a bit difficult to let go. I am programmed to guard, to protect, and if necessary, to destroy. But that has gotten muddled with Madeline's memories, and that makes it difficult for me to determine what I should do."

"I'm not even going to begin trying to unpack that particular statement," Lucian says, rubbing his forehead. "Forgetting for a moment that I'm somehow speaking with a robotic dragon that contains the memories of my mother and all the ridiculous amounts of hysteria that I'm ignoring right now… Inside, I'm screaming, you understand? But if we can't get the Council down here—and I really don't think we should even mention this to them yet—then how do we sort through all this information? And I'm sure there are recordings you'd rather not be seen by the Council…or the general public."

I frown. "But why would the public see them?"

"It will leak. Information like this always does. And even if you don't care if people see everything, there are definitely some things *I* would rather not share, aye?" Ghost flushes slightly as he reaches out to grab my hand. I take the hint and nod.

"So one of us has to sit here and go through it, right? But even so, what then?" I don't exactly relish the thought of having to sit through hours of my own past, or anyone else's for that matter, as fascinating as it might be. "And it has to be one of us. I wouldn't trust anyone else with it."

Lucian exhales slowly. "And we'd have to capture the entire picture in such a fashion as to make sense to anyone who watches it."

"Too much of that and we'll be accused of manipulating it," Ghost points out, frustration playing over his face. "But maybe we can at least cut it so it only shows the parts worth mentioning. The…breeding program." His face wrinkles in distaste. "I'm sure the Tithes are in there. Not to mention the Rot."

"There's no chance of any one human getting it done fast enough for the Council, so let me sort it out," IronHeart says. "I'll make sure it's only relevant footage as it applies to the Rot and the circumstances therein, and leave the more personal bits out of it." There's an impatience to IronHeart's words, as though she simply wants us gone, and the thought makes me uneasy.

I tap my fingers on my hammer in irritation. "I think all that information will be useful, aye, but it's not visceral enough. It's not enough to simply show them the basic things. They're horrible, yes, but Meridians so far removed up here I don't think it's going to change many minds. Joseph has brought up what he found in d'Arc's lab in the Mother Clock, and he is willing to argue on our behalf. But it would count for more if we could find another witness to corroborate his claims. Buceph himself told me they were utilizing our blood to look for an immortality serum, but he was giving his own blood to Lord Balthazaar's wife to keep her from dying of the Rot."

"Somehow I hardly think that's going to help us. He could have been lying, after all. Or they'll simply say the Meridians in the Pits were acting on their own, without outside knowledge." Lucian pulls out a small sketch pad from his pocket and begins scratching out some notes.

"Maybe," I say slowly, "and Joseph might be able to attest to the facts of that one way or the other. But..." I shudder, thinking back on the facility where Buceph ran his experiments on Moon Children. "I know Buceph was in contact with the High Inquestor—there was a tube where they sent wax messages to each other—and the facility itself was Meridian technology. What if they recorded what they were doing?"

Lucian's nostrils flare. "I can't fault your logic," he admits. "For the sake of science, of course they would record it in some fashion. But you said the facility was underwater by the time the caves collapsed. There would be no way to retrieve it, even if it somehow survived."

"Hmm." IronHeart makes a thoughtful hum, and the sound ripples through my chest as though my own heart wants to answer in kind. It's disconcerting.

"That's a dead end. But maybe the High Inquestor would be worthwhile. Undoubtedly he will have some records that would corroborate some of this," I say, though the thought of seeing that man again makes me nauseated beyond reckoning. "The Chancellor wouldn't let me speak to him, but maybe if Lucian can convince her to let Jeremiah at least interrogate him?"

"Indeed. That is a path worth investigating," IronHeart admits, snaking her head down for a closer look at Copper Betty. To her credit, Copper Betty doesn't flinch, but then, why would she?

Lucian pales visibly but straightens himself up, tugging on his waistcoat, as though the familiar gesture will somehow set things right in his mind. "All right. We have a part of a plan. How long will it take to retrieve the data?"

"Given the amount and the complexity of it, several days at least, if not a week or two," IronHeart says. "I'll want to make sure everything downloads without corruption, and that level of data checking can take some time."

"Good enough," Lucian says. "That will give us the time to put out feelers and work with the BrightStone Chancellor regarding a possible custody transfer of the High Inquestor." He tugs on my sleeve. " turns to look at Ghost and me. "You two had best stay out of trouble in the meantime."

"Where are you going?" Ghost asks, stepping a little closer to me.

"To speak with Jeremiah directly. Given the amount of evidence you've collected, we may need to request more time for the Moon Child case." He smiles ruefully. "The marriage issue is another problem altogether. Our family standing has fallen a bit with last evening's shenanigans, but I trust he'll manage something."

Lucian tugs on his coat again. "And I could do with a hot bath and a meal and some rest. So could you, I expect."

His words are more weary than accusatory, but guilt flushes through me all the same. One of these days we will have to sit down and hash out everything, but as per usual, there simply isn't time for what will surely be an extensive conversation.

"All right, children," IronHeart rumbles. "Run along. Betty and I have work to do."

The three of us take our leave then, though I can't help looking back. Copper Betty is staring up at IronHeart, the two seeming to commune on a level I am quite sure even my heart wouldn't be able to decipher.

Copper Betty turns her head toward me, her blue eyes flickering into what almost appears to be a wink, and then the two of them face the monitors, the work of sifting the data beginning.

True to his word, Lucian mutters a quick goodbye when we step out of the sewers and then dashes off to see Jeremiah. His coat flaps in the wind in the wake of his long stride, so reminiscent of Joseph.

A thin drizzle has started, leaving him a lonely figure walking in a sea of people heading off to various destinations in the early dawn. The weather seems to keep the conversations around us to a minimum, and I am just as glad for it. I wonder if we should simply go back to Joseph's to retrieve our clan but decide against it for now. Better to let them all sleep in a place of safety, and somehow, I don't think Joseph would look too kindly on us waking him up again so soon. They have my dragon if they needed me. For now, that will have to suffice.

"I'm surprised you have rain up here at all," I say to Ghost, gesturing to the dome above us. "I would have thought everything here would be under control."

"Probably a question for...well, you know," he responds. "But my understanding is that my mother wanted to try to keep biorhythms as normal as possible, and that includes the plants and the trees. Sometimes rain is good." He glances at me with a half-smile. "It reminds me of our time at Molly Bell's, you know? Listening to the water pattering on that roof."

I shiver beneath his suddenly hungry gaze, gently shoving him away. "Later."

He laughs then, and the sound uplifts me like nothing else could, as though we might really pull this off. His hand slips into mine, our fingers entwine, and we melt into the rainy morning, our hats pulled tight against our heads.

Hot water splashes over the edge of the tub, but I ignore it, focusing only on its warmth on my skin. Exhaustion has creeped over my limbs, making me feel heavy, and I sag against Ghost's chest.

"Well, this could have gone better," he says, placing a kiss on the nape of my neck.

"Could have been worse, though." He tips my head toward him. His mouth meets mine, carefully at first, almost shy, before he lets out a growl and presses harder, his lips seeking me out in quiet domination.

"I just want all of this to disappear," he says a minute later, pulling back regretfully. "None of this has gone the way it should have, or the way either of us expected, and now with IronHeart and this Lottie garbage, I just don't know." A shadow rolls over his face. "I never wanted to ruin things for Lucian."

"I don't think they're ruined." He leans his head on my shoulder, and I slide my hand up to run my fingers through his hair. "If you ask me, I think Lucian had a nostalgic fever dream about what life was like before you left. Even if it was true, things have simply changed too much—you, him, this place. All we can do is move forward and try the best we can."

"Mags the Philosopher," he quips. "But maybe you're right. Maybe all this was just a pipe dream. There's no way of knowing now, but if so, what do you want to do? Stay here? Go back to BrightStone?" He's silent then, as though he isn't sure he wants my answer.

I'm not sure I actually have one.

Underneath the glitter, some of the Meridians are just as corrupt and awful as those from BrightStone. Even being confronted with the reality of our lives led very few of the members of the Council to care beyond the few moments it took them to have something like an emotional reaction. So why am I still so adamant about staying here?

My heart whirs at the internalized question in the same way it seems to every time my thoughts strayed to Meridion when I was a child, as though this untampered longing for the floating city is beyond my control.

"I'm a bit disappointed," I admit. "I was hoping that once we showed everyone what was going on, they would…I don't know exactly."

"Welcome Moon Children home with open arms?" Ghost raises a brow. "Altruism would be expecting too much, I suppose. In the end, it's no better than BrightStone. They just have better technology."

"Maybe Bran was right all along and coming here was a mistake." I crack open a nearby bottle of beer that I'd brought up from the kitchens and sip at the sudden rush of bitter foam. "It feels disrespectful somehow to have all this wealth, these abilities, and to do nothing with them. We're a part of this, too, even if we don't really belong. But I think I was really hoping we would fit in, despite it all."

We both sigh then, his fingers threading with mine as we pass the bottle back and forth, taking a long sip here and there. The alcohol burns its way down my throat with honeyed smoothness. My mind drifts back and forth like an oscillating pendulum, remembering those few hours trapped beneath the rock of BrightStone, the two of us lying on a makeshift raft and watching the glow bugs shimmer on the ceiling of the caves, unsure whether we would make it out or die there, drowning in corpses. And now we're here, surrounded by dreams made of steel and stone and flight, and somehow, I feel as trapped as before, the weight of such power pressing down on me with all the force of the Pits, and I am a stranger to everyone, and everything is strange.

Except Ghost.

I rest my head on his shoulder, the tears sliding over the bridge of my nose. "I love you," I murmur, my voice somehow even smaller than it ever has been before, as though the admission of such a thing is enough to break the laws of the universe itself.

He leans against my head with his, his mouth brushing over my cheek to kiss my brow. "Was that so hard to say?"

"Been waiting, have you?" I half gasp a laugh through a sudden sob, and his amusement hums through his chest.

"Perhaps," he admits. "Though what I told Lottie was the truth of it. I don't think there really is a name for what we have. Maybe that's how it should be."

"No one really understands what we are, so that's fitting enough." I shiver as I move to wipe at my eyes. "What now?"

"Well, I suspect something to eat wouldn't be amiss. Might as well snag something portable in case we get embroiled in some other issue while we wait for my brother to return. And the rest of the clan—who knows when they'll wake up? I'm sure Joseph won't lead them astray in the meantime."

"*Mmmph.* I wonder when Josephine will come back after returning to BrightStone with the Chancellor. I wouldn't be surprised if she's managed to pirate a half dozen ships by now." I snort at the thought. "Can you imagine, sailing through the night, taking our plunder, and sailing off again? It sounds like a child's story."

"Sparrow would have liked it," he says, and I laugh, though the words still sting a bit. For all our wishes of Meridian grandeur, there is something so appealing about the pirates that I can't help but smile.

"Fairy stories later," I say, gathering myself to my feet and tugging him up. My stomach rumbles, bringing me back to the pressing need to fill my belly. We extricate ourselves from the tub, hastily rubbing down and changing into casual shirts and trousers. They're new and soft, and I can only wonder at the fineness of the weave.

The kitchen is mostly as we left it, and I take advantage of it by scrounging together a couple of sandwiches made of ham and cheese and some kind of sauce Ghost slathers all over the bread. We chew in relative silence, and part of me marvels that we are here, eating food that is available for the taking, in a warm kitchen with comfortable furniture. It's uncanny, really. I've almost never had anything that is really mine, and I'm not sure I'll ever be able to wrap my brain around it. But I will take advantage of it all the same.

Ghost pours us each a drink from one of the bottles of the Lucian's whisky stash, and we sip slowly before heading up to my bedroom. The sound of the rain is comforting, pelting the roof in a rush—nostalgic and maybe a little sad, if I'm to be truly honest about it.

The whisky burns pleasantly in my belly, but neither Ghost nor I drink more than a few sips. It's more to take the edge off our nerves than to truly get drunk, but at this point, I'll take anything. My fingers itch for a smoke, but I have nothing of that nature on me, so

I have to content myself with simply tapping them aimlessly upon my knee.

"Do you think we'll ever really manage to fit in here?" I don't know if I want an answer or not, but maybe talking about it will bring me that much closer to finding an answer.

He stretches out on the bed, his limbs graceful and lean. "Maybe. For the most part, the Meridians up here lack the rote cruelty of the Inquestors or the ones down in the Pits. BrightStone doesn't even exist as a real place to them. More like something out of a fairy tale where the bad people live. We could be goblins for all the reality they think we are. Irritating, but we should use it to our advantage." His eyes seem to darken when he looks down at me. "You know what else we should take advantage of right now?"

"Do tell." I set my glass on the nightstand.

It's barely touched the wood before he's tumbled me backward, our clothing scattering like the shadows of ghosts. With no one in the house this time, he's louder, more insistent in his demands, as am I.

By the end of it, I'm vibrating with soft pleasure, my body sinking into the blankets with a contented satisfaction I've rarely known. Ghost curls up next to me, half dozing.

"With any luck, we'll have more time for this sort of thing when this is all over, aye?" I press a soft kiss to his forehead. My lips are tender, but I find I don't mind the pain at all.

"Eager thing, aren't you?" He smiles slyly, chuckling at the hot flush that flares across my cheeks.

"I've earned it, I'd say. But maybe you're right," I admit. "Let's see how it plays out, shall we?"

"To the bitter end," Ghost says, lifting his glass in salute.

A slip of the tongue
And a taste of pain,
A moment of lies
And a lifetime of shame.

— CHAPTER TWENTY-THREE —

A series of sharp knocks at the door brings me back to consciousness, my head aching something fierce. My mouth tastes like something took a piss in it. If I were below in the Pits, I would assume something did. But judging by the extremely empty whisky bottle by my head, there isn't much else it could be.

I struggle to my feet, wiping drool from my lips. Beside me, Ghost groans and rolls over on his side. There's an imprint of a book corner pressed into his forehead, and he rubs it with tired hand.

The knocking grows louder, more insistent, and he groans again, clamping his hands over his ears. "Make it stop," he mumbles.

I get out of bed, and stumble down the stairs. My bare feet plop on the tiles with a homey sound. "Coming," I shout. "You can stop that anytime now."

The sun pours through the window, and the glare makes me avert my eyes with a painful wince as I open the door to see Jeremiah, his arms crossed in clear frustration.

"Are you deaf?" he snaps. "Do you have any idea what time it is?"

"Uh, no?" I shudder against the sudden pounding in my head and stagger to the kitchen to get some water. "And close the door, aye?" I call back. "The sun's killing me."

"What's the fuss now?" Ghost asks, appearing in the doorway with bleary eyes that look as bloodshot as mine feel. "Where's Lucian?"

"He'll be along in a few minutes," Jeremiah says, blinking as he takes in my state of undress. I sip my water and study him. The way my head's pounding, he might as well be nothing more than a fever dream. Lucian's paramour is handsome with a finely cut jaw, but there's a burning intelligence behind the pale eyes and fine lightning bolts flash across his dark skin, sudden and erratic.

The moment stretches out into something awkward. "Can you at least go put some clothes on?" Jeremiah asks in a strained voice.

Ghost snickers, handing me his shirt. I toss it over my head, the hem coming down to mid-thigh. "That better?"

"Barely," Jeremiah says. He moves out of the way when Lucian storms through the front door. "Thank the gods."

Lucian gives Ghost and me a once-over. "Go get cleaned up and dressed, the both of you. As formal as you can. We've got the betrothal hearing in a few hours, and you need to look as though you haven't spent the night drinking."

"I thought you said it would take a few days? And we spent the morning drinking, aye?" I correct him, avoiding any mention of IronHeart. Jeremiah might be on our side, but I have no idea how much Lucian's told him.

"I've filed an injunction on all the Tantaglio House's claims with the Council to halt the entire process."

I brighten. "That's good, isn't it?"

"It certainly helps," Lucian agrees. "But we've definitely made things a little worse with the stunt you pulled at the party. With any luck, they're no longer interested in a betrothal, and we can move on from this particular mess."

"Quickly please," Jeremiah begs as Lucian shoos us up the stairs.

I hesitate. "Should I even be a part of this?"

"I think you'll have to be," Lucian says. "Although you have nothing to do with the betrothal contract itself, the Tantaglio barrister has indicated they may want to call you as a witness to what happened during the party." His mouth purses. "We'll do our best to keep you off the stand, however."

"What about Christophe?" I cross my arms. "He's taking the blame for something he didn't do."

"The Slinter boy?" Jeremiah frowns. "I believe his family got him released. He'll be brought before the Council at a later date. It's considered more of a civil matter at this point, due to the retaliatory nature of the crime and the obvious bad blood between Houses." He pauses and then closes his eyes. "That was you he was talking to on the news footage, wasn't it?"

"Aye, it was. But I had nothing to do with the airship at all. I can swear to that part of it, if it helps." Technically, it was true enough. "But seeing as he told me his brother and uncle were the ones who poisoned and kidnapped me and that he wants to testify against them as to that fact, I would rather he not be falsely accused."

"But you know who *did* steal the airship? Wait." Jeremiah holds up his hand. "Don't say another word. The less I know right now the better."

"Probably." Ghost drags me upstairs before I can say anything else. I wash quickly, running wet fingers through my hair. Ghost does the same, and the two of us put on something more suitable for the hearing. His trousers are pressed, shoes polished shiny, and shirt collar stiff, and buttons flashing on his overcoat.

I find the only skirt I'd let Lottie help me buy, a long black one of a soft weave, and a crimson waistcoat. The color allows for the striking shade of my hair to stand out against it. "Almost decent," I note. "Though I wish I might simply show up as I am."

"I understand," he says. "But the Council won't see it as anything but disrespectful, and the less we can give them to pick on, the better our chances will be."

"Civilized monkeys, aye," I say darkly, tugging on a jaunty hat that somehow balances on my head.

"I don't think it's quite that bad, but I see your point." Ghost offers me his arm, leading me down to the foyer where the others are waiting.

Jeremiah nods at our appearance. "That will do. The Council will not find any fault with your appearance at least."

I stifle a snort. I doubt that very much, but no point in saying it aloud. I suspect everyone else is thinking it anyway.

"It's too quiet," Lucian complains. "Where are your partners-in-crime?"

"My clan, you mean? They haven't been back. I'm assuming they're still with Joseph." My gaze darts to Ghost and then to Jeremiah. "Should we pick them up on the way?"

"Ah," he says. "Lucian did mention there were several others of Moon Child lineage staying here. They don't have to attend for this part. At your Council hearing later, we'll need their testimony for the citizenship process, to help determine Meridian culpability in their plight, but for today, it's best to keep the audience small."

"We did send an invite to Joseph to attend, though," Lucian says. "I wanted him to observe in case there was anything about this betrothal process he might remember." The barrister purses his lips wryly. "Finding anyone from that time period willing to talk to us right now is extremely rare. Might as well take advantage of all the resources we have." He coughs impatiently, gesturing at the door. "Shall we? The last thing we want is to be late."

We take an airship taxi to the High Council building. This time I'm far less impressed with how high we fly or the small bridge we have to cross, but my heart whirs nervously. I reach for Ghost's hand, and he slows, falling into step with me. The double doors in front of us are etched with silver and gold, the filigree seeming to tell the story of Meridion's founding, complete with a dragon in the center of the city.

I stifle a smirk when I see it but stop a moment later. There, just outside the inner doors stands Copper Betty.

Lucian halts in his tracks, looking back at me and Ghost. I shrug at him. As far as I knew, Copper Betty was supposed to remain with IronHeart until the file transfer was done at least.

"Why is she here?" Lucian hisses. "How would she even know to come?"

"Perhaps our mutual friend had something to do with it," I say faintly. "I wouldn't be surprised if she sent Betty along to be a witness of sorts. I certainly don't think she has any direct information that would be helpful to the betrothal case."

Jeremiah's expression grows guarded. "Something I need to know?"

"Ah, our family automaton is a bit eccentric. She may have some data that will be of importance to the case regarding Moon Children." Lucian frowns. "I would have mentioned it earlier, but I thought we needed to focus on the betrothal issue first."

"I wish you had," Jeremiah says, his cheek twitching in what seems like annoyance. "Automaton evidence has to be submitted in a specific way or it isn't considered viable." My stomach sinks. Perhaps we should have spoken with Jeremiah before simply dumping Betty into IronHeart's domain. The thought of all my hard work being dismissed for a technicality makes me queasy.

"We'll just have her watch, then," Lucian says, his tone firm.

"If you say." Jeremiah waves us through, Copper Betty bringing up the rear.

I keep my steps as even as I can, the clicking of my heeled shoes reminding me of the sound horses make when they trot through the streets of BrightStone.

The group of us is shown into the same council room as before, rows of benches separated by a wide aisle. Lottie and her family are clustered together in the front of the room. I stiffen despite myself as we walk past, feeling Caspian's gaze shoot daggers into my back.

"Looks like Joseph's already here," Ghost says. I look toward the back of the room, and sure enough, the Meridian scientist is there, watching from the back row. His clothes are far more formal than I've seen him in before, but his expression is nonplussed, as though he's not quite sure why he's here. Our eyes meet briefly, and he nods in recognition, giving me an apologetic smile.

I want to ask him where the rest of my clan is, but Madam Councilor Greta is banging her gavel, and there is no more time. We take our seats as quickly as we can.

"Are all the parties assembled? House Tantaglio versus House d'Arc in the matter of a reneged betrothal, correct?" the councilwoman asks, surveying the two groups. Her eyes land on me for a half moment longer than I like, but I don't need Ghost's warning squeeze to make me hold my tongue. I've waited this long. I can wait a bit longer.

Someone sniffs, echoed by a fit of low giggling. Caspian Tantaglio strides up, full of self-importance, his shiny shoes echoing like a pistol shot on the marble floors. His barrister, a woman with a pointed nose and pointier glasses, keeps stride beside him without even a twitch of lightning on her face.

"We are here," she announces. "And we have brought the evidence required. Caspian Tantaglio will present it on his own behalf."

"Ah, your eminence," Jeremiah says coolly. "We are also ready."

"I see," the councilwoman says. "Well, then. We shall proceed with the initial task at hand. It feels as though we were just here, weren't we?" She eyes Ghost and Lucian before turning her attention toward Lottie's family. "I believe the initial grievance is yours?"

"Yes, that's right." Caspian makes his way to his podium as the rest of us take our seats. "We were promised a liaison between our House and the House d'Arc. Years ago, their mother and I made a deal: our monetary support for her...charity venture down below in BrightStone." He sniffs at us. "Not that we felt it was a worthy endeavor, but the d'Arc name is an old one, and surely the melding of our two lines would be genetically fortuitous."

I try to keep from rolling my eyes, biting my tongue so I don't shout something rude about their family line.

"Your eminence," Jeremiah interjects smoothly, "this grievance is immaterial. The Tantaglio House has no direct evidence of such a betrothal occurring. It is merely hearsay." His mouth purses. "They knew of Madeline d'Arc's problems and wished only to take advantage of her for their own gain. There is no record of such a betrothal, not in her sons' memories and not in any of her notes."

"I hardly think the memory of a child counts as evidence," Caspian insists, his face growing red. "Your protest means nothing—if you can't come up with a better argument than that you might want to consider giving up law as a career choice."

"Insults are the ploy of a schoolyard bully," Jeremiah retorts. "And if that's the only answer you have, perhaps we ought to remove this entire proceeding from the courtroom to the playground?"

"Order!" the councilwoman, bangs her hammer so that the sound rockets past us. I clamp my hands over my ears at the sharpness of the report.

"Does the sound of justice bear mocking?" Caspian points at me with disdain.

I cock my head at him, unable to stand down at his attack. "To be fair," I retort mildly, "living underground in the dark for months without end does not leave one unscarred. My senses aboveground are frightfully sharp. Often painfully so." I gesture at my dark glasses.

"Ahem, what my client is saying is simply a cause and effect of the mistreatment they have received by our people during their time in the city below known as BrightStone." Jeremiah shakes his head at me in warning. "A matter that we will attend to in a later trial. But she means no mockery or misunderstanding of the process, that I can assure you."

"Indeed," the councilwoman says tonelessly, her eyes clipping back to Lottie's father. "What evidence do you have in this matter of betrothal?"

"Since when is a Meridian's word not considered evidence enough?" he responds piously. "And one might question the opposing side's choice of council in this case. I seem to have heard that he has a personal bias. I don't think we can trust him to be completely honest when it comes to facts."

"That is uncalled for," Lucian snaps. "Jeremiah has never been anything but the most professional, even when he had no cause to be so. Your maligning him is stepping close to slander, sir."

"Oh, enough of this bullshit," Copper Betty snaps, standing up from her place on the bench behind us with a mechanical clang.

My head whips toward the automaton, my mouth dropping at the sound of her voice. Had IronHeart repaired her voice mechanism? But no...something in the way she moves is distinctly unlike herself. Her blue eyes are now a warm gold. My stomach drops as I realize Copper Betty isn't Copper Betty at all, but IronHeart herself.

Oh, but if she's here, where's the dragon, Mags?

The automaton saunters toward Caspian, her electric eyes flashing dangerously. "You know quite well we never agreed to such terms—not as things are now. And you only wanted to take advantage of my estate in the hope of furthering your own power. At least admit your duplicity. I might actually respect you for it." A ripple of disbelief spreads through the crowd, Madam Councilor Greta gaping, as IronHeart continues. "Besides, you know as well as I do why such a marriage would never work."

The councilwoman points at Jeremiah. "Explain this!"

Jeremiah makes a soft, questioning sound. "Your eminence, I have no idea…"

"He didn't know," IronHeart says, her metallic voice clear and sharp. "None of them did."

"What is this all about?" Caspian retorts. "As far as I know, automatons can't give direct testimony."

"Ah, but I am no ordinary automaton, am I?" She bows. "IronHeart, at your service. Or Madeline d'Arc, if you prefer. In the flesh, more or less." She looks at her metal hand ruefully. "Or at least a working facsimile thereof."

A low murmur of voices buzzes among the attendees of the proceedings, the members of the High Council frowning as they lean together, angry whispers and outraged words filtering through the room. I catch Lucian's attention, and in that instant, I can see both the sadness and despair in his face at the way things have turned. IronHeart or not, the automaton may have just completely upended everything we are trying to do. If the Council chooses to ignore her words or to stretch this out while they investigate her origins, who knows when it would be over?

"An unusual claim and one we do not have time to verify. That said, we cannot allow this breach of protocol," the councilwoman says finally, her mien thoughtful though her voice is shaken. "And you're turning these proceedings into a circus. If you have no direct legal evidence regarding the validity of the betrothal, then sit down and let us continue."

I can only give the woman credit for keeping her composure in the face of such incredulity. But it's clear this particular endgame of Madeline's isn't going to work as she hoped. Even a robotic representative of the scion of Meridion was not enough to dissuade the court from the task at hand.

"Oh, I've proof enough," IronHeart says dismissively, pointing to Ghost. "My son is all the proof you need."

"How so? What would prevent you from aligning your two Houses?" Councilor Tendou's eyes narrow.

"She's a selfish thief and a liar, that's what." Caspian's face has darkened to that of a beet, flaming hot as electricity nearly sparks from his skin.

"The hells she is," Ghost snaps, his own temper finally breaking beneath the other man's words.

"You heard me boy. I was a major supporter of her research into immortality. She stole my investment money and took off below after nearly destroying all the technological advances we made, simply because she didn't agree with how we were hoping to implement the serum. My shares in the project dropped so quickly I nearly lost all our holdings. It's taken me years to rebuild them, only for you and your brother to reappear, mocking me with your presence." His mouth curves into a sneer. "I merely want to ensure that my losses can be reclaimed by this marriage. That way my family won't have to suffer."

"So you admit this potential marriage has nothing to do with any sort of promise," Jeremiah presses. "It is simply an act of revenge?"

"It doesn't matter," Caspian retorts, pointing at Ghost. "He admitted he was one of those disgusting Moon Child creatures at the engagement party. My family is a laughingstock, thanks to him. Hells, how do we even know he's a son of d'Arc at all? He could be some beggar picked up on the side of the road."

Jeremiah's eyes narrow. "And if it was proven he was, in fact, Madeline d'Arc's child, would you still be willing to see him wed into your family, even knowing he might be sterile? That he might taint your lineage with Moon Child genetics, if he isn't?"

I frown. What in the hells is he trying to prove?

"If it would hurt the d'Arc family name in any way, I would do it in a heartbeat," Caspian says. "Moon Child or not." Lottie buries her face in her hands as she tries to sink into the bench beside her mother. I can only feel pity for her, to have her family revealed to be nothing more than petty monsters more interested in breeding stock than common decency.

IronHeart sighs. "How convenient a memory you have, Caspian. Of course, he's my child. But he *can't* marry your daughter. He's your son, too, you halfwit."

"That's im-impossible," Lottie's father stutters. "I would never have fathered such an abomination, let alone strayed outside my marriage."

Beside me, Ghost lets out a whooshing gasp, the color draining from his face. A bit of lightning flares briefly on his skin, and then he goes completely dark, his eyes shuttered. I reach out for him, but he avoids me, his head in his hands as though he means to shut out the rest of the world.

"Explain yourself, madam." Lady Tantaglio takes to her feet, incensed. "Do not think you will simply get out of the contract by throwing out baseless lies." Her mouth compresses sharply as she stands before the council, her tone imploring. "Why are we even listening to this? How do we know this isn't some trick by the d'Arcs to get out of a contract they agreed to?"

"It's hardly a lie," the automaton says. "But you don't need to take my word. All you need is a simple blood test and that should be more than enough. I'm surprised that wasn't one of the stipulations from the beginning, to be honest." She turns toward Lottie's father. "So you see, there's no point in him marrying into your family. By my reckoning, he's already the heir. Amazing. The scion of two powerful Meridian families, right under your noses all this time."

"Not that you saw fit to even let us know," Lucian says sourly.

"And how would it have helped you if I had?" She points to Lottie's family. "Do you think I would have let that man take your brother as some sort of collateral? Believe me, he would have tried." She turns toward the High Council. "I ran from Meridion, of course—everyone knows that—but not before injecting Trystan with the very serum I was working on to try to cure the plague that had erupted in BrightStone. A plague that we were instrumental in releasing, mind." Her voice lowers. "I would rather have seen my son abandoned below, mocked for what he was, than to have him used as some sort of pawn up here in a game played by degenerates more interested in their own holdings than using the technology at their fingers to help those worse off."

She clanks back and forth, clicking her fingers at me as she passes. "I know you thought I was crazy. Maybe I was. But I never left anything to chance. I have been keeping track of everything for nearly twenty years now. Believe me when I tell you that there is almost nothing I don't know about what certain people have been doing on our fair city."

She scans the room, her burning gold eyes impartial and deadly. "But that is for another date and time, I suspect. My body is long gone and there is nothing I can do to bring it back, so there is no particular hurry to discuss the current situation of my existence." Her voice turns smug. "I was never popular when I was alive. I expect I'll be less so in this form."

"This is preposterous." Madam Councilor Greta's nostrils flare wide, snapping her fingers at the automaton. "You will remove yourself from this hearing immediately. Do not return."

IronHeart snorted. "You don't have to tell me twice. My work here is done." To her credit, the automaton leaves the courtroom without another word, leaving only the droning murmur of the crowd in her wake. Joseph stares at IronHeart as she leaves, his mouth slightly agape. Somewhere in his mind, he is clearly trying to process the fact that his ex-paramour is currently walking around in the body of an automaton she built so long ago. It wasn't the way I wanted to tell him, but I have no way to explain that at the moment.

Madam Councilor Greta jabs her gavel at Jeremiah. "There will be an investigation into this, let me assure you. If we find any evidence that this was planned, you will be stripped of your right to practice law on Meridion, is that clear?"

Jeremiah bowed deeply in response. "Of course, Your Honor." His jaw is clenched so tight I'm afraid his teeth will shatter.

"Thank you, Madam Councilor Greta, for seeing the right of it," Caspian says, his mouth curving in triumph. "I'm glad to see that Meridion good sense is still a standard in which we can take pride."

"Let's end this little farce, right now." Madam Councilor Greta's expression grows resigned. "By order of the High Council, I request Trystan d'Arc be taken into custody for genetic testing. If it is as...the automaton has said, then whatever betrothal claims have been made will be thrown out. Otherwise, we will reconvene to determine further course of action."

Jeremiah holds up his hand. "Agreed, but he must be returned to us within the hour. The results will need to be documented with the city records either way."

"Very well. We shall take a short recess and then commence with the second part of this suit once the results are back." She bangs the gavel again, her face pensive as she and her cohorts disappear behind a set of thick velvet curtains.

The rest of the people file out to disperse elsewhere for a time, but I pay no attention to them or Lottie or her family at all as I kneel beside Ghost. He peers up at me through hair that's somehow suddenly wild, his dark eyes wide. His mouth moves, but I can barely hear him over the din, and I lower my ear to his lips.

"—out. Get me out of here, now." His voice is raspy and terrible. Lucian gives us a stricken look of his own that indicates he also had no idea. I gesture toward the exit, and he nods, so I grab Ghost by the hand.

"Come on. Let's get a bit of fresh air, aye?" Lucian helps him stand, the two of us leading him out one of the side doors to where a large balcony overlooks the Inner Spiral. It's empty of people, and there's a small nook to one side, some sort of artistic pot emblazoned with flowers sitting in lone decoration.

"I'll buy you a few minutes of time to calm down." Jeremiah ducks back into the chambers to head off the guards who are approaching to take Ghost into custody.

Ghost is almost panting now, turning away from me to violently vomit into the flowerpot, his chest continuing to heave for several moments after he loses everything he ate for breakfast. "I just… I can't… What?" He stares blankly at me and Lucian. "I don't understand. How… how could he be my father? Why would she ever…?"

"Moon Children have no fathers," I say, warning Lucian with a shake of my head. "And rarely mothers. Clan is clan is clan. That's all that matters. Prince or pauper, lineage means nothing to us."

"But I'm not even a proper Moon Child at all, am I?" He scowls. "She may as well have made me in a lab."

"You may not have had a clan growing up," I admit. "But there wasn't one of us who wasn't a bit envious of it. And there wasn't one of us who didn't know who you were. You were always a Moon Child, Ghost."

I wrap my arms around him then, pressing his face into my shoulder. He's on the edge of breaking down. I can feel it in the very air trembling around him. But he doesn't, and when Lucian taps him gently to tell him it's time, he lets me go and follows his brother without a word.

Inside, I can hear Lucian arguing with the guards. "And I'm a doctor so I'll do the damn blood draw!" he roars. "Take that stipulation or forget the whole thing." The response is lost to me, but Lucian hasn't been thrown out so I can only assume they accepted his terms.

I pace the balcony, staring out at the Inner Spiral with a fleeting wish that I might become a magpie in truth, wings and feathers and a mournful cry, meant to fly from here and all the ridiculous trappings of a society mired in stagnation.

It's deathly quiet when we retake our seats to await the results. Lottie's family has returned, but she is noticeably absent, thankfully.

Jeremiah has his head bent down next to Lucian's, the two men whispering furiously. IronHeart is still gone, but that's just as well, my fury at what she just did to Ghost making me nearly incoherent with rage every time I think of it.

At last, a woman in a white coat appears from one of the many doors on the far side of the hall. The tension of the room fills up and up, making it hard for me to swallow. Drinking a mug of poison would be easier than the long wait while she walks up to the High Council. Her heels *tap, tap, tap* on the marble, my clockwork heart echoing in matching time.

Madam Councilor Greta watches impassively, nodding when the bonewitch hands her a sheet of paper. She scans the page in a matter of seconds, slamming the gavel down. "The results are undisputable. They are as the automaton has said: Trystan d'Arc is also the scion of Tantaglio House and, therefore, may claim inheritance rights to either House…or both."

Lady Tantaglio lets out a weeping cry and is immediately rushed out the door by her attendants. Caspian stares after her, his wild-eyed gaze jerking to the Council, then to Lucian, and then to me.

"This isn't finished," he snarls, gathering his hat and coat. He storms from the courtroom, a burning flush turning his face red.

"Wouldn't it be a shame if he dropped dead of apoplexy?" I say to no one in particular, earning me a sharp look from Lucian

"Order!" Madam Councilor Greta calls out, whipping the hammer out to bang it again. She points to Jeremiah with it. "Your client is released into your custody, and the Tantaglio House case is dropped. If you wish to talk inheritance rights, you will have to file another motion."

"That won't be necessary," Jeremiah says quickly. "My clients have indicated they do not want to pursue family rights at this time."

"Well and good. Court adjourned," she says. Her face is suddenly weary as she removes herself from the bench.

A moment later, the court guards escort Ghost from the side door through which the bonewitch had retreated, his eyes quiet and hollow.

Lucian looks at him and then exhales softly, helping Jeremiah gather up the evidence folders. "Let's go home."

The sea is a saucy maid
Her foam a dress of white,
A shadow in the deepest depths,
And a dancer in the night.

— CHAPTER TWENTY-FOUR —

I remove the fancy clothes I was forced to wear and wiggle my toes from the confines of my boots. The loose trousers and a sleeveless shirt I put on suit me far better. Ghost is already half-asleep on the bed. He didn't even bother changing at all, his exhaustion written over his face.

The mattress creaks beneath my weight as I sit, my fingers ruffling through his hair. He leans into me for the span of a couple of breaths before withdrawing. "I'm sorry," he says, the words at odds with the emotional quell of his face. "I think I need a little time alone. It's a lot to process."

"I understand." And I did. Some things are simply too big to have anyone else be a part of.

"I love you, Mags," he says softly as I shut the door behind me.

I head down the hallway, my calves aching. I escape to the kitchen to stuff my face with some sort of leftover pasta and bread pastry that someone was kind enough to bring home with them. It settles in my nervous belly like a ball of lead, but it tastes wonderful, so I focus on that little bit luxury and sip at a bottle of beer.

Jeremiah and Lucian are talking in the other room, the rhythm of their voices soothing one moment and anxious the next.

Planning their strategy for our upcoming process, no doubt. When their tones drop into furtive whispers, my ears prick, and I cautiously make my way to the parlor where they've set up a bit of a war room.

Papers are scattered everywhere, a mishmash of parchment and inks, a typewriter and some other technology I don't quite recognize. IronHeart is there now, too, her arms crossed as her golden eyes flash in irritation. "Stop being so petty."

"That was about the cruelest thing I've ever seen," Lucian snaps at her. "And I don't care if it was for the theatrics of the thing or whatever strategy you have. You destroyed him in that moment. If he has any memories of his mother at all, I can only pray he'll forget them and forget you."

"Caspian wasn't going to listen otherwise—not him or his family," IronHeart points out. "They had their minds made up about it. Now they'll hide away and hope we forget our claim upon their House." She snorts. "Not that I ever wanted it to begin with. Some people simply can't help thinking their shit is plated in gold and that somehow makes it worth wanting. In the end, it's still nothing but shit."

"That doesn't mean you couldn't have given him a heads-up," I say, emerging from the hallway. They startle at my appearance, though IronHeart doesn't seem to register my presence, as fixated as she is upon Lucian.

I take a seat in one of the overstuffed chairs, curling my feet beneath me, my hair glowing faintly in the burnished light. I catch Jeremiah staring at me, and I gesture at him. "Go on. Ask."

"No, no. It's not right. And it doesn't matter anyway. Lucian has told me much about you and the time you lived with him below in BrightStone." He pauses, eyes suddenly bright and warm, his lips curling into an amused smile that seems almost sensual. "You're a very brave woman, Mags. The bravest I've ever met."

I almost flush beneath his words, unsure how to react in the face of such brazen charisma. He would make a formidable foe, and I say as much out loud. "To think Lucian willingly invites you to his bed. He's far braver than I am," I mutter.

Lucian rolls his eyes. "And how is Trystan?"

"Not great. Today wasn't exactly the best of days, as I'm sure you're all aware." I take another swig of the beer, glancing over to see IronHeart watching me. "Yes?"

"Nothing," she says shortly. "I almost wish you'd been my daughter, you know. You've got the backbone I need."

"No thanks. I'm just as happy not to know who I'm related to." I gesture with the beer bottle at the group of them. "All this shows me is that families are nothing more than beacons of drama held together by a thin fishing line of, what? What is it? Genetics? Far better to have a family of your own choice, aye?"

"Your perspective would be a fresh breath of air on the floor." Jeremiah taps his finger thoughtfully on one of the files laying on the desk.

"Mags has an interesting perspective on a great number of topics," Lucian says dryly. "But they may not be words that will help much."

"Too graphic for the pearl-gripping ladies of the court, I suppose. And you"—I nod at Jeremiah—"what in the hells did you mean about asking if the Tantaglio House would still accept a betrothal with Ghost even if he was a Moon Child? Why would you even entertain that?"

Lucian and Jeremiah exchange a look of lofty amusement. "It was a trap," Lucian says finally.

I frown. "How so? Caspian clearly doesn't think much of Moon Children. All he said was that he would be willing to consider it for revenge. How does that accomplish anything?"

"Because by saying he would take a Moon Child in as marriageable, the Council must now admit that your people are, in fact, worthy of being considered citizens," Jeremiah says softly. "Though Caspian's reasons for doing so might not have been particularly noble, the fact of the matter is that if such a great House would find it acceptable, we can make our arguments accordingly."

I gape at them. "Was…that planned?"

"Not exactly," Jeremiah admits. "But Lucian and I had discussed it if the possibility came up, especially after Trystan admitted it in the middle of the masked ball. With so many witnesses about and then with the blood test to confirm that he was of Meridian lineage after all, it simply allows us to get our foot in the door. No promises, mind."

"But it is a start." Lucian reaches out to cover Jeremiah's hand with his. I look away from this little act of intimacy, feeling like I ought to leave them be.

"Perhaps." Jeremiah smiles gently at his lover before turning to me. "As far as the Moon Children's case goes, we will be starting with Chancellor Davis. She will have the…stylistic grace, perhaps, to make them understand the gravity of the situation in a way we cannot. As leader of a city, she is uniquely qualified to explain the issues at hand."

"And what of my clan? The other Moon Children?" I ask it, knowing I'm probably not going to like the answer.

"You'll be called as witnesses, or as a sort of living evidence," Jeremiah explains, "so we can show the scale of the corruption in BrightStone and how it was directly influenced by Meridion. The more sympathetic you look, the better off we'll be."

"And when does all this take place?" I ask. "We left my clan at Joseph's, so we should probably inform them if they're going to be needed."

"I believe they've given us a start date next week," Jeremiah says. "But make no mistake, this isn't going to be finished in a single day." He points to the piles of papers. "We have many witnesses and a lot of evidence to present. Doing so in a cohesive fashion will take time."

Lucian hesitates. "There's something else, Mags. You should probably tell the other Moon Children when you get a chance."

My stomach sinks. Lucian's sudden burst of honesty means nothing good. "What?" I bite out, bracing myself for his words.

"The High Inquestor... The Chancellor agreed to our request that he be present to take the stand, if need be. To confirm our testimony." My eyes narrow. "But it won't be without cost."

My voice rises a few notches as I try to quell the panic scratching down the length of my spine. "What did you promise him?"

"A plea deal that will allow him to return to Meridion permanently," Jeremiah says. "I know it's not ideal. Lucian has told me how much you've all suffered at his hands, but I do think we will get a better result if we—"

Smash!

The glass of the beer bottle shatters just behind his head. He ducked just in time. "That's disgusting," I snarl. Lucian doesn't meet my eyes, and that infuriates me further.

IronHeart flicks a bit of broken glass from the table in front of her. "We wanted to tell you the truth. I do think this is perhaps the best choice in this situation."

"Aye, and isn't *that* rich coming from you?" My upper lip curls at her. "Where was all that honesty years ago when you left Meridion without a trace, without telling your family the truth of who and what they are?"

"I assure you, my organic originator had her regrets, as I've said," IronHeart says stiffly.

"I'm sure. Where's the real Copper Betty, by the way?" I start to pace in front of the fireplace, every instinct in me screaming to flee. "Locked up in a drawer somewhere?"

"Of course not. She's in my previous body and settling in quite nicely." IronHeart taps a metal finger on one of the folders on the table. "She's sorting through the video evidence even as we speak, arranging it in the proper order for the maximum impact for presentation. I have no doubts about her ability to do that. She knows what's at stake, after all."

"How convenient for you." This situation is making me far more uneasy than I like. IronHeart seems more than a touch mad at times, but then maybe she had reason to be. "Too bad you couldn't have let us in on your little plot before this morning. Might have gone a lot further if we'd known what to expect."

"It wasn't part of the initial plan. I was only there to observe the proceedings directly." She waves her hand. "No one really cares except those old-blood Meridian families that can't think their way out of a paper bag. They can accuse me of stealing money all they want, but I went down to BrightStone because I was hoping to force them to start working with other groups of people, utilizing other resources."

Her voice trails away as she looks at me, her mouth pursed. "Well, not your sort of resources, of course. Using Moon Children as test subjects... I don't know what that idiot Buceph was thinking. He completely corrupted my plans."

"So mighty, so misunderstood." It's obvious that expecting IronHeart to take responsibility for the emotional turmoil she helped create is too much. Copper Betty had more empathy in her electric eyes than IronHeart could ever have.

The alcohol burns deep in my belly as I debate what I need to do, my balance shifting precariously. Lucian reaches out as though to steady me, but I evade him. "You know, you talk about family and my bravery as though it's something to be proud of. It's not. When I talk about family of choice, I mean that I would do anything for my clan and they would do anything for me. No one can dispute that. Ever. But the truth of it is, they are not my family of choice and I'm not theirs. We were thrown together by your people, manipulated by your people, controlled by *your* people. There was no choice of any kind, save the sort you make in the dark when you're trying not to die."

"And that's no choice at all," Bran says softly from the doorway.

I blink, surprised to see him there. Our eyes meet and I let out a plaintive whistle as my dragon wings into the room to land on my shoulder. "You're back? All of you?" I crane my head to peer past him, but I don't see any of the rest of my clan.

"In a manner of speaking." He inclines his head, ignoring Lucian's querying grunt. "Let's go."

The night air sifts through my hair like a melancholy song. Bran and I are sitting on the roof of the house, and he's letting me ramble on about the events of the day, my head resting on my knees as I let the words pour out of me.

"Seems like we missed a lot," he says quietly. "We slept for a long time at Joseph's apartment. I don't think we realized how much stress we were all under until we found a spot where we could relax. We were still there when Joseph came home from the hearing, but he didn't seem to want to talk about what happened. We took that as our sign to leave and came here. By way of another noodle shop, of course."

"We'll need the others," I say. "Listening to Lucian and Jeremiah, they'll want us to be there to present ourselves as evidence since we are the only Moon Children who made it out of the Pits alive. While the rest of the Moon Children in BrightStone can certainly share their experiences, it's not the same."

"No." He pulls out a cigarillo and lights it up, taking a deep pull on it before passing it to me. "Is there an actual plan at this point or is it going to be a fly-by-the-seat-of-our-pants shitshow?"

I smirk despite myself, blowing a perfect smoke ring. "How do things usually go for us?" He laughs, and it's an ugly bitter thing, echoed in my own halfhearted chuckle. "I have no idea. The way the High Council was talking, I don't even know if the evidence Copper Betty has will be allowed. Jeremiah said it would have to be submitted a certain way, but if IronHeart messed that up today, I don't know where that's going to leave us."

"Nowhere at all. Like usual." He takes the cigarillo back and crushes the stub on the copper shingles. "When is this particular bit of hell supposed to take place?"

"Next week. Jeremiah and Lucian are still sorting through Joseph's data and Madeline's notes. Chancellor Davis is going to testify on our behalf, though I don't know how much good it will do." I stretch my arms out and slowly roll onto my back to look up at the stars, a soft coldness taking root in the pit of my belly. "They're also bringing up the High Inquestor to testify—in exchange for his freedom. Or at least he'll get to stay on Meridion."

He stares at me. "I see."

"Don't blame me," I snap, ignoring the dragon hissing in my ear. "It wasn't my idea at all."

"I know that." He scowls at the cigarillo ash as though he regrets putting it out. "He's a master manipulator, that one. It's a bad idea. I should have killed him when I had the chance."

"Maybe," I concede, trying to ignore the uneasy roil in my belly. These are waters I don't know how to begin to swim.

He stands up. "I've got something to show you."

I cock a brow at him. "Why, Bran, I didn't know you felt that way." He snorts, moving toward the edge of the roof. "What about the others? Where are we going?"

"They're still at that noodle shop, I suspect." A smile flickers over his face. "This place does have good food, and plenty of it. That part is nice."

A small twinge strikes me at their sudden independence, but it's tempered by pride. Like raising babies, maybe. It's bittersweet, but if they can get by without me, so much the better. "Hold on." I duck inside to check on Ghost. He's out cold, snoring slightly. I scrawl out a small missive and leave it on the pillow beside him: *Out with Bran. Back soon.*

I press a kiss against his forehead and slip out the window and down to where Bran is waiting for me. "Where are we going?"

His mouth purses slightly. "You'll see."

The view from the airship is spectacular as we weave in and out of the buildings, the speakers below blaring out a thumping beat that I suppose passes for music. It thrums its way into my head, the flashing lights making my vision blur. I push my smoked lenses closer to my eyes, scanning the inside of the airship.

It's enormous, and clearly very heavily modified with a dance floor inside that reminds me a bit of Molly Bell's brothel, although obviously far more technologically advanced. It has its own noodle shop, run by a crystalline automaton with hair that lights up with each pulse of music. And yet, for its great size, the airship is mostly empty of people, except for my clan scattered about various windows and the Heart of the Sea herself, holding court in the upper deck, framed by a balcony looking down below. I can see the glow from Bran's hair as he perches on the spiral staircase that separates the two levels.

I sidle up to Rosa. "Noodle shop, eh?"

She smirks, tugging on one of her braids, which has fallen loose beneath her woolen hat. "It wasn't exactly like we were asked to participate in the Council stuff today. And frankly, we were bored."

"And since Bran apparently had an open invitation from a certain celebrity, he decided to accept," Dafyyd adds. "We tagged along, of course."

"Of course," I repeat dryly. "I'm glad it didn't turn out to be an actual trap of some kind. What's her angle?"

Gloriana frowns. "I'm not sure she has one. She saw what went down at the party, and I think she was intrigued. She didn't know how to get in touch with us directly, hence that odd little song the other night, and— Well, maybe it's easier if you simply go up there and talk with her, aye?"

I nod and head up the stairs, passing by a wide-eyed Haru, who is apparently fascinated by one of the video screens illuminated with images of the ocean, a flash of sunlight sparkling through the waves to show some great monstrosity breaching the surface. I shudder at the thought of that enormous maw swallowing me up, but I say nothing. Who am I to disturb him in his moment of happiness?

Bran moves out of the way as I climb the stairs past him. The Heart of the Sea is seated on what appears to be a throne of iridescent seashells, a swarm of chambered nautilus thrumming around her head.

"I'm so pleased to see you here," she says, smiling broadly. Her dress hangs like translucent seaweed, draping over her torso in ragged strips. "I thought we might take advantage of the privacy here to discuss a few things."

"I'm a little confused," I admit. "What's this all about?"

"Me," says a quiet voice from behind us.

I flinch, turning to see Lottie sitting in an overstuffed chair, clutching a stuffed toy to her chest. Her eyes are bloodshot and swollen from crying, but there's a set to her jaw that wasn't there before.

"I…left my House," she says, her mouth trembling. "I want to help you."

"What does that mean?" I ask. "And help me how?"

"She abandoned her family, like I did." The Heart of the Sea's face glows with pride. "It means casting off the support she has known all her life, giving up a chance at inheritance and possibly even acceptance within Meridian society."

"I know you have no reason to trust me. I hurt you and Trystan, even though that was never my intention." Lottie looks me square in the eye. "But I want to try to fix it. Why do you think Christophe took the fall for the stolen airship? He wants to help you, as well. In part to make up for his family's actions, but also because he simply thinks it's the right thing to do. We both do."

I can't help but be skeptical at her confession, but I trust Ghost's opinion of her more than my own. He is less quick to judge. If he were present, he would hear her out. For the moment, I will do the same.

"And how do you plan to do that?" I cross my arms and lean against the wall.

"Meridion is dying. Anyone with eyes can see that," the Heart of the Sea says. "The system here is antiquated, and we're tired of these old customs ruling our lives." She inclines her head at Lottie. "It's why I left my House. Of course, that came with its own challenges, but the reward was worth the risk. There's a certain amount of notoriety I have as a celebrity, and I use that to my advantage." A rueful smile crosses her face. "I've been building my following for some time. I believe now is the moment to make a move."

"But I thought the whole point of all these betrothals was to keep the families here from crossing bloodlines," I say. "Or at least, that's what Lucian always told me."

The Heart of the Sea waves her hand dismissively. "That may have been the case, but honestly, at this point we're running out of options. And since it's clear that we can, in fact, breed with citizens of BrightStone, why not attempt to bring in some fresh blood, so to speak?"

"But we're sterile," Bran says, his tone far gentler than his usual wont.

I pause, unsure of how to process this. One on hand, more allies are always welcome. But still… "And where does that leave Moon Children? Our fathers were Meridian criminals injected with the serum, unwanted by their own people. Even if you do start wedding and bedding BrightStone citizens, that leaves us in limbo. Still unwanted. Still unneeded."

"And what happens if we're actually immortal now? Or close to it?" Bran shakes his head. "I can't say I fancy an entire lifetime of living on Meridian or BrightStone scraps, aye?"

"Though if we ourselves are somewhat long-lived due to the serum, perhaps we simply need to wait everyone else out." I tap my chest. "Or, you know, I can restart the city and fly us all away."

Lottie stiffens. "You can what?"

Bran rumbles a warning sound in his throat, but I ignore him, pulling my shirt down to display the panel on my chest. "Courtesy of Madeline d'Arc. I can open any Meridian lock, and in theory, I can restart the city. I'm not entirely sure of how it works, but as a bargaining chip, I imagine it might be worth something, aye?"

"Why haven't you come forward with this yet?" The Heart of the Sea's hungry gaze grows even more intense, as though she's imagining myriad uses for me.

"I was poisoned simply for being a Moon Child," I point out. Lottie mumbles an apology, but I ignore it. "Why would I expose myself so early? Some Meridians know, and the Council is aware of the rumors, but they appear to not care much."

Lottie frowns. "Then what was the stunt with that automaton? She called herself IronHeart, claimed she had Madeline d'Arc's memories. Surely she could tell you about your heart?"

I pause, not sure I want to open this can of worms just yet. "I'm not at liberty to share those details."

"Still, it's a hell of a marketing tool," the Heart of the Sea says thoughtfully. "Given a bit of time and some effort, I could make you a virtual star up here. The Council may have their day in court, but they can't sway the masses like I can."

"I don't want to be a star," I say firmly. "I simply want my people to have a place and a chance to survive on their own, to succeed or fail on their own." I point at Lottie. "The university, for example. I don't want us to be able to attend as…as part of a sideshow attraction, but as students, as people. There is a difference between being given an opportunity and being made into one."

"I understand," she says, turning to Bran. "I saw there were others of your clan here. Would it be okay if I went and talked to them?"

He shrugs. "If they want to. But don't make promises you have no intention of keeping," he warns her.

"I won't. I only want to meet them." She disappears down the steps, her head high as she sucks in a deep breath to approach Gloriana. Good. She can make or break those relationships on her own—and so can the rest of my clan.

"What's your plan exactly?" I ask the Heart of the Sea, wondering if I should put her in touch with Josephine. The two women were formidable in their own respective rights. Between the monstrosities of their airships alone, they would be downright terrifying.

"The Moon Child hearing is coming up in a week, is it not?" The Heart of the Sea chews on the tip of her pinky, and Bran stifles a groan beside me.

"Assuming things stay on schedule, yes. I don't have all the details as far as who is presenting what and when, but I might be able to find that out if you're looking for something specific." A moment of uneasiness strikes my gut. Trusting her is hard, but I so desperately want to believe in someone, anyone, who might possibly be sympathetic to our cause.

"These sorts of things are usually off-limits to the public," she says, tapping her chin. "I'm sure there's a fair amount of dirty laundry they'd rather not have aired, especially given the sorts of things that are bound to come out. We should change that." Her face grows sly. "Leave that part to me. Just make sure your barrister knows I'm planning to attend. I'll be very discreet, of course."

"And when it leaks to your fans that you were seen attending and they show up, too?" Bran says, skeptical.

She idly studies her perfectly manicured nails. "Ah, well, who can control what my fans will do?"

"Of course." I glance over at Bran, whose face is a study in longing, and then down at the others, their expressions animated as they natter on at Lottie. There's still a wariness there, but they're just as hungry for something new as I am, and my heart sings to see it.

"All right," I say to the Heart of the Sea. "Let's do it."

A scrap of longing
And the loss of bliss,
An echo of time
In a bittersweet kiss.

— CHAPTER TWENTY-FIVE —

Today the court is packed. The councilors haven't emerged from their chambers, but the benches are full of curious Meridians. The Heart of the Sea was true to her word. Snippets of information casually layered in conversation, hints broadcast upon her floating ship, whispers on the wind—whatever she did, her adoring public figured out the rest. Suddenly, Moon Children and our historic plight is the favored topic dropping from Meridian lips as though it is the only thing to talk about, raising the awareness of me and my clan until we are miniature celebrities, as well.

Over the past week, Lottie and the Heart of the Sea ushered us about the floating city. They introduced us at all the proper parties, offering small exclusive interviews that revealed nothing of our potential testimony, but created enough approval until even I was getting packages of baked goods and whisky delivered to the d'Arc estate by would-be supporters.

Ghost and I have become an entity of star-crossed lovers—the Moon Children who defied Meridian tradition for love. Ghost's bemusement at the concept has only made him more endearing to the citizens, the lost scion of d'Arc sacrificing his own lineage to embrace that of Moon Children. The stories aren't accurate, of course, but the Heart of the Sea doesn't concern herself with the truth so much as what generates the most interest. And in this we are unbeaten.

So now Ghost and I sit on one of the benches in the council room, our clan in the row behind us as we wait for the Council to start the proceedings. Unlike the private matter of House betrothals, we now have row upon row of supporters and witnesses. Joseph. Chancellor Davis. The Heart of the Sea. My stomach flutters with a basket of butterflies holding court in my gut.

Jeremiah and Lucian are beside us, the two of them conversing with their heads together, planning some sort of last-minute strategy, undoubtedly. Jeremiah smiles at Lucian as the doctor laughs, but whatever else he's about to say is cut off as the Council sweeps into the room from behind their curtain, taking their seats with prim satisfaction. Jeremiah rises to approach the bench, speaking earnestly to Madam Councilor Greta, who raises a skeptical brow at whatever he says, but finally nods.

Jeremiah bows courteously to the crowd. "Thank you, your eminences. We are here today to call the witness Chancellor Davis of BrightStone. We believe she can provide relevant testimony as to the plight of the Moon Children and their lives below."

The councilwoman gestures to Chancellor Davis to come forward.

The BrightStone Chancellor does so, her arms full of files. She drops the thick binders on the table in front of Jeremiah, lifting the Inquestor Tithe book and flipping through the pages. Line after line of names and numbers, each one a sacrificed Moon Child, sent below and never to return.

The back of my neck prickles as she starts to name them off, stopping after the first two pages. Her gaze sweeps the now silent court and closes the book. "This is far more than a simple scientific experiment, and I think everyone here knows it. The systematic abuse of our people and our city has come at a truly dreadful cost, and we seek reparations from both the High Inquestor and the Meridians as a whole."

"That's a pretty tall order," Madam Councilor Greta says. "Not that it is unwarranted, but you must admit it's an extremely loaded charge. Are you sure you'd not rather simply settle?"

Chancellor Davis raises a brow, gesturing at the Moon Children seated in the rows behind us. "It was an *extremely* loaded result, wouldn't you say?" She thrusts her chin out defiantly, her skirts like leather armor as she taps her gloved fingers on the table. "Let's get to the bottom of this, shall we? As I understand it, there is evidence to present gathered from both BrightStone and Meridion. All of it is relevant, and nearly all of it can be told by the parties who suffered beneath it." Her mouth compresses as she looks about the room, determined.

"Well then," says Madam Councilor Greta. "Begin."

Hours. Minutes. Months. After a while, it's hard to tell how much time has passed as the Council hears our plea. There is too much evidence and there are too many witnesses to simply wrap things up quickly. When the group of us finally drag ourselves to the d'Arc house and into our beds after the first day, there's a part of my brain that is numb with the thought that we will have to do it all over again the next day. And the day after that.

But there is no choice in the matter.

The weeks blur together as Jeremiah provides piece after piece of evidence. Joseph's testimony of his time in the Pits. Madeline d'Arc's notebooks from her lab beneath the Mother Clock. Lucian's and Ghost's testimony of their time in BrightStone. Chancellor Davis also returns to the stand to indicate the hardships of BrightStone in minute detail. The handling of the Rot. The terror of the Tithes.

The audience makes various noises, sometimes dissenting, sometimes scandalized, but through it all, I still get the sense that the Council simply does not care. Every day it's becoming more and more of a spectacle, and I am merely a clown for the viewing.

I've tried everything, from trying to appear small and invisible to projecting a confidence I barely sustain. Each of our arguments has been shot down again and again. For each bit of ground we gain, more is lost in the sweep of political laws that I cannot understand and that frustrate me almost beyond my patience.

The worst of it is when the Council declares the evidence previously collected by Copper Betty to be invalid due to possible footage corruption, though I'm certain the real reason is the stunt IronHeart pulled in regards to the betrothal. The public is not allowed to view it, and we are instead relegated to firsthand accounts only.

The lawyers bicker back and forth until even the Council grows weary enough to declare another recess. The Moon Children hoot derisively as the Council members retreat to their curtained alcove.

Our group is ensconced in a private room to debate our strategy as a small supper of ham sandwiches and watercress soup is delivered. I don't care what I put into my mouth, and I eat it automatically, barely tasting it.

Jeremiah and Lucian are arguing about how things are going. "We're running out of options. I think we need to put her on the stand," Lucian insists, gesturing at me. "Mags has some of the most direct information witnessed both by her time in BrightStone and in the Pits. Surely that has to count for something."

"It's risky. But I'm not sure what else we have to lose. The High Inquestor will be called to make his statement next, and I fear he will discredit anything she says," Jeremiah points out. "Her reputation right now is not the greatest, and they may not believe her.

Or any of them, really," he admits, gesturing at my clan as they shovel sandwiches into their gullets as fast as they can.

Old habits die hard.

I finish up my own sandwich, my fingers itching for a smoke. "If having an automaton with Madeline d'Arc's memories embedded in it doesn't convince them, I'm not sure what my testimony would do."

Chancellor Davis's mouth curls into a scowl. "I have an affidavit by Molly Bell as to the nature of her establishment's services. That alone should be enough to prove that this was a highly implemented plan furnished by the High Inquestor to funnel subjects for his heinous little science experiments."

Joseph flinches slightly in his seat on the far side of the room, his eyes meeting mine with a weary acceptance. I actually feel sad for him. In some ways, he is as lost as any of us, stripped of whatever he believed in, betrayed by the woman he loved, and living with the knowledge that he helped to murder hundreds, if not thousands of people with the Rot.

I head over to where Jeremiah and Lucian are. "How is it possible to have this many witnesses, this much evidence, yet they still don't seem to understand it?"

"Because the High Inquestor, for all his crimes, is still a Meridian," Jeremiah says, without a hint of mockery. "Banished or not, his word will simply be taken at a greater face value than yours. Even with those interviews by the Heart of the Sea...I know she means well, but you're a circus act, not a citizen."

He goes silent as I stare at him, the other Moon Children setting down their lunches. "I see," I murmur, something snapping inside my brain.

"He didn't mean it like that," Lucian says, making a soft sound of annoyance at his lover. "It's simply that they can't see past your otherness, and the fact that you seem to have made it out alive makes it look as though maybe it wasn't really that bad."

"And frankly, some of them probably approve of the methods behind the science experiments," Jeremiah admits. "The idea of immortality is not as far-fetched at it might appear, and it certainly is seen as desirable from at least some of their perspectives."

"And even more to the point, the High Inquestor may have been calling the shots from BrightStone, but he wasn't the person actually doing the worst of it. Some consider his to be simply a crime of bad management and implementation as opposed to actual malice." He glances at Joseph. "In some ways, they would consider Joseph to be far more culpable."

"Even with Joseph's testimony about Buceph? And the notes? Surely someone up here had to know what was going on, had to approve it. What else do we have to go by?" I thrust my fingers through my hair in frustration.

The other Moon Children have pushed their heads together and are whispering furiously, except for Bran who sits with a deep scowl on his face. "Fucking. Waste. Of. Time. All of it. I know you wanted to do this the 'proper way,' Mags, whatever that means. But you have to admit, we're never going to get a fair shot like this. Let's just take whatever they'll give us and get out."

"And where would we go?" I retort. "If we leave now, we give up everything we've fought for."

"Maybe it's not worth fighting for," he says quietly. "Maybe it never was." He turns on his heel and stalks from the room, the door slamming shut behind him in a way that sounds desperately final.

"We knew this was a risk, Mags. Any time a trial occurs, there's always a chance it won't go your way." Jeremiah takes a seat in front of the fireplace, flipping through a thick dossier of notes on his lap. "That's why the High Council asked if you were sure you wanted to pursue this."

"And I still am." I turn toward him. "I won't back down from that walking piece of garbage that pretends to be human, aye?"

"And if they find him innocent? Release him? Then what?" Lucian cocks a brow at me. "Will you take your army of Moon Children to dispense your own brand of justice?" He sighs. "I understand how you feel. Nothing would make me happier than to see him hanged for his crimes, but this goes so much deeper than just a single person. It's like a sickness in the entire city. They're so far removed from what the rest of the world is like..."

"I don't give a shit about the rest of the world," I snap. "I care about the shithole I came from, the people I live with, died with, nearly died *for*. The rest of the world can sod right off." A sobbing breath escapes me. I can see my hopes slipping through my fingers like ribbons made of sand. "The world is hard enough. Surviving for most of us is just that—surviving." I glare at Jeremiah. "But while you were up here dreaming your dreams of immortality, we were trying not to die in a game rigged entirely against us with no way out."

"And yet, here you are," Jeremiah says softly.

The walls of the room seem to press down upon me, suddenly suffocating. I need some air. "Here *we* are." I stand and let out a short whistle, calling the others up from their benches. "And here we go."

Before Lucian can say anything, we slip out the door and down the hall.

There's no sign of Bran at all. It doesn't surprise me any. He's lost his patience with me, and the entire situation. I can't blame him.

"Mags!" Ghost slides up behind me, taking my wrist to slow me down. "Where are you going?"

"I don't know." My dragon hisses from my shoulder, spooking a random Meridian walking in the other direction. There's a small crowd on the far side of the courtyard we're crossing, paying homage to the Heart of the Sea as she holds court among her fans.

But I'm not in the mood to be more of a sideshow than I've already become, Jeremiah's words stinging me harder than I thought. "I just need to catch my breath. I don't know. I half think maybe it's time we went home."

He frowns. "To our house?"

"To BrightStone. At least there we've got our own way of doing things. It may not be remotely perfect, but the Chancellor seems to want to work with us." A sad smile flickers over my mouth. "I'm sorry. I know this isn't what you were hoping for. If you want to stay up here, I'll understand."

His faces softens as he touches my cheek. "Oh. Oh no, Mags. I told you, didn't I? Where you go, I'll follow. Forever, aye?"

I swallow a lump in my throat, pressing my face against his palm. "Aye."

"You leave now and I'll probably kill you myself," drawls a slow voice as we make our way down the steps to where the airships are docked.

I startle. "Josephine. I didn't expect to see you here."

"Been busy ferrying the Chancellor around." A hint of reproach tinges her voice. "And keeping tabs on the clan down below. Doesn't leave much time for sightseeing. I hear you've been rather busy, Magpie. The Chancellor's been picking my brain in the evenings over the way Moon Children are being treated these days and how she might better accommodate us."

"At least she's trying," I say. I gesture toward the Heart of the Sea. "We have our allies up here, too, but when it comes to legalities in Meridion, I'm not sure how much help they'll be in the long run."

Josephine snorts. "If revolution were easy, Magpie, everyone would be lined up to do it whenever they stubbed their toe on the sidewalk. Change is like the sea. Sometimes it's a hurricane, and sometimes it's a slow roll of the tide. It's all the same to the starfish on the rock. It still gets wet either way, but fewer people get hurt with the latter, aye?"

I blink at her. "I didn't realize you'd taken up philosophy."

"Life *is* philosophy," she says.

"Bran come by this way?" Rosa peers past Josephine. "He looked kinda mad."

"He's onboard. Wants me to take him to BrightStone." She crosses her arms. "Anyone else want to go?"

A pang hits me, that he would leave us, but hadn't I felt the same way just now? "He probably needs to burn off some anger," I say.

"He said something about the High Inquestor testifying today. Can't blame him for not wanting to be around for that." She spits at her feet. "Maybe we'll be lucky and he'll take a long walk off a short plank, aye?"

"We can but hope," Gloriana says fervently. "So we stay?"

I exhale sharply. To have come so far, to turn back now would be admitting defeat. *At least if things didn't work out, I'll know I did everything I could. At least maybe I'll be able to make peace with myself.* "Until the end."

"Beware IronHeart's teeth and IronHeart's claws, for when IronHeart roars..." Ghost begins, his expression softening when he looks at me.

"Meridion falls..." I finish up the odd little prophecy. "Maybe that's what they meant." I think back on IronHeart and cringe at the unexpectedness of her true appearance.

"Well then," Josephine says with a toothy smile. "Let's roar so fucking loud they'll hear us all the way in the bloody Pits!"

By the time we make our way back inside, most of the seats are already packed with eager lawmakers and the usual Meridian gawkers. The High Council emerges from their alcove, a tension flaring about them for a reason I can't quite fathom. Madam

Councilor Greta, in particular, seems to be struggling to keep her usual composure, flashes of lightning starbursting along the edges of her jaw.

"Let us begin." She pounds the gavel when she sits, as though wanting to get this part over as soon as possible. I can hardly blame her. I feel much the same. "We call the next witness, High Inquestor Nicholai, formerly of House Montrice."

The side door opens, and all heads swivel toward it as the man in question emerges, flanked by two guards. For some reason, he doesn't look nearly as terrifying without the red cloak of his office. But the gleam in his eye is no less calculating when he spots me in the crowd, his mouth quirking up in a mocking half smile. His black hair and mustache have been neatly oiled, raven's-wing smooth. He hasn't been back on Meridion long enough to start the skin lightning, but he's so pale he might as well as be made of it.

I'm thankful for my glasses so that he cannot see the way I shut my eyes against him, even as I stiffen beneath his scrutiny.

Ghost lowers his head to my ear, lips brushing my skin gently. "He can't hurt you anymore, Mags."

"I know." I shift to the memory of him cracking the whip upon my naked back in the square in front of the Pits. The scars seem to burn, as if I can feel the weight of his cloak when he draped it around my shoulders, wrapped in the cloying scent of his cigars. I nearly vomit from it, squeezing Ghost's hands hard.

"The witness will now take the stand, and the prosecution will make their statement." Madam Councilor Greta announces it as simply as if she were ordering bread from a street vendor. The High Inquestor bows his head ruefully, allowing himself to be led to the chair in the center of the room. He takes his seat with a smooth authority that almost makes it seem as though he's the one running the trial.

The councilwoman eyes him disdainfully. "Well, it has been a bit of a time, hasn't it? I would have hoped sentencing you to exile below would have smoothed out your temperament, Nicholai, but it does not seem that way, does it?"

He smiles. "How nice to see you too, Grandmother. Pity it couldn't be under better circumstances. Like your funeral, for instance."

I startle at the familiarity of the exchange, my head snapping toward Lucian, suddenly understanding the councilwoman's reluctance. He's biting the inside of his cheek, but there's no surprise on his face. Common knowledge, then. But how can we possibly get a fair trial this way?

"Indeed," she says, her face unreadable.

Fury lances through me, my hands shaking as I grip the bench hard enough to leave marks on my palms. The utter indifference to our plight nearly plunges me into despair. To have come so far…

Jeremiah bows courteously to the crowd, obviously trying to move the process forward. "We are here today to call the witness Nicholai Montrice, formerly the High Inquestor of BrightStone, formerly the scion of House Montrice, currently charged with crimes against the BrightStone populace—the reckless creation of Moon Children, the spread of the plague known as the Rot, and the attempt at a potential coup against BrightStone's government."

He paces lightly, his coat flaring as he turns in animated eloquence. "As you also know, it is not the first time he has been so disposed here, hence his previous banishment to BrightStone years ago. It would appear he has learned nothing of remorse during his time down below."

Madam Councilor Greta nods. "And what evidence do you have of these crimes?"

"I call Lucian d'Arc, as the current expert in the plague known as the Rot," Jeremiah says, moving to allow Lucian to take his place. "He will present counterarguments and evidence to indicate Nicholai's role in the unleashing of the plague upon BrightStone and his conspiracy with the Meridian named Buceph Aubrey to utilize the Moon Children as test subjects created specifically to further research into the creation of the immortality serum."

The High Inquestor's face remains smug as Jeremiah finishes his final statements, his eyes bored as Lucian explains the mechanisms of the Rot. He interrupts to insert his plea that he was merely trying to assist the Meridian people with a chance of immortality.

"I am, of course, full of regret that we have wronged these people so," he goes on. "But perhaps we can agree that it hasn't been all bad, has it?" His eyes linger on me, his smile growing pious. "After all, look at the plight of the Moon Children. Where would they be without us? Living in squalor, no doubt." He gestures broadly with a well-manicured hand. "And yet here she sits, surrounded by luxury, with every amenity she could think of. What more could she possibly want?"

Nods of agreement all around, from the Council to the observers in the balconies above, and I grit my teeth against shouting every foul word I know.

"To be fair, there's a difference between being given a choice and receiving reparations after the fact. How about allowing them as part of a family?" Jeremiah asks mildly, ignoring the tapping of my feet. "These children have been created by us and abandoned by us. Do we think so little of ourselves that we can assume they are better off now simply because a chosen few are allowed the grace to live here?"

"If that is the way you wish to argue," the High Inquestor shrugs. "To invite them to reclaim a possible family here would be no different from adopting a dog as a child. Will you marry them off? Allow them to inherit?"

Jeremiah ignores the scandalized outcries all around us. "At least one family here did indicate that it would be acceptable," he points out. "The Tantaglio House went very far indeed to see Trystan d'Arc wed to their eldest daughter, despite his Moon Child lineage."

"And look how that panned out," the High Inquestor retorts. "A House in disgrace, a daughter abandoned. Should all such Meridian Houses expect the same? Moon Children live in the sewers in BrightStone like rats." He smiles at me again, something cruel and calculating flashing within the depths of his eyes. "Perhaps living in the filth is truly what they desire, even when surrounded by such wealth beyond their imagining."

I nearly launch myself at him in front of the entire court, my fingers itching to strangle him, to pull out his tongue like the slimy piece of garbage he is. But before I can make a move, the rear doors of the courtroom are kicked open, the sharp report of the wood slamming against the walls making everyone jump.

It's Bran. He's carrying something in his arms, wrapped in a black cloak, as he storms up the aisle to my bench. "Move," he snaps, edging Ghost and me over so he can sit down. His mouth is set in a terrible expression, as though he holds a dam of grief and anger set in bone.

"Is that...?" I reach out as though to touch him, withdrawing when he turns his face toward me. The cloak slides away to reveal Alora's hair, her face nestled in the crook of Bran's arm. The smell hits me then, the awful scent of the Rot, and it takes everything I have not to recoil. Beside me, Ghost stiffens.

Lucian peers around us both. "Is that what I think it is?" His voice is low and dangerous and trembling.

"Yes." The word cracks out of Bran like a bullet. "Call me as a witness."

Lucian's face draws up in a panic. "Why? Why would you bring her here? Do you know what kind of havoc this could potentially create?"

"What are you talking about?" Jeremiah demands, his nose wrinkling. "What is that smell?"

"Call. Me. As. A. Witness!" Bran roars, the rest of the court gone silent as the Salt Temple in mourning. Alora stirs in his arms, her head wobbling on a neck gone weak.

Jeremiah gapes at the girl, cupping his hand over his mouth as though he might vomit. Lucian leans in close to him, whispering something I cannot hear, but based on the way the lightning flashes beneath the other man's skin, I can guess.

"Is everything all right?" Madam Councilor Greta frowns at us, her expression confused.

"Ah...yes." Jeremiah straightens and tugs on his waistcoat, his slender fingers nervously playing with one of the buttons. "I know this is rather out of order, but we...believe this to be a time-sensitive witness. I would like to call Bran...of BrightStone."

The High Inquestor almost seems to snigger. "Should I remove myself?"

Jeremiah shakes his head. "No need. I don't think this will take long."

Bran's mouth trembles as he stands, carrying Alora to the center of the chamber. He ignores the High Inquestor utterly, kneeling down with the utmost care. "I know you people refuse to see anything that your nose isn't wiped in," he says, his voice cracking as he sets the girl down, pulling the cloak from her shoulders. "So here's the Rot, aye? See what your immortality has cost us."

A low gasp ripples through the room. Alora is no less sweet or confused than the last time I saw her, tottering on crow legs, but her skin is now so sheer and luminous you can see right through to the purpling organs beneath. Her heart flutters, a bird in a cage of dying flesh. Her smile at Bran is that rictus I remember so well, her teeth already starting to fall from gums that are gray and pulsing. But Bran's face never loses its gentle mien, even when he pats her gently on the head, watching as clumps of golden hair float to the floor. Alora seems not to notice, her gaze solely on to her champion.

The stench is almost unimaginable, and it fills the space of the council room with a thickness you could wrap around your shoulders like a coat. The High Inquestor's condescending smile is gone, wiped away as he struggles not to retch in full view of his audience.

I can see the blood vessels on the girl's eyes growing tight, the pupils clouding over. "She's changing," I breathe, knowing it all too well.

"You should have told me, Mags," Lucian says, tears welling up in his eyes. "I would have tried—"

"The time for trying is long past," Bran grinds out. "I know where the selfishness of Meridion starts, because this is where it ends—in the ruin of babies and a living death for which there is no cure." He turns about like a caged lion, ready to take them all on. "Three years. I spent three years underground with the Tithed. Three *years*. I ate rats. I watched my people die at the hands of yours. My sister, dead at *your* hands. Innocent Tithers rounded up in pens, without the dignity of a simple death, rotting away as they walked the tunnels."

The Council members can't quite seem to look him in the eye, so absorbed are they in the way Alora suddenly struggles to breathe, a soft rattling gasp that throws me straight back into the Pits with Anna and the way she begged me to kill her before the Rot took over.

Bran does a final pace around Alora before pulling her back into his arms. He nods at me, tears streaming down his cheeks. "Please," he begs. "Please. You promised me anything within your power."

Bile rises in my throat. "You want me to...set her free?" The phrase is a ridiculously laughable euphemism. In the Pits, I was the executioner for the Tithed Rotters, offering them the choice of a quick death instead of slowly going mad, trapped within the shell of their own rotting corpses. For most of them, it wasn't even a choice. They took my offered mercy without question. I briefly close my eyes against it, swallowing hard before I stand. Lucian snatches at my hand, but Ghost pushes him away, blocking his brother from stopping me. I don't know what sort of expression is on their faces, and I don't want to know.

I approach Alora, wincing as she sees me. "Mag...pie? Did you bring me...bring me something?" Her voice is already a whisper, a butterfly on the breath of the moon, and her lack of understanding at what's happening nearly undoes me.

"Not this time, sweetheart," I say softly, tipping her chin up so I'm looking at her. It's the final bit of dignity I can offer her in the quiet of the last act.

Her breathing rattles in her chest, her nearly sightless eyes white and rheumy.

Bran whistles a soft query at me, pressing something into my hand from beneath his shirt. I know what it is without looking, though the fact that he's kept it all this time makes me ill. I grip the blade tightly, ignoring the way it fits in my palm like a second skin.

How many have I set free this way?

What's one more?

The moment hovers in infinite time, stretching, stretching, stretching away, and I grow smaller and smaller inside myself. No matter how many times I do it, I will never get used to it, never take pleasure in it. Only that sad sort of knowledge that I was freeing the damned from their pain.

"I'm sorry, darling," I whisper. With a quick flick, the blade emerges from my hand. I'm no bonewitch, but I know the best place to slide the edge to kill her the fastest.

"Mags!" Lucian's voice comes out of nowhere, but it's too late.

The black, slick Rotter blood pumps sluggishly, spattering over my face. Bran lets out a low cry as she dies, holding her tightly, heedless of the filth sliding over his shoulder, the desiccated skin starting to peel from her skull.

The knife slips from my fingers to clatter onto the marble floor. Bran is weeping like a child, clutching Alora's body with ugly sobs.

"This is what your research got you," I say quietly to the High Council. "This is the fruit of your labors. Is it worth it?" Some part of me remains in the darkness, not ready to see what I've become reflected in the eyes of those I love. "What else can you possibly do to me? To us? You Meridians are crueler than anything I ever lived through in BrightStone. All this beauty and it's simply a shell, hiding your ugliness." My jaw trembles despite myself. "If I hit you, you'd shatter. That's how hollow you are."

"The world is hollow, Magpie," the High Inquestor says, sitting back to look at me with an intensity that somehow seems both smug and sad. "Only those who can lift themselves above it are worth anything. I think you know that."

I turn again, and this time I pull open my shirt and point to my chest, heart-shaped panel gleaming in the lights of the council room. "This is what Madeline d'Arc did to me," I say. "Opened up my chest cavity to hide a piece of Meridian technology so valuable you tried to kill her to get at it." I raise my eyes, meeting the High Inquestor's with unflinching certainty. "I can make the city of Meridion fly again. I could have made your entire city bow to my whim for a chance at this." I thump my chest in emphasis. "So don't you *dare* talk to me like I couldn't have lifted myself."

"Spoken like a criminal in the making," he sneers.

"And what was *your* crime?" I shoot back, as though somehow knowing the reason will make his sins against Moon Children more palatable. Or at least understandable.

"My crime?" He blinks, startled.

"The one that got you exiled to BrightStone in the first place." The High Council should have stopped this whole thing by now, but they seem fascinated by how things are unfolding, like cats watching a bird get disemboweled in the hopes they might feed on the scraps.

His smile grows crooked. Perhaps I've hit a nerve. "My crime? I was the first-born son in a Noble House."

"That doesn't exactly seem like something you should be punished for," I say, confused.

"It is when you're not able to have children," he points out. "I was wed off, the same as in most families, a match made of a specific advantageous lineage. I do believe you've had a bit of a run-in with such things yourself."

I shudder beneath the mocking tone. Coward that I am, I can't even look at Ghost or Lucian, but I'm horrified all the same that I've been forced to show them what I've truly become, what I was molded into, all for the sake of my clan. The High Inquestor chuckles, an ugly sound that creeps down my spine like a nest of beetles.

"We may pretend to be better than you common folk, but we're just as petty, it would seem. And once my infertility became known, my wife's family quickly moved to break off the marriage. It wasn't a love match by any means, but I'll admit I was a bit fond of her." He rolls his eyes. "Somehow my parents managed to convince them it would be easier to have her wed my brother. At least that way things would stay within the family, and they wouldn't have the shame of it stain either House."

"How dreadful," I say imperiously, suddenly wishing I had a cigarillo.

His face shadows. "Do not mock me," he snaps. "You have no idea..."

"Don't I? I have a *very* good idea what it's like. But just because you can't produce children doesn't mean you can't be productive." I pause. "Unless maybe it's an issue of a more personal nature?"

He actually flushes. "It makes no difference. I was forced to leave my family for the shame of it."

"And so you went to BrightStone in the hopes that you could create an immortality serum with Buceph and then be welcomed back with open arms, is that it?" I shift, the old whip scars on my back burning again, as though to remind me of what he'd done. "Or did you think you might sell it up here and make your fortune that way?"

"Nothing so altruistic." He slumps in his chair. "No, my revenge was more to gain such a gift for myself. And then, when I had it, my family could come crawling back to me with the knowledge that I would never grow old, and therefore, I would take control of our estate."

"That's what all this is about? Your fucking estate?" My hands tremble with rage. "You know, I almost get the idea of doing this for money. People always do the worst things for it. But simply because they shut you out?"

"It's mine! It belongs to me. My name. *My* estate. Not that pissant little brother of mine. Who knocked her up quite quickly," he adds darkly. "Maybe too quickly, given how fast she separated from me. I was no longer welcome home. I could come back to work for them, of course, but I would not be considered an heir."

I step toward him, my heels clicking like the claws of some predatory beast. "So you helped make an entire generation of half-breed orphans, generated a plague, used us in experiments, murdered us, and kept the entire city of BrightStone in ignorance, not allowing anyone in or out, save by your approval, simply because your carrot couldn't impregnate one of your inbred city girls?"

A bout of nearly hysterical laughter wheezes out of me. My body shakes with it, this screaming cackle of disbelief and anger and grief. That I had been so afraid of this person, that he had ruled over my people with such terror, and for what? *For what?*

I wipe the blood on my skirt, leaving black stains smeared over the fine fabric. My fingers jolt when they brush up against the hammer at my waist. Somehow, even in all the finery, I cling to those items that bring me the most comfort.

Before I realize it, the hammer is in my hand, the handle flashing silver as I twirl it between my fingers. I whirl on the High Inquestor, still perched on his chair and staring down at my broken clanmate. "I told you once I'd dance your bones into dust," I say. "Let's change the tune, aye?"

And the hammer flies from my grip.

The mirror of my soul
Is reflected in my dreams.
The halves that make the whole,
Cracking beneath the seams.

— CHAPTER TWENTY-SIX —

The jail cell is about as nice as I might expect. Meridian prisons don't seem to want to make things too uncomfortable for their guests, and why would they? In the past, they'd simply exiled all their bad seeds to BrightStone where they became Inquestors, free to live out their own special brand of tyranny on the people who deserved it least.

Jeremiah sits in a chair outside my cell. They don't use anything as mundane as bars here—nor locks, for that matter. That would have been too simple for me to escape with my heart, anyway. Instead, it's an electric force field that keeps me at bay. It's similar to the gates of the Pits. Those *were* metal but were also electrified, and I saw what they could do to rats, let alone a person.

Not to mention I have no idea what such a thing will do to my heart, and I am not about to take that risk.

"Are you finding it comfortable in there?" Jeremiah asks, all professional and smooth. He can't quite mask the wariness in his eyes, but he doesn't have to tell me that we are quite obviously being watched. "Are they feeding you well enough?"

"It's a fair step up from shit-covered hay," I admit, gesturing at a cluster of wilted grapes in a paper bowl on the edge of my bed. "Food is...interesting. Edible but not particularly fresh. And it smells of astringent, but I'll take it over the other. When do I get out of here?"

"I'm not sure you do," he says, jabbing notes into one of his many volumes of parchment books with an ornate fountain pen. "Your actions have complicated the situation by a rather large amount. Frankly, the Council sees you as a danger, and to be honest, I rather agree with them."

I lean back on the cot and close my eyes. The jail uniform they've given me is bright red and itchy. "Oh, aye. Dangerous me."

"You slit the throat of a dying girl on the floor of the council room," he points out. "And Nicholai still hasn't woken up. That hammer took out an eye. They're afraid even if he does come to, the brain damage may be extensive."

I pause in my imaginings of this. "Should I care?" It sounds callous enough to my ears, but it's certainly true enough. "Where were your sensibilities when I was getting whipped naked in the streets? When my friends were being murdered by Inquestors simply for being alive?"

"Mags, that's not—" Jeremiah gapes at me helplessly.

I hold up my hand. "Spare me the pearl clutching. I've been here for nearly a day and a night now, aye? Are they planning on keeping me here until he awakens?"

"I don't know. The High Council is still trying to decide if you were intending to murder him or simply wound him." His mouth compresses. "And as you can guess, they can be slow to deliberate, not even counting the fact that his grandmother sits on the Council. Bad blood between them or not, you nearly murdered one of their own in front of them. I don't think this is going to go well."

"Then maybe they should stop letting deviant criminals go simply because they're Meridians," I snap back. "If he's so trustworthy, why did they send him to BrightStone in the first place?"

Jeremiah leans in, his voice soft. "That's just it, Mags. Whatever he told us in the council room, he volunteered. He simply needed the space in which to do it, and with no oversight from the Council. He comes from a very powerful House. There is almost nothing they don't have their fingers dipped into on Meridion. If the Council missteps here, they all stand to lose."

"Forgive me if I cannot find the strength to care about what you all consider a misstep." I tap on the mattress, trying to keep my blood from boiling at the outrage. "So now what? What about Ghost? Lucian? Don't I at least get visitors at some point?"

"That's not up to me. I've tried. Believe me, I have. But we've never had a Moon Child in custody before. The laws are getting a bit muddled." Jeremiah pauses. "The most I can tell you is they are doing as well as expected. They aren't in custody exactly, but they are on house arrest for the foreseeable future."

"That's ridiculous! They didn't do anything." Now I do sit up, glaring at him. "What sort of barrister are you? Aren't they Meridians? If the High Inquestor is somehow taken at his word, why aren't they?"

I'm pacing now, half shouting as he shushes me. "If your outburst brings the guards, I won't be able to talk to you. And Trystan's linage is that of a Moon Child now—at least on the surface of things. You've managed to make a lot of enemies here in a short time. Between House Tantaglio and the High Inquestor's family, they don't care much about your innocence or lack thereof. Right now they simply want to see someone punished."

"And I'm it, aye." I sit back down on the cot, pinching the bridge of my nose. "What of the Moon Children? Bran?"

"Gone," Jeremiah says carefully. "To be honest, he left with the girl's body after you were taken into custody, and we haven't seen him since. In fact, we haven't seen any Moon Children at all since you've been locked up here." He frowns. "And we've been looking. But it's as though the security footage from our camera drones has been wiped somehow."

"Mmmph," I say, staring up at the bland blue of the cell ceiling, considering where they could have gone. IronHeart's lair, perhaps. Or some other safehouse provided by the Heart of the Sea. Or maybe they stole away to BrightStone on Josephine's airship. Regardless, they know not to be found until it's safe enough. "I'm sure they're around somewhere."

"You don't seem overly concerned," he says. "Rather unusual for you." When I don't say anything, he gives me a questioning look.

But I'm certainly not going to admit anything here. "Don't ask me. I've been in jail all this time. I could hardly give orders from within my little electric cell, could I?"

Jeremiah grunts. "Well however it's being managed, it's making people nervous. Some families have taken to leaving out bread and milk on their doorsteps." He lets out an unhappy chuckle. "They're terrified."

I put my feet up on the wall in a most unladylike manner. "Of what? That we might break in and borrow a bed? Pillage some food? Please."

"No. Mags, they're afraid you're going to steal their children." He seems almost offended by the concept, and I can't tell if he means it seriously or not. "That's the most recent rumor, anyway."

"Who said anything about taking babies? Luring a few children to our side would be fun, but not exactly worth the trouble."

"How so?" Based on his askance expression, he clearly doesn't trust me, but I don't care.

I pop a wilted grape into my mouth. It's sour, the acid making my lips curl. "Oh, well, there's that theory that we don't really age, right? It's never been tested because none of us have ever lived long enough to really know. I mean, most of our population is under twenty, but...what if it's true? What if we hit thirty or forty and simply stop aging? Buceph seemed to think it was possible. He hadn't stopped it exactly, but he definitely had slowed it down."

"What's your point?" There's a cautious thread in his voice that makes me think he's not remotely going to like my answer and is bracing for it.

"We'll outlive all of you, technically," I say with a brusqueness I don't really care for. I've never been so mercenary as to suggest such a thing, and yet the concept dangles like a needle on a thread. "It almost makes no difference at all what any of you decide. All we have to do is wait you out."

The blood drains out of Jeremiah's face. "I highly suggest you don't mention this to the Council, Mags. If they thought Moon Children were dangerous before, there's no telling what they will do if they hear you are entertaining such a notion."

"Round us all up and put us somewhere to forget about us, aye?" My smile is humorless, brittle. I pretend not to see him flinch, and we ride out the rest of the meeting in silence.

I don't watch him go, turning on my side to face the wall before etching a mark in the bedpost with a ragged fingernail. "And here we are again," I mutter, wondering what new hell awaits me tomorrow.

Not that I get any answers the next morning. Or even the next week, in fact. Based off the scratches on the bedpost, I'm in the cell for at least another two weeks. The guards take some pity on my pacing and give me leave to walk about in an outdoor cage once a day after Jeremiah visits me again. It's inside a courtyard so there's no chance of escape, but the air is fresh, even if I'm still imprisoned.

I haven't seen my dragon since I was dragged away in chains so I can't send messages that way. Sometimes I whistle on the offhand chance that a passing Moon Child might somehow hear me and at least know that I'm still alive, still unhurt.

Here, here.

If any do pick up the signal, they don't bother responding, but that's all right. I eat my wilted grapes and pace in my cage and dream of running on rooftops without end.

"What have you done?" The words startle me awake from a dead sleep, and I wince as the ceiling lights flare to life above me. I feel around for my smoked lenses, blearily putting them on so I can focus as the electric barrier of my cell is shut off.

"Huh?" My eyes water at the abruptness of the sudden onslaught of questions as I try to make sense of the people outside my cell. Madam Councilor Greta is there—the High Inquestor's grandmother. She looks less like a retainer of the law and more like a frightened family member. "Did he die?" The bluntness of my words makes her wince.

"Yes, you stupid girl, but I'm talking about this!" She snaps her fingers, one of her aides pulling up a small screen with one of those videos playing on it. "*This* just happened nearly twenty minutes ago. What is the meaning of it?"

"Maybe you can let me see what in hells it is you're talking about, aye? And get those damn lights out of my face." I rub at my temple as I take the screen from the aide and bring it closer. It's a security feed like the ones IronHeart showed me in her lair. This one is from the Inner Spiral, which, given the hour, is still ridiculously busy, clusters of citizens still out and about.

"What am I looking at?" I ask finally, trying to figure out what she's getting at.

"Just watch," she says sharply. "Turn up the volume so you can hear it."

I do as she asks, noticing that the largest screen in the Inner Spiral flickers once and then goes dark. The Heart of the Sea's airship floats into view, and her voice emerges into the night air over the loudspeakers.

"Today, the Meridian High Council found a Moon Child guilty of the murder of Nicholai of House Montrice, formerly known as the High Inquestor of BrightStone."

I startle, stopping the video. "Someone planning on telling me I'm guilty at some point in all this?"

"Not important right now." Greta turns it on again.

The Heart of the Sea continues. "They kept the evidence of his crimes related to the Moon Children and BrightStone's Rot under wraps, not wanting to release it to the public for fear of your reactions, especially if you understand the reality of the situation. But tonight we're about to change that..."

Ghost's picture appears briefly on the airship's video screen, and he begins to speak, his voice soft and warm and calm. "I am Trystan d'Arc, a scion of the House of d'Arc...and a Moon Child. Many years ago, I was exiled with my brother to BrightStone for the crimes committed by my mother, Madeline d'Arc. But before that..." On the screen are images of BrightStone before the Meridians arrived. It's a BrightStone I don't recognize. It's cleaner, for one. The people look less bedraggled. Then the history unfolds, narrated by Ghost. The Meridians' arrival, the Founding. The mysterious plague, the salting of the earth, the birth of children who changed as they grew, the Tithes, clips of branded necks and white hair, clans being rounded up, the bells ringing at their wrists, Rotters being led into the Pits. Molly Bell's brothel, the dancing girls, the babies, the ledgers of Inquestor fathers, stacks upon stacks of records, names, dates...

And then me, my shaved head, my bruised and bloodied face, my naked back as the High Inquestor flogs me in front of the Pits. It narrows in on the metal plate on my chest, then rises to my eyes, filled with such rage and despair that I nearly forget it's me. The dirty creature crouched in front of the crowd is a half-feral animal, bloody, caked in filth, and draped in the High Inquestor's crimson robe like some sort of queen, mocking and murderous. It's no wonder I'd picked up a bit of a following when I returned.

The screen goes black as my form is shoved through the gates of the Pits.

"What happened next was an ordeal most people could never comprehend..."

From here there is no actual direct imagery—the dragon hadn't been able to follow me belowground—so there are scatterings of Madeline d'Arc's notes, Joseph's notes, witnesses from BrightStone being interviewed by Chancellor Davis, and even Molly Bell, her monstrous teeth snapping shut in the face of the camera.

And then the explosion of Rotters erupting from the gates of the Pits, something I hadn't seen before as the swarming mass of starving, dying people slide through the city streets, ravaging citizens in an awful fury. Screams and groans, the sound of flesh being torn from bones. Mortally wounded men and women staggering, crying out, gunshots echoing through the streets. The sound makes the hair on the back of my neck stand up, and I'm already reaching for the nonexistent hammer at my belt as if I were back there, blind and weeping for breath as the fresh air thunders into my lungs.

The camera pulls back, and I *am* there, me and Bran, back-to-back among a horde of Rotters. We swing our makeshift weapons in practiced rhythm, borne of months and years down below where my name, my job, my entire being focused only on the act of execution, killing, releasing the damned from the last of their lives, the shackles of the bodies that betrayed them again and again.

A soft voice rings out. "Mag...pie? Did you bring me...bring me something?"

My head jerks up as Alora appears on screen, tottering over the marble in the council room, her eyes beginning to cloud over, her skin pulsing with a fetid heartbeat that no longer seems to want to sustain her life. The camera pans to me and Bran holding her as she dies, my bloodstained hands stark against the pale marble.

And then the footage goes to the council room and the chaos exploding between me and the High Inquestor, overlaid with images from what is probably an interview during his incarceration in BrightStone. The High Inquestor smirking, insisting he's done nothing wrong, that the sacrifices he made were for Meridion's greater good, that the medical experiments were his way of honoring the Noble Houses, and that of course some collateral damage would have to occur. All great movements with certain fields are expected to have such. Without risks, where would we be?

"After all, when it comes down to it, they're nothing more than animals…"

Me again, an ugly sound escaping my throat as I whip the hammer at his face, the scene fading to black.

And then it flickers again, a date appearing to show a more recent meeting as the High Council confers in an empty council room. Madam Councilor Greta slams down her gavel. "Moon Children are not, nor will ever be considered part of Meridian society, and while we will certainly do our best to make sure they are comfortable down below, they are no longer welcome on Meridion. As for the one known as Raggy Maggy, she is found guilty of murder, with a sentence of death, to be implemented within a week."

The silence as the screens go black is thunderous. If there are passersby, I barely notice because the entirety of the city has suddenly gone dark but for a cluster of Moon Children standing in the center of the Inner Spiral, their hair glowing gently to light up the area around them. My clan.

Bran lets out a piercing whistle. *Come, come, come…*

And they do. My ears pick up on the sounds from the darkness, the cautious feet slipping from the darkest shadows and the roofs, from allies and buildings and from drainpipes. Each one of my

Moon Child brethren sliding from the edge of night to illuminate the darkness we've found upon the greatest of cities.

The screen flickers once more, but now the cameras are panning over them as lights descend like odd bits of snow to illuminate the hundreds of us, staring at the screen with feral faces and angry smiles, Tithe bells hanging from each wrist to jangle like an accusing chorus of the damned.

"But we are already here..."

The screen goes dark. A moment later, the city flickers back to life, the neon screens proclaiming beauty products and ways to harvest one's eggs for future generations, but the Moon Children are gone, melting silently into the shadows with no hint of their presence at all. The Meridians gape at one another and then at the screens, and then the entirety of the city erupts into chaos as the video shuts off.

The aide snatches the screen from me before I can even process what I just saw. I still have the wherewithal to realize I am probably totally fucked. Yet I cannot help the brimming rush of pride at seeing what my clan, my people, did without me.

That doesn't mean I'm going to let the Meridians simply lead me off in chains without some sort of fight. I've been studying this room for more than two weeks by now. I know all its angles, and while there's no chance of escape from here just yet, they might get sloppy about it once we're outside the room.

And all bets will be off then.

"I can't imagine why you'd think I had anything to do with this," I tell the councilwoman mildly. "As to your grandson, and his death, well, of course I did that. But he deserved it."

Her eyes narrow at me. "Prepare her for travel," she commands. The guards rush past her to grab at my arms and legs. I don't bother fighting them. There are too many, and the room is too cramped.

"Where's Jeremiah Brasheen? I'm fairly certain you can't remove me from here without notifying him." I'm bluffing, of course. I don't have a damn idea how any of this works.

"Not another word from you," she says, raising her hand. "Cooperate and I'll consider letting you go. Fight me and not only will I have you executed in the most public and brutal of ways, but I'll ensure that the same happens to the sons of d'Arc." Her brows lower. "Am I clear?"

She's lying. I can feel it, even if I can't see the lightning bolts under her skin. Or maybe lying is too harsh, but something isn't quite right here. Better perhaps to let it play out a bit before I attempt to make a move.

The councilwoman says nothing else, whirling out of the room. The guards each take a shoulder and strong-arm me from the cell and down the hallway. I can see lights from outside streaming through the front doors, but I force my arms to relax. They'll know something's coming if I tense up.

But as the front doors open, I'm rewarded with a crowd of Meridian citizens trying to shove their way into the building. Demands for my death. Demands for my freedom.

"What is this?" I shout at Jeremiah, who is valiantly trying to press his way through the crowd, his usual suit and tie replaced by what looks to be like a pair of silk pajamas. Clearly he had been awakened abruptly, speaking volumes as to the legality of the current situation.

"Don't say a word, Mags! I'm trying to get a contin—"

Whatever else he says is lost as I'm whisked into one of those taxi airships, though this one seems to be more of a private vehicle. The seating is several levels above what I remember from the last one I was in.

Madam Councilor Greta sits across from me, tapping on the window to indicate the driver should move on. She's flanked by two of her guards, neither of them looking as though they possess anything close to a sense of humor.

"So where are we going" I finally ask her. "And why all this?" I gesture about the airship carriage. "If you wanted to kill me, I would have thought you would have simply done it back there."

"I would not stoop to be so petty," she says, glancing out the window. We're approaching the LightHouse, and a nervous tremor ripples over my skin. Did she discover IronHeart's secret? "You murdered my grandson. I should thank you for that. He was an embarrassment to the family anyway. But I won't."

"I don't understand." Is every Meridian batshit crazy?

"His death bothers me less than the current mess you Moon Children have created for me. I would be just as happy to never see your faces again, but now we have calls for a proper investigation into the BrightStone Rot. The civilian population is slow to anger, and mostly ignorant, but when it's riled up, sometimes it's simply easier to give them what they want."

"So you're going to let me go?" My eyes dart between her and the guards, still unsure.

"In a manner of speaking. If Madeline d'Arc truly made you the key to our salvation, well...I don't really believe in it myself, but I've been wrong before," she adds mildly. "I'll be happily surprised if this works."

"Where are we going?" I ask as we drift over the Inner Spiral.

"You're not asking the right questions," she says, impatient. "It's not where you're going, it's what you're doing." She points to the LightHouse. "You're going to make Meridion fly again."

Panic lances through me, and I begin to struggle despite myself. "Make me," I snap as one of the guards lurches toward my seat and presses his forearm against my windpipe.

"No need." He pulls out a small mechanical box from his pocket, his thumb rubbing over a shiny silver button. I hear the vibrating sound of a pig-sticker before I see it, steeling myself against the shock.

"You can't keep me here," I say. "I can unlock anything on Meridion, haven't you heard?"

"Oh yes," the guard says, almost sadly. "I'm counting on it." There's something familiar about him, and I try to place his face, even with the hat pulled down tight over his brow. The High Inquestor.

"But...you're dead," I mumble. The words slip out of me, slithering from my lips like a snake shedding its skin.

There's a soft buzz, but I can't tell where it's coming from, and then I realize it's coming from me. I suck in a breath, but my head is already growing dizzy. My heart clicks frantically for half a second and then stops completely.

Falling.

Am I falling?

Yes, I am falling. My eyes shut as though that's enough of an explanation, the air tickling around my face. Stars shine in my vision when I try to see past the darkness. Glowing eyes or not, there is nothing at all that I can see.

Am I in the Pits?

A momentary lapse of terror slithers over me, snakelike in its constriction. I cannot breathe. I cannot breathe.

My blood beats sluggish and tired through my veins, my lungs screaming for air. And yet, no matter how wide my mouth, how deep my breath, it's as though someone has shoved cotton into my throat, blocking everything short of a thin bit of oxygen.

I struggle and discover my limbs are blocks of cement, unmovable and stiff. Even my neck flops, my head sliding forward and back. I'm being carried? The tiniest wheeze escapes me, whispering over my tongue.

"Awake, are we? Good. I was afraid you were actually going to die back there. Should have shut down that energy burst a little faster." The voice of the High Inquestor natters on at me, but my brain can barely comprehend the noises he's making as words, and most of them drift past me like foam on the tide.

"I never really intended for things to go this far, you know. I simply wanted to weaken you a bit. Scare you up some." His voice grows warm. "Did it work?"

My mouth moves, or tries to, but I can't even form a word, let alone ask a question. Somehow my eyes flick open for a half second, but it's so bright I have to immediately shut them again, pain lancing into my skull from the illumination.

Am I outside?

My eyes water, vision blurring as I stare at him through my tears. His left eye is covered with a patch, his head still wrapped in bandages. His mouth droops as though he can't quite get it to cooperate.

I'm not crying so much as trying to squint through the light, but he doesn't seem to know the difference and he shushes me with an almost tender kiss on my forehead. "You're the key, my magpie. The key to making everything right."

"And how's that exactly?" I wheeze, finally able to catch a bit of my breath. "I killed you."

"You tried," he amended. "My grandmother, as much as she hates me, decided it would be less shameful for the family if I simply expired. That was leaked so there wouldn't be anything too suspicious later. Of course, not that it matters. My grandmother has lived far too long as it is. She'll make a beautiful corpse when they find her body." He lets out a giggle as he touches his face, tearing the bandage off his eye. A gaping blackness appears, oozing and raw. "I love what you've done here. I just want you to know."

"Happy to oblige." I cough, gasping for air as my heart stutters.

"The flight drive in the LightHouse is empty. When that bitch Madeline shut it off, she took out the power source so there was no way to turn it back on. But then you showed up with your mechanical heart, and all that garbage at the trial about just what your role in all of this is..."

I struggle faintly, but it's not more than a gentle sway of limbs, as though I'm wrapped in seaweed. "Fail-safe," I sputter. "That's what she called it."

"Indeed. But a fail-safe from what?" the High Inquestor asks darkly. "The worst has already happened. We've been stuck here for ages. To be truthful, that part hasn't bothered me so much. I used the time as I could to develop the serum, even though it has not been as successful as I need it to be. But you think I'm going to just let my grandmother use you to restart Meridion's engines? I don't think so. At least not on her terms." And with that, we're out on the deck of the airship, a gangplank leading to the top steps of the LightHouse. The light is on, of course, golden with a welcoming warmth that belies the cold glass through which it shines.

The bodies of two guards, ceremonial by the looks of it, lie sprawled out on the balcony in a bloody tangle of limbs. "Don't need anyone making a fuss," the Inquestor notes, shoving them out of his way with a booted foot. His smile grows more excited. "And here we are."

The door to the inner chamber is already open, and he deposits me into a chair. "The main mechanism is down below, of course, but this is the bit that actually turns it on. The steering is handled in a different chamber. If I recall, there were multiple teams in place in various locations around the city to ensure things were managing okay, but it has been quite a while, I admit."

In the center of the light mechanism is a tube, solid and metallic. He points to it. "Open it."

"Open what?" I blink at it blearily, not really comprehending his meaning.

"Use your heart. Unlock the LightHouse." He snaps his fingers, impatient. "That thing you do." He pushes me closer to the tube.

My heart sputters, causing me to gasp. "Might work better if you didn't fuck it all up," I say, wincing at the way it lurches. "Buceph almost broke it once, and it nearly killed me."

"Well, to be honest, I don't really care if you die," he retorts pleasantly. "I simply need you to turn this on. I'll take it from there."

I snarl at him, but the tube is already reacting, a panel lighting up on its surface. I hesitate, tapping out the matching pattern. The tube creaks, the entire LightHouse seeming to shift and turn, shuddering with an awful, screaming wail.

"We need to get your heart open, clearly," the Inquestor says, bending down to look at the panel in the tube. "It isn't enough to simply turn it on here. Anyone could have done that, if they knew the proper code. So what is it about your heart that makes you special?"

He leans down toward me, and I can feel his breath on my face. "You were just a girl who happened to be in the right place at the right time and one of us performed an experiment on you. That's it."

"Chance is a fool's game," I shoot back. "And fate cares nothing for fools or chance. I am what I am." He presses me into the chair harder. My heart is whirring in a new way that I'm unfamiliar with. As though it recognizes the panel, yearns for it, is trying to go…home.

A cold realization shoots through me. The chair that's carved into the wall isn't really a chair at all. But even as I'm lashing out at the Inquestor he's shoving me into it, my legs and arms strapped into thick metal fastenings. My brain snaps with panic, my body remembering being held down in similar fashion in Buceph's lab, fighting for my life when the Meridian scientist tried to pry my heart open.

I let out a whimper as the visor snaps down over my eyes. "Let me go!"

"Too late. You're home, Magpie. In Meridion, where you always wanted to be." His words mock me, echoing through the visor as my heart begins to hum. It's nearly musical in its cadence, and the city seems to respond, a harmonizing cacophony that shivers through my bones. I'm crying out with it, unable to contain the sound, giving voice to the city as it tries to speak through me.

"Free! Freefreefreefreefree!" The words sing through my lips, until my throat is hoarse. The High Inquestor is shouting something, but I cannot hear it properly through the song of the city. My heart thrums in response to Meridion's call, the notes growing closer and closer until they meet up. My body is rigid, an electrical current running through my systems that keeps me locked to the chair. I can feel the lightning bolts emanating from my skin. Is it a warning?

"Enough!" IronHeart's voice rumbles through me, echoing past the visor so hard I can barely keep my head up. The clanking of metallic footsteps can only be Copper Betty's body forcing her way into the room. "How dare you? Do you have any idea of what you've done?"

The High Inquestor lets out a high-pitched scream, warbling like a deranged bird. I struggle to see, unable to get past the visor until I turn my neck at some impossible angle, the barest edge of my eyes peeking through a small opening where the edges of the metal don't quite line up.

IronHeart stands there, her hands wrapped around the High Inquestor's neck, the bronze fingers curling into the flesh of his throat. His feet dangle as she lifts him higher and higher, ignoring the soft wet sounds he makes as he struggles to breathe.

Blood spatters over the automaton's face when his throat explodes beneath the force of her grip, his life leaving him with nothing more poetic than a surprised gurgle as she drops him.

"What a damned mess." She clanks over to me to remove the visor. Her golden eyes study me, but a moment later, I'm overwhelmed with information, stimuli of all sorts, assailed by images, smells, sounds, a carnival of noise that has no beginning and no end.

Somewhere in the back of my mind I'm screaming, realizing I'm essentially plugged into the nervous system of the city itself, as though it has become its own entity, my heart the last bit it needed to right its song and wake it up.

And Meridion *is* awake now. And it seemed rather pissed off, though for all I know, it's my own anger feeding into it. How does a city have emotions, anyway? Perhaps IronHeart would be able to tell me.

The thought drifts away as I attempt to focus on processing the information. It's as though I can see through the cameras themselves, catching glimpses of people as they move about the city. The network of information spreads out and out.

A child huddled under her bed crying. Clusters of panicked people pointing at the video screen in the Inner Spiral. Moon Children scattering to the shadows...

My attention pulls to them, terrified for their safety. How will the city react to their presence? And Ghost... Where is he? I flip through the cameras trying to find him, but it's like finding an ant in a colony. Too much information and I can't comprehend it.

My heart continues to thrum. For a moment it feels as though someone's grabbed my arm, but it's gone a moment later.

It doesn't matter anyway. I am Meridion, and I am alive.

Time passes, I suppose, but it's a hazy thing. I don't know if I'm asleep or awake. My body seems to maintain itself in some fashion, but I'm not eating or drinking or taking a piss. Suspended animation, maybe, as though the electricity flowing through my heart is enough to keep me going. Am I even breathing?

Sometimes I catch voices, but I don't know if I'm hearing them through the city itself or if they're in the LightHouse. They're familiar enough. Ghost. Lucian. IronHeart. Rosa. Bran or Josephine.

Their words are harsh and afraid, and I don't know why. I'm here, after all. And yet...and yet...

"Look at her! She's wasting away!" Ah, Lucian. "She'll die if we don't do something."

"This was not the intended solution. But I don't think you would have liked the answer when I came up with it." IronHeart's voice is almost soothing in its metallic cadence. I understand her now, more than I thought would be possible. "I'm not sure she even wants to wake up. It's a seductive thing she's doing—a web she may not be able to untangle. Perhaps it would be kinder to simply let her be."

"Then why was she whistling for help?" Ghost snaps. "Some part of her wants to get out. I know it!"

"Whistles." She sniffs. "As if that means anything. She's dreaming."

"No, he's right." Bran's voice is dripping with condescension. "I realize you suck-tits don't get Moon Child language, but she's absolutely been trying to communicate with us in some fashion. She's only stopped because her mouth is bleeding. Look at the cracks."

My eyes flicker open so that I'm looking at them—or more like I see their outlines. The visor is missing, as though someone has torn it off. Everything is clear, and yet, I have trouble making out their faces. It's as though I comprehend the mere suggestion of a mouth or an eye, a warped bit of emotional expression that becomes merely another data point within my recesses.

Ghost gasps when he notices me, launching himself to my side. "Mags? Mags! Are you there? Can you hear me?"

His words slam into me like a wave, loud and frightened, but it's like I'm underwater, a hazy noise that gets lost in the din of Meridion's singing.

"I hear you," I say finally, my mouth struggling to form the words. How much easier if I could make the walls talk, perhaps, but I have no mechanism for that.

"You're dying, Mags. You need to let go. You need…" His voice drifts away into the song, my attention already being pulled somewhere else. Another thread in the warp and the weft of the city.

"I cannot die, foolish thing. I am Meridion. A song within a song within a song. I take care of it all." My voice is rusty and creaks like old leather, the edges of my lips cracking and burning.

"This was never intended for you," IronHeart says gently. "It needs an automaton, Magpie. Not a body of flesh and blood."

"My heart… My heart…" I murmur, raspy.

"A mistake on my part. That core was to have gone to the body I wear now, but it was too dangerous. I had no choice but to hide it, and your birth defect gave me a perfect opportunity. I never figured you would survive this long. I'd meant to retrieve it after you died, but here you are."

That caught my attention, and my head turns toward her. Why did my neck hurt so much? "I don't understand. I read your medical notes. I was the fail-safe."

"You were. You are still, technically. Or you house it inside yourself." Her metallic face seems to muse it over. "Have you never wondered why you always longed to come to Meridion, for nearly the entirety of your life? So badly you could taste it, even though at times it made no sense?"

"My heart…" My brain stutters at this bit of information. That perhaps my need to be here wasn't driven by anything more than my heart trying to come home. The thought makes me sad.

"Yes," she says softly. "Remember when I told you it sounded like it had been tampered with? I would have known it even if I hadn't heard it."

"What are you talking about?" Lucian interrupts, the loudness of his voice making me wince.

"The mechanism in that heart should have driven her straight to the LightHouse the moment she arrived—or at least straight to me. The fact that she wandered about here for days before she found her way below the city is proof enough that it was no longer programmed to do so."

There's a terrible pause. "Did you arrange for her to be poisoned so that she would come to you?" Ghost's voice is trembling with a sort of deranged terror, as though he didn't want to ask the question and doesn't want to know the answer.

"Of course not," IronHeart snaps. "I'm not as heartless as all that. What good would it have done me if she died outright? No, that was purely Meridian politics and dumb luck. I would have sent another dragon to her eventually or called the old one home when I deemed it necessary." The automaton sighs. "And now I'm not sure the best course of action."

My vision blurs as my sandpaper eyelids scratch. I look toward Ghost, tears streaming down his face. "What is it?"

"You've made the city fly again, but we're not the ones controlling it. You are."

"Where are we going?" I frown.

"We're not entirely sure, but you've somehow disabled our navigational system. If you leave the chair, the city will fall. Your heart is the only thing keeping us up. And if it falls, the resulting tidal wave will assuredly take out most of BrightStone, not to mention everyone up here."

My brain rummages through this information, testing the validity of it against several iterations of options. We are, in fact, flying. But we are still connected by the anchors so it isn't as though I'm taking us anywhere. Yet.

Solution? Meridion came up with the obvious one.

"Remove my heart and give it to IronHeart," I say, the voice of the city flavoring my words. "This body is dying anyway. You can wait or not, but the clearest path—"

"No!" Ghost fiercely. "I can't. I can't, Mags."

"What choice is there?" I struggle to keep my focus on him, some small piece of me skimming the surface of my thoughts, insisting I wait, trying to block out Meridion's song.

"There might be another way," IronHeart says thoughtfully. "In truth, I was supposed to have been in that spot all along. It's what I built this body for. I simply needed the more robust core of your heart to complete it." She pauses sadly. "But that doesn't mean I can't handle it for a short while on my own. It won't be enough, of course. Meridion *will* fall. But I might be able to slow its descent enough to keep from killing everyone."

Ghost nods at Lucian, the two brothers in seeming agreement. After all, she is the embodiment of their mother. There is no doubt she won't be coming back from this particular endeavor, though I suppose if her data is stored elsewhere, it won't be a complete loss. Though, there certainly has never been an automaton quite like this one.

She moves closer to me, one metallic arm brushing against mine as she tests the connection between us, lowering her head to my ear. "Magpie, when you leave here, run. As far away as you can. I won't be strong enough to hold Meridion back without your heart, and I *will* attempt to get it. You understand? Once you manage to get off the city, I'll be able to force it down."

I nod at her words, her warning. How difficult will it be for her to fight against her very nature? Against the thing she was built for? "Yes."

"One. Two. Three," I count down, my body bracing for the impact. I half shut my eyes as her terrifyingly strong fingers snatch me from the seat, breaking through the metal fixtures that hold me in place. I scream, and it's the city's scream, as well, echoing through every street, every house, every hidden alcove and high rooftop as the electric shock of it nearly stops my heart.

The city lets out a shudder of alarm as its main power source disappears from the chain. I fall into Ghost's waiting arms, he and Lucian carefully holding me up. My limbs are half-locked in place, my fingers gnarled with tension.

"Run," I gasp at them, my tongue a sanded desert. And then everything goes black.

My name is Raggy Maggy
And I've dragon in my heart
Big and bold, like songs of old
To sing of freedom as we part.

— CHAPTER TWENTY-SEVEN —

Thump, thump. Thump.

I'm being carried, legs pumping around me, boots slapping the ground. The air is shaking. I'm shaking. My heart is whirring madly as though it can't quite seem to settle, and all around us is this terrible musical wail. Meridion is crying out in anguish as the only thing keeping it alive is gone. But we haven't plummeted to the sea. Not yet. IronHeart is holding up her end of the bargain, but I can tell from the discordance in Meridion's song that its desperate attempts to get me back will be hard and furious.

We have to get off this city. But how to do so without abandoning the other Moon Children? We can't leave them here. "The others," I mumble. "Our clan..."

"They're still on Meridion," Bran says. "Josephine spent days trying to ferry nearly all of them up here for that little stunt the Heart of the Sea and Ghost pulled off, but we weren't expecting the High Inquestor to take you from the jail like that." He grunts as he narrowly avoids a drone. "Caught us all off guard, aye?"

"Where are they all staying?" I ask, confused.

"The Heart of the Sea and Lottie were stowing them away in various places, and a lot were in the sewers, hiding until things settled down," Ghost says. "It's been a bit of a mess the last couple of days as far as communication goes."

Relief settles through me. At least that much is in order. Something skitters past us, one of the drones buzzing wildly by our heads. IronHeart is on the hunt. Sirens blare, sending us down alley after alley. Whatever protections she afforded us before appear to have been lifted.

Screaming civilians pass by us, making it easy to lose ourselves in the crowd before taking shelter beneath an overhang. They set me down, and Ghost hands me a flask of water.

"Don't guzzle it," Lucian warns. "You remember what happened last time."

I reward him with a half-smile, too many memories blurring with the remnants of Meridion in my mind. But I sip it slow all the same, my limbs shaking as the liquid dribbles down my throat.

Bran peers around the corner, his eyes scanning the sky. "We've got a few minutes here, but the drones will find us again."

"Where are the airships?" I rasp at him.

Lucian shakes his head. "There aren't enough for the whole city. Those that have private ones will undoubtedly use them, but the crowds at the ports are far too full. We'd have no chance."

"So what do we do?" Jeremiah asks, his brows drawn in fear. I don't blame him at all. His entire world is crashing down around him.

Something sharp lands on me, hissing in my ear. I barely have the strength to be surprised, but it's my dragon, and an idea flickers to life in the quiet part of my mind.

"Copper Betty. Is she still below?" I glance at Ghost. "What did IronHeart say? The weapon inside her… Something about an electromagnetic pulse?"

"We do that and every system in the city will be shut down, Mags. Not just the engine. Everything." Lucian's mouth compresses. "I'm not sure that's any better than simply letting the city fall."

"Well we can't wait here," I say. "Let's at least see what we're working with. If she can fly, maybe we can ride her out of here."

The passageways into the sewers are dark and narrow. IronHeart will have surely guessed that's where we might head, but we don't have any choice in the matter.

Another drone sweeps past us, but my little dragon takes it down, smashing it to bits on the side of the walls.

"Useful thing, that," Jeremiah says approvingly. "And what's all this about a dragon?"

"You have no idea," Ghost says, nudging Lucian. "Did you tell him?"

"Not in so many words, no." His brother muffles a cough in his fist. "Whatever you see down here, try not to panic, love."

"Because that's so reassuring," Jeremiah mutters.

We arrive at the inner gate to the dragon's lair. It's locked, of course, but it is just as easily opened with my heart and swings open with a creaking whine.

We limp into the control room, and I'm struck at once by how dead it seems. Whereas before, even with IronHeart's metallic body curled around everything, there was still some semblance of life—the smoke, the oil, the whirring of electronics. But now everything is shut down, oddly quiet. Even Copper Betty herself seems lifeless, her eyes shut.

"What in the hells is this?" Jeremiah stares around him in wild wonder. "Some kind of hidden art installation?"

Ghost ignores him, carrying me over to the dragon's head. "Can you wake her?"

"I don't know." My brain is rushing, trying to remember how. "She's still connected to the city, aye? We'll have to free her before we wake her up. If IronHeart catches wind of my presence here, she'll try to stop me."

"Free...her?" Jeremiah looks doubtful, but I don't have time or patience to explain just yet.

Ghost and Bran set about looking for the anchor points for the chains bound to her hind legs. They give her a fair amount of movement within this chamber, but the way they're connected makes it quite clear she can't remove them on her own.

"I'm surprised she didn't try getting some of the little dragons to remove them," Ghost grunts as he attempts to pry one of the bolts off her. "Damn, this stuff is strong."

"I'm sure she had her reasons," I muse. Madeline never left anything to chance. Perhaps even the city itself isn't fully aware that the dragon is anything other than some forgotten bit of machinery left within its bowels to rot like a trash.

"There," Bran says, removing a bolt with a grimacing twist. "I suspect they were electrified when they were on. Might have been what prevented her from removing them before."

The walls suddenly tilt, turning us hard on our sides. The newly loosened dragon begins to slide toward us, and I let out a small whimper as Copper Betty's head rolls toward me.

"Whatever you're going to do, do it fast!" Bran snaps, his teeth gritting as he pushes hard on the metal scales with his leg to keep it from crushing us. And he's right. There is no more time.

I crawl to the dragon's head, my fingers sliding over the muzzle and drifting past the wicked teeth. But how to wake her? My heart whirs madly as I lean over her. Undoubtedly, she will work a bit like Meridion's core, though hopefully without me having to insert myself inside her.

The city lurches again. This time I feel the hum coming from the dragon's head, and I find a small button gleaming like an emerald-green scale that glitters with its own light. My fingers reach it, and I still. Just like that, my heart matches some tone I can't hear, and the dragon's eyes flicker to light with Copper Betty's familiar blue staring at me. "Ah, you're awake."

She shifts her legs beneath her as though suddenly realizing she is not bound by chains. Her head snaps toward me in wonder, and she struggles to stay upright when the city shudders.

"Wait!" I shout as she turns, her clawed feet scraping the sides of the room. Her tail lashes back, clipping Jeremiah on the head as he tries to duck out of the way.

Ghost pulls me back to keep me from getting the same treatment. Copper Betty scrabbles madly at the wall, the thrumming of the city growing more intense until my bones are vibrating with it, my heart whirring and chugging in counterpoint. What the hell is it reacting to?

And then it doesn't matter. The dragon tears through the walls on the far side, destroying the screens with their panicked flashing and sounds of alarm and bursts into the bowels of the city.

Lucian is cradling Jeremiah, wiping a bit of blood from the other man's face. "It's not deep," he says, "but I think he was knocked unconscious." His brows draw down in worry, but he waves me and Ghost off. "Go. Go figure out a way to stop...all this madness." There's a hint of manic despair in his voice, and Ghost and I exchange a look.

Bran squats beside them. "You two go. I'll get them out of here as quickly as I can."

Ghost and I sprint after Copper Betty, avoiding the razor-sharp slices of metal, the twisted pipes and half-melted debris. It's not a hard path to follow. She's gone straight for the outside.

"Do you think she can really fly?" Ghost asks. "She's bound to be heavy."

"We're about to find out. If we can catch up with her..." I am off-kilter, my limbs not moving like I remember. But I stagger along, unwilling to fall behind or make Ghost carry me.

By the time we find where she exited, the city is almost completely sideways. We emerge along the top. The anchor chains are squealing beneath the strain, groaning against the enormous bolts holding them in place. Below us the city of BrightStone is eclipsed in shadow by Meridion. How many people have already fallen off?

Ghost sees where I'm looking and squints. "The weather shields should keep most of us from sliding over the edge. I'm fairly certain there are fail-safes in place for such things. Assuming the city itself hasn't overridden them," he adds, worried.

"Fail-safe." I rasp the word, letting it flee on the wind. Tapping on my chest, I look for the dragon. Did she fly or plummet into the ocean?

The sun is so bright, and I squint against it. Ghost points above us. "There! In the clouds!"

Now I see her, uncoiled into her full beauty, a massive creature that seems to grow larger with every passing second. A magnificent, enormous model of my little shoulder dragon, a sweep of wings and a flash of lightning standing out against the darkening sky.

The city wails out its panicked challenge, trying to right itself, and IronHeart roars in response, an electrical buzzing that radiates toward us.

Well done, Mags. What have you done this time?

"Only released the very thing made to destroy the city," I answer myself pleasantly. "In hindsight, it may have been a truly awful idea."

"What is she doing?" Ghost shouts, his words nearly lost in the din.

"What she was probably programmed to do," I say. "Shit. I thought if Copper Betty was in the dragon's body, it wouldn't attack the city. But if your mother built the dragon to destroy Meridion no matter what..."

Copper Betty swoops past us, electrical pulses thrumming over the entirety of her metallic scales.

"Have you ever actually had a *good* idea?" Bran staggers up behind us, helping Lucian hold up Jeremiah. The unconscious man's head was bandaged using what looks like part of Lucian's shirt.

"Probably a concussion," Lucian says. His voice is low and tight, but controlled like it is when he goes into doctor mode. I can hear the panic rippling below the surface, the same sort I used to hear when he talked about Ghost after he'd been taken hostage by Lord Balthazaar.

Drones buzz by us but pay us no mind, fixated on some other task. "Too bad we can't get them to give us a lift," I say. Even if they could, there's no trusting them at this point.

Airships erupt from the city, scattering like rats on a sinking ship and we frantically try to flag one down. "There!" Bran points as a shadow flits by us, the airships roaring as Josephine pulls abreast. There's a tangle of Moon Children on deck, and I breathe a sigh of relief as I see the rest of my clan among them.

Quickly, they help us on board. Lucian and Ghost immediately whisk Jeremiah belowdecks for what will hopefully be a better shot at medical care. Bran, Josephine, and I meet up on the bow, clan leaders conferring as to the best course of action.

I'm sure that's what the stories might say anyway. In reality, the three of us make rude gestures and swear a blue streak about the ineptitude of the other two. Still, I start grinning all the same. Clan discussions are supposed to be rowdy things, and the normalcy of it grounded me.

"What the hell just happened down there?" Josephine demands. "One moment, I'm having high tea with the Chancellor, discussing possible transportation between cities, and the next everything went to shit." She thumbs behind her. "There's an entire Meridion army out there with more ships than I care to count currently rescuing people who are hanging off the edge of the shields."

"What about the Heart of the Sea?" Bran asks, his mouth compressed.

"Her airship is massive so she's picking up as many passengers as possible in the Inner Spiral. I think Lottie's set up a triage on board for anyone who's injured, at least until they can get their doctors in order, but right now it's nothing but chaos." Josephine points to the dragon sweeping through the clouds past us. "And whatever the hells that is sure isn't helping any."

I slump against the rail, feeling dizzy. Bran thrusts more water at me.

"All right. Let's stop this, if we can. The city, I can't help with, but that—" I point at the dragon rolling through a storm cloud "—that's entirely my fault."

"What do you need us to do?" Josephine eyes the dragon warily, carefully navigating against the headwinds. "If we get too close it's likely to blow us out of the sky."

"No need." I glance over at Bran. "Just get me high enough that I can basically fall onto her. It's still Copper Betty inside her. When we woke her up, she panicked, I think. But she's mine. She's made that overly clear again and again. The city doesn't want her here so maybe if I can persuade her to move off a ways, Meridion will calm down enough that IronHeart can force it to land. I doubt she'll be able to hold it up much longer."

The dragon was made as a weapon. IronHeart told me as much. So if Meridion is reacting to her presence as a defense mechanism in its own right, the obvious solution is to remove her.

I hesitate. "A pair of those fancy wings will come in handy, though. If I miss, I'd rather not plummet immediately to my death."

"I'll find you a set," Bran assures me, his mouth quirking in a crooked half smile. "Maybe even two."

I frown at him. "Why would I need two?"

"For me, of course," Ghost says, sneaking up on me in that quiet way of his. "Did you really think we would let you go alone?"

"But I'm the only one who can make her stop." I tap the metallic heart plate on my chest. "And you don't know how to fly. I can barely manage myself..."

"And that may be true, but I'll be damned if I let you martyr yourself in the meantime because you pass out, aye?" He leans closer to me. "I haven't exactly been sitting around languishing during my house arrest, you know. Bran's been giving me lessons." His eyes dart to where Bran emerges from below deck with a set of wings. "One way or another I was going to get you of here, so let me be your anchor this time, Mags. If you calm her down, great, but if you don't... At least spare me the vision of watching you die, if you don't mind?"

I flush at his brazen assessment. "Fair enough. Two sets of wings, then. How quickly can you get us up there?"

Josephine eyes the dragon. "If we come up from behind her, we may be able to glide past if we shut the engines off. We'd be able to hide in the clouds."

Meridion turns against the chains binding it, the metal squealing. "There won't be a city to save if it takes us much longer," Bran snaps.

I take Ghost's hand, and he squeezes it hard. "Let's go."

The air is ridiculously thin where we are. Without Meridian's atmospheric shields, I'm exposed to the full brunt of the temperature and the winds, and I shiver beneath my clothes. Rosa was good enough to find me something to wear other than my jail rags, and it helps though not enough. But it is the best I can do. I let a fond memory of the bath beneath the Conundrum flee from me. Maybe when all this is over, I'll have time for such luxuries, but for now...

I shift in the wing harness, adjusting it over my shoulders so it doesn't rub too much. The metallic struts flare out and back in as I test their responsiveness.

"We'll try to get you as close as we can," Josephine says. "Otherwise there's a chance you'll be blown off course by the wind." She's shut the engines off, leaving us to drift on the sails. Below us, Copper Betty glides back and forth in apparent confusion, and every time she attempts to approach the city, a bolt of electric fire emerges from the LightHouse as though trying to shoot her down.

The city has partially righted itself now, the Meridians doing their best to get people removed, but there simply aren't enough ships for the scale of the thing. In the end, they're concentrating on not letting anyone slide off the edge.

But that's nothing I can help with.

"All right," Josephine says. "We're coming up on the point now. You two go get into position at the stern, aye?"

Ghost and I quickly work our way to the rear, the other Moon Children quietly sliding away from us in a wave. I would normally expect whistles of encouragement, but until I have control of Copper Betty, there's no point in making her aware of us.

"I'll let you go first, Mags," Ghost whispers in my ear. "With any luck, she won't notice me landing on her after that."

"And if I miss?" I say it mockingly, though it's just bravado on my part.

"Don't miss, Mags. Don't miss." He kisses me briefly, a quick touch to let me know he's still with me, a promise of tomorrows to come.

And with that, we're there. The dragon hovers below us, snarling in frustration as she gets ready to launch herself at the city again. There is no more time.

Climbing to the rail, I suck in a deep breath, then leap forward with a soft whistle. The wings snap open, slowing me as I hurtle down, down, down.

Thump! My booted feet slam into scales—not at the head, which I'd been aiming for, but closer to where her neck meets her back, the webbing of her wings sprawling flatly with each flap. My instinct is to roll forward to break my fall, but there's no room. I take the brunt of it with my knees, letting the impact vibrate its way to my teeth as they nearly bite through my tongue.

"Betty!" I scream into the wind. She turns her head up as though she means to eat me, the razor teeth opening. "It's me, Raggy Maggy! I'm trying to help you!" I flinch as she arches her neck for a closer look. Somehow I detect her unhappiness at being forced into a body that isn't hers.

The electric-blue eyes flare wildly, and my heart whirs in response. Her confusion washes over me in waves, horror and sadness and the realization of the power built inside her. The electromagnetic pulse, the weapon that lies deep in her belly, is ready to be unleashed upon my command. And just as clearly, I can tell that by setting it off, it will be a death sentence for her.

IronHeart might have been willing to accept such a thing, but Copper Better desperately was not.

Ghost has not jumped yet so I whistle a warning to him to stay back, though I doubt it will reach him. The dragon rumbles beneath me.

"I understand." And I do. I am not IronHeart with a mission to destroy Meridion. My heart is no longer programmed to force me to run a city or be influenced by a long-dead scientist. I am Magpie. I am *me*.

Copper Betty swerves suddenly, knocking me off her back. I let out a scream of surprise, my wings trying to steady me back upright. I look up as she launches forward, swooping down with her mouth open.

I close my eyes and let her swallow me.

The currents sweep past us, Betty and me. I'm lodged somewhere within her belly, but like I did with the city, I've somehow merged with her, the power of my heart connecting me to her frame, her senses. It's far different from flying about on my own little wings. Now *I* am the storm come to life, slicing through the currents of the sky with razor-sharp swiftness. I surge upward past Josephine's ship, careful to avoid knocking it over.

My eyes catch Bran holding back Ghost as he struggles to get to me, filling me with a pang of regret. But how to tell him? The dragon's speech mechanism has been disconnected. I can feel that now. It's probably something IronHeart did when she switched to Copper Betty's automaton, though it can still make guttural roars and grunts.

Not particularly helpful for communicating with Ghost, but I manage to make a whistling sound at him, at all of them. *Stand down. Stand down.*

They pause, an incredulous expression crossing over their faces. *Danger,* I add. *Wait for me.*

One by one, they respond in kind, Moon Children whistling their signals back and forth like the chattering of birds. I sweep past them and head toward the city.

The LightHouse alarms claxon as we approach, but instead of what Copper Betty's been doing so far, which is nothing more than trying to approach the city, I weave past the electric attack. Having been part of the city myself, I have an intimate knowledge of how its defenses work and the amount of time it takes in between energy blasts. But more importantly, I know how to call for help.

A roar builds up, rolling out of me as I sweep past the frightened citizens clustered in whatever corner they can find, trying to pile into airships and wind balloons, their skin flushing with electrical pulses.

The LightHouse sounds its alarms, but my roar grows louder. In a matter of moments, hundreds of little drones pop out from every nook and crevice, humming in time. I have to fight to keep them from the city's command center, but I suspect as IronHeart's energy is running out, her ability to command Meridion's technological beings growing weaker. A smattering of little dragons darts here or there, the last of IronHeart's children, including my own. The drones pour from the city, flying far from us. But that's all right. I'll need them to survive the aftermath of the electromagnetic pulse.

I sweep past the LightHouse again, and this time the electrical fire is triggered, forcing me to narrowly turn up and out. But I've timed it right. She won't have a chance to fire it again. I bank, my wings spread wide. My mouth opens, and the sound that escapes me is a single manifestation of every hurt, every triumph, every sadness, every death. All of it explodes toward the LightHouse in a rushing roar so loud the buildings tremble, my heart whirring so hard I think it might simply disintegrate.

The LightHouse sputters, going dark immediately, as though IronHeart was waiting for this. Every light in the city shuts off, leaving its buildings in total blackness. The wail of triumph let out by IronHeart in the LightHouse echoes through the alleyways, bouncing off the city's domed environmental shields.

Meridion begins to sink, and I steer myself beneath the silver dollar bottom, whistling at the drones. They hum along at me, following my commands as they take up their positions all along the seams of the city. Their engines flare, the entire surface coming to life. It's not enough to keep the city afloat, even with my own straining wings, but that was never my goal. A graceful fall is all I want.

"Mags!" Josephine's airship has darted closer, sinking with us. Ghost is on the prow, whistling something dirty at me, and I reply with a rumble.

Ghost lets out a laugh of triumph, and the ship darts away again, the ocean rising to meet us with worrisome speed. I roll at the last moment, leaving the last of the work to the drones. They plant the city just offshore of BrightStone, the silver skyscrapers towering over the BrightStone streets.

I close my eyes inside the dragon's belly, my heart beating as though a bird resides in my chest as we land smack in the middle of the Cheaps. Limbs weary, I crawl my way to her mouth and step off her tongue when it uncurls to deposit me on the docks.

I take about two steps before collapsing, my body giving out at last. I get a glimpse of a concerned-looking whore, and then I let out an exhausted laugh, cackling like my foster mother, Mad Brianna.

Meridion has fallen.

EPILOGUE

Five weeks later.

The last of Madeline d'Arc's ashes flutter across the foaming sea, Lucian and Ghost gently spreading their mother's remains over the waters to set her free. Of IronHeart, there's nothing left, other than a melted hunk of metal wedged within the fallen remains of the LightHouse. We leave it there, a final memorial to the woman who both created and destroyed the floating city of Meridion.

And now there is only the half-sunken city of Meridion, its perfect silver towers reaching for a sky much lower than before. BrightStone remains nearby, the tentative beginnings of a bridge starting between the two, though ferries and airships can already be seen moving between them in a flurry of mercantile movement, forging an alliance of need over the last several weeks.

It may not be the merging of civilizations that Madeline hoped for so long ago, but at least it will start on somewhat equal footing and that will have to be good enough. I hadn't truly wished for anything particularly tragic to happen to the Meridians. Most of them lived in ignorance, but that doesn't mean they should die for it.

The Heart of the Sea's airship floats overhead, the celebrity's face appearing on the screen briefly as she announces information regarding housing assistance. I can't quite help but smile at this. Not even the destruction of her way of life is enough to stop her from pushing forward. I can only admire that kind of drive, wondering if I'd do the same in her shoes.

"Explain it to me again," Fionula says, walking beside us as we head up the docks toward the Cheaps. Somehow she continues to look like a living jewel, dressed in her emerald greens and blues. "I'm still not entirely sure what happened."

I laugh. "I'm not entirely sure of it myself. I only wanted to bring Meridion down. I didn't want to destroy it outright." I chewed on my lower lip. "I don't think Madeline expected us to set the dragon itself free. If we'd left her chained in the center of the city, IronHeart would have attacked us directly, leaving us with no other option."

"So she was manipulating you this entire time?" Her brows raise as though she can't quite believe it.

"Maybe in a manner of speaking, but I think when she, as the city, realized I wouldn't do it, she simply allowed herself to give up as gracefully as possible. Her body couldn't handle the power of the city for long, so once she saw I could control the drones, she stopped fighting the city. It took what it wanted from her, and she...died, I guess. A kind of suicide, for lack of a better term."

Ghost and Lucian are talking quietly, and I don't want to interrupt it, so I stretch my arms with a sigh, my dragon shifting on my shoulder. "That's all there is to it."

"And what will you do now?" Fionula looks over at the towers of Meridion with a melancholy expression. "What will any of the Moon Children do, for that matter? In the end, we failed you all again, as we always seem to."

"Ah well. I suppose we're used to that," I say ruefully. "But as far as the rest of us, that remains to be seen."

I let my thoughts trail away, already half-full of bittersweet memories. The Heart of the Sea, Lottie, and I have already had several extensive meetings with both Josephine and Bran to hammer out the best way to handle our various clans. Some of them will stay. Some will leave.

Of my own clan, I already know Gloriana will remain here, her wish to become a bonewitch a burning desire that overrides everything else. And she's earned her chance to do so, beneath Lucian's tutelage.

Haru's found a Meridian family. In fact, several Houses have taken it upon themselves to provide genetic tests and bring the lost Moon Children into their families as potential scions. It won't be an answer for all of us—not every House wants a Moon Child and not every Moon Child wants to find their House—but the option is there, should they choose to pursue it.

Rosa and Dafyyd have no such desire. Where I go, they'll follow, all the way to their dying days. And Bran? I might have thought he would do the same, but the way his eyes track the Heart of the Sea is desperate and full of a longing I can never hope to match. If his time has come to part with us, at least he'll do so on his own terms.

And that's more than I've ever hoped to ask for.

"And you're sure this is what you want to do?" Lucian stands on the pier beside me and Ghost, Jeremiah a short way off. In the distance, the Mother Clock bongs out the hour, and the familiar sound nearly makes me weep.

"I think we have to," Ghost says to his brother. "But it won't be forever, I suspect." His mouth purses in a bittersweet regret. "You're welcome to come with us, you know."

Lucian chuckles sadly. "My place is here. Jeremiah and I, Chancellor Davis, Lady Fionula, Joseph, and Lottie, and all the rest of us who want to try to turn this into an opportunity... Well, we also have no choice."

The three of us stare at one another for a long moment, memories of BrightStone and Meridion both wrapping around us like a silken cloak until we're hugging, my throat tight as I wipe at my suddenly hot eyes.

As farewells go, it hurts quite a bit.

"Will we be able to contact you?" Lucian asks me, hopeful.

"I haven't the foggiest," I say, petting my dragon with a finger. "But if we can manage it, we will get in touch. For now, I think we will simply see what else is out there. It's a big world, after all."

"I suppose you've earned that," he agrees. "And what of the other Moon Children? What provisions should we provide?"

"Anyone who wants to come with us can," Ghost says quietly. "But for those who haven't changed yet, we'll be back. Perhaps once a year or so in the beginning, to take anyone who wishes to come."

In all fairness, it's probably naive to think that either city will suddenly be bastions of altruistic goodness, neither to Moon Children nor one another. But with our allies helping to make things work together, I am confident they will at least find a way to balance it out.

On the other hand...

I gesture to where Copper Betty is curled up on the far side of the docks, her electric-blue eyes intently watching the city of Meridion. "If we hear of any abuse, any wrongdoing on our people, there will be a reckoning," I warn. "Make sure citizens of both cities understand that, aye?

"I'm so proud of you both," Lucian says, his voice trembling. "Who could have imagined this when we took in a ragged Moon Child after she'd been left for dead? It seems like only yesterday, doesn't it?"

"And good riddance." Bran pushes past our sentimental goodbye to embrace me in a tight hug of his own. "You better not die out there, Magpie. I'll kill you myself if you do."

"Same to you," I mumble, trying not to cry. "Keep an eye out for the Moon Children who are staying. They're going to need your guidance."

"I'll manage." He presses a package of cigarillos into my hand. "For the road."

"For the road," I say.

Ghost taps my shoulder with a quiet smile. "Are you ready to go?"

I squeeze his hand. "Always."

I am free, I think, for the first time in my life. Staring down at the fallen city of Meridion leaves me somewhat hollow inside, remembering how Sparrow and I crept on the rooftops below like insects, staring up at the sky to dream. I stifle a soft laugh. Dreams are the hollowest things of all.

Ghost presses his mouth against my ear, murmuring something I can't quite make out, but the sound warms me from the tips of my toes to the top of my head.

Around us sails Josephine and her flotilla of airships, Moon Children clinging to the rails, small dragons zipping here and there in an odd mechanical dance. Copper Betty's neck shifts beneath me as we climb the rising currents. I let out a whistle, clear and crisp, that shatters through the air in a flurry of echoing responses in the moonlight, ships sailing on a silver sea of clouds.

Together, we fly.

— ABOUT THE AUTHOR —

ALLISON PANG is the author of the urban fantasy *Abby Sinclair* series, as well as the writer for the webcomic *Fox & Willow*. She likes LEGOS, elves, LEGO elves...and bacon.

She spends her days in Northern Virginia working as a cube grunt and her nights waiting on her kids and her obnoxious northern-breed dog, punctuated by the occasional husbandly serenade. Sometimes she even manages to write. Mostly she just makes it up as she goes...